"I will pose . . ."

Emma said, pushing her spectacles farther up her nose, "but only fully dressed."

"I cannot paint what I cannot see." A dimple flashed in his smile. Sheer willpower kept her from smiling in response.

Chambers's intense gaze raked her form as if fact belied his words. Never had a man studied her with such intent, certainly not one as handsome and refined as this. His voice, soft and seductive, surrounded her with the rich scent of warmed brandy and his own unique essence.

"I need to see how light and shadow caress a woman's curves."

Immediately, she imagined a physical heat, flowing down from her chest and swirling around her waist and hips. Her mind insisted that modesty called for distance between them, but her feet refused to move.

Chambers turned abruptly, releasing her from his enchantment. She slumped slightly, catching her breath while he strode toward his easel. "I will draw a picture of an aroused man's private regions if you will remove just one article of clothing."

"I have already removed my cloak," she said, a bit short of breath.

He smiled, a subtle gesture. "And I have already shown you a picture of a naked man."

She considered a moment, weighing the advantages and disadvantages of compliance. "A boot," she announced. "If I had a buttonhook, I would remove a boot. However, as it is unlikely that such an instrument would be readily available in an artist's studio . . ."

Chambers stepped over to his desk and returned with a long hook fashioned from a metal replica of a woman's leg, complete with garter. "Perhaps this will help?"

THE EDUCATION OF
Mrs. Brimley

DONNA MacMEANS

BERKLEY SENSATION, NEW YORK

THE BERKLEY PUBLISHING GROUP
Published by the Penguin Group
Penguin Group (USA) Inc.
375 Hudson Street, New York, New York 10014, USA
Penguin Group (Canada), 90 Eglinton Avenue East, Suite 700, Toronto, Ontario M4P 2Y3, Canada
(a division of Pearson Penguin Canada Inc.)
Penguin Books Ltd., 80 Strand, London WC2R 0RL, England
Penguin Group Ireland, 25 St. Stephen's Green, Dublin 2, Ireland (a division of Penguin Books Ltd.)
Penguin Group (Australia), 250 Camberwell Road, Camberwell, Victoria 3124, Australia
(a division of Pearson Australia Group Pty. Ltd.)
Penguin Books India Pvt. Ltd., 11 Community Centre, Panchsheel Park, New Delhi—110 017, India
Penguin Group (NZ), 67 Apollo Drive, Rosedale, North Shore 0745, Auckland, New Zealand
(a division of Pearson New Zealand Ltd.)
Penguin Books (South Africa) (Pty.) Ltd., 24 Sturdee Avenue, Rosebank, Johannesburg 2196, South
Africa

Penguin Books Ltd., Registered Offices: 80 Strand, London WC2R 0RL, England

This is a work of fiction. Names, characters, places, and incidents either are the product of the
author's imagination or are used fictitiously, and any resemblance to actual persons, living or dead,
business establishments, events, or locales is entirely coincidental. The publisher does not have any
control over and does not assume any responsibility for author or third-party websites or their
content.

THE EDUCATION OF MRS. BRIMLEY

A Berkley Sensation Book / published by arrangement with the author

PRINTING HISTORY
Berkley Sensation mass-market edition / October 2007

Copyright © 2007 by Donna MacMeans.
Excerpt of *The Trouble with Moonlight* copyright © 2007 by Donna MacMeans.
Cover art by Leslie Peck.
Hand lettering by Ron Zinn.
Cover design by George Long.
Interior text design by Kristin del Rosario.

ISBN: 978-0-425-21830-3

BERKLEY® SENSATION
Berkley Sensation Books are published by The Berkley Publishing Group,
a division of Penguin Group (USA) Inc.,
375 Hudson Street, New York, New York 10014.
BERKLEY SENSATION and the "B" design are trademarks of Penguin Group (USA) Inc.

PRINTED IN THE UNITED STATES OF AMERICA

10 9 8 7 6 5 4 3 2 1

ACKNOWLEDGMENTS

As this is my first book, I have far too many people to whom I owe thanks and praise than I can list on one page. However, please indulge me while I pay tribute to a special few.

I wish to thank my agent, Cori Deyoe of 3 Seas Literary Agency, and my editor, Cindy Hwang, for believing in both this book and me. I am deeply indebted to Central Ohio Fiction Writers for the support and knowledge afforded me through good writer friendships over many, many years, and to Romance Writers of America for numerous opportunities and for awarding *Mrs. Brimley* their prestigious Golden Heart Award. Thank you. May I also acknowledge Christine Stahurski for her advice and support through good times and bad, Janet Ciccone for timely critique and advice, and Rosemary Laurey, who insists that writing goals must be met. A special thank you is extended as well to Berkley's art department for the fabulous cover. Wow!

Finally, I'd like to dedicate this book to my mother, Helen Lutz, who passed away before she could hold this, my first book, in her hand. She never faltered in her praise for her writer daughter. And to my wonderful, supportive husband who is my own personal hero. Love Always.

· One ·

PERCHED ON HER TRUNK, HER NOSE NUMB, HER toes paralyzed, the January cold burrowing bone deep, Emma Brimley huddled on an empty train platform agonizing over her decision to leave London for Yorkshire. She hadn't considered the hazards of living in such a remote wilderness, nor had she planned for the tardy arrival of a carriage.

The muffled thud of horses' hooves and the distinct rattle of wood and metal wrested her from her makeshift seat. A lantern swayed in the distance.

"Over here," she called, shaking off the settled snow. Relieved that she hadn't been forgotten, she waved her arms frantically overhead, even though she suspected it was too dark to be seen.

The light stilled, then moved in her direction, unleashing new anxieties. What if it wasn't someone from Pettibone? In the dark, an unaccompanied woman was vulnerable to any miscreant or footpad. Her heart lurched into a fierce rhythm. She quickly lifted the leather flap of her traveling bag and fumbled for the only weapon on her person: her prized volume of sonnets.

"Would tha' be the new teacher for th' Pettibone School for Young Ladies?" A gruff voice called.

"Yes." She relaxed, dropping the book back in her bag. "I'm Mrs. Brimley." The words hung in a cloud of moist vapor. "They told me someone would meet me, but I was beginning to worry."

"Aye. Tha'd be me. I come as soon as I could. Hurry along now. I'll get tha' things."

She hurried to the end of the platform, eager to escape the elements. Too eager to question the appearance of the well-appointed carriage, and too impatient to wait for the assistance of the driver stowing her trunk, she grasped the door handle herself.

"Don't mind his lordship, ma'am. He's mos' likely sleeping it off. He won't even know he has company."

"His lordship?" She released the handle as if it were blazing hot and not icy cold. No mention had been made of titled gentry in her correspondence with the school.

"Aye. Hissel' is why I missed th' train, late as 'twas. But I'll have thee at Pettibone in a wink." The well-bundled driver stepped to her side, opened the door, then helped her into the pitch-black interior. The door slammed shut behind her before the trapped warmth could escape. She had barely gained a seat before the lenses of her spectacles fogged beneath the protection of her black lace veil. The carriage lurched forward.

She sensed, rather than saw, the stranger's presence. His body heat transformed the shared air of the interior into something earthy and forbidden. Her heart raced. The polite world would never sanction an unmarried woman alone with a man in such confined, private quarters.

In a bit of a panic, she dug her fingers beneath the sleeve of her heavy pelisse, searching for her mother's handkerchief. She removed her spectacles, squinting in the dark to the opposite bench.

"My lord?" she inquired, her voice barely above a whisper.

A slumping bundle occupied inordinate space on the seat across from her. She swabbed her lenses with the recovered handkerchief, relaxing at his lack of response. Probably some old harmless member of the gentry who'd be more concerned with his hounds than an unattended woman. She slipped her eyeglasses back on the bridge of her nose, but the dark interior obscured details regarding the other passenger.

No matter, she sighed. Even if the man were awake, her widow's weeds afforded her a small measure of privilege as well as anonymity. As quietly as her petticoats allowed, she slid away from the slumbering stranger to the far end of the padded bench.

Pulling aside the window curtain, she gazed with curiosity on what promised to be her new home. The moon had risen, its feeble light magnified by reflecting snow, revealing a forlorn, bleak landscape, so different from her familiar London, yet intriguing in a fundamental way.

"I have looked out in the vast desolate night—" she recited.

"In search of him." A slurred voice completed the line.

He spoke! Her heart slammed into her rib cage. Emma tore her gaze from the window yet continued to hold back the curtain, allowing the moonlight to slip through the glass to the opposite seat. Her breath caught. She almost let the curtain drop, yet his face held her captive. Far from the old codger she'd expected, her companion was young, probably within a decade of her own twenty-three years. His fashionable clothes pegged him for an affluent gallant, right down to the silver-topped walking stick loosely trapped within his hand.

A dandy, she thought with a pang of disgust. She knew about dandies, those pompous, empty-headed peacocks who would cruelly snub someone like herself just to win favor with her pretentious cousin. This fashionable stranger probably knew only enough about literature to win a wager or two at some gentlemen's club.

"You are familiar with Lord Byron's poetry?" she asked, just to be certain she had not imagined his response. As she waited, watching the moonlight wash over his handsome features, a bit of unanticipated yearning tugged at her heart. How would it feel to be desired by someone like him? To be asked for a dance just once ahead of all the wealthy, gossiping debutantes who couldn't tell a verse from a stew recipe? To be envied and not looked down upon for circumstances not of her making?

Although his eyes remained closed, a half smile tilted his lips.

"Let us have wine and women, mirth and laughter, sermons and soda-water the day after." Slight slurring aside, his fluent elocution proved familiarity with Byron's work.

"That is not my favorite verse, sir." She frowned, disappointed by his choice. Still, he had recited more than she had anticipated and the prospect of conversation after her long trip from London proved too great a temptation.

"You are obviously a man of learning and appreciation," she said, releasing the curtain. She slid back to her original seat. "Do you share my passion for the great poets?"

A soft snore was her only reply. Whether he had truly been awake, or only dreaming, she knew not. That he slept now emboldened her beyond the realm of etiquette. A flash of excitement shivered down her spine. In spite of her general dislike of dandies in principle, she admitted a certain curiosity about one so well made who knew his way around a poem or two.

She leaned close to see more detail of his face, only to be repelled by whiskey fumes. Still, she had glimpsed black hair curling gently on his brow, lending him a cherub's sweetness that was challenged by a masculine thin sweep of mustache and a day's growth of stubble. A dark angel with a devilish brand, she decided, worthy of a poem himself.

Excited by the thought, she rummaged in her bag for a stub of a pencil and a scrap of paper but stopped abruptly. His eyes, fringed with long black lashes, opened with apparent difficulty. He blinked several times before squinting at her.

"Am I dead?"

An odd question, but then she remembered her mourning attire. "No sir, you are not."

He relaxed a moment, then turned his head slightly as if searching for other passengers. His brows dived in a scowl.

"Am I married?"

She wasn't sure how to answer. His kid gloves hid any evidence of his matrimonial state, but his expression of instantaneous alarm and regret suggested he was referring specifically to her. An old ache stirred in her bosom. Even in his drunken state, he could ascertain that she was no beauty.

"No sir, we are not."

"'Sgood." He closed his eyes and settled back in slumber, leaving her with a vague sense of insult and disappointment.

The carriage slowed, then turned. They must be approaching the school. With a bit of regret, she took a last long glance at his lordship, wondering whether to credit his pleasant countenance or his obvious command of the romantic poets for the piqued interest fluttering about her rib cage.

Silly girl, she could well imagine her uncle saying. *It's your stays that are too tight. No man with his looks would be interested in the likes of you.*

She banished the thought with a shake of her head. She had left both Uncle George and her cousin Penelope behind in London. If only she could leave her memories of them behind as well.

The carriage slowed to a halt. In a moment, the opportunity to share words with this handsome stranger would vanish. She took a deep breath.

"Thank you for your company, sir. I wish we—"

His audible snore scattered her words. Before she could gather them again, the carriage door opened. The sturdy arms of the driver helped her out.

"Mrs. Brimley." A stout woman with graying hair tucked neatly under a lace and ribbon cap waved enthusiastically from the steps. "We've been so anxious for your arrival."

Surprised, yet pleased by the warm welcome, Emma smiled. Perhaps her plan to come to Yorkshire had not been so flawed after all. The bulky pyramid of wool and petticoats rushed forward. Beneath heavy matronly lids twinkled eyes like those of a young child on holiday.

"We've been . . . oh, my goodness!" The woman's jowls dropped.

"Is something wrong?" Emma asked, trying to ignore the stab of alarm beneath her stays.

"You're so young. We were expecting a much older woman." Concern clouded the woman's features, then rapidly dissipated. "Never mind. My sister will simply have to adjust." She turned her attention to the driver. "Henry, take Mrs. Brimley's belongings upstairs, if you please. Cook prepared a basket for your troubles."

A cloth-draped basket passed Emma's nose on the way to the driver—warm hearty scones by the smell of it. Her mouth watered. Fleeing her uncle's household had left no time to fill her stomach with anything more than fear and anticipation.

"Come along, dear. Cecilia would like a word with you before you settle in." The older woman practically hauled Emma up the stone steps to the front door. Just before entering, Emma stole one last look at the carriage. She could have sworn she saw the flash of a silver-tipped walking stick holding back the curtain a moment before it fluttered back into place.

Her brows lifted. Had he truly been asleep? A man like that couldn't possibly be as intrigued with her as she was with him. Could he?

"This way, dear."

EMMA FOLLOWED HER NEW EMPLOYER TO A SMALL SITting room decorated with an overabundance of needlework doilies and lacy antimacassars, some the bright white of recent work, others with a yellowish tint of years past. Oval photographs of serious young girls covered the green walls. Emma studied their solemn yet fresh faces.

"Those are graduates of the Pettibone School for Young Ladies." A sharp voice, laced with pride, spoke from behind her. Emma turned to see a tall, stern-faced woman dressed entirely in black.

"You must be very proud of them," Emma replied. Another widow, she supposed. They must migrate to schools like this, the women without husbands and means to live in more fashionable locations. Perhaps that would explain why the school insisted its new teacher be a widow as well.

"Mrs. Brimley, I am Cecilia Higgins, headmistress of the Pettibone School for Young Ladies."

Emma rendered a slow and proper bow.

The headmistress nodded approval, then motioned her to sit before settling herself in a chair directly opposite. "Please remove your veil, Mrs. Brimley. I wish to get a closer look at you."

Emma worried her lip and complied. Although pleased to rid herself of the gauzy nuisance, the black lace had shielded her from close scrutiny. As she pulled the barrier back over her hat, she feared discovery of the fraud she portrayed.

The headmistress leaned forward, squinting. "Beatrice mentioned that you were much younger than we had anticipated. Sometimes my sister leaps to wild conclusions, but in this instance, I can see that she is correct. When exactly did your husband depart, Mrs. Brimley?"

"He died in a tragic carriage accident nearly eighteen months ago. We married young, but alas, we were not married long." Although she had rehearsed it well, the lie still warmed her cheeks. Emma dropped her gaze. With luck, the headmistress would interpret her blush as something else entirely.

The woman waited a moment, touching the tops of her steepled fingers to thin, dry lips. "The length of your marriage is not important to us, but as I explained in our correspondence, it is mandatory that our new teacher have experienced marriage in her lifetime. Perhaps the girls will relate to a young widow more than they would to an older one."

The woman's frown lessened, which Emma interpreted to signal acceptance. Her own smile born from relief threatened to surface, but Emma suppressed it, sensing it would not be appropriate.

The older woman rose from her chair and strode to her desk. "You have already met Beatrice. She teaches needlework and the French language. I teach proper etiquette, grooming, and household management. You will be responsible for—"

"Proper elocution and literature befitting young ladies," Emma interjected, the suppressed smile bubbling to the surface. "Indeed, I'm looking forward to it."

"Yes . . . well . . . there is one other subject you will be expected to teach. One that I did not mention in my letter but that should not be a problem given your experience."

The older woman avoided eye contact. Observing her uneasiness, Emma felt anxiety as well. Perhaps, if she reassured the headmistress as to the versatility of her own instruction, the conversation would return to its former easy discourse.

"Mrs. Higgins—"

"*Miss* Higgins," the other woman corrected. "Neither my sister nor I ever married. That is the crux of our difficulty."

Confused, Emma mentally revisited her own education, trying to imagine how spinsterhood might prove difficult in the conduct of a school. "I'm afraid that I don't understand."

"Pettibone School for Young Ladies serves clientele of the first order," the spinster said. "The wealthiest merchants and industrialists in the area send their daughters to us to mold into fine young women suited for marriage to gentlemen of the highest quality."

"Yes, yes, you mentioned that in your letters, but I still don't understand." Emma's concern blossomed into foreboding. The headmistress was clearly uncomfortable with this topic. Why would this unsettle her so?

"One of our patrons has suggested, quite correctly mind you, that the Pettibone School provides little in the way of instruction to prepare the girls for the intimacies of marriage, particularly the wedding night. Our patron quotes Mr. Copland's definitive work on practical medicine that successful procreation can only be achieved if both parties are . . . well . . . agreeable to the process."

High color stained Miss Higgins's cheeks. Fortunately, the older woman seemed oblivious to Emma's own distress.

"As the generation of heirs is a desired goal of marriage, we must prepare our girls for their ultimate responsibility." Cecilia brought her gaze in direct line with Emma. "And teaching this, therefore, will be *your* responsibility."

Emma's foreboding exploded to full-blown panic. "But what if—"

"I must say that I am not in favor of this course of study," the headmistress interrupted with a frown. "I believe certain behaviors"—she waved a hand in the air, as if to dismiss them—"should remain unmentioned in polite society. However, our patron was quite emphatic. Therefore, I must insist that if you are not agreeable to teaching this subject matter, we will make arrangements to send you back to London."

Emma's panic plummeted into despair. London, she knew, was not an option. This was not the time, she supposed, to confess she had no more knowledge about the subject of intimacy than the girls she was expected to teach.

"I am shocked," she stalled, trying to order her thoughts. "You never suggested in your letter . . ."

The woman winced ever so slightly. "I was afraid you would not make the journey to Yorkshire if I had confided the true nature of your responsibilities. I apologize for my deceit, but it was necessary under the circumstances."

Emma glanced at the headmistress, who stood as unwavering as the Dover cliffs. They apparently shared a common thread of deceit. Would that make Miss Higgins more accepting should her own hidden truth emerge? Emma squashed that thought before it could fully develop. The consequences of admitting her lack of experience remained too severe to chance confiding in Miss Higgins.

"Will I be teaching elocution and literature as well?"

"Yes, of course. Pettibone will profit from a teacher of your background and training."

Emma worried her lower lip. No training had ever prepared her for this situation. She took a breath, then glanced at the gallery of faces on the wall: kind, friendly faces. She'd need their kindness and friendship if she was to succeed.

"When do my classes begin?"

Miss Higgins's shoulders sagged in obvious relief. "I suppose you will need a day to organize before assuming your duties. I will alternate your classes with those of the dance tutor. Let us begin the day after tomorrow."

Miss Higgins picked up a little bell. "Now that the matter is settled, I shall ring for tea. Beatrice shall join us, and we will all become better acquainted."

The day after tomorrow! That didn't allow much time, Emma thought, fighting back rising alarm. Her fingers sought out her mother's wedding band and the sense of calm it conveyed. She had one day of reprieve. Every day away from London allowed her trail to grow a little colder. She'd use the day to think of something. Although she wasn't at all sure what.

The moment Miss Higgins opened the door, Beatrice stumbled in with all the tea elements on a silver tray. One side of her face had reddened as if it had been pressed against the door.

Emma suppressed a grin.

"We anticipated your need for nourishment after such an arduous trip," Beatrice explained in a rush.

"Mrs. Brimley has agreed to the teaching arrangement we discussed." Cecilia poured a cup of tea, then handed it to Emma. "I thought she might have some questions about Pettibone that we might answer."

"That is wonderful news." Beatrice's gray curls bobbed with approval. "Lady Cavendish's letter of reference praised your credentials to such high extremes, we would have been disappointed if you had declined our offer."

Emma smiled faintly, relieved that her forgery had been accepted as genuine, but still ashamed to have resorted to such deceitful measures. Fortunately, the likelihood that the true Lady Cavendish would learn of her transgression was as remote as Leighton-on-the-Wold itself.

"I'm so pleased to be here," Emma said, shaking her head to turn down an offer of sugar and cream. "I do have one question, although it's not specifically about Pettibone." Steam from the hot liquid warmed her nose and fogged her eyeglasses.

"What might that be, dear?" Beatrice asked.

Emma sipped and smiled, letting the languid heat spread from the inside out. "What can you tell me about the man in the carriage?"

"Henry, the driver?" Beatrice asked, sounding surprised.

"No, the gentleman in the carriage." Emma sipped a bit more of the fortifying liquid. Nothing could be so horrid that a good cup of tea couldn't improve. "The driver referred to him as 'his lordship.'"

Cecilia's cup clattered to the saucer. "Chambers was in the carriage?" She directed a glare toward her sister as chilling as the snow piled outside.

Beatrice wrung her hands. "Henry didn't say anything about his lordship. I didn't know he was there."

Cecilia turned to Emma. "Did he offend you in any way? What did he say?" Her eyes narrowed. "Did he touch you?"

Alarmed by their reaction, Emma placed her cup and saucer carefully on a side table. "Indeed no. He slept almost the entire ride. Is something wrong?"

"Pettibone School has been built on the most stringent

standards of respectability." Cecilia rose to pace the small room, wringing her hands. "Association with Lord Nicholas Chambers could place our pristine reputation in jeopardy. His behavior is not consistent with that of a gentleman." She stopped in front of Emma. "Did anyone see you enter the carriage?"

"He's an artist," Beatrice explained. "A painter. Tavern women come and go from his estate at all hours of the night." Her twinkling eyes widened with excitement and her voice lowered to a conspiratorial whisper. "They say he's extremely handsome. Did you think so, Mrs. Brimley?"

"Beatrice!" Cecilia hissed. "How many times must I warn you that such talk does you no credit? He is a dissolute rake who uses women."

Beatrice quailed before her sister, clearly chastised.

Cecilia turned to Emma. "Answer me, Mrs. Brimley. I must know if we are ruined."

"No one save the driver saw me enter, and it was extremely dark in the carriage. If I hadn't heard his breathing, I would not have known he was there at all," Emma said, quickly determining that her conversation with the attractive gentleman, as innocent as it had been, had best remain private.

Cecilia sighed. "Good. Henry knows to hold his tongue."

Beatrice leaned toward Emma. "His estate borders ours, barely a mile distant, riding through the woods."

"It is bad enough that we have need to borrow his conveyance on occasion. We should not be forced to endure his person as well." Cecilia sniffed, as if to suggest the demon lord had selected his estate for the sole purpose of taunting innocent Pettibone women.

"My sister believes Lord Nicholas Chambers allows us use of his carriage because he relishes the thought of decent folk sitting on cushions that have witnessed all sorts of debauchery." Despite Cecilia's earlier rebuke, Beatrice's eyes shone bright with curiosity.

The suggestion of debauchery, mentioned in connection with the man in the carriage, sent a ripple of interest deep through Emma. She shifted, uncomfortable with the foreign feeling, and tried to shift her focus as well. Still, the man's lazy half smile refused to abandon her thoughts.

"Needless to say," Cecilia said, raising her hand to interrupt her sister, "I will not allow that man's close proximity to influence our girls. Now that you understand the danger, Mrs. Brimley, I am sure you will be ever vigilant and do the same."

Emma nodded. As difficult as it might prove to forget the intriguing lines of Lord Nicholas Chambers's face traced in moonlight, or the unexpected thrill of their brief clandestine journey, those experiences were more in tune with those of a heroine in a light novel. Such flights of fantasy rarely touched her reality.

It was just as well. A man who spoke poetry even when not in full possession of his wits could prove only a distraction to her immediate problem. She must obtain sufficient intelligence to portray a convincing widow, else she'd be back on her uncle's doorstep. And that was completely unacceptable.

EMMA MET THE GIRLS AT THE SCHOOL THE NEXT DAY— too many to remember all the names and faces. They swirled around her in pretty frocks, giggling and whispering. Emma suspected she was the subject of those poorly hidden discussions. In her black bombazine and horn-rimmed glasses, she felt like a weed in a flourishing cottage garden.

She was introduced to many of the serving staff, none

of whom appeared to be married. She'd find no font of knowledge in those quarters.

Emma set out to explore the great manor that housed the school. With luck she hoped to discover a library with a text that might offer enlightenment on intimacy. She was proceeding down one hallway when her name, uttered in a low conversation, floated through the very air.

"Have you seen the new teacher?"

Surprised, she stopped just short of a turn in the hallway. As a new teacher, she probably should scold the girls for such vulgar behavior as gossiping, but curiosity got the better of her. She flattened herself against the wall paneling and listened. She couldn't see faces, but their voices carried clear and close around the near corner.

"She speaks funny," a younger voice said.

"That's because she's from London, you silly goose. They all sound like that, all hoity-toity down there."

One voice lowered to a near whisper. "I heard she arrived in a carriage all alone with Lord Bedchambers."

Emma's cheek heated against the cool paneling. How could news of her unorthodox arrival travel so quickly? Surely the Higgins sisters had not publicized the circumstances.

"If her belly starts to grow," the first girl said, "we'll know it's not from Cook's meals."

"Fanny, you are so wicked!" Laughter echoed off the walls.

"Girls!" Beatrice's voice interrupted the merriment. "Have you no better place to be?"

Emma shriveled inside. The years should have toughened her hide to the hurtful prickings of the privileged, but the unkind laughter still struck deep.

Emma silently tiptoed back down the hall before rushing to the opposite wing of the house. Embarrassed by the overheard conversation and by her equally improper eavesdropping, she pushed through the first door she encountered and stumbled into the library.

Her pulse raced from her hasty flight, while the girls' taunts still echoed in her ears. She sank onto a wooden chair and braced her forehead with her hands. She had come all this way yet still remained an object of ridicule. How foolish to run away from home, thinking to escape the whispers and scorn.

Deep in the recesses of her mind, she heard laughter, her uncle's laughter. The mere thought of him sent an icy chill tripping down her spine. Determined to rid herself of the memory, she pushed herself from the chair. She had managed to escape London without his notice. If she was to stay hidden, she'd best get to work.

The upper portion of three walls in the library were lined with bookshelves, more empty than full. Emma found a few dusty novels, mostly by the late Mr. Dickens, Mrs. Beeton's thick tome on household management, and several collected volumes of fashion magazines and needlework patterns. Just as she resigned herself to needing an alternate strategy, she spied a volume on a high shelf beyond her reach. It lay flat so as not to be obvious to the casual observer.

Pulling a small step stool into position, Emma stretched to her full height to retrieve the book, a sizeable medical text, and looked at the title: Mr. Copland's *A Dictionary of Practical Medicine*.

"There you are. I'd been hoping you'd be here." Delighted with her find, she stepped off the stool and took the volume to a nearby table. The book opened a bit too naturally to worn pages marking the discussions on conception. Although she readily discovered Mr. Copland's assertion regarding enjoyment of intimacy, she could find no mention on how that enjoyment was to be obtained.

Belatedly, she realized that had the information been

so available, Miss Higgins could teach the class as well as she.

"Have you found what you're searching for, Mrs. Brimley?" Cecilia asked, startling Emma from her examination of the text.

"Miss Higgins! Yes . . . I was checking to see what books I could use in my literature sessions." She readjusted her eyeglasses on the bridge of her nose. "Your novels complement my volumes on poetry. These shall do quite nicely."

Miss Higgins glanced at the open text. Her brow raised.

"Do you plan to discuss female hysteria in your literature class?"

Emma closed the book. "I was curious as to the ailments listed. I suppose in a remote location such as this, doctors are difficult to obtain. How far is the nearest village?"

"You rode through it last night."

Emma recalled passing a handful of buildings, a church, and at least one tavern.

"But if one of the girls is seriously ill, we send word to Hull or York. It may take several hours, but we are not without medical resources." Cecilia cocked a brow. "Are you planning to need the assistance of a doctor?"

"No, I was just curious," Emma replied quickly, although she certainly wished for a doctor's knowledge at present.

Cecilia gazed about the library. "I think this room will do well for your classes. Naturally, I've selected only a few of the older girls to receive instruction." She nodded to herself, apparently pleased with her decision. "I'll let them know to meet you here tomorrow, and Mrs. Brimley"—her gaze leveled on Emma—"I believe I will attend your first class."

Emma stared at Cecilia's retreating back. Tomorrow!

Her heart raced. In the space of a night and day, she could easily be unmasked as a fraud and sent packing.

She paced the room, trying to calm her frantic thoughts. Her needs were immediate, her resources were not. She paused, removing first a handkerchief from her cuff, then her spectacles from her nose.

"Cleaner vision means clearer focus," she recited, allowing her mother's familiar words and the repetitive action of polishing her lenses to calm her nerves. "Sharp focus on any problem leads to possibilities." She pushed the cleaned glasses back in place. "Possibilities lead to . . ."

Her gaze lingered on the title of a small treatise lying on a low table, *The Art of Arranging Cut Flowers.*

The word "art" reminded her of "artist." A memory of the dark angel stirred her thoughts. Only an educated man would have recognized Lord Byron's poem. An educated man would surely have books, and as an artist who painted the human figure, he might keep texts that addressed anatomical issues as well.

"Possibilities lead to solutions," she murmured, completing her mother's familiar stanza. A flame of hope ignited deep inside. Miss Higgins had mentioned that the distance to Lord Nicholas Chambers's estate was not far.

Miss Higgins. The tiny flame sputtered, uncertain. Emma recalled Miss Higgins's prohibition of association with the man in the carriage. She bit her lip. Calling on him might prove just as disastrous as not calling on him. Her stomach twisted in turmoil.

She resumed her pacing, mentally weighing the alternatives. It wasn't as if she was a complete bumbler. After all, she had managed to leave London with none the wiser. Surely she could do it again here at Pettibone.

A memory of Chambers's sweet face, rocking gently in the moonlight with the motion of the carriage, stirred her thoughts. Perhaps after he had provided the necessary materials, maybe they could again exchange a few more poetic verses. A quiver of anticipation tingled her nerve endings.

She took a deep breath, drawing confidence from her decision. She'd make a clandestine call upon Lord Bedchambers . . . er, Lord Nicholas Chambers. Tonight.

· Two ·

EMMA'S STOMACH LURCHED AS IF SHE WERE Blondin, the famous tightrope artist, suspended high in the Crystal Palace with nothing but a thin wire for foothold. One misstep and severe consequences would surely ensue. Behind her, the trodden path led back to the relative safety of Pettibone School. Before her stood the massive, many-gabled manor of Black Oak in all its gothic glory.

The confidence that had effectively carried her away from Pettibone somehow had eroded along the way. Now she questioned the wisdom of what could be an awkward intrusion. She hesitated to catch her breath and quell the uneasiness that roiled in the pit of her stomach. Then, like Blondin, she moved ahead one slow step at a time.

The path approached Black Oak from the back, past shrubs deformed by their heavy burden of snow and jutting skeletons of plants long past seed. The house appeared twice the size of Pettibone, with far more grandeur and far less warmth. No light shone through the windows. If not for the pale ribbons of smoke rising from several chimneys, she would have thought the structure uninhabited. A dog barked and she hurried along lest the hounds be set loose.

Circling around the manor, Emma discovered the front entrance. With one final deep breath for courage, she rapped sharply on the heavy oak door.

She shivered, more from dread than cold. The winter light had rapidly faded; already a pale full moon hovered over the horizon. Making this forbidden call, alone, under the cover of night, broke every tenet in *The Ladies' Guide to Proper Etiquette.*

A solemn-faced gentleman opened the door and looked her up and down.

"You're late." He ushered her swiftly inside.

Dumbfounded by the reception, Emma let herself be moved along, if only to escape the cold. Fog rapidly appeared on her lenses, making it difficult to see where she was going. "I couldn't send my card ahead for reasons I can—"

"No time for that," he said. "Give me your cloak. Quickly now."

Her numb fingers fumbled over the fastenings, much to his apparent agitation.

"This is a most puzzling household," she said, handing over the heavy woolen cloak. "I am given to think you were expecting me."

"We expected you several days earlier. You may wait there." He pointed toward a small salon near the front entrance. "I will let his lordship know that you've arrived." The servant left with her outer garment folded over his arm.

Fortunately, the condensation on her glasses had begun

to evaporate, or she'd never have been able to negotiate the dim salon with its clutter of furniture. She stretched her palms to the welcoming warmth of an inviting fire hissing beneath an ornately carved overmantel.

She had expected that country living tolerated less formality than the rigid manners of the city, but this reception had lacked even the basics of propriety. "A most puzzling household, indeed," she murmured to the flames.

"You're thinner than I recall."

Shocked by the proximity of a deep baritone voice, Emma spun about, then curtsied by force of habit to the broad-shouldered man framed in the doorway. She squinted, trying to imagine him slouched in the corner of a leather-bound seat. Was this really the man from the carriage? Without the soft slur and poetic refrains of the night before, his familiar voice held more authority and power. The fluttering about her rib cage, however, convinced her this must indeed be her dark angel. No one else had so affected her by mere presence alone. She inclined her head. "My lord."

"None of that nonsense. Come closer," he commanded. "Let me take a better look at you."

She winced. Manners were truly different this far north. Not only did he receive her without benefit of his neck cloth, but he also issued orders as if she were a servant. Clasping her hands together, she approached as requested. "My lord, I've come about a matter—"

"Sssh, don't speak."

Surprised, she stopped an arm's length away. She could understand his refusing to receive her due to the lateness of the hour, and her uninvited call, but commanding her not to talk? What manner of custom was this?

He stepped forward. The tips of his fingers reached toward her face and gently lifted her chin, pulling her gaze up to meet his. He was as attractive in the glow from the fire as he had been in moonlight, an image of tantalizing innocence compromised by sinful promise.

Her throat dried to ash as she took in long black lashes framing eyes so dark they reflected the leap of flames behind her. His fingertips must have captured the heat of the flames as well, for they warmed the sensitive underside of her chin.

Mesmerized, she felt as if her whole being were in his power, captured by the touch of his expressive hand. It was the most delicious sensation that she had ever experienced in her life. Her breath escaped on a sigh.

His eyes narrowed slightly. "Was I drinking when I hired you? I don't seem to recall—"

"Hired!" The spell broken, she stepped back, escaping from his touch. "Sir, you did not hire me."

His brows rose nearly to the defiant lock of black hair curled on his forehead. "Are you not the woman who agreed to model for my painting?"

"No," she answered, first shocked, then insulted by the absurd notion. "I've come to speak to you about a book."

"Rubbish." He stalked toward the hall, and she noticed, for the first time, that he leaned on a walking stick that moved in tandem with his left leg. "I haven't the time or inclination to discuss a book with you, Mrs. . . . Mrs. . . ." He stopped and turned, his brow furled. "Who are you?"

He'd forgotten their brief meeting in the carriage. She wasn't surprised. She rarely made a memorable impression on people. He had been well in his cups last night. Still she had hoped . . .

"I am Mrs. Brimley, sir. I'm a new teacher at the Pettibone School for Young Ladies." Now that he knew she was a fellow intellectual, surely he would listen. She followed him down the corridor. "I need to talk to you about—"

"Thomas, I need you," he bellowed toward the high ceilings before turning to address her in a more refined manner. "Thomas will show you out." He spun on his heel and disappeared into another room.

Stunned, she stopped in place, staring at the empty hallway. Disappointment stabbed deep. Even if her unanticipated appearance hadn't intrigued him, he shouldn't have dismissed her so rudely. The long cold walk back to Pettibone loomed, with nothing to justify her risk of coming.

He mustn't ignore me. He is my only hope. Resolve buoyed her. *He must be made to listen.*

"Wait!" She lifted her skirts and ran down the hall. "At least hear me out." She followed him into the room, closed the door behind her, then leaned against it to deny him exit.

Her gaze swept the room in astonishment.

It was as if the sun had been harnessed and made to shine exclusively in this magical place. Strategically placed mirrors in ornate, gilded frames reflected light from both the fireplace and numerous lamps. Riotous colored cloths and canvases, some painted, some not, lay scattered throughout. So much color and discord made her head swim. "What is this place?" she whispered in awe.

"You are trespassing in my studio."

In the midst of the color and confusion stood Lord Nicholas Chambers, rolling up the sleeves of his linen shirt like a circus ringmaster preparing to bring order from chaos. As a refined woman, she should have been shocked to observe such an intimate gesture, but the sight of his bared forearms caused her pulse to race. Tensed muscles gleamed with a fine sheen of black hair, rough yet alluring. An ache spread through her. How would it feel to be captured within those arms? She stroked the dowdy black bombazine sleeve that concealed her own forearm, silently wishing he'd roll the cloth back one more fold, expose one more inch.

A pounding ensued on the door at her back, breaking

the spell and reminding her of her desperate need. She raised her voice to a near shout.

"I have risked both my reputation and my employment coming here. The least you can do is listen to my plea."

"Plea, Mrs. Brimley?" One dark brow lifted in question. "As you are new to this area, I should warn you. Women in dire circumstances rarely come to me for assistance."

Another reference to his terrible reputation, though from his lips, the words sounded more like an invitation than a warning. Although she'd asked for his full attention, now that she had it, she wished it otherwise. His masculine virility was like a physical force, attacking her senses, and now he concentrated it fully on her. She could barely breathe. She crushed her bustle into the door, needing its support.

"It's all right, Thomas," he shouted, as the pounding continued behind her. "I'll call if I need you."

The pounding stopped, although her insides continued to vibrate.

"All right, Mrs. Brimley. As you appear to hold me hostage, to what purpose do I owe this pleasure?"

She was tongue-tied. What to say? How to begin to explain her awkward, embarrassing need?

He turned to a small table by his side. "May I offer you a brandy? It might loosen your tongue."

She stiffened her spine, annoyed with herself and her cowardice. "I don't indulge, sir."

"More's the pity." He began to pour from a crystal decanter. "My model has abandoned me at a most inconvenient time." He paused, then glanced at an empty canvas across the room. "No, I correct myself. At a time that is worse than inconvenient. At a catastrophic time."

He raised his arm to a prominent burgundy velvet divan situated on a raised dais in the center of the room. "As you can see, my model has failed to materialize. In her stead, a madwoman *with a plea* has assaulted my household to discuss"—he glanced back at her—"what was it . . . a book?"

He saluted her with his filled glass. "At this point, a stiff drink is about the only sensible course of action."

Her breath caught. He moved like a finely crafted poem: strong, fluid, purposeful. Watching him swallow the amber liquid, she was transported back to the intimacy of that shared carriage. Her throat felt as dry as the pages of her books. He swirled the liquid in his glass and looked to her, expectant, waiting. She shook herself from her reverie.

"I'm not a madwoman, sir. I've come in search of knowledge." He was a learned man, she reminded herself. And a talented artist, as evidenced by the dozen or so masterfully rendered landscapes and still-life arrangements scattered about the room. Surely he could help her. She smiled at the thought. Once he understood her need, he would most certainly oblige.

"Then you've come to the wrong place." He grasped the walking stick propped against the table, then carried his glass to a nearby easel. "Ask anyone. I have no knowledge of anything but debauchery." He sneered in her direction. "Surely a young widow would have no wish to learn about that."

The smile slid from her face. In one sense, this was exactly the knowledge she was seeking, but only the polite form of debauchery, the sort between a husband and wife. From the anger and disappointment in his voice, perhaps asking for his assistance would be tantamount to an insult. She searched in her cuff for the comfort of her mother's handkerchief. This was not proceeding according to plan.

"Let me begin again," she managed, searching for the right words. "This is most difficult to explain."

She moved deeper into the room, moving closer to the elegant divan, such an odd placement for an extravagant piece. Then she remembered Beatrice's and his mention of debauchery. Is that where it took place? On a raised elevated platform so others could see. She had heard rumors in London of such practices, but she had never encountered physical evidence. Her heart raced. She had indeed stumbled into the devil's den.

Feeling familiar warmth coddle her cheeks, she turned her back to the furniture, studying instead a painting of a bowl of fruit until her face could cool. "I . . . I was hoping you might have a book or some drawings that I might study—"

Laughter rumbled from his chest. He exchanged a small canvas at the easel for paper tacked on a board. "Are you a critic, Mrs. Brimley? Is that what you wish to discuss?" The humor left his voice. "I have critics aplenty. I don't require another."

"I'm not a critic," she said, surprised. "How could one criticize your obvious talent? Why I could almost pluck one of the cherries out of this painting and suck its sweet nectar."

He stared at her. "You think I have talent?"

"I'm not an art critic, my lord," she said, believing she may have trespassed the proper boundaries of pride. "But I do find this painting quite pleasing."

She glanced back at the painting. Indeed, his brushstrokes, alternately bold and delicate, were of a master's hand, obviously rendered by talented fingers. Her gloved hand reached to the very spot where his artist's fingers had caressed her chin. Heat resurged in her cheeks.

"If you're not a critic, then what are you, Mrs. Brimley?" His voice shocked her back to reality. She turned toward him.

"I . . . I'm a teacher in need of viewing a portrayal of a special subject," she stammered. "I had hoped you could direct me to a source."

He cast her a sideways glance. "What kind of special subject?"

"This is most difficult," she began, searching for socially acceptable words to explain her need. "The nature of the subject is such that I'm not sure there exists a proper way to address . . ."

His sigh signaled annoyance. Patience did not appear to be his virtue. She took a deep breath and, finding no other recourse, lowered her voice to a near whisper. "I need to see a painting of—"

"Speak up, Mrs. Brimley," he intoned in a particularly loud voice. "You are interrupting my work and unless you can articulate your purpose—"

"I need to see a painting of a man's genitals." Cowering in embarrassment at having to shout such a shocking request, she glanced again about the room to verify no one else had witnessed her humiliation.

But for the hiss of the fire, there was silence. Chambers stood deadly still, his face contorted in apparent disbelief. Suddenly, he laughed. Loud raucous laughter that erupted from his chest and shook his entire body in mirth. He laughed so hard, he knocked against the drawing board and it slammed to the wooden floor, but he didn't seem to notice. He laughed until tears rolled down his cheeks.

Never had she been so mortified. If only she had had the foresight to slip a fan on her wrist, she could hide behind its folds. Having mentally rehearsed this moment on her trek through the woods, she had anticipated that he'd be shocked, or disgusted, but not that she would be subject to ridicule. Her cheeks burned hot enough to melt wax.

"Mrs. Brimley, you jest!" He tried to drink from his glass of brandy, but he was seized by gales of laughter. His hand shook, splashing the liquid onto a set of charcoal sticks. He abandoned the glass for one of the charcoals and shook the liquid off. "Pray tell me, why do you wish to see such a thing?"

The grin on his lips, combined with her own mortification, did not encourage her to cooperate. She had been the subject of jests before, a cruel experience that she did not wish to repeat, especially with this man. Unfortunately, she suspected her explanation would only provide more fuel for his frivolity. "A gentleman wouldn't ask such a question," she snapped.

"Mrs. Brimley, you forced your way into my studio seeking assistance. You will humor me if I insist on an answer." The laughter eased from his face. He reached for the fallen board and propped it on the easel. "Why do you need to view such material?"

Despite her rigid training, her shoulders sagged. She turned away so he couldn't see her face, and removed her glasses pretending to clean them, needing time. Think. Think. What to say?

"Mrs. Brimley?"

She heard the impatience in his tone. Exasperated by her lack of courage, she turned to him, shoving the lenses back in place. "I'm to teach the girls at Pettibone how to prepare for their marital duties, and I'm lacking in essential information."

His hand moved freely over the paper in tiny arcs. His focus on his work and not on her person lessened her embarrassment almost to the point of gratitude. Words came easier without his laughter or his intense stare.

"How is it, *Mrs.* Brimley, that you lack such basic information? Has not *Mr.* Brimley provided adequate instruction?"

She removed a small handkerchief from her cuff, worrying it with her hands. She had hoped to keep her circumstances secret and not come to this revelation. However, given the nature of the requested assistance, she saw no escape. She lowered her gaze, as well as her tone. "There is no Mr. Brimley."

"You are a widow, are you not?"

Even though she could not see his face, she could well imagine one of those dark eyebrows rising.

She shook her head and waited for his reaction. Given her admission, he would be justified in demanding her departure. Without his assistance, she would have to admit her masquerade to the spinster sisters. She'd be back on her uncle's doorstep in a matter of days.

Chambers's silence encouraged further explanation. She took a breath for courage.

"In order to procure this position, I pretended to have been married. I had no idea I'd be expected to teach bedroom etiquette." There. She had admitted her deceit. She should feel ashamed, she supposed, but telling the truth actually made her feel a bit better. She had never anticipated how physically taxing this burden of lies and deceit would be. She lifted her chin but still avoided his gaze. "I suppose you must think me devoid of all honor."

Chambers chuckled deep in his throat. "You do not wish to know my thoughts, *Miss* Brimley."

His voice, low and seductive, brought her gaze round to meet his. A dark, forbidden knowledge smoldered deep in his eyes, fueling a resonant response within her. For the first time, she recognized her vulnerability, alone with this man. Awareness tingled up her spine. She stepped back, gulping a swift intake of needed air.

He chuckled deep in his throat. "Your secret is safe." A slight smile tipped his lips before he turned his attention back to the drawing board. "The ladies at the school wouldn't nay-say your instructions. Make something up. They won't know the difference."

"But I don't wish to lie to the girls," she insisted. "They trust me to tell them the truth." Granted she had already told more misrepresentations in the past two days than she had in her entire lifetime, but lying to the Higgins sisters was necessary. Lying to children, abominable. She glanced quickly about the room. "Haven't you a painting or a picture in a book that might assist me?"

He traded his piece of charcoal for his glass, considering her over the rim while he drank. He tilted his head slightly. "I may have something."

For the first time that evening, Emma felt a stirring of hope that this scandalous foray might yield positive results.

Chambers slipped the knob of the walking stick under his left palm and moved toward a desk pushed against a back wall. He shifted through a clutter of papers.

"I have a friend in Paris, Auguste Rodin, who created a bronze statute of a full-size nude male. Perhaps you've heard of him?" He looked back at her over his shoulder. "It caused quite a stir at exhibition."

She shook her head. Chambers's awkward posture suggested he'd be more comfortable if he allowed his walking prop to bear more of his weight. His pride, she guessed, disagreed. Her heart softened. She understood a thing or two about pride.

"Some time ago, Rodin sent a letter with a drawing . . . Yes, here it is." He brought several pages of the letter over to the dais. Shifting through them, he produced the one with a detailed drawing of a male figure. "Just as you requested, a picture of a man as God made him."

Proper etiquette demanded she couldn't acknowledge her observation regarding his altered gait. She couldn't even ask how his condition occurred, although she'd admit to being curious. Accepting the offered paper, she hesitantly pulled her gaze from his broadening smile.

She adjusted her glasses so as to see, then memorize, every detail. Anticipation fluttered in her chest. This, after all, constituted not only the purpose of her visit, but also the culmination of all the speculation of her youth.

The drawing portrayed an athletic man, an Adonis, she supposed. Her gaze skimmed the bare shoulders and slipped past the trim midriff, focusing instead on the forbidden area between the man's muscular legs—that very spot deemed improper for virginal eyes.

Her lips parted in surprise.

"Why, it's so small. I believe I could cover it with one hand." As if to prove her theory, she stretched her hand, base to tip. Although she wasn't exactly sure what she had expected, this appendage hadn't the menacing character alluded to in so many poems. Disappointed, she turned to Chambers.

"Why is there so much commotion over two small potatoes in a twisted sack?"

Chambers's eyes crinkled, his amusement at her inexperience evident. "This man is flaccid. An aroused man looks much different."

"Can you show me?" she asked.

He nearly choked. "You wish to see my manhood?"

"I thought you might have another picture." Emma's cheeks burned at her blunder, although she was shocked to realize a small part of her wished to answer in the affirmative. She pushed her spectacles up her nose trying to think prim, innocent thoughts.

"I need to let the girls know what to expect."

His lips thinned a moment before he pivoted smartly using the stick and retreated to his easel. Derision filled his voice. "I assure you I have no interest in retaining pictures of aroused men in my studio, in my house, or on my person."

"You are an artist," she insisted, not willing to let the opportunity pass. "Perhaps you can create a drawing for me, purely for scientific purposes, of course."

"A drawing?" He scowled, his gaze skipping from the easel to her face. He must have seen her sincerity, because the scowl softened as he returned his attention to the easel. Was that a twinkle she saw in his eye? A sly smile chased away his disdain.

"Miss Brimley, you may recall that the girl I hired to pose for me has not materialized."

She nodded. "Indeed, you thought I was she earlier."

"You have need of information, and I have need of a model." He smiled, reassuring her that his moment of displeasure had indeed passed.

Her hopes lifted.

"Perhaps we can design an agreement," he continued, "that will satisfy both our desires."

"You wish to paint my portrait?" Pleasure rippled through her. Great ladies had portraits painted. She could bend to this arrangement, especially if it required more time in his presence.

"I wish to paint you naked." A devilish smile played about his lips. "But I'll settle for painting you in a thin gown."

"Sir!" Shock paralyzed her. "Surely, you don't mean it!"

He positioned himself in front of her. "In exchange for information," he added.

"I've never been so insulted." She tried to step around him, but he continued to hinder her exit. Again she regretted the absence of her fan. She would have thrashed him with it.

"What kind of woman do you take me for?" she cried, frustrated at his efforts to thwart her.

"A comely one, I suspect, beneath all that black." Using the tip of his walking stick, he lifted the hem of her skirt an inch off the ground.

"Sir!" Shocked, she slapped the material back in place. The man was incredulous.

A bemused grin played about his mouth. He was playing with her, she realized, feeling the stab of disappointment. She had fooled herself into thinking this dandy was different, yet it was all mockery. Pain burrowed deep.

"I refuse to be the subject of your jest." Her lips tightened, her eyes burned. She tried to push by him, but he caught her arm.

"There is no jest."

If only that were true! She looked away, afraid he might see the yearning in her eyes. Her throat tightened making words difficult. "If you meant to compliment me, I assure you—"

"I meant no compliment."

Her head swung around, capturing his gaze. His brow lifted. "I was merely stating facts."

His ridiculous statement confirmed the joke. She jerked her arm from his grasp and turned her face from his scrutiny, before beating a hasty path toward the door.

"Think of the girls," he called behind her. "How are you going to prepare them for their marital duties without my assistance?"

She paused. Logic slowed her retreat. The headmistress was to observe her class in the morning.

"Do you have so many resources that you can abandon the one readily available to you?" His voice wove through her thoughts like rhyme through a stanza.

Indeed, that very lack of resources had inspired her visit in the first place. If she couldn't turn to him for answers, where could she go? She kept her back to him but listened to his calm, insistent plea.

"How can you mislead those young, trusting girls at this crucial juncture?"

She ignored his light mockery. He may not believe her dedication to her students, but then he wasn't familiar with the events that had brought her to this wilderness. Now that she was here, she could never go back. First, however, she must prove to the Higgins sisters that she had knowledge of a carnal nature . . .

"You would answer all my questions about intimacy?" she asked over her shoulder, hesitant to be reminded of his handsome visage. "No matter how difficult, and with complete honesty?"

"The difficulty, I suspect, will be yours in framing the questions." His voice moved closer, the exposed skin on the back of her neck prickled in response. She imagined he was an arm's span away. "Yes, I will answer all your questions," he said, "completely and truthfully."

She turned to face him, surprised to find him even closer than she had approximated, uncomfortably close. She studied him anew, mentally assessing her adversary. The London popinjays had always underestimated her intelligence. Although it pained her to place him in that category, she suspected he would do the same.

"If you will answer my questions first"—she hesitated to emphasis her sacrifice—"I will pose for you."

"You must think me daft." A smile tilted his mustache. He raised one brow and shook his head. "After I fulfill your needs, what assurances do I have that you will fill mine?"

"You have the word of a lady," she said decisively, although in truth she suspected she could avoid meeting his demands.

"No, I don't think so." His eyes narrowed. He tapped an idle rhythm with his prop on the wooden floor.

She bit her lip, suddenly wondering if she had been the one to underestimate him. She studied him anew.

"Let us strike a bargain," he said, overlapping his hands on the top of the silver-knobbed cane. "My needs are for a model to pose in the Grecian fashion. You, on the other hand, require answers to questions of a personal nature."

He stepped closer, engulfing her in a subtle atmosphere

of forbidden magnetism. She could almost taste his determination in the shared air between them, but she refused to give ground.

"I propose that I will answer one of your questions"—his raised finger almost touched her nose—"for every item of clothing you remove as my model."

Her knees threatened to buckle. Surely, he could not desire her, by her uncle's estimation a scrawny scarecrow devoid of a woman's charms, as a model. She was no beauty. To suggest otherwise was cruel.

"I will pose," she said, pushing her spectacles farther up her nose, "but only fully dressed."

"I cannot paint what I cannot see." A dimple flashed in his smile. Sheer willpower kept her from smiling in response.

Chambers's intense gaze raked her form as if fact belied his words. Never had a man regarded her with such intent, certainly not one as handsome and refined as this. His voice, soft and seductive, surrounded her with the rich scent of warmed brandy and his own unique essence. He lured her much like the famed mythological sirens. Lord help her, she could happily drown in this assault.

"I need to see how light and shadow caress a woman's curves."

Immediately, she imagined a physical heat, flowing down her chest and swirling around her waist and hips. Her mind insisted that modesty called for distance between them, but her feet refused to move.

"I need to judge how proportion is modified by the angle of the pose."

Emma thought of the paintings she had viewed of women languishing in forest bowers, bending in some trivial task. Even if she were fully attired, those poses would be too risqué to consider. Still, her insides quivered at his indecent proposal.

Chambers turned abruptly, releasing her from his enchantment. She slumped slightly, catching her breath while he strode toward his easel. "I will draw a picture of an aroused man's private regions if you will remove just one article of clothing."

She should run. She should escape now while she still had her dignity, and yet . . .

"I have already removed my cloak," she said, a bit short of breath.

He smiled, a subtle gesture. "And I have already shown you a picture of a naked man."

She considered a moment, weighing the advantages and disadvantages of compliance. "A boot," she announced. "If I had a buttonhook, I would remove a boot. However, as it is unlikely that such an instrument would be readily available in an artist's studio . . ."

Chambers stepped over to his desk and returned with a long hook fashioned from a metal replica of a woman's leg, complete with garter. "Perhaps this will help?"

Her bluff called, Emma hesitantly accepted the bachelor tool, then sat on the only seat available, the velvet divan. She worked on her side buttons. Who would have thought the man stocked his studio as another would equip a boudoir? Beatrice's voice slipped into her thoughts. *Women come and go at all hours of the night.* Emma's hands froze in the effort to remove the loosened boot.

Chambers placed a fresh piece of foolscap on the board and drew some quick lines on the page with his charcoal. "When a man is aroused, his manhood grows long and hard."

"Hard?" The word interrupted her thoughts. Her boot fell to the floor with a resounding thud. From her vantage on the dais, she couldn't see Chambers's face until he leaned to the side of the board. A knowing smile teased his lips.

"He must be hard to penetrate the woman."

She may have doubted his answer, but he had promised to be truthful. A shiver danced up her spine at his words. Penetrate. One being inside another.

"Is it painful?" Her voice quivered.

He looked pointedly at her other still-shod foot. Resigned, she began to unhook the buttons.

"Not if the man properly prepares the woman," he said. "With preparation, the act is most pleasurable."

Emma removed the boot, then rubbed her stocking-clad foot, debating whether to pursue the concept of preparation.

"Some men find a well-turned ankle very alluring." His voice punctured her thoughts. "Yours are especially so."

Her lips tightened to hide the effects of his compliment. She dropped the hem of her skirt removing the sight of her ankles from his view, then stepped off the platform to view his drawing.

"That . . . that's grotesque!" She quickly covered her gaping mouth with a gloved hand. "That thing would frighten my poor girls to death."

"And what of you, fair lady?" The heat of his breath stirred the tiny hairs on the back of her neck and slid all the way down to her clenched toes. "Does the sight of an aroused man frighten you?"

She forced herself to focus on the charcoal rendition and not the delicious tremors his words initiated. Truth be told, the turmoil created by his close physical proximity frightened her more than some paper image of an object she would likely never encounter. She edged a few steps away.

"Don't run away, Miss Brimley. This is what you are preparing your girls for, but it is not something to fear."

"I am not afraid, sir!" she offered with false bravado.

"The union between a man and a woman is pleasurable

beyond imagination," he said, his knowing smile spreading to his captivating eyes.

"Perhaps for the man." Emma pointed to the daggerlike drawing. "That . . . thing . . . appears as pleasurable as a birch rod."

His soft chuckle held an intimate quality that heated her cheeks. "I promise you, the union is pleasurable for the woman as well, *if* she has the knowledge to handle the man." He stepped closer.

"Isn't that why you came here, Miss Brimley?" He stood behind her. Fissions rippled throughout her body. "For the knowledge?"

Emma knew undeniably that she was in dire trouble.

His lower lip dragged across the tip of her ear. "Let me teach you."

The tips of her breasts tightened. He had touched her! With his lips! Panic blasted through her shock. Without further hesitation, she grabbed two fistfuls of skirt and dashed to the door.

"Will I see you again, Miss Brimley?" His question chased her across the room.

Her unshod feet beat a fast retreat down the wooden hallway in response.

SO HE HADN'T MERELY IMAGINED HER INTELLIGENT and determined spirit on that ride home in the carriage. He was so foxed, he wasn't sure if his initial impression of the new teacher was dream or reality. Probably a little of both. He smiled, feeling more invigorated now than he had before her visit.

Miss Brimley's curiosity amid frequent bouts of blushing had proved surprisingly refreshing. Her cheeks colored quite nicely, a bit of rose madder mixed with pale cream. It had been a long time since he had enjoyed time spent merely talking with a woman. He chuckled a moment before summoning Thomas with the bell pull. The servant appeared immediately.

"I suppose you've realized that she was not the one we anticipated," Nicholas said, walking to the dais to retrieve her boots.

"I'm sorry, sir. I wasn't aware you were expecting anyone else but the model."

"I wasn't." His fingers slipped inside a boot. He frowned, noting it was still damp. "Is her rig outside?"

"No, sir, she arrived on foot."

"The fool woman must have walked through the snow." He shook his head. Most of the women in London society wouldn't cross a street if it meant their slippers might be muddied. It required courage to call on him as she did, and desperation to come through the woods and snow. He glanced toward the hallway. A bit of guilt deflated his pleasure. Perhaps he shouldn't have teased her as he had. "See that she gets home safely, Thomas."

"I'll alert Henry."

"Tell Henry she's to be delivered discreetly," Nicholas added. "No one is to know she's been here." He handed the boots over to Thomas. "I'll warrant the old biddies would have a fit if they knew she'd been consorting with the likes of me." That returned the smile to his face. "And see that she gets something to eat. She's too thin by half."

"Will we be entertaining the young woman again, sir?" Thomas asked.

"I believe I scared her half out of her wits. I doubt she'll return." That realization drained his high spirits. Even though he had suspected he was challenging the teacher's sensibilities as never before, he found he could not stop. There was something unaffected about her that pulled at his baser instincts.

"I'm sorry, sir," Thomas said. "I know you hoped to

start on *The Seduction of Antiope* for the spring exhibition."

"Antiope?" His brows lifted. "Not for that one." He looked back at the empty dais and reflected, almost to himself. "No, I think Artemis, the virgin goddess, would be a better suit."

His fingers twitched with creative energy. Miss Brimley would be perfect for Artemis. Her rich brown hair loosened from that prim braided bun softly curving past the firm mounds of her breasts. Her sweet, wide-eyed expression in perfect contrast with the sensuous lines of her feminine curves. Her winsome body positioned at his every command. His groin tightened, much as it had when he had urged her to stay.

Of course, that was before his rash actions caused her to flee. Perhaps his father was correct. He always managed to sabotage his opportunities for success before they could be realized. Bloody hell, he should never have gotten close enough to smell her winter-apple scent of wholesome innocence. He ground the tip of his stick in the floor in self-reproach, then glanced to Thomas. "I suppose if she does not return we shall have neither."

"I've always found your Yorkshire landscapes quite pleasing to the eye, sir."

Chambers glanced at a primed empty canvas leaning on the far wall. "I appreciate your assessment, Thomas, but it's common knowledge that the Academy is only interested in paintings of Greek mythology. Another landscape is tantamount to another rejection." He grimaced. "I've collected enough of those already."

"Will you return to the tavern to find a model, sir?"

Chambers paused. He doubted he would discover a suitable model at the Bleatin' Ram. Now that he had found and lost the one model who awakened his creative juices, he had little interest in settling for less. The time spent with

Miss Brimley, however, had resulted in a need of a more physical nature. The tavern women would welcome him with open arms and provide the needed relief. He tapped the floor with his stick.

"That is an excellent plan," he said. "Let Pettibone lock up their young innocents. An experienced woman looks the same and talks far less." Thomas looked confused, but Chambers saw no reason to elaborate. "I've had enough challenge this evening. Tell Henry I will need him once he returns."

• Three •

THAT NIGHT, ALONE IN HER SPARSELY FURNISHED bedroom, Emma tossed and turned, alternately reliving the sensual excitement of Chambers's attentions and the shock of his indecent propositions. How could her simple plan to escape her uncle have dissolved into such disaster?

She was right to flee Chambers's studio, she reassured herself; any proper lady would have done the same. The spinsters hadn't lied; that man would sully everything he touched.

Still the thought of those very talented fingers called forth the memory of eyes that sparked with humor and a secret knowledge, lips that beckoned with improper suggestions, and a manner that infuriated, yet beguiled. Beneath all the masculine allure beckoned the greatest seduction of all: he wanted her for his model, not her cousin Penelope, or some other properly born lady. He wanted *her*. Emma clenched the sides of the narrow mattress while longing burned through her chest.

Stop that! she ordered herself. Who better than she understood the dangers that lie along that path? Hadn't her uncle and cousin reminded her on a daily basis that she was born on the wrong side of the blanket? Hadn't she seen with her own eyes the injustices dealt her mother, and felt the stinging insults and alienation of a child born outside of marriage? She bit her lip and turned on her side. Hers was a lesson well learned. Attraction to a man of Chambers's standing could lead to no good.

Thoughts of her heritage stirred a niggling suspicion. Was her lack of ancestry somehow visible to a man like Chambers? Why else would he have offered his devil's barter? Her fingers curled into fists. Panic roiled in her stomach. He knew her secret. If he suspected she wasn't worthy of a promise kept, he could reveal her charade to the spinsters.

No, she thought, fighting the tears burning her eyes. Chambers was different from other men. She wasn't sure why, but she trusted him in this. Her secret was safe, but she wasn't as convinced of her reputation.

Emma punched at her pillow, hoping to force the thin stuffing of feathers into some semblance of a mound. She was wrong to go to his residence, wrong to step into his lair, his studio. She would simply not make that mistake again. A sob caught in her throat. Memories would fade and she could continue a quiet respectable life in the country with her poems and students. A part of her heart cried in protest, but she closed her mind to arguments. The plan was set. Starting tomorrow she would ban thoughts of Chambers, but tonight . . . his face loomed in her thoughts . . . tonight there could be no harm in dreams.

The next morning, still tired from lack of sleep, Emma faced an equally daunting prospect: her first class. She walked into the library filled with apprehension. Two of the five young faces waiting for her seemed eager and delighted with her appearance. Two others appeared a bit shy and embarrassed, and one, a girl with pointed features and reddish brown hair, looked downright defiant. Behind them all, a dour-faced Cecilia stood as imperious and regal as the gilt-framed image of the Queen hanging above her left shoulder.

"I'm pleased to see that you've recovered from your headache, Mrs. Brimley," Cecilia said. "We missed you yesterday evening."

A modicum of panic jolted her already frayed nerves. The driver had been careful not to deliver her to the front door of the school. Instead she had walked the final short distance intending to explain that she needed a bit of fresh air if anyone inquired about her entrance.

"I had hoped not to impose, but I'm afraid the long trip from London was more demanding than I had anticipated." Emma paused; the long trip was but a minor inconvenience compared to the demands that awaited her here. "The fresh air and extra rest have done wonders. Now, however, I believe we should leave yesterday behind and concentrate on the matter at hand."

Turning the conversation from her mysterious disappearance to an equally uncomfortable subject was a bit risky, but she was better prepared to discuss the latter, at least for this one class.

"Yes." Cecilia looked unconvinced. "Perhaps we should." She clapped her hands.

"Ladies." All faces turned to Cecilia. "It is our goal at Pettibone to prepare proper young ladies to assume their place in society, and to secure by virtue of their refined manners and appearance, an excellent prospect for matrimony."

The word "matrimony" inspired tittering and fidgeting

among the girls, but Cecilia regained control with another swift clap of her hands.

"Although you are properly trained to assume a household and accompany a husband as society dictates, we feel additional instruction is necessary to prepare you for your wifely obligations. We have specifically obtained the expertise of Mrs. Brimley to discuss those issues with you. I trust you will treat her with the grace and propriety with which you have been prepared."

"I'm so glad you've come," gushed the oldest of her students, a tall blonde named Elizabeth. "My mother says I should be engaged by the end of next season. I have so many questions."

"Did you ask your mother for answers?" Emma silently prayed the answer would be yes. Then perhaps Elizabeth could instruct them all.

"Oh, no, no." Elizabeth shook her head so violently her blonde curls swung with the motion. "That would never do. The subject would be too awkward for dear Mama."

Emma surely understood that. Her own mother never saw fit to discuss such topics. Perhaps because her mother realized Emma's prospects would be limited without a large dowry to compensate for obvious deficiencies. "I see. What sort of questions do you have?"

"I have a question," Alice, a younger girl with expressive brown eyes, interrupted. "I've lived here as long as I can remember so I haven't little brothers like Charlotte." She squeezed the hand of the girl sitting next to her. "My question is . . . what do they look like? The boys, I mean."

The other girls, except the loyal friend Charlotte, dissolved in hearty laughter.

Emma clapped her hands to quiet them down. "Ladies, ladies, that will be quite enough. Miss Higgins could substitute another course of study if this one proves too disruptive."

The girls hid their laughter under smug smiles. Cecilia smiled approval from the back wall.

"I think that is a very good question." Emma patted the hand of a furiously blushing Alice. "I haven't any brothers either. Perhaps if I had, I would have been less surprised on my wedding night."

After viewing Lord Nicholas Chambers's drawing, she could well imagine how shocked and unprepared she would have been had she actually experienced a wedding night. Perhaps the spinster sisters had the right idea. Unfortunately, they had entrusted the wrong person.

"That was courageous, Alice. Thank you." Emma was rewarded with a timid smile. "As the rest of you believe yourselves to be quite knowledgeable, perhaps someone can answer Alice's question?"

"They have a snake in front like a dancing cobra," the defiant one said. Emma instantly recognized the voice as belonging to the girl the others in the hallway had called Fanny. She committed the face to memory.

Fanny continued her discourse by holding a curved arm close to her chest. "If you don't keep the snake caged, the snake will strike."

Her hand lunged at poor Alice. Both Alice and the one next to her shrieked. Fanny laughed at their reactions.

"That's quite enough, young lady," Emma scolded before turning her attention to Alice. "Young gentlemen do not have snakes, but they do have an appendage where we do not."

Emma straightened, assuming her teacher stance. "The great poet, John Donne, once said—"

Several girls moaned in unison beneath their breath. Emma continued, undaunted by their lack of appreciation for poetry.

" 'Love's mysteries in souls do grow, but yet the body is his book.' Perhaps we shall let the body be our book and begin with a description of the masculine form." Especially as this was the only information she had to impart. Despite her resolve not to think of him, she issued a silent thank you to Lord Nicholas Chambers. The mere thought of his name initiated a flutter low beneath her stays. She shifted uncomfortably and forced her focus back to her students.

She glanced back to Cecilia, who stood behind the girls. "May I draw an illustration?"

The older woman cautiously nodded before taking a step closer. Emma selected a seat in the midst of the girls and did her best to reproduce the intimate components of Mr. Rodin's statue. The girls crowded around her shoulder; even Cecilia ventured a peek.

Fanny screwed up her face. "How can they prod you when it's curled up like that?"

Elizabeth's eyes widened. "What do you mean, 'prod you'?" She glanced at Emma in alarm. "Can they do that?"

"Why would they want to?" another asked.

"Does it hurt to be prodded?"

The cage door opened and all manner of questions burst forth, flapping about Emma's ears like gulls diving for fish. An incessant clapping of hands silenced the girls. Cecilia towered above them all.

"We will have order in this room," she demanded.

The girls quickly dispersed back to their seats.

"I believe Mrs. Brimley has covered quite enough new territory for one day. If these sessions are to continue, I shall expect to see more structure and discipline."

The girls lowered their heads, avoiding eye contact. Although grateful that Cecilia had saved her from proving her own ignorance, Emma nevertheless felt the sting of her reference to class discipline.

"I suggest each of you write down your questions, so Mrs. Brimley can present the answers in an organized, civilized fashion. And Miss Barnesworth"—Fanny looked up—"you will resolve to keep your vulgarities to yourself."

Charlotte hid a giggle behind her hand. Fanny cast a sideways glare at Emma. However, all heads peaceably bent to the task of writing questions. Questions, Emma worried, she didn't have answers for.

Cecilia signaled for Emma to join her in the hall. Emma rose, her stomach churning at her anticipated chastisement.

"We owe our patron gratitude for suggesting education in these intimate matters," Cecilia said once they were safely out of earshot of the young pupils. "The girls' enthusiasm and desire prove the necessity for such information."

"Yes, madam," Emma said, surprised not only by the lack of reproach but also that Cecilia's attitude closely mirrored her own. "I appreciate your suggestion of the lists," she said, regarding the older sister with new appreciation. "I will definitely use them to advantage."

Cecilia nodded. "So you shall. I will give you my list of questions in the morning."

"Your list?" Emma stepped back. "Does that mean you will be attending the rest of the classes?"

Cecilia smiled, turned on her heel, then continued down the hall.

AS THE GIRLS SILENTLY FILED OUT OF THE LIBRARY, Emma collected their papers, pages and pages of carefully penned lines. After the last student handed over her assignment, Emma slumped into a chair and scanned the collection of questions. Most of the inquiries echoed her own, and she hadn't even seen Cecilia's list.

Despair overwhelmed her. Only one person could provide sufficient information to answer these questions and he—she shuddered—he demanded an exorbitant price. She shuffled through the papers. Even if she were so desperate as to accept Lord Nicholas Chambers's outlandish offer, she didn't have enough items of clothing to garner all the needed answers. She ticked off on her fingers the layers of petticoats, her drawers, chemise, and corset. Remembering how he allowed her to ask a question for each shoe, she added four fingers to accommodate her stockings and gloves. She ran out of digits and started a quick count on paper. Her propriety would unravel long before the questions expired.

She retrieved her mother's handkerchief from her cuff, squeezing it briefly before she proceeded to clean her lenses. A faint essence of rose petals, her mother's fragrance, drifted to her nose. "I wish you were here, Mama. Oh, the questions I would ask."

She gazed at the crumpled linen, hoping for spiritual guidance, but thoughts of a practical nature intervened. Would the handkerchief count as an item of clothing? Her spectacles? She replaced the glasses on her nose. She wore both on her person, did she not?

And if the handkerchief counted, what else could she layer to barter for answers? A victorious grin bubbled from deep inside. In retrospect, perhaps she possessed enough clothing after all.

She would pay another visit to Lord Nicholas Chambers, only this time she'd be prepared for his devil's bargain.

· Four ·

"BLOODY HELL, THOMAS, WHAT COULD POSSIBLY induce you to wake me at this infernal hour?"

Chambers resisted opening his eyes. For two evenings straight he had made a foray to the Bleatin' Ram but in both cases returned with only a hangover for company. The women had welcomed him with great enthusiasm. Yet even after several drinks, none seemed to satisfy. Ever since that curious widow had trespassed . . .

"It is eleven o'clock in the morning sir, and you have a visitor."

Chambers groaned. "Don't tell me William has descended upon us again. For all his good intentions, I do wish my brother would lavish them on someone else."

"You are the Marquess's only brother, sir."

Chambers opened one eye. "Surely, we have some disreputable cousins hiding closer to London. Can't he visit them?"

"This visitor is a woman, sir. The widow Brimley has returned."

"The widow Brimley?" Both eyes opened, blinking rapidly until they adjusted to the sunlight streaming through the window. A spark of sensual awareness ignited deep inside him, chasing away the last remnants of sleep. "I thought we had frightened her back to London."

"Apparently not, sir."

The sarcasm in Thomas's stoic reply brought a smile to Chambers's lips. He pulled himself upright, then braced his body while his head struggled to find balance.

"I took the precaution of bringing your head remedy, sir."

"Thomas, you are a saint." Chambers accepted the offered restorative and downed it quickly before the taste registered. Grimacing, he handed back the empty glass. "I'm getting too old for this."

"Nonsense, sir, you are in your prime."

"William would beg to differ."

Thomas poured hot water into the basin and stacked fresh towels by the bowl.

"If the widow has returned," Chambers said, following the progress of his valet, "perhaps she plans to accept my offer." Why else would she return? His chest expanded with tingling anticipation. If his head didn't already pound so much, he'd crow with triumph.

"What offer is that, sir?" Thomas asked.

"I'm attempting to barter her services as a model." A smile tilted his lips in spite of the resulting throbbing at his temples. *She was such a challenge, seducing her will be pure delight. I wonder if that pretty blush travels down to her toes.* He stopped short. Where had those thoughts come from? He glanced to the pillow indented from his slumber. He must still be dreaming.

He started an unsteady course toward the basin, the aftereffects of the previous night's activities affecting his gait more than his weakened leg. "Naturally Thomas, I'm trusting the household to keep her presence here a secret."

"I shall remind the staff to be discreet. Do you need my assistance to dress for the day?"

"No, no. Don't tarry here." Nicholas rubbed his hand over his chin stubble, anxious to hurry through the morning rituals. One didn't squander precious daylight when there was painting to be done. Miss Brimley . . . rather, Artemis awaits!

"Go pull the draperies from the studio windows. And Thomas," he said, bracing his arms on the table supporting the basin, "do find the young widow something to eat. We have squirrels in the garden better fed than she."

"From all appearances, the widow Brimley has plumped since her last visit," Thomas offered from the doorway.

Nicholas winced. This was not a morning for sudden motions or deciphering riddles. "What exactly do you mean by 'plumped'? She's not a pigeon, Thomas."

"With your permission, sir, when Mrs. Brimley called two nights ago, I noted her attire appeared a bit large for her frame."

"Yes, I noticed that as well. She was drowning in all that ill-fitting black cloth," Nicholas said, remembering his own desire to view her free of all that baggage. Heat flared in his groin. Seeking relief, he splashed water on his face.

"This morning," Thomas said, stepping back into the room to drape a towel over one arm, "she can barely fasten the buttons on the same garment."

Nicholas stopped his motions and glanced over his shoulder toward Thomas. He ignored the offered towel, preferring the stimulation of the water dripping down his chest. How could she fill that monstrosity of a dress in so few days? Even gluttony required time to pad one's figure . . . *pad*? Instantly, he recognized the reason for her "plumping." The chit hoped to best him at his own game.

Appreciation of her ingenuity pulled at his lips. It was no small wonder he enjoyed her company, a challenge at every turn. But if she thought she could thwart his purposes with his own terms, then she underestimated the extent of his desires. Now, what to do about it?

He pulled a cloth from Thomas's arm and turned back to the mirror, scowling at his reflection.

"Did you place Mrs. Brimley in the front salon?" He watched the mirror for Thomas's nod. "Is the fire lit for her comfort?"

"Yes, sir, I prepared it myself."

"Excellent." He smiled, blotting his face with the cloth. The plump pigeon was set for roasting.

"I would like breakfast served in the salon. Please set the table for the widow and myself directly in front of the fire."

Thomas's brow creased in an unusual display of puzzlement. "But won't that be rather hot for—"

"Directly in front, Thomas." Nicholas insisted, swabbing the cloth over his chest hair to catch the clinging droplets.

"Yes, sir. I will attend to it immediately."

Nicholas smiled, choosing not to elaborate. It was time for the teacher to be taught a lesson. "Please inform Mrs. Brimley that I shall be down presently."

EMMA PACED THE LENGTH OF THE SALON, NOT AN EASY task given the weight of the garments journeying with her. Dismissing the tingling excitement coursing through her veins at the prospect of seeing him again, she schooled herself to focus. Her feminine desires mustn't interfere with this educational opportunity.

She mentally rehearsed the series of questions she planned to ask his lordship, assuming his offer was still available.

Dear heavens! What if he had found another model to meet his needs? Another woman, a comely one well endowed with feminine attributes, could be disrobed in his studio this very minute. She stopped in her tracks. Rejection tore through her belly. It wasn't as if she hadn't been rejected before. The few suitors who had offered tepid kisses during her lackluster season had balked at the prospect of marriage. That was not correct, she amended. They had balked at marriage to her, as both had married someone else within a year's time. The pain from those prior snubs stabbed at her anew. Her fingers tried to curl into a fist, but the layering of gloves of various lengths made the motion impossible. Instead her fingers leaned into a fat claw.

Still, the possibility that Chambers would choose someone else to model for his painting disturbed her beyond the pale. She would lose her bartering position, that was certain. But, she had the distinct impression she would lose something else as well. She bit her lip and crushed her linen handkerchief in her palm. He must still need her. He must.

Thomas appeared carrying a wooden table that he proceeded to set before the fire.

"His lordship shall appear presently. May I offer something for your comfort?"

Relieved, Emma shook her head no. If Lord Nicholas Chambers planned to receive her, he must still require her services. Her trip to Black Oak was not in vain.

Although the prospect of unfastening buttons and removing layers of fabric in Chambers's presence kept her nerves on edge, she remained satisfied that her multiple layers would protect her from revealing anything of an intimate nature. The thought offered a semblance of control. She could do this.

Thomas returned with linens, china, and silver and proceeded to arrange the table for a meal. Emma chose to study the landscapes lining the salon's walls while she waited. The room had been too dark and she too nervous on her prior visit to notice them.

A shift in the current of the room prickled the back of her neck and lifted gooseflesh on arms buried beneath three layers of sleeves. With sharp awareness, she knew the cause. Lord Nicholas Chambers had arrived.

"Widow Brimley, I had not anticipated seeing you so soon."

She turned and curtsied, her stomach twisted into tight knots. Why did the sight of him, the mere sound of his voice, reduce her insides to warm mush?

"I have been admiring your collection of artwork." Her words stuck and scraped her throat like dry toast. "Particularly these charming landscapes."

His lips thinned. "*Charming*, Mrs. Brimley?" His eyes glittered dangerously. Her chest tightened. Somehow her words had given offense, although she wasn't sure why.

"They were produced by a local painter, not worthy of much notice." He frowned.

For just an instant, she thought she saw a flash of pain, of vulnerability. However, it quickly passed behind a façade of confident arrogance. She readjusted her glasses. Perhaps she had been mistaken.

He moved toward the table, his walking stick not in evidence. "Would you care to join me for breakfast?"

"I've already eaten, thank you." It was a lie, of course. She couldn't eat and expect to squeeze into all these clothes, but he wouldn't know that.

"Then please do me the honor of sitting with me by the fire. We can talk while I take a bit of refreshment." He motioned her toward a chair with an assertive sweep of his arm.

The seat he had indicated was too close to the fire for comfort, but she couldn't politely refuse. Hopefully, his lordship was a quick eater. The warmth generated by his presence alone could melt the waxworks at Madame Tussauds. She negotiated her multiple layers into the breadth of the chair.

"Am I to assume by your visit this morning that you have reconsidered my offer?" he asked, after both had been seated at the table. She smiled nervously, reminding herself that her overdressed state allowed her to play the vixen without compromise to her virtue.

"The girls had more questions," she stated. Beatrice and Cecilia had questions as well, but she didn't mention them. "I have little choice but to accept your proposal."

"I see." His gaze slowly swept from her eyes to momentarily rest on her lips, before a prolonged appraisal of her clothes-inflated chest. She shifted a bit on the chair, afraid he might see too much.

A tight smile pulled at his lips before he carefully, and oh-so-slowly, slathered cream onto some hearty scones. He offered one to her, but at her refusal, placed it on his plate, proceeding to carefully dish eggs, potatoes, and various meats.

The scent of the lavish fare set her stomach to complain. She bit her lip, hoping Chambers didn't notice. A rivulet of moisture raced between her shoulder blades down to the small of her back. Her black bodice held the heat from the fire too efficiently. What the top layer captured, the two below retained.

"I am honored that you have placed your faith and trust in me by accepting my proposal fairly and honestly," he said after what seemed to be many protracted moments. "I believe honesty to be one of the great undervalued virtues.

Don't you agree, *Miss* Brimley?" A dimple flashed for a moment before his face settled into a more serious expression.

"Honesty is important," she replied. Although at the moment, garbed in every piece of clothing that she owned, she didn't feel very honest in her representation. She tried to ignore the moisture dampening the first layer of undergarments.

"William Shakespeare once wrote that 'honesty coupled to beauty is to have honey a sauce to sugar.' " Lifting a small jar, he poured a thick stream of amber honey onto a waiting scone. He placed the sweetened biscuit on her plate. "Sugar, *Mrs.* Brimley?"

"Shakespeare!" Enthusiasm displaced some of her discomfort. "You read the bard as well as Lord Byron?" This was the conversation she longed to share. She leaned forward. "I'm partial to sonnets myself. In fact, I am teaching literature appropriate for young ladies as well as"—she averted her eyes—"other courses."

She returned her gaze to his. How unfortunate that after today, after she had secured all her answers, she'd not be allowed to talk about literature, or art, or anything else with him again. A pang of remorse twitched at her lips.

"I'm sorry," he said, his eyes a study of empathy.

Shock sizzled across her chest like snowflakes on heated skin. She pulled back in her chair and stared. Had he read her thoughts? What else did he know?

He reached for the teapot. "I thought Thomas had offered you tea. Allow me to pour. A nice hot cup of tea on such a cold day should warm you for the work ahead."

He was just well mannered! Almost giddy at her false impression, she shook her head no. He poured the hot liquid anyway. She almost giggled. He certainly wasn't as perceptive as she had credited him, otherwise he would have honored her refusal. Without thought, she sipped the hot liquid.

Steam from the cup added to the gathering moisture on her face. She resisted the urge to retrieve one of several handkerchiefs tucked up her sleeve to mop her forehead in an unseemly fashion. Instead, she snapped open the re-membered black fan that dangled from her wrist, and waved a frantic current. *This must be what inferno feels like.* Although she'd brought the fan as another item of clothing to barter, she sorely needed its comfort. How apropos she should experience inferno in the midst of her deceit.

"Perhaps we should get started on your painting," she said, anxious to escape the sweltering room. "I have many questions to present to you."

His eyes narrowed slightly. "I can see that."

Still seated at the table, he selected a poker from an as-semblage of implements, then stoked the fire, releasing even more heat into the room. "First, however, I wish to learn your philosophy on honesty and deceit. You recall I promised that your secret regarding your lack of experi-ence is safe with me."

"Thank you for that, sir." Her words, to her mind, issued slow and heavy as if she had to push them through the very air. Indeed, everything seemed heavier, her clothes, her eyelids, even the fan. She concentrated on waving it faster.

"I need to know if my secret is safe with you." His gaze leveled on her face. There seemed an unusual intensity about him, though exactly why she couldn't discern.

"Your secret?" Had she heard him correctly? "You haven't shared a secret with me, sir." She gave into temp-tation and attempted to discreetly blot her forehead with a lacy scrap of linen. The heat numbing her senses. "Perhaps you've mistaken me for another, as before?"

"My secret lies in my art," Chambers continued, holding

her gaze captive. "The creation of a painting is personal beyond measure. If you come to this bargain lightly, it would render my art trivial. I would be deeply offended. I must know that you come to this agreement honestly and that you trust me to create a painting worthy of your sacrifice."

"I'm not a critic, sir." She struggled to keep annoyance from her tone. Why wasn't he as anxious to begin painting as she was to shed some of these superfluous layers? "I would not make light of your art."

"But are you a believer?" He leaned forward, emphatic in his discourse.

Albeit a bit woozy, she looked deep into his eyes. Confidence resided there, as well as arrogance, but she glimpsed deeper emotions as well. Remembering his childlike innocence in the moonlight, she recognized both his yearning and his need for approval. Her heart expanded. He was not unlike her young charges at Pettibone: eager, trusting, and vulnerable. In those eyes, his eyes, all things were possible.

"Yes." Her lips spoke for her heart. "I believe in you."

"Excellent." His wide smile shattered the brief spiritual connection.

She blinked, trying to bring Chambers into focus. What just happened? His vulnerability collapsed behind rakish charm. Or was it all her imagination?

The heat in the room, combined with the weight of all her garments, pulled the blood from her head. "Before we begin, my lord." Her voice sounded slurred to her ears, distant. "There's something I should tell you." Was she even speaking?

His brows descended, puzzlement chased across his face, then alarm. He drifted slightly to the right, along with the table and the fire.

Light-headed, she tried to stand but her knees buckled. Her world dissolved to black.

· Five ·

CHAMBERS STARED IN DISBELIEF AT THE BUNDLE of wool and trimmings that had crumbled into his arms. Good Lord, he'd meant to harm the girl.

His hands caught her about her rib cage, but the garments thus captured slid up while her body slipped down. She hung from his hands like a drunken sailor.

"Mrs. Brimley?" He gave her a gentle shake. The effort dislodged her spectacles while her head lolled to one side. The peaches and cream complexion he'd noted earlier drained to a stark white. Her hat slipped from its proud mooring and settled at an absurd angle just above her closed eyelids.

"Thomas!" he bellowed, his heart hammering in his throat.

The voluminous garments negated his awkward attempts to pull her to a chair. Finally, he straddled her spineless body like one might a racehorse and hauled her to a seat cushion. If he hadn't halted her continued downward progress, she would have easily tumbled out of the chair and onto the floor.

"Thomas!"

"I'm here, sir," a calm voice answered from the doorway.

Chambers half turned while supporting the woman in place. "I think she's fainted," he gasped. "Hold her for me. Mind her spectacles. They've fallen somewhere on the floor."

Once Thomas kept her positioned, Chambers moved his ear toward her mouth. The gentle puff of warm sweet breath brought instant relief, draining away his heightened anxiety.

"She's breathing, thank God." He straightened, wiping sweat from his brow with the sleeve of his shirt.

"What happened, sir?" Thomas asked, holding Mrs. Brimley in place.

"It must have been the heat. Those clothes weigh at least a stone, probably more." He grimaced. Bloody fool. He should have known better than to enter this child's game. He could almost picture William's disapproving countenance. This time it would be well deserved.

Nicholas slipped one arm beneath the general location of her knees and the other around her back. "Let's move her away from the fire."

"Are you sure, sir? Won't you let me do that?" Thomas asked an instant before Nicholas scooped her into his arms.

"No. My leg will hold." He grimaced, dismissing the pain that shot up his thigh into his hip. He alone was responsible for putting the poor girl into this predicament. He alone would see her through. Her head tipped back exposing a long fragile neck. A gentle lift of his forearm adjusted her head back into his chest.

He looked down, letting her body reposition in his

arms. She was like a bird. A poor, broken bird injured by his hand. All the weight of her garments left his arms and settled heavy about his heart.

"Where to, sir?" Thomas asked, breaking into his thoughts.

"Arianne's room at the top of the stairs." Nicholas moved awkwardly toward the door.

"Bring me some water and smelling salts, if you can find them," he called over his shoulder. "She'll need a maid to remove some of these clothes."

"I sent the maids away for the day," Thomas said behind him. "You didn't want any word of Mrs. Brimley's presence traveling back to the school."

Bloody hell, he'd forgotten about that. Another bit of poor judgment to add to his growing list. "Then have Henry get that wife of his. She'll know what to do and stay mum about it." He took the steps as best he could, taking care to avoid the copious quantities of fabric that threatened underfoot. It was a wonder the woman could move with all this ghastly wool wrapped insidiously about her.

Once Nicholas cleared the stairs, Thomas hurried in front to open the door and pull back the bed coverings. Nicholas laid Mrs. Brimley on the bed, then sat down beside her to catch his breath. The pain in his leg screamed bloody murder, but this was not the time for the solace of a numbing brandy. Hearing Thomas's footsteps pound back down the stairs, Nicholas leaned over his prone companion.

"Mrs. Brimley, wake up." He removed the silly hat and lightly tapped her cheek, watching for a flutter of her lashes.

She lay unconscious like a sleeping child. Not quite like a child, he amended, casting an eye down her definitely feminine curves. Hesitant to risk bruising her skin with a more substantial tap, he ran a knuckle instead along a delicate cheekbone, and leaned closer, lowering his voice to a gentle entreaty. "Mrs. Brimley?"

Still no response.

"Confound it, woman." He pulled back before calling over his shoulder. "Thomas, where's that water?"

He attacked the large buttons on her bodice jacket, pushing the jet buttons through tight buttonholes. Once the jacket was unfastened, he still faced the task of pulling it off her limp body. He did so as delicately as he could, then tossed the jacket to a nearby chair and proceeded with the next item. Rocking her from side to side to track down elusive hooks, buttons, and ties, he managed to wield his way through the jacket, two skirts, a dress, and a horsehair bustle. He paused long enough to wipe the sweat from his brow.

"A man could use a bloodhound to find the woman in this mess. Children do less unwrapping at Christmas." He proceeded to apply his aching fingertips to the unfastening of tiny buttons lining a high-neck gray blouse. His endeavor was rewarded with a glimpse of pale white skin.

"Thank God. You are in here after all, Mrs. Brimley. I had begun to suspect otherwise."

Beneath his industrious fingers, her chest rose and fell with easy breaths. A little color seeped back into her cheeks. He worked faster, revealing a few layers of fetching lace, and then a pale pink corset, the color of dewy English roses in the early light of dawn. A smile lifted the corners of his lips. "My, my, Mrs. Brimley. What have we here?"

He hurried to finish unfastening the drab black buttons, then splayed the fabric wide. Before his hands could touch her creamy white skin, a knock at the door summoned. He was about to tell Thomas to enter but reconsidered. Mrs. Brimley wouldn't approve of being viewed in such a manner, of that he was certain.

"Just a minute, Thomas." He pulled a single sheet across her barely attired form. "That will keep the chill off." He left the room, closing the door softly behind him.

IN A SEMICONSCIOUS STATE, EMMA HEARD A RATTLING and could well visualize the carriages and cabs outside the window, all the sounds of the bustling streets of London . . . London! She lurched to her elbows in the bed, her eyes widening to a fuzzy out-of-focus yellow room filled with bright winter sunlight, not the drab green walls of her uncle's residence in London.

She gulped air, waiting for her pulse to slow and her head to clear. Wind gusts rattled the windowpanes, pulling her attention to the cheerless winter sky and bare tree skeletons outside. Her uncle's windows looked out on the bricks and stones of other buildings, not sky and country-side. She wasn't back in London, thank heavens. She sighed relief.

But if not London, she thought glancing quickly about the room, she wasn't at Pettibone either. Unless, of course, her bed had magically tripled in size and grown mahogany posters at each corner.

Confused, she twisted toward the side of the bed, searching for her spectacles on a bedside table. The sheet slipped to her lap, exposing her shocking state of undress. Her breath caught. Merciful heavens!

She fell back to the mattress, frantically pulling the sheet to her nose. She remembered stifling heat and suffocating layers of wool . . . and Chambers! She groaned. How was she to escape this predicament?

The door creaked open. Emma quickly squeezed her eyes shut, feigning sleep. Although, in truth, it proved difficult to master the slow breath of slumber when her heart raced like a hackney driver in pursuit of a tip.

Uneven footsteps clamored across a wooden floor until muffled by a carpet. Water splashed in a basin not far from her ear. The faint scent of bacon rashers and coddled eggs nearly made her eyes water. *Go away*, she prayed. If left alone she would locate her clothes and spectacles and leave this disastrous turn of events.

A damp cloth stroked her forehead.

She flinched, a mere reflection of the vast distance her heart ventured in its leap to her throat.

"You can open your eyes, Mrs. Brimley. I know you're awake." Chambers's tone spoke neither concern nor displeasure.

Embarrassed by her situation and irritated by his apparent dispassion regarding same, she shook her head from side to side.

"Come now. It does no good to pretend. We need to talk."

She sighed and opened her eyes, easing the sheet to uncover her mouth, but pulling it taut beneath her chin.

"That's better. I thought the cool water would help." Chambers bent over her, his eyes searching with a surprising degree of urgency, while his voice modulated to a soothing tone much as if he were addressing his dog. She almost expected him to scratch her head, but instead he tenderly swabbed her cheeks.

"What happened? Where am I?" she asked, already dreading the answer to the second question.

"In my bed." His eyebrow cocked. "At least in one of them. The house has several."

The skin on her arms prickled. Although the differences between London life and Yorkshire had been significant, surely lying about in a man's bed, scantily attired, was not acceptable in either city.

"This cannot be proper." She pushed back into the mattress, trying to create a little more distance between them.

"Perhaps not, but in this case it was necessary." Chambers reached for a glass on the side table. "Here, drink this."

He held the glass and let the liquid slip between her lips. She swallowed.

Liquid fire surged down her throat, exploding in a ball of flame in her empty stomach. Her torso whipped upright into a sitting position, the top of her exposed corset barely missing Chambers's nose. Gasping, she recovered the fallen sheet and settled back, waving her hand in front of her face.

"What was that?" she rasped.

"Just a little brandy." The corners of his eyes crinkled betraying his amusement. His obvious enjoyment made her particularly wary.

"Try a little more." He held the glass in position. "It goes down easier the second time."

She waved his offer away, opting instead for a deep draught of cooling breath. Her lungs filled with precious air laced with his exotic essence. She coughed, but the taste of him remained.

"Why are you doing this?" she asked, grasping control of her breath.

"You fainted," he explained. "The brandy will put a little color back in your cheeks."

"I suspect my cheeks are bright enough." Indeed, her face bathed in heat generated by sheer humiliation. He offered the drink again, but she shook her head.

"No? Then I'll just place it on the table." He settled the glass, then dabbed at her cheekbones with the moist cloth. "You might change your mind when you consider your situation."

Her situation! Practically naked, neatly installed in a bed he probably used for scandalous endeavors, the last thing she needed was to examine her situation. She shriveled beneath the cover of the sheet.

"Oh, Thomas recovered these from the carpet." He reached in the pocket of his morning jacket and extracted her spectacles. Peering through the lenses, he hesitated a moment before polishing them with a cloth from his pocket.

Irritation stabbed at her, although the reason escaped her at the moment. She released her death grip on the sheet momentarily to reclaim her glasses.

"I was not in this room when I fainted," she stated pointedly. Her lenses quickly brought his impossibly handsome face into focus, unnerving her further. The enormity of her situation sharpened along with her eyesight.

"Nor was I undressed." She glared at him. "I distinctly recall being dressed."

That insufferable eyebrow cocked. "Dressed enough for several people if I recall. You fainted from the heat of all those garments." His smile widened. "Although tempted to leave you prone at my feet, I carried you here for your comfort."

For her discomfort more likely, she thought as another wave of embarrassment radiated from her cheeks.

He shifted his balance, resting one hand on the bedside table.

She glanced pointedly at his leg. "*You* carried me?"

His smile dissipated; he responded with a curt nod.

"But how . . ." She glanced to see a scowl settle on his face and decided now was not the time to inquire about his injuries. "Who undressed me?"

"I did," he answered, his lips pulled to a straight line.

She groaned, turning her face away from his scrutiny. Was there to be no end to this torture? God must be punishing her for her foolish attempt to win his devil's bargain.

"You would have preferred someone else?" Chambers

asked. "Thomas? Or perhaps old Henry?" She heard his haughty undertones and well imagined that cocked eyebrow. "I'm afraid there are no women in residence who could assist. I sent for Cook from Pettibone but expediency demanded—"

"Expediency?" she sobbed, turning to face him. "That is your justification?" Tears welled in her eyes. Cook would surely tell her new employer. Her whole fabrication would unravel and her past would be revealed. She'd be returned to London, where her uncle would delight in subjecting her to his perverse and inhumane "corrections," much as he had her mother. All because she thought she could trick Chambers into answering some questions.

"Where are my clothes?" The words barely squeezed around the lump in her throat.

Seemingly unmoved by her outburst, he stepped aside, revealing that what in her unfocused state she had assumed was a chifforobe was actually a chair piled high with crinolines, overskirts, and bodices, in essence the remainder of her entire wardrobe.

"I know Londoners have some strange customs," he said with barely concealed ridicule, "but here in Yorkshire, we tend to let the fire provide the warmth and save portions of our wardrobe for another day."

A swath burned from her rib cage to her hairline. She understood his taunt. He recognized full well the extent of her foolish trickery.

After tossing the damp cloth into the bowl, he nodded in her direction.

"I should mention, that for the sake of your little masquerade, pink is not the color of a widow's corset."

She gasped. Of course he had witnessed what no one was meant to see. It was her one concession to her youth and innocence, her one true expression in a world of forced deceit. That he should be privy to her secret and give voice to her indiscretion added further mortification.

"I was tempted to remove that as well," he said, a smile playing about his lips. "But the color suits you. I wonder if I had removed those petticoats, would I have found practical flannel or the thin gauzy drawers of a temptress?"

He looked at her cover-bound legs as if in moments he would decide the answer for himself.

Emma sucked in her breath, both humiliated and shocked by his insinuation. "How dare you!"

Her fists tightened on the sheet covering her to her chin. She wanted to flee, much as she had at their last encounter. Of course then she was only missing her boots; this time she was missing much more.

Hoping to chase him away instead, she grabbed the nearest item at hand, a pillow, and threw it at him, but he ducked, allowing the pillow to knock askew another "charming" landscape on the wall.

"Have you no shame? No remorse for what you've done!" Tears raced in tracks down her cheeks. "I'm ruined. I arrived in this desolate place with only my honor and integrity intact, and now you've taken those, leaving me with nothing."

Chambers's face twisted from flippant humor to a dark scowl. Within seconds he grabbed her wrists and forced them overhead, pinning both wrists to the mattress.

Shock momentarily paralyzed her, but once she recognized her restraint, she twisted and struggled to no avail.

"Let me go!" Her attempts to kick her way free skewed her glasses down her nose and brought the sheet to her waist. "Let me go! You, you, blackguard!"

He leaned low, the black silk of his neck cloth teased the base of her throat, while his face formed a dark thundercloud of malice.

"I have done nothing to defile your character, *Mrs.*

Brimley," he seethed. "You have no claim. You may call me all the names you wish, but if you believe this little charade will coerce a marriage proposal, I assure you I have dealt with such threats before."

"Marriage?" She stopped struggling, wondering if she had heard correctly. Had he just proposed marriage? She glanced at his face, trying to read his expression.

His features remained as hard and frozen as the ice topping the puddles on the road. An unanticipated lump of disappointment smothered the tiny spark that had briefly flared deep inside.

"I have no expectation of marriage, sir," she said, trying to catch her breath. "I abandoned that course long ago." She swallowed hard. In truth, the prospects of marriage had abandoned her, not the other way around, but he didn't need to know that.

"My present concern is for my reputation. My widow's pretense allows certain liberties, but this . . ." She looked pointedly from side to side at her arms still clamped in his grip.

"Oh?" She noted the exact moment awareness penetrated. His narrowed eyes widened and a moment later his ironclad hold lessened, though not enough that she could retract her arms. From her unique position beneath him, Emma watched disbelief chase the storm from his eyes. She waited, a bit breathless from her earlier struggle. His gaze slipped from her eyes to her lips as though he couldn't believe her words.

She smiled tenatively, feeling control shift in her direction even though she remained physically trapped by a man more powerful than she.

With each breath, the lace of her chemise scraped against the starched linen of his shirt. If she filled her lungs deeply, she imagined she would feel the press of his wide, hard chest. For the briefest of moments, she longed for that pressure. Just to know . . . just to feel . . .

She licked her parched lips.

"Oh," he said again, releasing his hold on her wrists and straightening slightly. She let her arms slide to her side but otherwise remained very still; his close physical proximity left room for little else. No etiquette book gave guidance for this exact situation. His gaze dropped to the rise and fall of her exposed corset.

Heat smoldered deep in Emma's chest. She knew she shouldn't desire Chambers's prolonged stare. But her fingers remained frozen by her side, unable to tug the sheet further between them. The distant toll of the mantle clock broke the spell.

Emma reached for the sheet, but he was faster. He pulled the sheet up to her neck and tenderly tucked it around her shoulders.

"I . . . I apologize," he said, averting his eyes and clasping his hands behind him.

She wasn't sure whether he was apologizing for his brusque behavior or his provocative stare. Either way, she surmised such pronouncements uncommon for him.

The room felt colder, less welcoming. Even with the addition of the sheet, she was chilled.

"I'd like to get dressed now," she said softly.

"Yes, yes, of course." He edged toward the door, fidgeting with the lapels of his jacket. "Perhaps you'd like something to eat? You didn't touch the food downstairs and you need to recover your strength."

She nodded. Indeed she wondered if his question was more motivated by the faint rumbling of her stomach as opposed to an excuse to escape her presence.

"Come when you are ready. I'll wait downstairs." He turned to open the door but stopped and commented over his shoulder. "And, Mrs. Brimley, only one gown this time?"

"My lord?" She stopped his progress out of the room. He opened the door but didn't turn around.

"How long have I been here?" The excuse given at Pettibone would have enabled her only enough time to secure answers to a few important questions. She hadn't counted on the morning's developments.

He sighed. "I daresay not long enough."

Six

NICHOLAS PACED IN HIS STUDY WITH THE ASSIS-
tance of his stick, waiting to hear her footfall on the
stairs. What an idiot he had been. He hadn't intended for
his little game to lead to her complete collapse. Although
his actions were motivated by his desire for her rapid recovery, instead he had embarrassed the overripe innocent.
It would be his own fault if she vowed never to return to
Black Oak. He stabbed at the carpets with the tip of his
stick. His own damn fault.

"Brandy, sir?" Thomas stood at the ready with a full
glass on a silver tray.

"Thank you, but no. I believe I'll need a clear head for
this one," Chambers replied. "I'm afraid I've ruined any
chance of retaining Mrs. Brimley as a model."

"Are you sure, sir? If I'm not mistaken, you thought you
had discouraged her on her last visit and yet she returned."

"Yes, but this time, I pinned her to the bed like a common trollop." The memory refused to leave his mind. Mrs. Brimley, tendrils of her rich brown hair loosened from her struggles, thrashing beneath him. Her breasts swelled and pressed above a corset that mirrored the same color of her flushed cheeks.

"I suppose that would frighten the girl," Thomas said with a patient monotone.

"It wasn't intentional. I was angry," Chambers explained with a dismissive wave of his hand. "Still, there was something about her reaction . . ." He remembered her eyes, open wide and trusting, and her smile, so accepting even as he held her captive, and her lips . . .

His own body had responded immediately with a jolt that had traveled from the tips of his fingers straight to his groin. He had to turn and leave before she recognized the result of their encounter. He winced. She would recognize it. After all, he had drawn her a picture of his very condition.

Reflecting on both of their reactions, a faint hope glimmered amid his otherwise fumbled handling of events. He glanced at Thomas, perplexed. "The thing of it is . . . I rather think she may have liked it."

Thomas raised his brows. "We are discussing the widow Brimley, are we not, sir?"

Chambers nodded. "What do you make of that, Thomas?"

Thomas lifted the glass of brandy and took a swallow, grimaced, then said, "I suppose we shan't require the assistance of Henry's wife, after all." He turned on his heel and continued down the hall.

IMPATIENT, CHAMBERS HEADED TOWARD THE ENTRY BUT stopped just shy of the opening. Mrs. Brimley, burdened by an unwieldy bundle of garments gathered in her arms, silently descended the circular stairway in her old-fashioned, ill-fitting black bombazine. The hem of her skirt fluttered with her advance, briefly exposing slim ankles encased in black boots.

Delicate ankles, he remembered, that marked the start of a long stretch of shapely calves and what promised to be well-proportioned hips hidden beneath frilly petticoats. Bloody hell!

What was he thinking! He straightened and readjusted his jacket. Blast her pink corset! He had no right to be entertaining such thoughts about one of those Pettibone women. Indeed the young chit could well be a spinster-in-training. She said as much. He frowned. That would be a waste.

She paused midway down the stairs as if she could hear his exasperating thoughts. She glanced toward his hiding place before performing a more intense study of the wide expanse of floor between the foot of the stairs and the door.

"Are you planning to run away again, Mrs. Brimley?" he challenged, allowing free reign to the irritation stirred by his mental scolding. He stepped into the spacious entry. "At least this time you've retained your shoes."

She blushed, drawing that winsome pink to her cheeks that stirred a reaction in his private regions.

"I'm afraid I shall have to decline your invitation for refreshment," she said, straightening as if she balanced Dickens's complete works on her reordered topknot. "I'm long overdue at Pettibone and the spinsters will ask questions." She continued her downward progress toward him.

He lifted the bundle of garments from her arms. "Then I shall escort you to be certain that you don't faint en route." He stilled the beginning of her protest with his hand, lowering his voice to a more intimate level. "Were you planning to leave without bidding me farewell?"

"I . . . I . . ." Her lower lip fell in apparent distress as if she couldn't choose between good manners and good sense. Chambers smiled to himself. He'd wager she'd choose good manners.

"Lord Chambers," she said, pushing her spectacles higher on the bridge of her nose, "our bargain is obviously forfeit. I think it best if I leave immediately."

"Why should our bargain be forfeit?" he asked with an innocent air. "Have you suddenly discovered all there is to know about relations between a man and a woman?"

Her green eyes, luminous like polished emeralds, narrowed behind the cover of the lenses. Her lips pulled to a taut straight line.

"You've undressed me, much to your amusement and my shame," she said in a voice akin to a harsh whisper. "You've accomplished your goal as men are wont to do. The spinsters warned me about you, and I didn't listen. It's time to end this play. It's past time for me to leave."

How had the trusting girl in the pink corset transformed so quickly into a judgmental prude in an ugly black dress? He could accept, perhaps, chastisement over pinning her to the bed. However, to accuse him of wanting to merely strip her naked, as if he were not already intimately familiar with a woman's body, that was beyond contempt. He tossed her pile of garments into a nearby chair, letting them fly pell-mell over the furniture. He advanced on her, effectively backing her toward the wall.

"Don't come near me," she said, panic affecting her voice.

"My mission, as you call it, is to complete a painting, Mrs. Brimley. A painting that I cannot hope to finish without your assistance." She could not retreat further, yet he still pressed on, perversely enjoying the alarm flashing in her eyes. Let her be worried. Her fool trick had cost him several years growth as it was.

"My purpose in undressing you was not part of a schoolboy's prank, but rather to alleviate the intense heat you suffered while wearing an inappropriate amount of clothing."

He braced one arm against the wall, blocking her means of escape.

Her eyes widened. "What are you doing?"

He braced his other arm alongside her, trapping her in the narrow space between his chest and the wall. "If I'm to be accused of being dishonorable, I'm bloody well going to get something for the trouble."

She was trapped, much like a fox in a hole. Just as he had manipulated her in his bed upstairs, she was once again ensnared by his arms. She looked toward the hallway for assistance, but the broadcloth encasing Chambers's well-muscled arm blocked her view.

Emma turned her gaze back toward Chambers, intent on pointing out the inappropriateness of his behavior. Before she could say a word, his lips crushed down on hers. She tried to shake her head, but his hands moved quickly to hold her firmly in place. Once the shock of his actions passed, she eased her struggle, focusing instead on his kiss.

His kiss! She had dreamed of precisely this moment from the day of her arrival at Pettibone. Poets wrote odes about the power of a kiss, though her limited experience in this area had shown the fireworks at the Crystal Palace to be far more exciting. However, with a man like Chambers . . . emotions should swell to dizzying proportions, desire should explode at the meeting of their lips. She waited . . .

Nothing happened. No bells rang in the heavens. No outpouring of rhyme engaged the spirit. Perhaps she was what her uncle had implied her to be: a cold fish. Her euphoria faded in a crush of disappointment.

The pressure eased, taking with it the discomfort of having her lips plastered to her teeth. She willed herself to relax. After all, stealing a kiss was hardly akin to stealing her virtue. His hands gentled on the sides of her face. She felt the soft tracing of his thumb edge along her cheek. His lips teased hers with playful little tugs.

"Open for me, sweet lady." He whispered before kissing her eyebrow. "Let me show you how it feels to be truly kissed." He kissed the other eyebrow. "Then you'll have an experience to share with your girls."

"Really, sir, I hardly think—"

He seized the opportunity her words afforded him. Instantly, his lips joined hers in the most delightful fashion. Half out of curiosity, she pressed back with wondrous results. His hands found her waist and pulled her tight against his solid chest. She had to move her hands to his forearms to avoid having them crushed. The strength in them reminded her that just a few hours earlier, these very arms had carried her up the steps. Heat, ignited earlier by his intense stare, spread at the thought of being lifted by his arms and cradled by this chest. Tingles raced to her fingertips.

Suddenly, his tongue touched hers, then teased and coaxed an interchange of play. *A strange sensation to have someone inside a part of one's body,* she marveled, *exciting and surprisingly delicious.* Curious about this unique stimulation, she allowed her tongue to trace the length of his. A low rumble vibrated throughout his chest. He pulled her closer still, bending her frame into his. She could have lived a lifetime in that moment. Surrounded by another, sharing a breath.

After too short a time, he withdrew, and Emma, believing it was part of the play, followed the retreat of his lips. Somewhere her disappointment had disappeared.

"So you like my kisses, Mrs. Brimley," Chambers said with a superior lilt.

Her eyes opened to his dazzling smile. "It appears I like kissing," she admitted. It would do no good to deny that fact when she had so enthusiastically responded. Who would have thought that the mating of two lips could set other parts of the body to simmer and hum?

"I don't know if my enjoyment has to do particularly with your kisses, Lord Chambers. I simply don't have enough experience to compare." Although her response had been honest, she silently admitted to enjoying the surprise that widened his eyes a moment before his laughter shook her frame as well as his own.

"I have the experience you lack, madam, and I've been told my kisses are better than most."

"Proper etiquette would demand no less of a response." Although in truth, none of her texts addressed such an issue.

"Yet etiquette didn't prevail upon *you* to praise my kisses." His hands dropped from her waist. She felt an instant sensation of loss.

"I apologize, sir. My manners must have deserted me." As well as any sense of propriety, she mentally added.

"Come," he ordered, tugging at her elbow. "You need to eat."

He guided her to the salon and to the very table she had visited earlier, only now she noted it had been moved a reasonable distance from the fire. She picked up a piece of toast and slathered a swatch of butter across it. He, in turn, picked up a glass of amber liquid and drank with great swallows.

"You gave me quite a fright," he said in a low, hypnotic voice.

He held her gaze a moment, then returned the empty glass to the table. He cocked his head and scowled until she popped the buttered toast into her mouth and speared a bit of jumbled egg on her fork.

"Mrs. Brimley, I have apologized for my rash behavior upstairs—"

"Yet not below?"

His lips turned in an indulgent smile. "You, however, have not apologized to me for your deceit."

Her mouth tightened, and by the satisfied expression on his face, he knew he had struck the mark.

"I had a number of questions. More than what the apparel of a typical day would allow," she said.

His shuttered eyes stared at her without expression, his mouth thinned, and his dimple was a fading memory. She had hoped to close the discussion, but he didn't believe her. An ancient ache pulled at her as if she were once again a little girl caught stealing a forbidden sweet.

"In truth," she confessed, "I did purposefully overdress. I did not wish to disrobe to a dishonorable state."

"Yet, you wanted honest answers from me."

She nodded, more embarrassed at acknowledging her deceit than she had felt appearing in her corset. The irony was not lost on her. She dropped her gaze to the plate.

"Mrs. Brimley." He reached across the table and stroked the underside of her chin. With gentle pressure, he raised her gaze to his. Her pulse quickened at his touch. Already she had experienced a degree of unsought intimacy with this man. She should feel a deep repulsion, or at minimum, a deep resentment. But as her gaze met his, a longing expanded with a dangerous pull of promise and intrigue.

"I still require your assistance to complete my painting, and I assume you still require mine. I propose we continue our original bargain, with a stipulation that no matter what, we will be honest with each other. No more deceits," he scolded lightly. "Are we agreed?"

She watched his lips, wondering if brandy still burned if tasted from a man's lips. She wanted . . . all the things a proper lady shouldn't desire. *Ah, but you're not a proper lady, are you?* her uncle's voice intruded. *You're a tramp like your mother was a tramp. It's in the blood.*

She pulled back from the soft stroke of his fingers. "I have a stipulation."

"What is that?" He asked, his eyes caressing her as if his fingers still made contact.

"Under no circumstances will you touch me with your person."

His eyes widened a moment before his brow dived in a frown. He crossed his arms in front of him. "I recall no complaint when I carried you upstairs."

"I was unconscious, sir." Heat singed her cheeks before she could marshal control. He would choose the very incident that had so entranced her moments before. "The circumstances of our meetings are immodest at best. I only seek to minimize the improprieties."

An eyebrow lifted, giving him an imperial air. "No more kisses?"

"Especially no more kisses," she said, hiding her disappointment. Too much of that tactile knowledge would land her in the "desperate straits" suffered by her mother.

Chambers studied her a moment before a satisfied smile lifted his mustache. He rose, assumedly to check the fire. However, upon his return to the table, he stepped behind her, slowly easing his hands down the sides of her chair.

She stiffened, uncomfortable with him hidden from her sight, yet intrigued by his close proximity. His heated breath stirred the fine hairs on the nape of her neck, coaxing gooseflesh to rise on her arms.

"Perhaps you should experience my touch before you so casually dismiss it?" His whisper drew shivers up her spine, while his hand stroked an invisible barrier near her forearm.

She held her breath, afraid her true desires would respond rather than her refined intellect. He waited a few more agonizing seconds, then stood. "As you wish, Mrs. Brimley. Agreed."

"I have one more request, a favor, actually," she said, a little giddy from her small victory. As long as he couldn't touch her, she was safe from the disastrous consequences suffered by her mother.

"In all the activity this morning, I haven't had the opportunity to ask you some questions. I know that if I hadn't tried to deceive you, I would have received information to present to my girls. But I'll be expected to teach them something new, and now . . ."

"Mrs. Brimley, one consequence of undressing you today is the discovery of all the incidentals that women wear for the pursuit of fashion. You have cuffs and collars, panels and skirts . . ." He pointed to the various items, then paused. "I propose I answer one question for each of the representative items that I removed today, provided they are promptly removed when next you enter my studio."

"Promptly?" She cringed at the idea of starting their sessions in such an undressed state. "Can you define 'promptly'?"

His frown conveyed more than words. He jabbed a finger toward her plate.

"Agreed," she said with little enthusiasm before finishing her eggs with two quick bites. She patted her mouth with a napkin, sipped the tea warming by her plate, and then delved into the matter at hand.

"I'd like to discuss the issue of pain."

HENRY BROUGHT HER BACK AS BEFORE, LEAVING HER A discreet distance from the school. She walked the final distance, climbed the stone steps, then paused a moment. Full-bodied chords of an awkwardly played piano piece escaped through the stone and mortar.

Talent night, she remembered. The girls were required to demonstrate their musical progress. Every proper young lady should have some musical talent either through voice or instrument.

Emma was taught to play the piano, primarily to accompany Penelope at various dinner parties and outings. Actually, everything Emma was taught was meant to show Penelope to advantage. She was raised with enough knowledge of social mores to be Penelope's companion, foil for her beauty, fodder for her conversation. At least in music Emma found a bit of revenge. Penelope never could carry a tune, a fact that was nevertheless blamed on Emma's crude abilities. Penelope's performances always signaled the end of a dinner party, which worked to Emma's advantage. Why prolong an evening of gossiping debutants, lewd laughter, and awkward stares?

An off chord grated on Emma's ear, rousing her from reminiscing.

The weekly recital should offer a diversion from her entrance. Congratulating herself on her bit of fortune, she opened the oak door as silently as possible. Once inside, she slipped out of her boots and tiptoed across the hall toward the stairs.

"Mrs. Brimley." Cecilia's voice stopped Emma in the process of avoiding the squeaky floorboard in the second riser. Her stomach roiled at the summons, but she dutifully turned.

Cecilia stood just outside the music room, a frown etched deeply in her face. "We were beginning to worry about your prolonged absence. Come here please." Cecilia looked pointedly at her borrowed valise. "Now."

Just as Emma made slow silent progress toward her, Cecilia left the gathering in the music room and led the way toward the sitting room that doubled as an office.

Without the accompanying clatter of boots, Emma sailed by the music room with only the soft rustle of crinolines. Yet to her own ears, each of her silent steps rang loudly as if someone were tolling a death knell. Sparring with Chambers had exhausted her reserves for intellectual combat. She feared she'd be no match for Cecilia if the older woman challenged her shield of deceit.

The labored repetition of practiced chords slowed as she approached the office. Cecilia waited at the far end of the room. "Close the door," she said.

Emma noted even the lack of feigned courtesy. Just as she was about to comply with Cecilia's order, Beatrice hurried in with a piece of handiwork. She quickly glanced at Emma, her eyes wide with alarm, then rushed to a seat near her sister, her head bent over her round embroidery hoop. Emma closed the door.

The headmistress did not bid Emma to sit or in any way make herself comfortable. Emma's toes wriggled in discomfort on the cool, drafty floor.

"Mrs. Brimley, it is difficult enough to monitor and oversee the whereabouts of our twenty-seven students. I should not be forced to do the same for my teachers. You were hired for your presence, not your absence. Do I make myself clear?"

"Yes, madam," Emma answered, feeling much smaller than the loss of her boots allowed.

"I realize life here may be vastly different to the life you enjoyed in London. One might even say difficult in comparison." Cecilia motioned to the valise. "Were you running away? If so, you are headed in the wrong direction."

"No, madam. I was not running away."

Cecilia waited, then sighed in apparent frustration. "Good heavens, child, where were you? We have been worried sick."

Cecilia's evident concern made Emma's admission all the more difficult. She stiffened her back and fixed her gaze on a spot on the wall. "I was visiting Lord Nicholas Chambers."

Beatrice gasped. When Emma allowed her gaze to drop to Cecilia's face, she recognized the shocked expression of betrayal. It was the same look that had graced her own features a time or two in the past. Emma's posture softened, wishing to ease them of the discomfort she had caused, but Cecilia held up a restraining hand.

"Did you not understand that we disapprove of association with Lord Nicholas Chambers? That his reputation could easily tarnish ours?"

"I knew you would disapprove. That is why I didn't tell you before that I had need of inspecting his library." She should be alarmed at the ease with which these mistruths rolled off her tongue. She would worry about that later. Right now she needed to pacify the sisters. "Once there, we engaged in a conversation about art, and I lost track of the hour."

Beatrice continued to punish her captive linen at a frantic pace. The porcelain filigree clock on the mantle ticked in rhythm to the tapping of Cecilia's foot on a patch of wooden floor. In the elongated silence, Emma realized the notes from the music room had mercifully ceased.

"If it hadn't been for Lady Cavendish's claims that you were a lady of high deportment and ethics," Cecilia said half to herself, "I believe I would have insisted you return to London the minute you inquired about Lord Nicholas Chambers. I knew that brief association would come to no good." Cecilia stared across the short distance of the room, alternately squinting her eyes and shaking her head in an internal battle. Having apparently come to some conclusion, her face softened. "Still, I suppose your widow's status does allow a certain latitude. Perhaps this transgression is not as grievous as it would have been otherwise. As this is an isolated incident—"

"I will need to see him again." Emma braced herself for Cecilia's reaction.

Beatrice cried out in pain, drawing all eyes her way. She placed her bleeding finger between her lips and shrugged an apology. Cecilia turned back to Emma. "Surely one trip should have been sufficient to take stock of Chambers's library."

"He has offered to give me lessons and I have accepted."

"Art lessons?" Beatrice asked around her finger, her wide eyes suddenly inquisitive. "Lord Chambers is teaching you to paint?"

Emma hesitated, watching enthusiasm build in Beatrice's eyes. The sisters would believe this falsehood more than the truth. They had already accepted her other deceptions. She worried her lip. One more small lie could conceivably save her position at Pettibone. But this, she silently vowed, would be her last. She nodded.

"Oh, Ce, the best schools offer art lessons for their students." Beatrice tossed her handiwork aside and grasped her sister's hand. "Wouldn't it be wonderful if Mrs. Brimley could teach the girls to paint?"

Conflict played across Cecilia's stoic features. Emma wasn't sure whether the lure of offering a better education or purely indulging her sister swayed Cecilia more. It didn't matter. Emma's spirits lifted at the chance of reprieve. Surely, she could learn something about painting from her unique vantage as a model.

Cecilia glanced at the valise by Emma's side.

"Lord Chambers lent me an artist's smock to modify for my fuller skirts." Emma quickly improvised, knowing full well it only contained her own excess garments. "As well as some other materials to study before our first lesson."

"Let the girl go," Beatrice urged Cecilia. "As long as Lord Chambers doesn't come to Pettibone, what harm can come of Mrs. Brimley taking art lessons?"

Cecilia relented in the face of the double onslaught.

"As long as the school benefits from her education, I suppose we can make an exception in Mrs. Brimley's case." Beatrice clapped her hands gleefully.

"However," Cecilia said, turning back to Emma, "we must know when these lessons are to occur, and suitable transportation must be arranged. It does no good to have you traipsing about the estate."

"Lord Chambers has offered the use of his carriage for the lessons. The timing can be arranged through Henry," Emma said, slumping a bit in relief.

"Look at the poor girl," Beatrice said with sympathy. "She's exhausted. Let her be off to bed, Cecilia. She has a class in the morning and we have plans to make."

"Thank you," Emma replied, feeling the weight of the tumultuous day on her shoulders. Now she needed to figure how to paint, as well as how to be painted, and still maintain her integrity and honor. "I am exceedingly tired."

The wooden floor vibrated with the quick padding of several feet dashing down the hallway. She doubted the sisters noted, already absorbed in their plans for art education. She might not have noticed herself if she had been wearing shoes. She opened the door to the beginning refrain of a new recital piece. At least the sisters weren't demanding demonstration of her talents in that area.

•

THE NEXT DAY, THE GIRLS CROWDED AROUND EMMA AS she reproduced, in her own hand, a drawing of an aroused man, as per Lord Nicholas Chambers's earlier instruction. A moment of silence ensued, as all studied the swordlike appendage.

"That looks uncomfortable," Beatrice observed, screwing her plump face into a scowl.

"Yes, I suppose it is," Emma replied, then added, "I never thought to ask."

She had asked so many other questions though, and Chambers, true to his word, answered them all in an intelligent and thoughtful manner. She could only hope they were truthful answers, as she had no knowledge to prove or disprove his information. But there was something about Chambers's eyes, about his smile, about his acceptance that made her trust him implicitly in this. Even though her experience with her uncle and would-be suitors had suggested that no man could be trusted, she suspected there might be exceptions.

"Why does the man need to change like that?" Hannah's soft voice broke into Emma's reverie.

"Good question," Emma said, remembering how Chambers's compliments about her own questions had made her feel less awkward. Indeed, he had made discussing an uncomfortable topic somewhat enjoyable.

"The man needs to change in order to plant his seed. Now girls," she said as she looked around the group, "you are all old enough to have your monthly cycles." Heads nodded in almost perfect unison. "So you know the place the man inserts his manhood."

Elizabeth whitened and collapsed on a chair. As the girls had just completed their class on the language of the fan, four brightly painted vellum arcs flashed before Elizabeth's face, producing a powerful current that straightened her finger curls. Beatrice opened a vial of salts that quickly revitalized poor Elizabeth. Once Elizabeth's eyes fluttered open, the girls promptly shifted their attention back to Emma's illustration, abandoning Elizabeth in the process.

"Please, Mrs. Brimley," Alice asked, "how does a man do that?"

"Anyway he can," Fanny snickered.

"There are several ways insertion can be accomplished." She frowned at Fanny to secure her silence. "But we'll discuss those at a later class." Although considerable knowledge was gained as a result of yesterday's discussion with Chambers, Emma had avoided asking questions about the positions used in coupling. After all, she needed to begin her posing sessions with at least some garments intact. "Let's return to the issue of pain. That topic appeared on everyone's list."

Silence descended on the group as all eyes turned to Emma. "Some girls, not all," she hastened to add, "experience some brief pain the first time they couple with their husbands. This is because of a thin piece of tissue inside the woman that blocks the man's entrance. He has to push through it." She swung her fist to punctuate the image. That tidbit of information had cost her both detached sleeves.

Elizabeth moaned again, but everyone ignored her.

"That's why there's blood," Beatrice said, entranced.

Emma nodded. "There's a little blood. It's one way a man can tell if his new wife is innocent. But it only happens on the first time. After that, the portal is open."

"What does it feel like when it breaks?" Alice asked.

Although Chambers had offered his opinion, she thought she was on her own for this question. "Do you remember how it hurts when you jab your embroidery needle into your thumb? It is a quick pain, a sudden pain, but then it's over and done with and soon forgotten." At least, she hoped so.

"After the first time, the sensitive parts of the woman's body might be a little uncomfortable, but a warm compress helps." She'd sacrificed her caged crinoline for that information.

"Is there anything else that might ease the pain of the man's entry?" Elizabeth asked with a desperate gleam in her eye.

"Yes, but we'll talk about that another time." Emma had

a few more questions about the concept of juices, something she still didn't understand, even after sacrificing her overskirt and jacket. "When a man is aroused, his body produces the seed that will ultimately grow into a baby if placed properly inside a woman's body. The important point to grasp from today's lesson is that a man must be aroused to enter his wife and plant his seed. In future classes we will discuss ways to arouse the man."

"That shouldn't be difficult," Fanny said. "My brothers get aroused looking at the sheep." The other girls laughed.

"Let us not forget the other important lesson," Beatrice intoned. "Beware of the aroused man who is not yet a husband. His seed could bring forth a child while stealing the proof of a woman's virtue. If you believe you are in danger of falling victim to an aroused man, you must run away as fast as you can."

The girls shared sidelong glances and barely suppressed smiles.

"Yes, run," Emma agreed, perhaps a bit too emphatically. "One moment's indiscretion can cost a lifetime of woe," *for more than just the mother.*

But what does one do when there's nowhere to run, nowhere to hide? She supposed she would discover soon enough at her next meeting with Lord Nicholas Chambers.

· *Seven* ·

"GOOD MORNIN', MRS. BRIMLEY. DON'T THA' LOOK lovely today."

"Thank you, Cook." Emma selected a seat at the dining table, pleased to see that she was alone, save for Cook. She had a demanding day before her, complete with teaching a literature class for the younger students, and being taught in turn by way of her art class with Lord Chambers in the afternoon.

"Henry brought a copy of yesterday's *Times*. Would tha' care to see it?"

"Yes, please." Emma said, anxious to keep abreast of news of London. The sisters received an assortment of ladies' journals. Most addressed society news, fashion, and etiquette in that order. Political news, as well as the more graphic police blotters, apparently had no place at Petti-bone. Emma made do with the secondhand edition of the *Times* purloined from Chambers's residence. At least she liked to think it was stolen. "Purloined" sounded far more romantic than "discarded."

She had barely finished eating when she saw the small notice at the bottom of the page preceding society news.

> **MISSING:** Emma Heatherston was reported missing from her London home in the Kensington District on January 12th. Miss Heatherston is a medium-sized woman of normal proportions with brown hair and green eyes. Her uncle, Mr. George Heatherston, has offered a reward for any information that might lead to her successful recovery.

"Mrs. Brimley?" a tiny voice asked.

Emma looked up, half expecting to find her uncle standing in the doorway. Instead she found Alice with her brow furled.

"What's wrong, Alice? Shouldn't you be in class?"

"I told Miss Beatrice that I didn't feel well, so she excused me from needlework. I really wanted to talk with you about Charlotte. I thought maybe before you taught literature you could perhaps spend a few minutes with me?"

"Yes, of course, dear. I just . . ." She glanced down at the newspaper before returning her gaze to Alice. She smiled. "Miss Beatrice dismissed you to your room, did she not? Perhaps it would be better if we talked there. Let me just take this plate . . ."

She allowed the remnants of her breakfast to slip onto the paper in a runny mess.

"Oh dear, look what I've done!" For good measure, Emma pretended to be shaken by her loss of propriety and let the tea in her cup slosh over the side onto the paper as well.

Alice gasped and rushed forward to help, but Emma held up her hand to keep the young girl at bay. "I wouldn't want anything to spill on you."

Cook bustled into the room. "Now, now, Mrs. Brimley. I'll see to that. You needn't bother with such things. Did tha' get anything on tha' dress?"

Emma bit her tongue, tempted as she was to reply that a spot of color on the drab black cloth would be an improvement. "No," she said instead, "everything appears to be confined to the paper. I'm afraid no one can read the *Times* in this condition. I'll just . . ."

In one swift motion, Emma slipped the newspaper from the table into the nearby fireplace. The pages quickly browned, curled, then were reduced to ash.

"Miss Cecelia will be upset she can't read those society pages. I could've blotted off the mess," Cook said, watching the resulting flames.

"It's too late for that," Emma replied with a mock frown. "Tell her that I was startled by my own clumsiness and overreacted. I'm sure she'll understand."

"I'm sure she won't." Cook crossed her arms and looked at Emma with speculation. She shook her head with an audible sigh. "On tha' way then. I'll clean up the rest."

Emma and Alice slipped out of the parlor and quietly up the stairs before their association could be discovered. "Now, what is it that you wish to discuss?" Emma asked once they reached the empty room shared by Alice and Charlotte.

"I think Charlotte's planning to run away," Alice said mournfully.

"What makes you believe such a thing?" Emma sat on one of the narrow beds.

"She doesn't like it here. The other girls make fun of her. They say her parents are too poor to offer a dowry and she has no business being here. She wants to go home."

Alice's words pulled at Emma's heart. She understood too well how it felt to live where one was not wanted. Although her uncle settled a small dowry on her, and claimed to keep the circumstances of her past secret, Emma was constantly reminded that she was far too plain, too clumsy, and too solitary to be desired by any potential suitor. If it hadn't been for an ability to hide in an empty wardrobe below stairs with her books and poetry, Emma wasn't sure how she would have survived those years.

"Is there nothing here that makes her happy?" Emma asked. "Maybe something at which she excels?"

Alice's brow crinkled in thought. "She's good at embroidery." Alice smiled. "Charlotte keeps a scrapbook full of pictures of animals and flowers and uses them in her designs. She's really clever at that. And she's the best croquet player in the school." Alice beamed for a moment, then frowned. "But we can't play croquet in the winter."

"No, we can't," Emma agreed. She looked closely at Alice. "And Charlotte's good at being a friend to you, isn't she?"

Alice nodded. "I don't want her to go."

"How about you?" Emma asked, noting the grim sadness in Alice's eyes. "Do you want to go home too?"

"I don't have a home," Alice said simply. "I'm an orphan. No one wants an orphan."

The girl's misery stabbed at Emma's heart, reminding her of herself at that age.

"Alice, that simply isn't true." Emma put her arm around Alice's waist. "The sisters wouldn't allow you to stay here if they didn't want you."

Alice bowed her head, studying her shoes. Obviously, Emma's attempt at comfort did nothing to alleviate the girl's concerns.

"I want you here," Emma said emphatically.

Alice looked at her, puzzled. "Why?"

"Because you care so much about your friend that you're telling me about her concerns," Emma said, softening her tone. "There are too many people who don't give a farthing. I want people around me who care about others."

"So what are you going to do about Charlotte?"

"I'll talk to her. Then I'll talk to the girls who are mean to her. Do you know who they are?"

Alice bit her lip before tilting her head toward the far wall. If Emma wasn't mistaken, that was the room used by Miss Barnesworth. She smiled, not entirely surprised by the revelation.

"I'll see to it."

"I knew you'd help. Thank you, Mrs. Brimley." Alice executed a little curtsy.

"You just mind that you don't get such silly fancies in your head, young lady," Emma lightly scolded. She left for her waiting literature class. She'd only managed a few steps down the hall when she heard Alice's soft voice.

"I can't. Where would I go?"

ALICE'S SAD REFRAIN STILL ECHOED IN EMMA'S EARS later that afternoon when she stepped down from Chambers's four-wheeler with the assistance of Henry's offered arm. Although years separated her from the lonely child, she and Alice shared a similar refrain. One that Emma silently invoked while raising her eyes to Black Oak's weathered door. She couldn't refuse Chambers's demands, for if she were to be exposed for the charlatan that she was, where could she go? Certainly not back to London.

"Mrs. Brimley, how wonderful to see you again." Thomas stepped aside to allow her admittance. She wondered just how much the man knew of her role at Black Oak. But then again, she might have difficulty facing even the butler if he understood her circumstances. She continued to pretend that this was just another social call.

"Lord Nicholas Chambers is in his studio. May I show you the way?"

"I remember, thank you." Indeed, how could she forget?

She passed the wide curving stairway that Chambers had used after she had fainted, and then the cozy salon where they had engaged in intimate conversation on her last visit. The memory ignited a spark of awareness of the abundant knowledge Chambers possessed of the feminine form, and of the absolute certainty of that knowledge as it related to her own. Her throat inexplicably dried to the texture of ash. Her step faltered. She stopped, took a deep breath, then knocked on his studio door.

"Mrs. Brimley." Chambers opened the door wide and stepped aside. "I'm pleased you have arranged to see me again."

For a moment, she forgot how to breathe. He had dispensed with his jacket, cravat, and even the collar of his shirt. The half-dressed man looked as handsome without the confinements of fashion as he did with them. She swallowed with difficulty.

"Yes," she managed to squeeze through her constricted throat. "I have questions."

"I'm sure you do." A mischievous twinkle in his eyes launched a slow engagement of each facial muscle, deepening his dimples and pulling back his lips to show even, white teeth. She discovered her own lips curving in response to his contagious smile so she pressed them tightly together. He mustn't know his own power.

She took a deep breath and willed herself to relax. "I find I also have need of your instruction in another matter."

"My services are yours to command."

She ignored his joviality. "The spinsters have discovered that I have been meeting you, and I confessed, by way of explanation, that you are giving me lessons."

"And so I am." His eyes twinkled impossibly brighter.

"They expect me to teach the girls."

"And so you are." His perfectly aligned teeth gleamed beneath the teasing curve of his lip. Teeth she recalled exploring intimately with her tongue. The missing moisture from her throat found its way to her palms, then spread throughout her body.

"About painting," she said with exasperation.

"Oh." Some of the mirth faded from his face. He shrugged. "Then we shall incorporate this topic as well into our lessons." He held out his arm as if to invite her to step on the dais.

"But will I still have to remove . . . ?" She hesitated, glancing down at her dress front. "I have so little left."

"Really, Mrs. Brimley, you do yourself an injustice." He peered at her bodice as if he could see straight through to the stays beneath. "We are losing daylight with this idle chatter. Perhaps you'd like to take a position on the dais." He turned his back to her and strode back to his easel as if she were no more than a servant bringing in the tea.

Stunned, she paused a moment, then remembered that he was probably used to women modeling in his studio on a daily basis. It should be no surprise that he took the act lightly. Perhaps she should draw on his resolve and act accordingly. She stepped on the platform.

"What am I supposed to do?" Shifting uneasily, she fumbled in the cuff of her sleeve for her mother's handkerchief.

Chambers, without a glance toward the platform, draped a sheet over his canvas and easel, then moved them aside. Only two feet of empty space and a mile of uneasy anticipation stood between them. He settled himself on the stool and glanced to the platform with a cocked brow.

"You may begin by removing your clothes."

Emma stood quite still, barely breathing. She knew this moment would come, but she had hoped . . . she had hoped he would dismiss her obligation out of compassion. Apparently this was not in his nature. She squeezed her handkerchief so tight, the lace dented the silk of her gloves.

Chambers crossed his arms and appraised her quite cruelly. "Is this a serious visit, Mrs. Brimley, or another subterfuge?"

"A serious visit, sir. I've come to honor my part of the bargain."

"Very well. The divan is there for your comfort."

She glanced at the rich velvet divan and waited while he positioned a piece of foolscap on a wooden board. Gripping the board in front of him, he settled back on the stool.

He glanced up once again and sighed. "Mrs. Brimley, this is becoming tiresome. We agreed on the terms of this arrangement, did we not?"

"Where do I remove these items?" She glanced about the room for a partition or perhaps a door to an inner chamber.

Lord Chambers held out his hand to indicate the stage.

"Here!" Her voice raised in alarm. "You wish me to disrobe here? While you watch?"

"I don't see why not." He shrugged. "I've seen your flesh before, Mrs. Brimley, or have you already forgotten?"

"Of course not," she snapped. Indeed, that memory wove into most of her daylight thoughts and all of her nighttime dreams. A familiar heat that had sparked the moment he opened his studio door began to spread to her extremities. She chanced a quick glance to Chambers. The lift of his brow suggested he remembered that last meeting as well.

With a feigned sense of urgency, she removed her hat and pulled at the fingers of her gloves.

"That is all you will see unless you do me the decency of turning your back. I am not an actress to be gawked at upon the stage."

He nodded, then shifted on his stool, presenting her with the broad expanse of his back. "Is this how you will teach the girls to disrobe in front of their husbands? If so, you are doing them a most serious injury."

"You are not my husband." Defiance tainted her reply

while her fingers hesitated on the top button on her bodice. Granted, he had already seen her naked shoulders, but she had been unconscious. No one could fault her for that predicament. But this . . .

She unfastened the first three buttons and held her breath, expecting a bolt of lightning to strike her where she stood. Nothing. No lightning, not even a curious glance from her tormentor. Her fingers trembled yet continued to work down the row.

"It is common knowledge that wives have the privacy of their own rooms in which to disrobe," she said, disappointed that her crinolines rustled louder than the crackling of the fire in the hearth, giving evidence to her activity.

"Heirs are not created in separate rooms. Clothes hinder the process as well. Indeed the artful removal of one's garments can arouse a young husband, making the evening pleasurable for both."

She had her doubts about that. This disrobing was not especially pleasurable, quite the opposite, in fact. She pulled her arms out of the bodice and laid the garment on one end of the divan, then hugged her bare arms. Consciously undressing with a man in the room was quite disconcerting, but she congratulated herself on her foresight to make him turn his back. Were she on display, this would be absolutely intolerable.

The room was quiet, not even the tick of a clock to distract from the sound of the unfastening of hooks and buttons. At least when they conversed she could pretend he wasn't aware of her actions. Perhaps she could covertly gather information while he waited for her to complete the disrobing process.

"You have mentioned both pleasure and pain in coupling," she said, unhooking the overskirt from the skirt beneath. "Can you assure me that there is more of one than the other?"

"Is that your question for our meeting?"

Obviously he was holding true to not giving free information. A more direct approach was needed. She took a deep breath and plunged forward. "I wish for you to explain how to mitigate the pain of coupling."

"You know the price."

She glanced to the back of the divan. "I've removed my bodice."

"I removed both a bodice and a jacket just three days ago," he said, holding up his fingers to tally the count. "As well as skirts and—"

"I forfeit a petticoat," she interrupted before he could complete the litany of her disgrace. She glanced down at the fastenings on her skirts, to avoid staring at the strong broad back of the man before her. Her fingers began to work. "Explain, please," she said, embarrassed by the tremor in her voice.

"A woman who has not experienced a man generally has a tight sheath, much smaller than the thickness of a man's shaft. The man may enlarge the passage by probing the area with something smaller, often his finger."

"He touches her? There?" For a moment, she forgot to breathe. She herself was hesitant to touch that forbidden area. That a man . . . that his fingers . . . She stole a glance at Chambers's long, agile fingers as they moved silently over the brushes and painting implements by his side, imagining them gliding up her thigh in approach to that most intimate of places. Even as she contemplated the matter, a stirring in that very region generated tiny tremors, like ripples in an internal pond. A shudder tripped up her spine. Dear heavens! How could she imagine such a thing about a man not her husband? If imagination alone generated such a powerful physical sensation, his actual touch would surely . . . Her skirt fell to the floor in an audible swoosh.

"I . . . I don't understand how a touch there would

mitigate pain." Oh, but she was beginning to. She fought for control of her voice. "If anything, I think it would be even more painful." If only from embarrassment, she silently added.

"More than a touch," Chambers continued. "The man explores her. He stimulates her, makes her slick with her own wanting."

At his very suggestion, moisture pooled between her legs. The juices! Was this what he meant by "slick"? She clasped her thighs tight together, appalled at her body's re-action. She was beginning to understand "slick," but what bothered her most was his use of the word "wanting."

"Often he'll use his hand to ease her passage wider to accept his manhood. However, if the woman is lucky . . ." He paused. "He'll use his tongue."

"His tongue!" After the initial shock, she laughed. "Now I know you jest. No gentleman would participate in such an scandalous activity." The idea was so absurd. Had he truly expected her to believe it? "You promised honest answers, sir. Perhaps I should demand you forfeit an item of clothing."

The moment she uttered the words, she wished to re-tract them. Her own curiosity aside, a proper lady would have bargained for the retention of her own garments, not the removal of his.

"I would happily oblige if I had indeed been dishonest, but I have not. Such a 'scandalous activity,' as you describe it, is mild compared to some of the diversions of the polite world."

He hesitated as if he were waiting for her request for elaboration. Although her curiosity was aroused, she glanced at the growing pile of clothes and decided to hold her tongue.

"Did you not explore me with your tongue when we kissed?" he challenged.

Indignation shot through her. "How rude of you to mention that indiscretion." She hardly needed a reminder of something that never traveled far from her consciousness: the texture of his lips nudging hers, the intimate sharing of a breath.

A sigh slipped unguarded from her lips. Remembering her audience, she renewed her attack on the stubborn knot of her bustle. "That . . . that was different!"

"Was it not pleasant?" he asked, his tone suggesting he knew the answer. "I assure you, I found your exploration most pleasurable. Should you wish to explore further . . ."

Yes! Yes! She bit her lip to sharpen her focus before such errant thoughts would find a voice. Surely her mother's experience had taught her not to wish for exploration of any man, without benefit of marriage, especially when that exploration involved the employment of one's tongue! An internal tremor shook the flounces of her petticoat. She took a breath to clear her thoughts. "Have you forgotten my stipulation so soon?"

"I had hoped you had reconsidered." Was it hope or laughter she heard in his voice? She almost wished she could view his face, but that would mean he could see her as well.

"I have not." She relaxed a little, empowered by those three words. He would honor his pledge not to touch her, of that she was certain. After this latest revelation, however, she was not as convinced about the truthfulness of his statements. For the girls' sakes, she must be certain.

She studied her fingers, afraid to raise her eyes and expose the warmth creeping into her face, even to his turned back. "A tongue is not as rigid as a finger. I do not believe a tongue can expand a passage."

"I would be willing to demonstrate," he said with experienced authority. "You could remain standing and I would kneel before you and—"

"Lord Chambers!" Her knees buckled and she grasped

the back of the settee for support. The image he invoked released vibrating tremors throughout her body, particularly in the area where his tongue . . . Sweet Lord, what was happening? "I do not require a demonstration," she huffed. "Just honesty in your answers."

Honesty demanded, however, that she continue her disrobing. She began work on her caged crinolines, avoiding the temptation to stare at his head. With her position on the raised dais, his head would be at the proper position if . . . No! She couldn't allow her thoughts to follow that path.

"Shall I continue to explain how this mitigates the pain?"

"Please do so." She could barely find breath to issue the words.

"A man employs his tongue to pleasure a woman as well as to introduce more moisture into the area."

"He spits into her?" This made more sense than inserting one's tongue.

"Moisture, Mrs. Brimley." His voice slowed as if speaking to an irate child. "The custom is not meant to degrade or show displeasure, quite the opposite, in fact. The additional moisture helps to lubricate the passage, much the same way a wheelwright would grease an axel."

The introduction of the wheel and axel allowed some much needed distance from the topic at hand. She slowed her breathing and let the air in the room cool her inflamed cheeks. For a moment she appreciated her lack of clothing. Adding wool to this incendiary topic would surely have rendered her prostrate once again. She stepped out of the crinoline cage.

"Do you believe my girls will be forced to submit to such practices on their wedding nights?"

"Only if they are very fortunate. Too many men look to their own pleasure before that of their brides. Your young ladies will most likely be expected to provide similar services to the man."

One minute, she thought she understood; the next he described something totally incomprehensible. "The man's passage will need expansion?"

"Is that another question, Mrs. Brimley?"

She hesitated in the process of removing her already forfeited petticoat. She only had one short one left. If she removed that last barrier, she would be forced to pose in naught but her corset, chemise, drawers, and stockings. He had already seen her exposed to her corset, but her drawers . . .

She thought of the slit between her legs that allowed her to tend to private necessities. If she kept her legs tightly together, he might not notice its existence.

"Mrs. Brimley, if we are to continue this conversation, I feel I should turn around. The back of my studio is not conducive to finishing my painting."

"No," she fairly shouted. "I'm not ready," she said, still considering.

She thought of the girls. She thought of herself. Would it be preferable to be knowledgeable about the expectations of coupling, including these "explorations," before confrontation on the wedding night? Or should mystery prevail? She mentally rummaged through her readings for guidance. Keats provided her answer.

"An extensive knowledge is needful," she softly quoted, "to ease the burden of the mystery."

"I'm sorry," Chambers said, his back still to her. "Did you say something?"

"I am removing my last petticoat."

· Eight ·

"I FEAR I'VE FORGOTTEN YOUR QUESTION," HE said.

The man was incorrigible. She occupied her hands with the removal of the final two petticoats. "You suggested a husband might require his wife to employ her hand, or . . ." this was most difficult to say, "tongue to a man's . . ."

"His manhood, yes. That indeed would facilitate his arousal, I should say. A husband would treasure a wife who aroused him in such a manner."

"This would be expected?" She thought of the drawing Chambers had provided earlier. Placing her hand on a man's manhood might be similar to grasping a low branch of a tree. There existed similarities.

"Expected by some, appreciated by all."

"A wife would be expected to taste the man with her tongue?" The image of the tree branch worked exceptionally well to keep her mind away from the human element.

However, placing one's tongue on a branch seemed ridiculous at best. One would only gain a mouthful of splinters.

"She'd be expected to use her hand, or her tongue, or both. There are many ways this can be done, but perhaps the most enjoyable is when the man and wife pleasure each other at the same time. She positions her nether regions about his head, and he does the same. Either the—"

"Merciful heavens," she gasped at the mental picture inspired by his words.

"Mrs. Brimley? Are you all right? Do you require some water? A brandy, perhaps?"

She couldn't look at him, much less answer. The muscles in the very areas he described tightened and shuddered. She could no longer focus on his broad back, his thick black hair, his narrow hips. His words and her imagination made every part of his body too provocative to consider.

Her gaze drifted to a spot just about his left shoulder. She gasped. The gilt-framed mirror on the wall captured not only her horrified expression, but Lord Chambers's smirk as well.

"How dare you! You've been watching me all this time? You positioned that mirror for the sole purpose of observing me while I disrobe. You . . . you miscreant!" Mortified, she looked to the door, but surely only further humiliation would follow if she were to arrive back at the school half-dressed. Fleeing the room wasn't an option, so she settled for crouching behind the settee.

"I assure you, Mrs. Brimley, that mirror has occupied that wall for so long, I had forgotten it had existed until you so delightfully reminded me." He turned to face her. "I use the mirror to reflect light unto my easel. However, today it reflected an innocence and beauty I can only hope to capture with my paints."

She would have hidden her face with her hands if they

weren't already engaged covering her chest from view. She couldn't meet his eyes.

"Come now," he soothed. "What harm has been done? You are the same chaste, untouched woman you were when you stormed my studio with your unusual demand. I saw nothing in the mirror that should prove embarrassing to you."

"A lady does not subject herself to public view. A lady doesn't . . ." The constriction in her throat prevented further explanation. She had violated so many of the constraints of being a lady, she wasn't sure if she still qualified.

"Mrs. Brimley, outside of this studio, I promise to treat you with all the accord due a fine lady. But inside this studio, you are a woman, nothing more than my model, and most certainly, nothing less."

His words gave her the strength to slowly stand up and step from behind the divan. Sheer willpower kept her knees from buckling. Her arms continued to wrap around her trunk, hiding her chest from his view. She slowly lifted her gaze to his, grateful to see that he appeared serious.

"You are a beautiful woman," he said. "I promise to—"

"You think I am beautiful?" She breathed through the gap between her lips a moment or two, then recognized what must be an unseemly expression. After a lifetime of scorn and ridicule, she'd never considered a different opinion regarding her appearance could exist. She held her breath, searching his face for confirmation.

He opened his mouth as if to reply, then hesitated, narrowing his eyes. "Has someone told you otherwise?"

Heat rose in her cheeks. She looked away. "Several people, in fact. I have an uncle and a female cousin who would most certainly disagree with your observation."

He frowned. "They have done you a disservice." He picked up his board with paper. "I propose to prove that to you, but first we must move beyond this issue of embarrassment or neither of us will progress."

"That is easier for the one dressed than for the one not." Her lips quirked. His admonishment of Uncle George and Penelope lifted her spirits, but her arms remained locked about her chest.

Before she could utter another word, he unfastened the remaining buttons on his shirt, letting the loose cloth hang from his broad shoulders.

"Lord Chambers!" she gasped. Proper etiquette insisted she shouldn't stare, but no ladies' training had prepared her for the sight of his exposed chest.

With a quick shrug, he removed the thin fabric and tossed it aside, presenting her with a wide expanse of hard muscle furred with the most intriguing mat of black curling hair that narrowed as it approached the waistband of his pants. She bit her lip; her chest tightened. She had seen the cartoons in *Punch* about men who wore corsets to narrow their waists and flatten their stomachs. Although Lord Chambers possessed those fashionable physical endearments, his manly shape was obviously natural. Firm muscles, not padding, filled out his jackets.

After her shock receded, curiosity advanced. Her fingers itched to tactically explore this forbidden region. Was a man's chest hair coarse or silky? Dense like a terrier, or softly accommodating like a . . .

"You are staring, Mrs. Brimley. I had thought to make you feel more comfortable." The tilt of his mustache suggested that had not been his intent at all. "Would you prefer I put the shirt back on?"

"No . . . Yes." She shook her head as if the action would empty it of her errant observations. "I appreciate your gesture. I apologize . . . I've never seen a man assembled quite like you, sir."

"I shall assume that is a compliment."

In her shock at his gesture her arms had dropped to her side. She had forgotten that he could fully view her in her partially clad state. It would do no good to hide from him now.

"My lord—"

"Nicholas," he corrected. "I believe we may dispatch with society's amenities." He stepped closer to her. Her heart raced. "I prefer that you call me Nicholas. And perhaps I may call you . . . ?"

"Mrs. Brimley," she replied without hesitation. She needed the distance that such formalities offered, especially when confronted with such manly perfection. She needed to hear the alias as well as a reminder that he didn't know her heritage. If he ever learned of her past, he would no doubt abandon her as unworthy of respect. The thought calmed her racing pulse. She adjusted her spectacles. "You shall catch a draft without proper covering."

"There are other ways to stay warm," he said, recovering his shirt from its resting place. The timbre of his voice warmed her indeed. "Perhaps in a later lesson, we can explore those options."

She was learning, she thought, squashing the question that rose to her tongue. He would not bait her into removing yet another item by asking for an explanation.

"What do you wish me to do now?" she asked, her voice rasped from the burning in her throat.

He smiled with an expression of gentle understanding. "I'd like you to position yourself in various postures so I might work on the composition."

"What sort of postures?"

"Are you familiar with the Greek deity, Artemis?" he asked, settling the white linen of his shirt over his shoulders.

"I am a literature teacher, sir," she huffed, reminding herself that she should incorporate Greek mythology in her literature curriculum. "Artemis, daughter of Leto and Zeus, and twin sister to Apollo, was a goddess of hunting and archery, and she was a defender of children as well." She smiled. "We have that last item in common."

She knew full well that as the virgin goddess, Artemis shared another trait with her, but she saw no need to remind Chambers. Every painting of the huntress she had ever viewed displayed her in a tunic that left her legs and arms bare. A bit of hope blossomed in her chest. Perhaps Chambers would allow her to remain partially clothed after all.

"Do you have a bow and arrow?" she asked, becoming more enthusiastic. "I could pose with that." She mimicked plucking a taut string on an invisible bow.

He chuckled. "Introducing a weapon into our sessions may not prove the most intelligent endeavor. I envisioned depicting Artemis's Revenge."

Her mind raced, mentally reciting the stories of Artemis. "Wasn't Actaeon turned into an animal?"

He nodded. "Actaeon spied on Artemis and observed her bathing. Artemis turned him into a wild stag as punishment for viewing her naked body."

"Surely, you don't intend—" Her cheeks heated again.

"Let us stick for the moment with the poses," Chambers said, a tight smile lifting one side of his mustache.

"You promised I could wear a thin gown." She refused to concede the point. "I remember distinctly. You said you wanted to paint me naked, but you'd settle for a thin gown."

"Mrs. Brimley, I remember our conversation." His smile disappeared, replaced with something akin to frustration. "At this moment, I am only thinking about the composition of the painting. Now, may we continue with the poses?"

She sighed. "What do you want me to do?"

"Pretend for the moment that you are a goddess, a

beautiful forest nymph preparing to bathe in a lake or a pond. How would you approach it?"

"I don't swim," she said sullenly.

"But you do bathe, do you not?" He, in turn, sounded exasperated.

Good. What was that line from Shakespeare's *Romeo and Juliet*? "One fire burns out another's burning; One pain is lessen'd by another's anguish." Perhaps his anguish would lessen her embarrassment.

"Play the game with me, Mrs. Brimley. Pretend you are a goddess. What would you do?"

"I'm quite sure I would have a large cloth towel wrapped about my body." Emma edged her voice with a bit of defiance, clutching one fist to her chest in mimicry. When his only response was a lowered brow, she closed her eyes and eased into the role. "Then I'd test the water with my toes to see if it was overly cold." She lifted one stocking-clad foot in pantomime.

"Would your hair be piled high on your head? Or loose, curling softly about your pale, sun-dappled shoulders?"

Sun-dappled. She liked the sound of that. With her eyes closed, she could easily pretend she was something she was not, a beautiful goddess above reproach, welcomed by all with open arms.

"Only a child or a woman in her chambers would wear her hair down," she said, caught up in the fantasy. "Artemis would wear her hair up but with bits of wildflowers and greenery as ornamentation." She imagined herself in a serene woodland setting straight from one of Wordsworth's poems.

"Yes, I can see it," his voice encouraged. "Are you alone? Or have you attendants about you?"

"I am alone," she replied. "Except for the forest creatures, of course." In her fantasy world, she watched a bird chase another across the pond. The rustling of squirrels stirred the trees overhead. The animals wouldn't judge her, criticize her.

"You approach the water . . ." His voice surrounded her as if he were part of the vision. She responded with a careful step, imagining water the color of the clear sky overhead, swirling around her calf. The sweet, refreshing water, free of London's dirt and grime, yet tempered by the sun's warmth, welcomed her into its depths. Filtered sunbeams beckoned her forward.

"The towel?" the voice asked.

She clasped both hands to her chest then flung them wide, imagining the towel billowing behind her like a sail. She lifted her face to the sun and arched her back. She was a goddess.

"Magnificent!"

The catch in his voice and the stab of a protesting whalebone stay shocked her back to reality. She opened her eyes and wrapped her arms around her chest as if they had transformed into her imaginary towel. Had she really stretched and arched in the immodest fashion of her fantasy? Heat flooded her face. She turned her back to him and searched for her discarded bodice.

"What are you doing?" Chambers asked, alarmed.

She slipped her arms through the black crepe sleeves as quickly as possible.

"Don't do that," he protested. "You were wonderful."

"Please, sir," she said over her shoulder, as she hastily worked the buttons through the holes. "I was wrong to think I could do this." Tears muddied her gaze as she looked down at her handiwork, dismayed to find that she had misaligned the buttons to their respective buttonholes. With a frustrated sigh, she unfastened and worked to refasten the closures.

"You've done nothing wrong. There's no reason to

hurry away." By the proximity of his voice, he was rapidly approaching her back.

"Do not touch me. Don't you dare touch me," she threatened with a sob. "You promised."

"I won't touch you. I just wanted to show you what we accomplished."

A board with paper attached edged around her side. She took it from his hand and looked at the sketch. The drawing was hasty and lacking in full shading and color, but the artfully crafted lines detailed the head of a gentle, beautiful woman with a long graceful neck. Elegant fingers reached as if to pluck a bloom from her high coiffure woven with ivy and pale flowers. The woman appeared too beautiful to be her likeness and yet it was. The embarrassment that had heated her face slowly receded.

"This is what you drew?"

"This is what I saw," he said. "To me, you were a goddess."

She turned to face him and handed back the drawing. "I am a teacher and, I fear, a poor moral stalwart of my students." She hastily pulled on a petticoat. "Do not look for me to return, Lord Chambers. I will not submit to the mockery of your sketches or to the lies you preach." The bottom of her bodice interfered with the fastening of her crinolines and her skirts, but experience led her fingers to the proper closures.

"What lies? What mockery?" Chambers asked, refusing to let her dress in peace.

Emma sighed, stopping her progress to point out the obvious. "I am not the beautiful woman you have presented in those sketches. My own eyes tell me that. And the nonsense you present about widening passages and the arousal of a woman's passions could truly be harmful to my girls. You should be ashamed of yourself."

"I spoke the truth," he declared. "I thought that was your purpose in seeking my counsel."

She searched for her boots, finding them half under the divan. With a tug on her skirts, she coaxed them out with a foot. "I will grant that a woman's body would not easily accommodate that aberration you drew for me earlier."

"Aberration!"

"So some sort of widening might be in order." She ignored the dangerous edge to his voice. "But I cannot accept that such a practice would be pleasurable, or that a woman could be aroused in such a way to make the act of coupling pleasurable."

She sighed heavily. To some in society the very act of bending at the waist to retrieve her boots would be considered indecent, but after this afternoon's activities, she no longer cared about Chambers's opinion of her proprieties. Her embarrassment was just too great. She plopped on the divan and bent over her boots, hoping the indecent posture would hide her face from view.

If the act of coupling were as pleasurable as he described, and a woman could be aroused to want to engage in such activity, even without the benefit of marriage, then her uncle could have been correct all these years. No! That couldn't be. That would make her mother a . . .

She faced Chambers, placing all manner of conviction in her words. "Arousal in the manner you suggest is a purely masculine state." *It must be. It must be.*

"You are so very wrong." His voice suggested he was enjoying the debate. Anger lashed through her. This was not something about which to bicker. She turned her back, preparing to leave.

"Women have the capacity for arousal as much as men," Chambers said, almost mocking her. "Perhaps more."

Enough! Emma clenched her hands into fists and spun on her heel. "My mother was not a whore!"

Silence filled the space between them. Emma clutched a gloved fist to her open mouth, appalled by her own words. She couldn't move. She couldn't breathe. Shock drained the laughter from Chambers's face. He appeared frozen, distant, cold.

A sadness slipped into his eyes, or was it pity? She had seen that expression before, most recently in her suitor's eyes a moment before he turned and walked out of her life. To see that same look in Chambers's eyes hurt beyond measure. Soon, she suspected, he would treat her with the same regard as the tavern women rumored to visit Black Oak. Her edict not to touch would be ignored, all because of the circumstance of her birth. With tears burning in her eyes, Emma lowered her gaze to push past him on her way to the door.

"Don't go," he said as she tried to brush past him. "I apologize if my words somehow implied a disrespect to your parentage. There was no intent. Please do not leave."

"You wish me to stay?" she asked, incredulous. "After what I've told you?"

"You've told me nothing, Mrs. Brimley. You just corrected what you perceived to be an incorrect impression." He stepped nearer; she could feel him along the small hairs on her nape. "You've been running away all your life, to the extent that you now live among strangers. You have nothing to fear here. Why are you running again?"

But she did have a great deal to fear, especially from Chambers. He had managed to reach deep inside her, like no other man, and make her yearn for a closeness that she thought was impossible. She could lose her position at Pettibone if the sisters learned of her illegitimate birth, but that was a mere complication compared to Chambers's inevitable rejection.

"Face your fears, Mrs. Brimley. It is the only way to be

free of them. No one beyond these walls will know what transpires here. You can trust me."

Could she? Chambers was unlike any other man she'd ever known. If she shared the nature of her past, would he look at her with condemnation? Or would they continue as before? She turned to face him.

"I was born on the wrong side of the blanket. My father had his way with my mother but did not marry her."

Chambers nodded. "It is a common enough tale. A sad one, indeed, but hardly enough to consider one's mother a—"

"All these years, I have believed that my father must have forced himself upon my mother," Emma said as if Chambers had not spoken. "I believed that he ruined her. That he was at fault."

"Society is often unfair in the way—"

She held up her hand to silence him. "Let me finish, sir. You have suggested that a woman can be aroused much like a man."

He glanced away and said something under his breath.

"It is said that a woman who enjoys intimacy with a man, outside of marriage, is a . . ." She couldn't bring herself to repeat the word. "Is not genteel. My uncle has often said that my mother enjoyed that single act of indiscretion, and indeed would so again if he had his way."

This time she heard Chambers's low curse murmured with malice.

"If what you said about a woman's arousal is true, then it stands to reason—"

"What has your mother said about this?"

"My mother died two weeks before I came to Pettibone. Indeed, that is one of the reasons I answered the spinsters' ad for a teacher." She lowered her gaze. "We never discussed it. There were many things that we never discussed. Now that she is gone . . ."

Tears burned her eyes. *Oh Mama, so many things I should have said . . .* She couldn't force words around the lump in her throat. She dug in her sleeve for her mother's handkerchief, but it wasn't there. The loss of that small piece of linen, one of the few remembrances of her mother, broke the barrier that held back the tears.

"Look at me," Chambers directed in a soft, comforting voice. She raised her gaze, and he gently blotted the tracks of tears on her cheeks with his handkerchief. She sniffed, pulling the full scent of turpentine and linseed oil into her consciousness. It was a scent she associated uniquely with Chambers, and now would be associated with this simple act of kindness. Instead of thanking him, more tears flowed from her eyes, causing her to remove her spectacles.

"You loved your mother very much," he said.

"She was a good woman, a kind woman," Emma insisted, eager to correct her uncle's impression. "She prayed at church every Sunday, and she never so much as smiled at another man, even though Uncle George tried to make her do it. She took care of me. She loved me." She sniffed. "And I loved her."

"Of course you did." He smiled, and dabbed at her cheeks.

She wanted to crawl into his arms and forget that with her mother's passing, she was alone in the world. Her gaze slipped from Chambers's eyes to his lips. What a fool she was for insisting he not touch her. Even now, he was careful to caress her only with the handkerchief. That pulled a weak smile to her lips.

"If your mother gave herself to only one man, it stands to reason that she loved him," Chambers said.

"Why then didn't he marry her?"

"Why indeed." He grimaced. "Some men aren't worthy of the gift they are offered. Had your father married your mother, you would not question her character."

"Yes, but—"

"Then it stands to reason that the fault lies with your father. His character is the one to question, not that of your mother." He used the tip of the handkerchief to coax her chin up. "Your uncle was wrong. Your mother was not what he suggested."

She managed a bit of a smile. His eyes softened and his face brightened.

"Well then," she sniffed, tasting again his exotic essence. She slipped her glasses back on her nose. "I think I should be going."

He handed her his handkerchief and she used it to dab at the corners of her eyes one final time before slipping it into her sleeve. Before she could leave, however, she needed to settle one final matter.

"The things you've told me about a woman's arousal . . ." She gave him a sideways glance. "Are they true?"

She suspected she already knew the answer. What else could explain that strange fluttering in her chest or those tremors emanating from her private regions whenever she saw Chambers? Up till now she thought they might have been something else. Perhaps they evolved from fear that she really was her mother's daughter even to the extent of depravity. She corrected herself and smiled. Thanks to Chambers she would work not to link those two words, "mother" and "depravity," again.

"Yes, they were true," he said quietly. He glanced at her with a look of uncertainty, almost as if he expected her to resume weeping. Her timid smile must have convinced him otherwise.

"Remember, we were talking in the context of arousal between a woman and her intended husband. Your girls should be judicious as to how they practice their newly acquired knowledge."

"Yes, of course," she replied, exhausted from the emotional exchange. She turned to leave and managed a few steps.

"Mrs. Brimley," he called. She turned, half in a daze. "You will return, will you not?"

"Yes, I believe so," she said, then paused. "May I ask one more question?" She glanced at her fully dressed figure. "As I have recently dressed, I would ask that I be permitted not to remove an item of clothing."

Chambers smiled. "Although it was not of a nature that would profit my painting, your courage this afternoon has revealed a bit of yourself to me. Let us count that as a clothing forfeiture."

"Thank you." She smiled, accepting his generosity. She worried her lip a moment before raising her gaze to his. "Can a respectable woman be aroused by a man and yet still remain virtuous?"

"Are we speaking of yourself, Mrs. Brimley?" His eyes crinkled in a soft, sad smile.

She blinked behind the cover of her lenses. "Naturally, I am asking for the girls."

"Naturally . . ."

AFTER SHE LEFT, CHAMBERS EASED HIMSELF ONTO THE stool and gazed at his charcoal sketch. A quiet, relaxing warmth spread through him.

So Miss Brimley had been borne out of wedlock. It was an unfortunate statement of the times that this could hardly be conceived as a unique situation. Indeed, another woman's face crept into his memory. Another honorable beauty who like Miss Brimley's mother was abandoned with a tiny life growing in her belly. However, she never lived long enough to see her daughter come into society. Given the confusion and contradictions that he had witnessed tormenting Miss Brimley today, this may have been a blessing. What fool cur of an uncle tortures a niece with misrepresentations of the mother? Why convince her that she was plain? Obviously the man couldn't see beyond his nose. Loathing filled his chest. If the uncle saw his niece as Chambers did, he glanced again at the sketch, it's likely the uncle would never let her go.

Any doubts Chambers may have had about the suitability of the young widow for Artemis had dissipated the moment she had imagined herself in the role. She had transformed before his eyes from a charming, though prim, intellectual into an exciting, sensuous goddess. Her strong, lithe body held enough womanly curves to make a painter yearn to try sculpting. When she arched her back in the act of dropping the towel, it was all he could do not to throw himself at her feet. Modeling obviously unleashed the goddess within, and he probably was the only man alive privileged enough to know of her existence. He smiled, feeling a bit of self-satisfaction at his discovery, a privilege indeed.

With the schoolteacher as his model his success at the Royal Academy show was virtually guaranteed. His talent would be validated. How he'd love to see his father's face when he heard the news.

Thomas appeared at the door with a tray. "Henry has taken Mrs. Brimley back to the school, sir. I thought you might be in need of a bit of refreshment."

Chambers waved him off. "I think I shall just sit here a bit longer. The young widow has given me some things to consider, plans to make, and so forth."

"She will be returning then, sir?"

Chambers smiled. "Yes, I believe so." *She'll be back in my studio if I have to drag her myself.*

"Very good, sir." He left.

Yes, Chambers thought, very good indeed. Miss Brimley would return. When she did, his painting would prove to her what a true beauty she was. If along the way she discovered for herself that a respectable, virtuous woman could indeed be aroused—his grin spread wider—so much the better. Her own feelings of arousal would help her understand and forgive her mother for the circumstances of her birth. The challenge, of course, would be to find a way without touching her.

The problem with you, my son, is that you always run from a challenge. You sabotage your chances before you begin. His father's words echoed in his head, but for the first time, his words brought forth a smile. His father never understood that not all challenges were worthy of pursuit. But this one—Nicholas looked back at his sketch—this challenge he would not fail.

· *Nine* ·

A WINTER STORM SETTLED IN THAT NIGHT, MAKING trips to Black Oak impossible. It was just as well. Chambers had challenged her to think of her mother and a woman's passions in a much different light then that suggested by her uncle. Those thoughts kept her in a daze, forcing her to move through her classes like one of those clockwork toys on exhibition in London. Even beginning a new topic in her literature class, Greek mythology, failed to rouse her from introspection.

One day ran into another without reprieve. Unsure how long the storm would keep them confined indoors, Emma doled out her newfound knowledge about intimacy in dribs and drabs to her eager students. The inclement weather tested everyone's reserves, making for short patience and quick tempers.

Emma found partial respite by joining Cook in the kitchen before Henry arrived to take her home in the evening. It was a quiet, settling time. She could plan her lessons, listen to Cook's pleasant banter, and sometimes, after Cook had left, attempt her hand at a poem or two.

"I think Yorkshire winters suit thee, Mrs. Brimley. Tha' cheeks have a pinch more color and a little more flesh in places becoming a lady."

Emma smiled. "I suspect the additional flesh is a testament to your cooking more so than the winter, but yes, Yorkshire and Pettibone agree with me." She could have added Chambers to her list of "agreements" but suspected Cook would not approve.

"I'm pleased to hear that," Beatrice voiced behind her.

Emma turned around, surprised at the newcomer. It just showed how unobservant she'd been of late, as Beatrice's perfuse lavender scent tended to arrive long before the woman herself.

"Would you care to join me for a cup of tea?" Emma asked, more out of politeness than a genuine desire for company. She had hoped to work on a new poem dedicated to her mother after Cook's departure.

"Yes, thank you," Beatrice said. Cook hurriedly slipped a fine porcelain cup in front of the younger sister. Emma removed the flowered tea cozy from the pot Cook had left by her elbow, and poured hot liquid into the cup. She offered Beatrice sugar and cream.

"This is quite pleasant, isn't it?" Beatrice said, once all the little ceremonies surrounding the preparation of a proper cup of tea were complete. She waved away an offered plate of sweets. "Have to mind my girlish figure, you know," she said, patting her ample hips.

"Begging th' pardon, Miss Beatrice, is there something that'd be wanting before my man comes?" Cook asked with a bit of concern.

"No, no. You go along home. I was just a bit restless and saw the light. Don't let me keep you."

Cook's face brightened. "Thank thee, ma'am, then I'll be saying my good nights. God willing, I'll be back in the mornin'." She hurried out the door before an afterthought could call her back.

Cook's enthusiasm to join "her man" warmed Emma more than the hot tea. Since her discussion with Chambers about her mother's demise, the world had seemed a lonelier place without someone to confide in.

After abandonment by two suitors, she had assumed marriage was not to be her destiny. She hadn't regretted that conclusion as she only had to look at her uncle and his wife to see that marriage was not all fat-cheeked cupids and lacy hearts. They may have been morally correct and properly married by society's standards, yet neither party showed the least bit of enthusiasm for the other.

"How long have Cook and Henry been married?" Emma asked, thinking they must be recently wed given the enthusiasm Cook displayed on rushing home. The nuptials must be too fresh for reality to have set in. "She seems so very happy."

"I believe it's been twenty-some years," Beatrice replied with a sigh. Emma noted the subtle shift in her voice, the longing in her sigh. This was a different Beatrice than the one who bent her head by candlelight to finish an embroidery project. "Henry has been good for her," she said wistfully. "And she for him. They're two of a kind, perfectly suited."

"And you, Beatrice? Have you never found someone for whom you were perfectly suited?" Emma asked, suddenly curious about the younger spinster sister.

A spot of color bloomed in Beatrice's cheeks. "Many years ago, there was a young man I was fond of. I thought perhaps . . ." She shook the memory from her face. "But my parents felt it was not a good match and that I should wait for someone more worthy." She smiled thinly over her cup. "I'm still waiting."

They sat in silence a moment before Beatrice asked, "Tell me of your husband. Was it a good match?"

"I suppose we weren't married long enough to truly test the union," Emma improvised, quickly gathering her guard. "But I would prefer not to discuss it. It's still too painful." With a practiced bow of her head, she pretended deep sadness.

"I'm sorry, dear, I didn't mean to intrude. I thought talking might help a bit." Beatrice patted her arm in sympathy. "Truth be told, I'm a bit envious. Your marriage may have been brief, but at least you have experienced one." She withdrew her hand. "Some things, I fear, Cecilia and I will never sample."

A chilled current, set in motion by Cook's departure, swirled about the room. Beatrice pulled her shawl tighter about her shoulders. "Sometimes on these cold nights, I wish I had a man to go home to, like Cook."

Emma glanced at her. Could that be true? Would she, herself, grow to resent not having experienced a man's attention in her later years? Did her mother, after all the pain and suffering, *not* regret her indiscretion? That proved a novel thought, one she would have liked to share with Chambers. What would he say to the concept? Emma felt her own cheeks warming. She could well imagine his lazy smile, his cocked brow, and a quick offer of assistance to remedy her own lack of experience.

"Enough ruminating," Beatrice said with a slight shake. "What's done is done. Cook would say, 'Everyone must row with the oars he has,' and we have you now to provide our missing oars." Beatrice patted Emma's hand. "So tell me, what do you think of our young ladies?"

"They seem very young," Emma said with a smile. Although her physical years were not far past those of Elizabeth, her experiences of late had aged her beyond measure of months and years.

"Yes." Beatrice laughed. "Young and ready to take on the world. How do you compare our young ladies to those in London? Can they compete?"

Her eyes glittered with affection. Emma wasn't fooled by the lightness of the question. "They have charm," she said, "when they wish it, and pleasant enough features." How could she say that the Pettibone girls lacked the sometimes cruel determination of the social set in London? That cold shoulder was hard enough to experience and impossible to teach. "I'm sure they will make fine wives."

"Yes," Beatrice agreed with the satisfaction of a proud mother hen surveying her brood. "If we can just gain them the exposure to catch the eye of potential husbands."

"Are there no suitable gentlemen in these parts to court the girls?"

"Merchant's sons and farmers." Beatrice shook her head. "Fine, strapping young men, but not the sort our ladies are aiming for."

"And that would be?"

"Why landed gentry, of course." Beatrice drew back in surprise. "A gentleman with a heritage to fall back upon in hard times. A gentleman who can offer our ladies the kind of life we've prepared them for." She leaned in closer to Emma and lowered her voice. "Many of the girls have generous dowries. They have the means within their grasp."

Emma wisely kept her opinions to herself. A merchant's son, trained in business, should not be overlooked in favor of a perceived bloodline. A paper lineage didn't always guarantee a substantial future. A man with his wits about him, however, could carve out a satisfying life for himself and his family.

"Have you thought of a ball to display their talents?"

Emma asked. "That seems to be the way of it in London, although in these parts I suppose—"

"A ball? That's a wonderful idea!" Beatrice's eyes widened as if she were a young girl once more, anticipating her first ball. "We shall have to get some musicians, but Monsieur Philippe is sure to have some ideas. I'll have to talk to Cook about the refreshments. Cecilia will adore the idea."

Beatrice glanced quickly to Emma, but that rushed glance confirmed Emma's dawning suspicions. "You've been planning this for some time."

"Balls are not unheard of here in the country," Beatrice confessed. "We were unsure of how to proceed. But with your knowledge of society, I know a proper ball would be a successful endeavor."

Realizing she had once again been effectively manipulated, Emma sighed. First, she'd discovered she was to teach bedroom etiquette, a subject she knew nothing about. Then she'd been cornered into teaching painting, another area of which she knew little. And now she was to arrange a ball. At least this was something she had some experience in, even if all her experience was of a derogatory nature. Penelope had made sure of that.

"And Cecilia?" Emma asked. "Does she support this proposal?"

Beatrice fidgeted with her shawl. "I told Cecilia that you were the answer to our prayers, and I was right. We had hoped to attract a simple widow to teach our girls the requisite skills needed for the marriage bed, but when we read Lady Cavendish's glowing letter of reference regarding your fine social abilities and manners, we knew that such a woman with a fine London address, no less, would give our girls the advantage they needed."

Beatrice hurried out of the kitchen to seek Cecilia. Emma prayed Cecilia, keeper of the household accounts, would recognize the folly of this enterprise—a considerable expense for no guaranteed profit.

The wind howled down the chimney in the kitchen. Emma drained the last of her tea, letting the germ of Cecilia's imagined reaction take root. She sighed a breath of relief. Cecilia, the practical one, would put the idea to rest, sparing Emma the additional duties of organizing a ball.

THE WHOLE SCHOOL RALLIED BEHIND THE PLANNED ball with enthusiasm and determination. Even Emma eventually found pleasure in the girls' bubbling enthusiasm. The date selected for the endeavor, early May, remained sufficiently distant to dismiss. Much could happen in March and April that would render the idea of a ball unpalatable. Too distracted with maintaining her charade, Emma could not project that far into the future. She was contemplating how to maneuver her way out of this latest predicament when Cecelia discovered her in the library.

"I wonder, Mrs. Brimley, if you could accompany me into town. I'd like to order the ball invitations and your expertise in this area would be appreciated."

Cecilia's stern countenance combined with the capricious nature of a ball rendered her almost comical. Emma raised her brows.

"My expertise?"

"Although my sister and I have received invitations in our youth to many formal occasions, our knowledge is somewhat dated as to what is appropriate under modern circumstances." Cecilia hesitated as if her next words were troublesome. "I'd like your opinion on the style and fashion."

"Of course," Emma replied. It would do no good to protest on the grounds that years had passed since she had last seen an invitation of any sort. As much as she felt removed from London society, the sisters would be even farther along the path.

"Be sure to wear a heavy cloak," Cecilia cautioned. "We'll be taking the school's rig. The winter sun, though bright, is rarely warm enough."

A well-bundled Emma joined Cecelia in the open rig. Cecilia handled the reins in her heavy gloves as expertly as Henry, directing their route over frozen roads and ice-filled ruts.

"I suppose Lord Nicholas Chambers had need of his carriage today," Emma observed, pulling the lap rug over her knees. "I must admit I appreciate his past generosity of sharing his closed vehicle on a cold day such as this."

Cecilia sniffed. "It's hardly generous to let a neighbor use an implement that would be wasting away for disuse otherwise. He doesn't know how to associate with decent folk." She glanced at Emma, a frown at home on her face. "Quite frankly, Mrs. Brimley, I don't know how you manage on your visits."

"We speak of art and painting," Emma said. It was on her tongue to say that Lord Nicholas Chambers had been a perfect gentleman, but that was hardly true. Although he had not touched her beyond that one kiss, as had been their agreement, one could hardly call him a "gentleman" when his female guests were expected to disrobe in his company.

Emma eagerly observed the passing fields and low stone walls. Having studied Lord Chambers's paintings at some length, she was anxious to see what lay beneath the snow, mud, and ice. The landscape was hardly as desolate as she had first perceived, but rather teeming with life, dormant now, but waiting to burst through the hibernating season in vibrant greens and lavender hues. The dales and downs would roll forth as far as the eye could see, and see it she would, she promised herself. "It's really quite beautiful, isn't it?"

"What did you say?" Cecilia asked, pulled from her own thoughts.

"The countryside. It's beautiful in its own way, isn't it?"

Cecilia smiled, a rare sight. "Very much so. Not everyone appreciates it. I'm glad that you do."

"I had thought the girls would enjoy some of the poems that captured the beauty of this region. William Wordsworth traveled these parts, did he not?"

Cecilia nodded. "I met him once, when I was a little girl."

"You met William Wordsworth?" Emma repeated in disbelief. She had trusted so many of his poems to heart that she imagined the poet to be something far grander than a mortal man.

"It was well known that he liked to walk the countryside, you see," Cecilia said with a look that traveled far beyond the road ahead. "I was about seven years of age and he found me playing by a stream. It was a beautiful morning, fresh and new."

"Did he write you into his poems?"

"That would be foolishness." She scowled. "No, I did not inspire his work. But you are correct about the unique beauty of the shire. Wordsworth's poems do speak to me. I remember there was one about the river Dove."

" 'She dwelt among the untrodden ways/Beside the spring of Dove,' " Emma recited, having just read the poem the night before. Indeed, it was one of several that she had planned to offer the class. " 'A Maid whom there were none to praise/And very few to love.' "

Cecilia grimaced, clicked the reins, and recited the third stanza. " 'She lived unknown, and few could know/When Lucy ceased to be.' Yes, that's the one I remember. Sometimes I suspect that I'm that maid."

"But you said—"

"I said I was seven years old when I met Wordsworth. I

am not his Lucy." She snapped the reins as if to call attention to her denial. "Still, that poem speaks to me."

"How can you say that?" Emma scolded. "How many girls have you helped find a place in the world? I am sure they would sing your praises." Cecilia had her faults, but no one could fault her love for "her" girls. Emma continued her rally.

"How many women would turn their home into a school, just for—"

"Pettibone is not our property," Cecilia interjected.

"It's not?" Emma stopped, perplexed. "I had assumed—"

"My sister and I run the school in exchange for room and board and a few extra shillings. Much like yourself."

"But who?"

"Our patron keeps his identity a secret. All is handled through solicitors. But I will say this: I do not believe it is by accident that we are located where we are."

Emma did a quick mental survey of the adjoining properties. "You believe Lord Nicholas Chambers is responsible for the school?"

Cecilia screwed her face tight as if she had bitten into a bitter fruit. "Not him. Not the younger. He would sooner spend his coin at the tavern than for gently bred women. No, his brother, the Marquess of Enon, he's a man with a good heart and a pocket for charity."

"Lord Chambers's older brother?" Of course, he'd have to be the oldest brother to carry the title of Marquess. She hadn't thought to inquire as to Chambers's relations.

"He has never admitted as much, mind you. But we invite him to visit the school every year, and every year he comes." Cecilia had a youthful gleam in her eye. In that moment Emma could see the family resemblance between the two sisters.

"Perhaps he will come to the ball," Cecilia mused. "He would be a nice catch for one of the girls."

"Will you invite Lord Nicholas Chambers as well?"

"I suppose we shall. Although I can only hope he will decline." Cecilia's lips thinned in her consideration. "Yes, he must be invited. He is providing painting lessons."

And much more, Emma thought.

"Ah, we're almost there," Cecilia said. Smoke and the tops of a dozen or so chimneys loomed just over a hill.

Emma glanced over at her companion, whose disciplined and taciturn expression masked the regrets of a past lifetime. Imagine living a full life and believing no one would remember you when you left earthly cares behind. It was a burdensome thought, and unfortunately, a taste of her own future if she were to follow the Higgins sisters' footsteps.

"Miss Cecilia, you are not the maid in the poem," Emma stated with conviction and compassion. "I shall remember you."

"Of course, dear," she said, her voice falling to a whisper.

ALTHOUGH MINUSCULE BY LONDON STANDARDS, THE village with its shops and traffic warmed Emma's spirits. Neighbors nodded greetings as they passed, harnesses jingled as carriages rumbled by, children chased dogs that chased children around houses and in between the strangers on the walkways.

Cecilia pulled into the village and left the rig in the hands of a capable liveryman. She made her way purposefully toward the stationer, nodding and exchanging polite words with several villagers. As the two women walked side by side, their crinolines made a formidable wall that swept the cobbled path from one side to the other. Should Emma and Cecilia encounter another woman, the two would surround the stranger in such a way that other women would need to wait for the exchange of a few pleasantries before they could pass unimpeded.

Men, however, would step out in the street to provide ample room for the ladies to pass. That is, all the men, except for the preoccupied one barreling his way in their direction.

"Don't speak to him," hissed Cecilia. "It wouldn't be proper."

Indeed Cecilia plowed ahead and didn't acknowledge Chambers with as much as a nod. He, however, came to a complete stop in front of Emma.

"Mrs. Brimley, how nice to see you so unexpectedly." He perused her from head to toe in a most familiar, and therefore disrespectful, fashion.

"I'm surprised to see you as well, sir." Emma dipped in an informal curtsy, trying to hide the thrill at seeing him again.

"Mrs. Brimley!" hissed Cecilia. "Someone will see you."

"What brings you out of your studio?" Emma asked, knowing the question was in clear violation of Cecilia's dictate.

Chambers knew it as well, judging from the slight curve of his lip. His eyes sparkled. "New paints, among other things. My order from Paris has arrived."

Wishing to prolong their encounter, Emma kept her hands enclosed in her muff, her arms tucked tightly to her sides, suspecting that Cecilia would willingly pull her along like an errant child if she could find a handhold. Even now, she tugged impatiently on Emma's skirt.

Emma glanced toward the low clouds. "The weather appears to be on the mend."

"Henry managed the roads without difficulty." His eyes searched her face. His brows lifted as if he were waiting for an answer, or perhaps a question.

"Emma!" Cecilia hissed.

"I must go," Emma explained, wishing she could stay. She'd missed the sound of his voice, his quick wit, and even the slight tilt of his head. Most especially, she missed the way she felt with him, although she hadn't been able to put a word to describe it.

He nodded and placed a gloved hand to his tall hat as she continued up the walk with Cecilia.

"Mrs. Brimley," he called after she had passed. She stopped and turned. "I almost forgot. I have something of yours."

A smile leapt to her lips and she took a few steps back, leaving Cecilia to stew a short distance away. Chambers fumbled through the layers of his elegant frock coat, until he pulled something from the vicinity of his breast pocket.

"Here it is." He slowly withdrew a folded bit of lacy cloth embroidered with the letter "W" from inside a breast pocket.

"My mother's handkerchief!" she cried, taking the cloth from his gloved hands. "Where did you find it?"

Instinctively, she pressed the cloth to her bare cheek, absorbing the warmth that had come from his person. The faint scent of linseed oil filled her nose. She smiled.

"It smells like you." She lowered her voice so Cecilia couldn't hear.

"On the contrary." He bent his head closer as well. A smile tipped his lips and warmed his eyes. "It reminds me of roses." His gaze shifted low to her bodice. Suspecting he referred to the color of her corset, Emma felt her cheeks heat. The man knew no restraint; they were on a public street!

"I thought you might find comfort in it," he said, his gaze warming her more than the winter sun.

"Yes. Thank you." She quickly slipped the cloth in her

muff. The return of her mother's handkerchief meant more than she could express in public.

Chambers looked past Emma's shoulder. "I believe your presence is required elsewhere."

"Yes, I'm afraid it is." Disappointment pulled at her throat. She wanted to say something to keep his attention, but he tipped his hat and continued down the street. Emma watched with a sense of loss, until Cecilia grabbed her by the crook of her arm and turned her to their destination.

"Why did you speak when I clearly said you shouldn't?" she scolded.

"To do otherwise would be impolite, and a lady is always mindful of her etiquette." That would silence Cecilia. She should have stopped there, but added, "Perhaps Lord Nicholas Chambers doesn't visit Pettibone because he perceives he is disliked."

"He would be correct," Cecilia snarled. "He is probably en route to the tavern as we speak. His kind always finds a warm welcome there."

Emma tried to turn to measure Chambers's direction, but Cecilia tugged her into a shop.

THE TWO WOMEN ARRIVED BACK AT PETTIBONE IN THE fading light of the short winter day, pleased with the success of their mission. Although Cecilia had seethed to vent her displeasure at Emma's familiarity with Chambers, Emma had proper etiquette on her side. Cecilia's anger eventually dissolved in the procurement of various household necessities at a fair price. The invitations were properly ordered and the ride home swift and cordial. Emma still carried a warm glow from her chance encounter with Chambers. She had barely stepped down from the rig when Alice bolted out the door running in her direction.

"She's gone, Mrs. Brimley. I knew she wanted to run

away. I can't find her anywhere. She's gone." Alice ran into her arms, knocking Emma slightly off balance and into the side of the rig.

"Who's gone, Alice?" Cecilia demanded.

"I fear it is Charlotte," Emma replied. "I promised Alice I would talk to her, but I haven't had an opportunity."

Beatrice followed in Alice's wake, carrying a woolen shawl that she draped across the girl's shoulders. "Charlotte didn't come to her needlework class. We've searched the house from top to bottom. We had hoped you would have passed her on the road."

Emma looked to Cecilia, whose dour expression said more than the negative movement of her head.

"We should inform Lord Chambers of the missing girl," Emma said. "Perhaps he can be of assistance." Cecilia frowned. Emma pulled her recently returned handkerchief from her muff to wipe the tear tracks from Alice's face.

"Inside, all of you," Cecilia said. "We can plan our course of action in the warmth of the house."

Once they had closed the door on the cold and dark, Cecilia turned to Alice. "You knew Charlotte was planning this and you did not inform me?"

Alice pressed tighter to Emma's side. "I didn't think she'd try so soon. I thought she'd listen to Mrs. Brimley."

"Alice did what she thought was correct. Now is not the time to assign fault." Emma squeezed Alice's shoulders with a reassuring hug. "The concern must be to find Charlotte before the temperature drops much lower. How long has she been gone?"

"Two hours," Alice answered. "It's been at least that long."

"Go put on some warmer clothes and I'll do the same," Emma directed Alice with a gentle push to the stairs. "Meet me back here as soon as you're ready."

"What are you going to do?" Beatrice asked. "The light

will be gone in another hour, and there's not a moon in the sky tonight."

"We'll take lanterns and search the back path to Black Oak. The path provides the only break in the trees." Thank heavens neither sister asked how she had come by that information.

"We know she's not on the road to town," Cecilia said. "I'll take Miss Barnesworth and search the road in the opposite direction. I suspect she has a hand in this." Cecilia lifted her skirts to hurry up the stairs.

"What should I do? Where should I look?" Beatrice asked, wringing the life out of an unlucky piece of embroidery.

"You have the hardest job of all," Emma said, anxious to dash outside in search of the missing girl. "You need to stay here in case Charlotte returns on her own. The younger children will need someone in authority to calm them and keep order. That will be your mission. To keep order and to make sure the tea is hot and ready when we return home."

· Ten ·

THE FIERCE DARKNESS CONSUMED THE HEAT AND light like a hungry animal cast out in the wild. Emma and Alice concentrated on remaining upright as the light from their lanterns caught obstacles only moments before they were underfoot. Their throats were hoarse from crying out Charlotte's name. Even sound disappeared beyond the circle of the lamps, supplanted by the cracking of frozen twigs underfoot and the scurry of unseen feet inches from their own.

"Do you think we'll find her?" Alice asked after an unreturned volley of calls.

"I hope so." Emma pulled the wool of her scarf tighter around her neck. "I wouldn't wish to be out alone on a night like this. I do hope Charlotte thought to dress appropriately."

"She missed her family. If I had brothers and sisters, I would miss them too." The longing in the girl's voice twisted Emma's heart. "I suppose it would be rude of me to ask if you have brothers and sisters, Mrs. Brimley?"

"Indeed, questions of such a personal nature would be considered intrusive," Emma replied, ever mindful of her responsibilities to mold the girls to society's standards. "However, rather recently I have learned that speaking of one's personal nature can sometimes prove . . . helpful, so I will answer your question. I have neither brothers nor sisters."

She gazed about into the black void around them and shuddered. She hoped Charlotte had found shelter. On a night like this, the woods was no place to be by oneself.

"The world is a sad place when you are all alone," Alice lamented with a heavy sigh.

As much as Emma could empathize with that statement, it was not the future she would wish for Alice.

"You are a beautiful young lady," Emma comforted. "I'm sure you will find a suitable husband and begin a family of your own."

"I have no prospects, no dowry, and no family to speak of. I'm afraid your special etiquette classes shall be wasted on me," Alice said with a deep sigh.

"Then I shall be your family, and you shall be mine," Emma pronounced. "And at the darkest of times, we shall run toward each other, as we pray Charlotte will do to this lantern." She raised the light high.

Alice smiled. "I shall like that." She called again for Charlotte, yet received no response.

"Look!" Emma pointed to a spot between the trees. "Those are the lights of Black Oak. We must have traveled the full path. We can stop there and warm our hands a few moments. Perhaps there's news of the search."

"Not there." Alice stopped dead in her tracks, refusing to budge. "Miss Higgins says we are never to visit Black Oak. To do so is to be ruined."

"That's ridiculous. I've visited numerous times for les-

THE EDUCATION OF MRS. BRIMLEY 141

sons, and I have always been received with warmth and cordiality." To say she'd been received warmly did injustice to her elevated temperature whenever she confronted Lord Chambers, but that was an improper subject for Alice's young ears.

"But you are a widow. I am an innocent."

That brought a small smile to Emma on such a comfortless night. If only she knew. "Alice," Emma said, "you are in no danger at Black Oak, especially when accompanied by your family."

Alice smiled and moved forward.

"MRS. BRIMLEY, WE'VE BEEN EXPECTING YOU. AND YOU have brought a visitor." Thomas greeted them at the door.

"You were expecting us?" Hope blossomed in Emma like a sip of brandy. "Have you found her?"

"His lordship is waiting for you. This way, please." Thomas led them round to the back of the manor house and pointed the way to the stables. Emma and Alice grabbed fistfuls of skirts and ran the short distance to the brick and wood structure. Leaving their lanterns outside the stable doors, they ventured in, drawn by voices and a light in one of the back stalls.

"That one, I think, has a special affinity for you." Chambers's deep voice drew Emma like a bee to honey. "I can't even entice this one to—oh, there he goes."

Emma peered around the stall to see Chambers lying on a bale of hay, his head propped by a bent elbow, trying to lure a tiny gray kitten to jump at a dried wheat sprig. Charlotte sat in one corner, a fuzzy ball of gray and white fur curled contentedly in her lap, laughing at the resulting flurry of tiny paw pats. A third kitten crouched by her knees, preparing to lunge at the tip of the twitching tail of Chambers's pet.

"Charlotte Hawkins!" Alice charged into the tranquil

scene. "We've been worried ill." Emma noted the accurate imitation of Cecilia's censure, complete with her hands on her hips.

Chambers looked up at precisely the same time the kitten leapt for the dangling stalk, missed, and landed on Chambers's face. Everyone laughed except Alice. Chambers removed the gray furry mass and returned it to the curve of its mother's swollen belly before crossing the stall to stand next to Emma.

"Come see the babies, Alice," Charlotte called. "They're barely four weeks old and they're ever so tiny."

"It seems I've found one of your strays," Chambers murmured to Emma. The delicious warmth of his breath swirled in her ear. Indeed she wasn't sure what pleasured her more: finding Charlotte or watching the impervious Lord Chambers playing with kittens in a cozy, fragrant stall.

"We found her half-frozen in the back garden. I couldn't convince her to come inside the manor, so we compromised on the stable. She looked at me like I was the devil incarnate."

He scowled as if offended, although she knew he enjoyed the role well enough when she stood half-naked in his studio. However, after seeing him with the kittens, she supposed she would have difficulty thinking of him in such evil terms in the future.

"She said she was making her way to the train station." He crossed his arms, watching the girls play with the future mousers. "Thomas warmed her up with tea and biscuits." Chambers lifted an eyebrow in her direction. "Do they not feed you women at that school?"

Emma was so thrilled to find Charlotte that words managed to swell in her throat and render her mute.

"And who is this young lady who has chosen to join our party?" He smiled at Alice, who looked at him somewhat circumspect,

"Lord Nicholas Chambers, may I present Miss Darlington," Emma managed to say around the lump in her throat. Alice rose to her feet and curtsied on cue, but still gazed in fear and awe at their host. Not surprising. Emma had had a similar reaction to Chambers after listening to the tales of the Higgins sisters.

"Miss Darlington?" Chambers's eyes narrowed slightly as he studied her face. "Could that be Miss Alice Darlington?"

"Have we met before, your lordship?" Alice asked.

"I believe I knew your mother many, many years ago," he said in a wistful tone.

"You knew my mother?" Alice's eyes grew as wide as saucers. "Please, sir, I know so little. Would you tell me about her?"

Chambers gently cupped her chin and smiled into her hopeful eyes. "She was very beautiful and very talented. You look exactly like her when she was your age."

Any fear or apprehension on Alice's part apparently evaporated at his touch. "Did you know my father? Were they from around here? In what way was she talented?" Questions long suppressed quickly bubbled to the surface.

Chambers's gaze slipped to Emma. Something akin to pain flashed in his eyes. "I imagine you are anxious to return the girls to the school."

Although puzzled by his reaction, Emma recognized the cue. They had overstayed their welcome. "Girls, the hour grows late. We must return to Pettibone." Charlotte protested, wishing to spend more time with the kitten.

"When it is old enough, and as long as the headmistress allows it"—he winked in Emma's direction—"you may take her back with you to the school.

"Please allow Henry to return you to Pettibone," he added to Emma. "He's waiting inside, I'll warrant."

• • •

"HE'S NOT AT ALL WHAT I EXPECTED," ALICE CONFIDED the moment the carriage door shut and the horses began the long walk back to the school. Due to the moonless night, Henry walked in front of the horses with a lantern to light the way.

"I like him," Charlotte said, with a loud yawn. "May we come back to visit?"

"Yes, we must come back," Alice pleaded. "Please?"

"We will discuss the matter with Miss Higgins," Emma replied, pleased that Chambers had made a good impression on the girls. "I expect she won't be inclined to allow you, Miss Hawkins, to go visiting anywhere for quite a while."

Charlotte hung her head. "I'm sorry. I didn't mean for you to worry."

Emma patted Charlotte's hand. "Everyone was worried, not just me. The whole school turned all topsy-turvy when you were discovered missing. But you're safe now." She squeezed her hand. "That is what is important. I suggest the both of you close your eyes and attempt to get some sleep. At this pace we shall arrive back at Pettibone long past your bedtime."

IT TOOK SEVERAL DAYS FOR THE SCHOOL TO RETURN TO normal. Emma heard Lord Chambers's name mentioned in hushed whispers in corners and alcoves throughout the school.

Although visits by the girls to Black Oak continued to be strictly forbidden, the furrows in Cecilia's brow no longer touched the bridge of her nose at the very mention of Chambers's name.

A week passed before Emma could return to Black Oak. The carriage body rocked from side to side, tossed by the howling winds that carried a fresh layer of snow to coat the sleeping countryside. The time spent negotiating the distance from the school to Chambers's residence doubled. Poor Henry, she thought of the bundle of wool coaxing the pair of horses onward. Perhaps she should have listened to Cecilia's suggestion that she miss another art lesson.

Beatrice went so far as to volunteer to accompany Emma to Black Oak to personally thank his lordship for his role in Charlotte's recovery. Before Emma could think of an appropriate protest, Cecilia nay-sayed the idea. "Mrs. Brimley is capable of extending our gratitude under the circumstances."

Although Emma insisted it was the courtesy of conveying those sentiments that drew her to Black Oak in such adverse weather, she knew another deeper desire spurred her action. She needed to see him again and would have braved rain, hail, and ice to return to Black Oak.

Thomas allowed Emma access into the studio even though Chambers had not yet arrived. She gazed about the room, sensing a change in the atmosphere, a shift in some basic fundamental. The room still overwhelmed her with light and color; the scent of oils, turpentine, and pure creative energy continued to dominate. Freshly painted canvases leaned against the wall, though she detected a change in subject matter. The landscapes had slipped into the minority compared to some studies of clothed human figures and even a painting of kittens in the straw.

The mirror that had telegraphed her artless removal of garments hung in the same place on the wall, but the addition of a three-paneled screen in the corner caught her attention. She smiled, feeling almost comfortable in her surroundings. The room no longer terrified or intimidated her. She amended that thought. The room itself had never threatened; it was the absent master. Coming here today still set her heart to pounding, but her palms remained dry beneath her gloves, and her throat retained some semblance of moisture.

"I had thought you would have arrived earlier," Chambers said, joining her. "How am I expected to paint without a subject?"

"I am here now, sir." She smiled, appreciating the fashionable waistcoat that spanned his chest. Something else was different about him, she thought. A new vitality, a restlessness, seemed to vibrate the air around him.

"Did you notice I added a screened panel for your comfort?" He pointed toward the back corner of the room. "I ordered it after you modeled last."

Emma wondered at his chattiness. He fidgeted with his brushes, selecting one and testing it against the palm of his hand.

"I was most disappointed when it arrived yesterday. Not only because I find it totally unnecessary, but because the unannounced delivery was an innate object"—he glanced up, tapping out a rhythm in his palm—"and not a certain ladies' English teacher."

The hurt in his eyes bruised her heart. *He had missed her.* She was scarcely able to credit the idea, yet she couldn't deny the subtle change in his character. *He had missed her, the cold fish, the intellectual, the plain by-blow whispered about in dark corners.*

In spite of the scowl on his face, a smile threatened to blossom on hers. Such an expression would have frightened her before, but now that she knew him, she relaxed in his presence. She clasped both her hands together in front of her as would a demure miss and calmly explained. "The weather impeded my earlier return, but I'm here now."

She took two steps toward the new screen but stopped and turned. "Before we begin, sir, I'd like to thank you for your assistance in rescuing poor Charlotte. It was foolish for her to run away on such a cold night, but good fortune brought her to your garden and you brought her back to us." She ended her speech with a deep curtsy, pleased with the execution of her practiced show of gratitude.

The brush stopped its downward arc, his eyes narrowed slightly, his lips thinned. "I offered a frightened, freezing child shelter and nourishment. Do not elevate me to sainthood, Mrs. Brimley."

She stood, a bit hesitant. She had thought he would be pleased with her expression of appreciation, not insulted. Her brow furled. "I did not suggest you were a saint, sir."

"Good. Because I most certainly am not." He stared at her with an arrogance that welcomed dispute.

"But you—" She wanted to enumerate evidence of his kindness: the return of her mother's handkerchief, the shelter offered to a scared little girl, the kittens, the screen, but he interrupted her before she could begin.

"What then is to be my reward for my *uncharacteristic* charitable act?" His eyebrow cocked, a slow smile shifted his features.

"Uncharacteristic? Why the kindness you have shown time after time . . ." Her gaze caught his sly smile and cocked eyebrow. His wanton expression should have chased her to a hasty retreat. Instead her chest tingled with fervent anticipation. Appalled at her body's reaction, she felt a telltale warmth spread to her hairline.

He walked around her slowly, like a fierce jungle cat stalking its prey.

"I think you do understand. Doesn't one act of kindness deserve another?" His voice flowed over her, as smooth and potent as the amber liquid in the crystal glass waiting by his easel. "You, of all people, should realize that everything has a price."

· *Eleven* ·

EMMA BIT HER LIP, AFRAID OF WHAT HE WOULD demand. Now that he had time to consider her mother's indiscretion, perhaps he would expect the same from the daughter.

"What do you wish?" she asked around the lump in her throat.

"I wish you to undress in front of me, without the benefit of my turned back and without the benefit of the screen." His eyes burned hot as they raked over her form.

"I assume our earlier condition remains in effect?" She struggled to control the catch in her voice. "You will not touch me?"

"Only if you ask me to."

She bristled at his self-confidence, even as she released her pent-up breath. "That, sir, will not happen."

With a bit of resolve, she raised her hands to remove her hat, but he stopped her. "First, your blouse."

She stiffened, then demurred. The garment would have been eventually removed anyway. "As you wish."

Emma supposed his edict toward her hat applied to her gloves as well. They made the unbuttoning a bit awkward and slow. She continually reminded herself that he had seen her like this two times before. This should be nothing new, yet an expression in his eyes begged different. As she wrestled with the bodice buttons, her arms brushed the hardened nubs of her breasts pushing at the pleated satin ribbon ringing the top of her corset. A tremor rippled through her chest. Was her body's reaction to his intent stare visible to his eye? An appreciation tugged at his lips, suggesting an answer. The tremor dipped lower.

She pulled the fabric off each arm, never once breaking eye contact. She held the garment out to him. "I have no place to put this."

He draped it over his arm. "Now the hat."

Unfastening the pins holding the hat foundation in place required the use of both hands. She raised her arms. Her chest lifted and pulled against her confining corset. His swift intake of breath pulled her glance, only to be rewarded with an intense stare that singed her skin and burrowed to her spine. She handed him the hat.

"The skirts," he said, his voice huskier than before. "And lean forward as you lower them."

A shiver of fear raced through her, as if he had threatened a dangerous consequence if she did otherwise. True to his word, he remained rooted in his spot near his easel, one hand clenched by his side, the other smothered in her discards. He had not moved to touch her, yet the change in his voice and demeanor proved he was not unaffected by her actions. A sense of power emboldened her.

She unhooked her double skirt and leaned forward slightly, testing the results.

"More," he said, his voice thick with a hunger that shot straight to her core.

She bent lower, tugging at the black wool. A bulge pushed the front of Chambers's pants. Arousal! And she was the cause of it! Remembering Beatrice's observation that a man's arousal appeared uncomfortable, she glanced up to his face. He grimaced. How ironic that when he had turned his back, she was the flustered one. His current state of discomfort put her in control. She smiled, congratulating herself on obtaining this bit of information without risking additional clothing.

"You smile, you minx? Are you enjoying the effect you have on me?"

"I believe I am, sir." Indeed, now that she thought of it, this reversal of authority pleased her a great deal. But it was more than that. His adoration made her feel intensely wanted, desired, as if she were the only woman who could satisfy his needs.

Moving her legs a little further apart to give greater stability, she dipped as low as her corset afforded. She unfastened her petticoats, pulling the garments slowly over her protruding derriere. "Is this low enough for you?"

He growled. The man growled! Little ripples of appreciation shimmered along her nerve endings. She straightened very slow and deliberate, leaving the petticoats to lay where they fell. His bulge continued to expand.

"Are you uncomfortable, sir?" she asked with a knowing smile.

"Extremely," he replied.

His answer delighted her, though she wasn't sure why. She still needed to remove her gloves according to the terms of their agreement. She unfastened the buttons on each then began to pull on the tips.

"Use your teeth," he said.

"You wish me to bite my gloves?" This request made no sense.

"Use those sharp little teeth to pull at the tips of your gloves."

She did as he asked, placing each finger routinely between her lips, loosening the glove tips until she could pull on the middle finger alone. She tugged, allowing the silk to slowly slide down her wrist. To gain a bit more leverage, she arched her back ever so slightly.

Chambers collapsed on his stool, his legs spread wide.

"Mrs. Brimley, if you were any other woman, I'd beg you to ride me to our mutual pleasure." His voice was strained, as if he were under some great exertion, yet he only sat on a stool.

Giddiness spread through Emma like warm honey. Chambers's evident desire blasted her uncle's criticisms to perdition. Obviously, she possessed the ability to arouse a man and make him want to do things for their "mutual pleasure." Although the exact nature of those things still eluded her.

"I don't understand what you mean," she said, although she suspected his reference referred to that crude world of which she had little experience, but suddenly longed for more.

"I'll explain if you remove one of your stockings."

"Is this something my girls will have need to know?" With so few garments left, she needed to use them judiciously.

"We are discussing the possible positions for coupling, Mrs. Brimley. Indeed, for both stockings I will tell you of two positions."

Positions! That was one of the questions on her list. She nodded agreement, then bent to unfasten the first of the two long garters that secured each black silk stocking. She stopped.

"Was there a particular way you wished me to remove my stockings?" Her lips lifted in a smile. "I'm afraid I am not agile enough to bite them off."

"You learn quickly, Mrs. Brimley." His eyes crinkled in a slow, lazy smile. "The artful unveiling of one's attributes would whet any man's appetite." He pointed to the divan. "Can you raise your foot unto the cushions? I wish to see a full expanse of your leg."

Wonderful! This was exactly the information she needed for her girls. She stepped up on the dais and started toward the divan until she remembered the slit in her drawers. Raising her leg would expose the flesh beneath the resulting gap, the very flesh Chambers implied could be stimulated by hand, or tongue, or . . .

Heat flooded her face and regions below. "I'd prefer not, sir. I'll just bend low as before." She unfastened the front and back garters and began to roll the first stocking down her leg. "You owe me an explanation of one position."

He cleared his throat. "There are many, many positions to facilitate the act of coupling. I can think of at least four for which your girls should be prepared."

"I will settle for two." Indeed she originally had only five items of clothing with which to barter, and now she had lost two.

"The most common position is not my favorite, but it is efficient. The woman lies on the bed and spreads her legs wide, giving open access to her feminine core. The man positions himself between her legs and inserts his manhood. Sometimes he will lie across the woman while he thrusts deep inside her, or he might lift her hips and manipulate her while he thrusts."

"The woman just lies there?" She stood briefly on one foot to tug the stocking over her heel. She imagined herself lying on a bed in such a vulnerable position while a man, who remarkably resembled Lord Chambers, approached. Her knees buckled and she quickly clasped the divan for support.

"Many do," Chambers said, "particularly the ones that wish their husbands would seek their pleasure elsewhere. The wife who desires her husband's fulfillment as well as her own actively thrusts in rhythm with her husband." He paused. "Which kind of woman are you, Mrs. Brimley?"

Emma was still considering the meaning of the word "thrust." How exactly did one thrust one's lower regions? She tried to discretely *thrust* her hips and succeeded in hopping forward slightly, like a player in the child's game of hopscotch. A strangled gurgle issued from Chambers's direction.

"I beg your pardon," she said glancing up. "Did you ask a question?"

"Yes, but I've already deduced the answer."

Something in his expression made her cheeks burn. "You said there was another position, one that you preferred?"

"I prefer to lay on the bed and let the woman sit on top, her legs astride me. She can take my manhood as fast or as slow as she wants, and I can lie back and enjoy her efforts."

Emma tried to visualize, being careful this time to avoid the face of her fantasy lover. "This is what you meant by 'riding'?"

"When the man is fully involved, the motion is similar to riding a horse."

"Well, then, that position should not be too difficult for the girls to learn. They are all capable horsewomen. We'll start with riding." She nodded to punctuate her decision, and attacked the second stocking.

"I should warn you," Chambers cautioned. "Not all men enjoy this position."

"Why not?" She paused. "Does it not give pleasure?"

He smiled. "It most definitely gives pleasure, but it also places the woman in a position superior to the man. He is at her mercy, so to speak."

She rather enjoyed that expression, "at her mercy." It suggested that the woman was not as powerless in the act of coupling as society suggested. Indeed, it was an apt description of Chambers throughout her artful removal of garments. She filed that away for reflection at a later time. At the moment, she needed to focus her attention on his answers. Emma tugged the second stocking free with a jerk of her hand.

"There is another position your girls may need to know," he suggested with a lift of his brow.

"What might that be?"

"I've given you the two positions promised. I believe you know the price of a third."

She hesitated; she had so little left. "Is this a common position?"

"Some men prefer it above the others."

If she were to sacrifice her corset, her fitted camisole would still serve as a barrier between his eyes and her skin, but her breasts would be unrestrained. "The girls should not be unprepared for the demands that may be asked of them," she said more to herself than to him.

She reached behind her and pulled the loop that unfastened her corset. With the back thus widened, she eased the silk and whalebone concoction over her head.

"Lord, have mercy," he gasped.

She clutched the empty corset to her chest. "Did I do something wrong?" A lump formed in her throat. *Have you finally noticed the shapeless, ugly body that my uncle insisted could hold no attraction for a man?*

"Mrs. Brimley," he said with a seriousness that shot straight through her, "if you were any more perfect, I should die on the spot. You lack only wings to be an angel."

"Oh." Relief and appreciation made her a bit light-headed. She suspected his flattery to be less than truthful, but his reassurance reinforced her earlier revelation that she was desirable. Tears welled in her eyes. She blinked rapidly to keep them at bay. "Thank you," she whispered.

"In the third position," Chambers's voice cracked. He laid Emma's garments on a nearby chair, then paused for a sip from his glass.

"In the third position, the woman is expected to lower herself to her hands and knees. The man kneels behind her and inserts himself into her opening. Then he pulls on her hips to rock her back and forth."

"He cannot see her face?" She would want to see Chambers's face when he made love to her. The thought did not shock her as it had earlier. Nicholas was worthy of love, of her love, though coupling would occur only in her imagination.

His gaze lifted to her face, unleashing a fresh surge of yearning in her heart. His eyes crinkled. "Not without an appropriately placed mirror."

She glanced at the gilt-framed mirror on the wall. "I can see why you'd be familiar with this position."

He laughed, then groaned. "Have pity on me, Mrs. Brimley. You have already reduced me to this lamentable state. Further discussion about intimate relations between a man and a woman may be my total undoing."

Although she wasn't sure why the slow removal of one's garments would excite a man to such a state, she could not deny the proof before her. Chambers's suggestion that mere discussions regarding intimate relations could be stimulating should not have surprised her. Hadn't her own body reacted in the most alarming, though somehow pleasing, way to his words? She filed that thought away for further consideration. For now, she smiled. Chambers had given her a wonderful gift: freedom from her uncle's criticisms. She felt lighter, attractive, and at the moment, generous.

"What can I do to assist you, sir?"

"I suppose your stipulation that I not touch you extends as well to an unwillingness to touch me?"

She almost laughed at the hopeful lift of his brows. His sad, soulful eyes reminiscent of a bloodhound denied a tasty treat implored her mercy. She was tempted to ask him to explain how a touch would restore his vitality, but something in the tilt of his lips reminded her of the birch branch. Her eyes widened. She shook her head from side to side.

"I thought as much." He swiveled around on his stool and pulled back the drape from the canvas on his easel. "Perhaps it's time we turned our conversation to other matters. If you'll assume the pose of Artemis, we can utilize the light while we talk."

Although relieved that her most private areas would remain concealed from Lord Chambers's view, she experienced an unsettling stab of disappointment. She had found such pleasure in their engaging banter, she was hesitant to leave it behind.

She stepped into the pose, splaying her hands wide as she imagined herself as the goddess. Interesting that she had found even this posture so difficult on her earlier visit. Now she reveled in her newfound power and smiled inwardly at Nicholas's hungry gaze. *Hungry for her!* The realization weakened her knees. She bobbled a bit on the dais.

"Don't move," Chambers implored, a brush held aloft in the air.

She nodded, her throat suddenly too dry for words. If she continued thinking about Chambers's desires specifically for her, the resulting fidgeting would end their session too soon. She searched her brain for a safer topic to explore.

Alice had begged and pleaded with Emma earlier to find out more about her parents. Chambers seemed to hold the key.

"You've mentioned before that you knew Miss Darlington's parents," she said, pleased with her use of opportunity.

Chambers didn't respond, focusing intently on the canvas he'd positioned on the easel.

"What can you tell me about them?"

"Alice's mother was a beautiful young lady who fell in love with the wrong man." He dabbed at the canvas with his brush. "She died in childbirth."

"And the father?"

He frowned. "This is not a subject I care to discuss. Pray, choose another."

"But the poor child deserves to know something about her mother. She's so lonely." And relentless in her pursuit for more information, Emma thought silently.

"Having a family does not prevent one from loneliness. You should know that." He scowled.

"Me?" Shock loosened her jaw. "Why should I know such a thing?"

"Because you are running away, are you not?" He scowled, resting his brush on his knee. "You left the comfort of London for the wilds of Yorkshire. You are pretending to be a widow when you most certainly have not experienced the touch of a man."

His attention returned to the canvas. "Sometimes, knowing one's family induces loneliness."

Only the crackle of the fire broke the silence.

Granted she had told him some of the details of her past, but she had been careful not to mention names. If he had discovered her family, others might as well. A shudder rippled through her. She'd need to run again before her uncle could find her. Her throat tightened. "You know of my family?"

"I was speaking of my own."

He tossed his brush in a murky jar, then lifted the crystal glass for a deep swallow. Brandy glistened on his lips.

"Who are you, Mrs. Brimley? Why are you here?"

"I don't know what you mean," she said, hedging for time.

"I think you do. I know you have secrets. Women do not masquerade as widows and flee their domiciles without secrets. Granted you have some sad excuses for relatives, and a difficult heritage, but you could have managed. Something chased you from London, did it not?"

She gnawed at her lip, thinking of how to change the topic of conversation. How did discussion of Alice's parents swing scrutiny back to herself?

"No one knows the nature of your visits to Black Oak. I have kept my word. I will keep your secrets safe. But I need to know. Tell me. Who are you?"

It was true. The sisters held no suspicion that her visits were less than honorable. He hadn't touched her, even to steal a kiss, after giving his word. Perhaps she could trust him in this, as well.

"My name is Emma Heatherston," she admitted.

"Emma," he said, testing the name on his lips. "It suits you."

"I overheard a conversation not meant for my ears." She rushed forward, not bothering to explore the pleasing sound of her name on his lips. "My uncle is planning to sell me to another man to rid himself of the burden I placed on his household. He has secured the buyer. The arrangement awaits only delivery."

"To sell you with benefit of marriage, I assume?" His scowl suggested another possibility.

"I determined not to stay and find out." Indeed, that part of the conversation had occurred before she stumbled upon the two men speaking in the library. She had the foresight to draw up short and not announce her presence.

"My uncle is not a kind man. He cared little for my mother or for me. Once my mother died, he resolved to rid himself of me as well." She didn't add that she feared he was responsible for her mother's death. It was enough that she suspected.

"So you removed yourself from his household." Chambers nodded in approval. "Will he look for you?"

"He would not pass on an opportunity for profit." She lowered her gaze to meet Chambers's. "And I will not be tied in servitude to a man not of my choosing."

"An interesting choice of words, Mrs. Brimley." He cocked his brow. "Would you be willing to be tied in servitude to a man *of* your choosing?" He rubbed his brush on a cloth.

He had that same look as when he had invited her "to ride." She narrowed her eyes. "I fear you are twisting words beyond my scope of understanding."

"I have displeased you." He smiled an apology. "Let us attempt a less personal topic. I believe you asked me to teach you about painting?"

She sighed. "That's another subject I'm to teach the girls for which I'm not experienced."

"Then we shall remedy that." He dipped his brush in a small puddle of paint and lifted it to the canvas. "Let us discuss the theories of color."

He bent behind the sizeable canvas, hiding his scowl from Emma's gaze. What fool in his right mind would plot to sell a woman like Emma to settle a few debts? The man must be mad!

"There exist two types of colors, primary and mixed." He carefully modulated his tone to conceal his thoughts. *And two types of men, those that can be trusted and those that should be tossed into the Thames with no questions asked. Emma's uncle would enjoy the company on his way to the murky bottom.*

"Only God and certain talented London and Paris colormen firms can reproduce the primary colors of red, blue, and yellow." *Yellow. Her uncle most likely had a yellow streak down his back. Only a coward would use a woman's skirts to settle a debt. Red, the color of blood and the color that will run freely if I catch up to that miserable maggot of an uncle. Blue . . .*

He noticed that in his anger he had pressed too hard on the brush, distorting the shadow beneath Emma's graceful neck; he reached for a palette knife to scrape away the excess paint.

Careful, he cautioned himself, *the uncle can be dealt with later. No sense in letting him affect the painting.* He studied the painted neck, checking to see if the correction was adequate, then shifted his position on the stool so as to see the real thing.

Her neck was one of the first things he had noticed about her, that and her dogged determination and refusal to be frightened out of his studio. Of course, an appreciation of the delicate planes of her cheekbones, her glowing skin, and the expressive depth of her eyes soon followed. He smiled, and what man couldn't appreciate her need of an education. But that neck should be worshipped with tender kisses and . . .

An uncomfortable shift in his groin brought him back to the painting.

"All the other colors can be created by mixing in some measure those three." He resumed his lecture. "For example, I can mix a light red and blue to paint fields of lavender. Or I can mix a deeper red with a light yellow and create the blush you see on a perfect English rose." Or on Emma's cheeks. He shifted to see her face and followed her gaze to the pile of clothes on the divan. Topping the pile lay her pink foundation.

"Or a corset," he added with a smile. Emma's cheeks followed suit.

LATER THAT EVENING, EMMA SAT ALONE IN THE EMPTY kitchen with a warm cup of tea and her poetry journal. She glanced at the line she had just written: *Love's soft whisper entered the innermost Chamber.*

Perdition! All her poems these days seemed to contain that single word, and once again she had inadvertently capitalized "chamber." Using the freshly carved quill, she tried to subtly correct the error. Was it any wonder that the man who dominated her thoughts and dreams found his way into her poems? Ink pooled on the journal page, rendering the line unreadable. With a sigh, she blotted the page and set the journal aside to dry. Another page ruined by her daydreams.

Still she couldn't be angry. Something magical had transpired between them today. A ruined journal page was but a passing gray cloud on a brilliant sunny day.

She felt safe and secure even though another knew of her true identity. Upon reflection, she had to admit Nicholas had given her far more than she had ever imagined. With his clever words and long smoldering glances, he had brought her to life, much like the landscape beyond the kitchen walls. She smiled. Maybe that explained those internal explosions whenever he came near: she herself was bursting into bloom.

This time she laughed out loud, wondering what kind of flower she would blossom into.

A perfect English rose. His voice, low and full of promise, whispered in her ear. She gasped and glanced frantically about. But only cleared work surfaces and empty corners met her gaze. She sniffed, disappointed to find only the redolent scent of candlewax, warmed brick, and gathered apples in the air. Clutching the ends of her woolen shawl, she pulled it tight around her. A soft warmth slowed the heightened beat of her heart. It was just her active imagination. She smiled. Even though she was alone in the kitchen, Nicholas Chambers stayed close in her thoughts.

THREE WEEKS LATER, THOMAS STOPPED BY CHAMBERS'S studio late on an early March evening. He rapped sharply on the doorframe. "May I enter, sir? I thought I might tidy up a bit before retiring."

"Of course, Thomas, come in." Chambers continued his work on Artemis's Revenge. "I'm just finishing up myself."

"I must say, sir, that is an extraordinarily large canvas. Much larger than your previous endeavors."

"That appears to be the trend at the Royal Academy exhibitions. Last year, some of the full portraits were life-size, a tremendous opportunity for detail." Thomas's eyebrows rose a notch, which Chambers construed as expressing surprise.

"It's true. The landscape painters are planning equally large canvases to compete for wall space."

"May I presume that all proceeds well with your painting?" Thomas picked up a tray of plates and teacups used earlier and moved it nearer to the door.

"All proceeds very well, thank you." Nicholas smiled. "Mrs. Brimley has proven to be a most adept and inspirational model." Thoughts of their modeling sessions filled him with a warmth he hadn't felt in years. "I'm almost hesitant to finish this for loss of her company."

"The winter snows have passed; the roads improve daily. You haven't visited a tavern in several months."

He glanced up quickly. "I hadn't realized that. I just

haven't had the desire. Do you suppose I'm maturing, Thomas?"

Thomas smiled, a slight curve of the lips. "I noticed the large blank canvas against the wall. I thought perhaps you were planning to render a painting of one of the tavern ladies, sir, as you have in the past."

"This?" Chambers reached out to grasp a primed canvas of the equivalent size to *Artemis's Revenge*. "I stretched two canvases just in case something proved unsatisfactory with the first. However, now I'm thinking about using this one for a landscape."

"A landscape, sir?"

Chambers scrutinized the blank taut fabric. "I'm thinking on taking Mrs. Brimley on a picnic." He looked up. "Did you know that I'm teaching Mrs. Brimley how to paint?"

"I had no idea, sir."

"Of course, so far we've only discussed theory. I think it's time she got in some actual brushwork." He glanced to his jar of brushes, the rudiments of an idea stirring in his mind.

"That sounds like a brilliant idea, sir." Thomas picked up a gray and white kitten off the desk and dropped it unceremoniously into a nearby cushioned basket. The kitten yowled a protest, then settled in quietly. "Henry mentioned a strange story yesterday."

"Hmmm . . . what was that?" Chambers only half listened, his imagination heading in an opposite direction.

"It appears there's been a rash of clothing mishaps at the school. Several of the young ladies have rips and tears in their gloves, just in the fingertips, mind you. According to Henry's wife, it's almost as if they've been bitten. What do you make of that, sir?"

Chambers's smile broadened. "Mrs. Brimley."

· Twelve ·

EMMA'S OUTSTRETCHED ARMS ACHED FROM holding the same position. Her ribs hurt, her legs trembled. The posing sessions had become physically demanding and downright boring. After so many hours of standing before Chambers in naught but her chemise and drawers, that particular experience no longer assaulted her sensibilities. True to his word, he hadn't tried to touch her, not even to steal a kiss, preferring to use his lips to speak incessantly about art. She considered revoking her no-touching edict, but feared it would make little difference. Outside, rain lashed against the windowpanes, thunder rumbled the sleepy countryside. Inside, all remained calm, hushed. Her shoulders slumped.

The movement attracted his notice. Chambers's eyes softened. He laid down his brush and palette. "Perhaps a period of rest is in order."

"Thank you," Emma gasped, stumbling the few steps to

the divan. "You failed to tell me that posing required so much effort."

"The flowers and rocks never complained when I painted them," he said with a sympathetic smile. "I suppose I hadn't realized how difficult it could be."

Emma massaged her aching calf muscles and glanced toward the tea service on a side table. "Do you suppose Thomas could bring more tea? I believe this has grown cold."

Chambers started for the corner bell pull but stopped midway and turned to face her. A hesitant smile teased his lips. "Before I do that, there is one thing more I'd like to teach you about painting."

She would have groaned, but etiquette forbade it. After so many weeks learning about various color combinations, canvas preparations, and composition concerns, she had hoped for a respite. She was even tempted to ask a question about that other subject of which he was so knowledgeable, but with only her chemise and drawers left, she hesitated.

"Before one can master a craft, such as painting, one needs to be familiar with the tools, in this case, the brushes." He approached his table of implements, most notably a jar full of upended brushes. "Different brushes produce different effects."

Emma tried to hide a yawn behind her hand.

"Various animals have sacrificed their hide to produce these tips." He drew his fingers across the bristles. "Just as each animal's fur has a unique appearance and texture, so do the resulting brushes. Let me show you . . ." He picked up several brushes and stepped toward her.

"Our agreement," she reminded him with a bit of trepidation. He hadn't stood this close for several weeks. A spark of excitement ignited in her rib cage.

"I haven't forgotten," he said with that same mysterious

smile, the one that sounded warning bells in her head. "Extend your arm and tell me how this feels." He jabbed at the underside of her arm with the bristles of one stubby brush.

"It stings." She pulled her arm away from his reach and watched an indignant red spot rise to the affected area.

"When used harshly, this brush can bite," he admitted, without apology. "It's made from ox, but if I stroke it slow and soft . . ." He motioned for her arm again. Hesitantly, she extended it. "It has a different effect."

The thick black bristles produced a tingling path up the underside of her arm, teasing dormant nerve endings and leaving a faint blush of pink in their wake. "That's not as unpleasant," she admitted.

Chambers slid to the side, then to the back of the divan, all the while dragging the bristles toward the sensitive skin exposed by the armhole of her chemise. A shiver danced down her spine. She attributed the reaction more to Chambers's near presence than the strange experiment he performed with his brush. "I fail to see—"

"A man can feel like this." His low voice seduced her senses like fragrant hot chocolate on a cold winter morning. "Imagine this is a man's whiskers. Perhaps, my mustache." The brush dragged slowly across the top of her back, lightly scratching the delicate skin, before dipping between her shoulder blades, tugging at the thin silk chemise. The blunt bristles stimulated more than irritated.

As suggested, in her mind, she allowed the bristles to transform into Chambers's mustache. She imagined his lips a mere breath away from her skin as he forged a path of sweet torture. The trembling in her legs shifted upward, bringing a renewed vitality to her lower regions. When the brush pulled at the back of her chemise, she imagined it was Chambers's fingers that lifted the lace from her skin. *Oh please, let it be his fingers.*

Instinctively, her shoulders lifted, as if pulled by a string. Gooseflesh tingled down her arms.

Suddenly the sensation changed. A smooth silky texture replaced the harsh bristles.

"What did you do?" she gasped.

"This is sable." His moist breath bathed the back of her neck. She couldn't see him, but by the sound of his voice, she judged his lips to be near the curve of her neck, else her nostrils wouldn't quiver at the faint scent of fine-milled soap and exotic spice. If she turned her head, ever so slightly, she might force his touch. She breathed deep, inviting his scent deep in her lungs.

"Feel how the brush glides and strokes the canvas."

"That is not a canvas, sir. That is my shoulder," she said, holding her breath while the mesmerizing brush drifted from one shoulder to the other.

"Your delicate skin is a canvas for my imagination." Chambers slipped around her side, returning to her front. His voice, combined with the delicate fine brush hairs explored all the curves and valleys of her shoulders and throat, igniting fissures beneath her skin.

She should move. She should stand up and walk to the changing screen. But she remained riveted to the divan, afraid any motion on her part would end the exquisite sensation.

"As smooth as silk and creamy white." He dipped the sable lower, skimming beneath the top of her low-cut chemise. Her breath caught. Dormant nerve endings exploded, stimulating riotous sensation. Her head tipped back, too heavy to remain supported by her hypersensitized neck. The back of the divan cushioned the fall.

"Do you like the way this feels, Mrs. Brimley?" His lips moved a breath away from the underside of her chin. She could barely breathe much less reply, but she suspected he already knew her answer.

"Imagine that the brush is moist," he whispered, "like a pair of lips."

In her mind's eye, she imagined his lips, his tongue, licking and playfully nipping at her throat, just as he had with his kiss so long ago. Why, oh why, did she make him promise not to touch her? But a proper lady couldn't very well ask to be kissed, could she?

The brush slipped beneath the lace of her chemise, jolting her nerves in ways she never could have imagined. The whisper-soft tease of the brush head swept her breasts, reaching almost to the tip of her tight, constricted buds. Her jaw slackened with an unspoken cry of pleasure.

"Imagine this brush is a man's hand."

Please let it be his hand! Let him swirl, and tease, and rub with his talented fingers, not an inanimate brush. The long, wooden brush handle tugged at her chemise as the velvety head stroked the fullness of her breasts. She gasped. This could not be decent, but she couldn't bring herself to stop his manipulations.

Her back arched, seeking more. Fabric pushed beneath her breast almost as if . . . She opened her eyes. The brush handle had pushed the cloth beneath one of her breasts, leaving it exposed to Chambers's entranced view. He licked his lips, a fraction of an inch from her straining nipple. He looked up through the veil of his long lashes.

"Are you moist for me, Emma? Do you feel an ache deep inside that longs for the satisfaction only a man can provide?"

Dear Lord above, her body reacted as if in tune with his orchestration. Her woman's core vibrated with urgency to an unheard note. Her hands clenched tight in her lap, longed to wrap around Chambers's back and pull him close enough to feel the chaos he had released in her virgin body. Was this how her mother felt? Was this love? She took a quick breath, watching the turgid tip of her exposed breast lift to delicately touch Chambers's lower lip.

"Release me from my pledge, Emma. Let me whisper sweet strains of poetry over your skin. Let me show you . . ."

"Yes." The word slipped through her lips yet her entire body strained in answer. "Touch me."

His lips encircled her nipple. She gasped in wild tumultuous pleasure. The brush fell to the floor as both his hands paid homage. He suckled and nipped at her breasts till she cried out in pleasure. Her hands tangled in his thick black hair, pulling him closer, not willing to let him go.

"Magnificent!" He repeated over and over again, kissing his way up to her lips. A fierce desire tugged at her, wanting him closer, needing him closer. Her hands slipped to his back, feeling the powerful knead of his muscles as he stroked and massaged her breasts. She pulled him closer, wanting him nearer. He obliged, pushing her back on the divan till he was lying atop her, between her sprawled legs. His bulge pressed against her exposed tender flesh.

Merciful heavens, this was one of the positions he had told her about. She should stop him. She should demand this go no further. She would be like her mother, ruined and shamed.

Her body hummed with a primitive need. She remembered Beatrice's words: *At least you've experienced what it is to be loved.* Never had Emma desired anything more in her life than this minute. She needed that experience, that love, with this man and no other.

His fingers slipped under the straps of her camisole, tugging it down her arms. His kisses followed the retreat of the material.

"You are so beautiful," he whispered. "Who knew such treasure lay beneath all those layers of dismal black."

"And pink," she added, remembering her discarded corset.

"And pink." He smiled, chasing her hesitations away in the process.

He slipped down her body until his knees hit the floor, shifting the burden of his weight in the process. She tried to pull her legs together in a more ladylike pose, but he braced his arms between them pushing them even further apart.

Her drawers offered no protection, the slit providing ample access to her inner core. His fingers slipped inside, entering her in a way she herself would never consider.

Her entire body instantly tensed. She bit her lip and tried to close her legs

"Relax, Emma. I won't hurt you," he said, his voice a comforting balm. "I just want you to experience one of the pleasures that can be achieved between a man and a woman."

Before she could reply, he lowered his mouth to the slit and probed her with his tongue. Lightning ripped from her groin to the tips of her breasts and back again.

She hadn't believed a man would really do such a thing. She swam in a sea of moisture of her own making. His fingers pulled at her nether lips, exposing more of her private areas to his assault. Her hands found the edges of the divan and held tight.

Need, pressure, and desire built one upon the other like the stones in the walls defining the pastures. Increased need, increased desire, increased pressure, until suddenly an explosion blasted them all away. Wave after wave of languid heat poured throughout her body, seducing, calming, titillating even to her fingertips.

Chambers pulled back, grinning at her over her drawers. "That is the kind of pleasure that can exist between a man and a woman."

"I . . . I had no idea," she gasped, struggling for control over her vocal chords. She slipped her hands over her midriff. "I fear something exploded deep inside."

"That is what I wished you to experience." His lips pressed against the thin linen covering her thigh. A tremor rippled through her, reminding her of the series of tremors she had just experienced.

"You are whole," he assured her. "Nothing has ruptured."

"Are you quite certain?" Whole? How could she ever be whole again? The experience had fractured her innocence beyond repair. She pushed herself up to her elbows so she could see his face, to see if he was appalled by her wantonness. "It felt so . . . powerful."

His eyes crinkled, his grin broadened. He appeared quite pleased with himself, and by extension, her.

"I assure you, everything is as it should be. You have no cause for alarm." He drew back, allowing her to close her legs.

Of course she had cause for alarm! Was this not the very thing that led to her mother's demise? Still, as the tingling faded from her extremities, she was grateful she had experienced this incredible sense of intimacy at least once in her life. She drew in a deep breath and glanced to Nicholas. If she was indeed destined to be ruined like her mother, at least Nicholas had been the one.

"Is that how it felt to you," she asked, curious if men and women were similar in this regard. "Like a captured burst of thunder?"

"Not this time." He smiled. "But I enjoyed bringing pleasure to you." He held out a hand to help her rise to a seated position.

Pity, she thought, feeling far superior and immensely pleased to be a woman. With Nicholas's assistance, she pulled herself upright, then glanced to her lap. "Why isn't there blood? I told the girls there would be blood their first time."

His eyes widened a moment before he sat beside her. "Emma, I didn't penetrate you in that way." He took her hand in his and stroked it softly. "You are still a virgin, although a very knowledgeable one."

The shame of her ignorance heated her cheeks. "You mean, this was not the coupling for which I'm preparing my girls?"

He shook his head. A rueful smile shaped his lips.

"And I am not ruined?" she asked, adjusting her glasses.

Compassion drained from his face. He averted her direct gaze and stood, suddenly searching for some unnamed object. "I . . . I wouldn't discuss this incident with anyone else, Emma. They might misconstrue what has transpired. Another man would not appreciate that you had been pleasured—"

"Another man?" She asked, feeling shame wash over her. He assumed she would allow another man the same liberties she shared with Nicholas? Earlier she had thought her innocence had shattered in a loud tumultuous explosion. She knew better now. Life-altering events cannot be measured by the noise they make. Her heart had just been crushed with barely a sound.

She rose and walked swiftly to the corner Japonaise screen in order to dress.

"Emma, don't be angry with me. I've done nothing to harm you," he pleaded beyond the screen.

She didn't reply. She couldn't. Her constricted throat made it impossible.

"I gave you pleasure. I took nothing away from you."

"Just my heart," she whispered, doubting that her voice carried beyond the screen. She could hear the tap of his walking stick accompanying what she assumed was his pacing. With practiced efficiency, she pulled her black bombazine skirt over her head so it could settle on flounced petticoats. However, her trembling fingers couldn't manage the tiny fastenings needed to secure the garment. She covered her face with her hands, choking back the sob that burned her throat.

What had she done? Chambers had suggested that he had changed nothing about her, that she was still innocent. Yet if that were true, why did her private regions still tingle and throb as if awakened after a long slumber? Why did her chest feel empty and hollow and devoid of the happiness and excitement that had inhabited it that very morning. Chambers said he had changed nothing about her, but in fact he had changed everything.

The tapping stopped. He was near. Her fingers shook as she fumbled with the necessary hooks on her skirt before slipping her arms through the bodice.

"The painting isn't finished, Emma. We're not finished."

She looked toward the ceiling, trying to draw a deep breath. Heavenly Father! How could Chambers expect her to continue after suggesting other men would enjoy the very liberties she had permitted him? *You're just like your mother,* her uncle's voice said. Emma retrieved her mother's handkerchief, holding it to her mouth to hide the sound of ragged breathing. Was this how her mother felt? Used by a man and then tossed aside for the next man to enjoy? A half-garbled cry rose from her throat.

"Emma? Emma, are you all right? Speak to me."

She could not, her throat too constricted for words. Instead she drew in breath as best she could and proceeded to button the front of the bodice. If in truth he had left no tangible evidence of the day's activities, perhaps she should be grateful as he suggested. Her heart may always belong to Nicholas, but from this day forth she would never allow herself to be alone in his company. His compassionate eyes might tempt her, his voice might lull her, but now that she knew his true nature, she was steeled against his seductive ways. She drew a calming breath and stepped out from the screen.

The sight of Nicholas leaning heavily on his stick twisted her heart as if it were broken anew. Her breath caught. Recognizing that she would never be completely able to resist him, she lowered her gaze and hurried for the door, ignoring his outstretched arm.

"Emma, wait. You don't understand. Emma!" He called after her.

She paused long enough to look back over her shoulder. She sniffed. "My name is Mrs. Brimley."

THE MOMENT THE DOOR CLOSED BEHIND HER, HE ground his stick into the floor. She left. He couldn't believe it. After the experience they had just shared, she still walked out the door.

The ungrateful wench! Hadn't she tempted him with skin so soft and delicate that the sable brush proved harsh in comparison? She teased him with breasts that begged to be initiated to a man's touch. Hadn't she implored him with her own words, *touch me*?

A groan slipped from his lips as he remembered the moment. His manhood had throbbed to bury itself deep in her lush body. She laid open to him, his for the taking. Yet he restrained himself. He sacrificed his own pleasure for her maidenhood. He gave her everything, everything!

He turned abruptly and stalked up to his painting of Artemis.

He raised his stick, planning to destroy the canvas, but the sight of Emma's sweet innocent smile slashed through his rage-induced haze. Her compassionate iridescent gaze, so reminiscent of the sea with all its mysteries, stilled his hand. Her eyes had held that same guileless expression when she asked, *Am I ruined?* His hasty response had turned those compassionate orbs to emerald hardness. What was his reply? He had been so caught in her web of inexperience, in furthering her education, that he hadn't been thinking . . .

Bloody hell! He was no better than that miserable maggot of an uncle. Did he really suggest that she would enjoy intimacy with another man? As if she were a bit of a light-skirt offering her charms for pleasure? What a bloody fool he'd been, a blithering idiot better suited for an asylum than the company of gently bred women.

"Emma, wait!" He hobbled after her, as fast as a man with a cane could run. But he was too late; she was gone into the downpour outside.

THE NEXT DAY, A PACKAGE ARRIVED AT PETTIBONE FROM Lord's in London. Inside, lay ten pairs of white silk gloves in various sizes, as well as a pair in black silk and another of black lace.

Cecilia ruffled through the box. "Who ordered these gloves?" She scowled. "Beatrice can mend the old ones."

Finding neither a card nor a bill, she sent an inquiry to Lord's only to learn by return post that an anonymous donor had extended the gift.

Frowning, she fanned the card in front of her face. "Curious," she commented to no one in particular. "Most curious, indeed."

•

· *Thirteen* ·

NICHOLAS WORKED FURIOUSLY ON HIS PAINTING. Easter came and went with little fanfare at Black Oak. The Chambers's carriage returned empty time and again from the scheduled pickup at Pettibone. According to Henry, a rash of coughs brought on by "forgetting winter stays out the welcome" kept Emma at the school. But Nicholas suspected his own improprieties kept Emma at bay. She was avoiding him.

The thought twisted in his gut. If he ran into her in the village today, as he had earlier, would she still speak to him? Or would she hurry by with a vinegar expression, offering not even a silent nod in acknowledgment? The unanswered question nagged at him in a way that only working on *Artemis's Revenge* could alleviate. In painting he found her acceptance and so devoted every waking moment to his art.

His sketches from earlier sessions allowed him to continue to work without a live model. He could easily paint Emma from memory, and frequently did. He couldn't pen a letter to a colleague without a study of Emma's seductive eyes or the long sweep of her neck drawn in the margin. As much as he longed to witness Emma transform into the goddess in the privacy of his studio, the deadline for entering the exhibition loomed near. Chambers bent all his energies to finishing *Artemis's Revenge*.

A dour wet spell proved particularly productive. By the time the weather broke, Nicholas determined he needed a break as well. With a thought that Emma might be of a similar mind, he sent a note inviting Emma on a painting expedition. Her acceptance brought with it relief, gratitude, and great anticipation.

"Henry has been dispatched to Pettibone to pick up Mrs. Brimley, sir," Thomas announced.

"Excellent, excellent." Nicholas smiled, surprised at how invigorating that simple news could be. He pranced about his studio like an expectant father. "Is everything ready?"

"I have a hamper packed with food, drink, a cloth for sitting, and a bit of libation, should the need arise," Thomas answered in dry humor.

"Very good." Nicholas smiled again, imagining the cloth appropriate for other means of repose beyond mere sitting.

He busied himself gathering painting supplies, his large primed canvas, and a smaller one for Emma. He had just draped *Artemis's Revenge* when Thomas advised that the carriage had returned. After tucking an easel under one arm and grasping a canvas with the other, Nicholas hurried to the front door, anxious to greet Emma after a long absence.

Although Henry was to collect Emma from Pettibone in the carriage, just as he had for modeling sessions, Nicholas had planned to use a more intimate conveyance to transport just the two of them to a favored painting spot.

Instead, Henry stood by the open carriage door. A quick glance at the colorful array inside the carriage meant either Emma had declared the end to her period of mourning in no uncertain terms, or she was not alone. As much as he would have preferred the former, he suspected the latter.

"Mrs. Brimley, I see I have visitors," he said, irritated. Not only did guests mean Emma would remain buried in that ridiculous, ill-fashioned black garment, but the woman dared to test his carefully constructed reputation for avoiding society. Under the circumstances, he should be the one dressed in mourning.

"Not visitors exactly, fellow artists," Emma announced with great enthusiasm. "I've brought some of the girls along so they might benefit from your talent. You remember Miss Alice Darlington and Miss Charlotte Hawkins."

He bowed slightly as each was reintroduced. "Of course, I remember." *Well played, Emma.* One had to admire her ingenuity. With the girls in attendance, he would have to forgo his other planned pleasurable pursuits.

"I hope you forgive my liberty in extending your invitation to these talented ladies." Her smile conveyed her purposefulness. *Well done, indeed.*

Nicholas handed the easel and canvas over to Henry for proper stowing. "Allow me to collect a few more supplies for my unexpected guests, and I shall immediately return."

Nicholas returned to his studio for some drawing pads and charcoal. She may have won this round, but an afternoon with Emma would be far superior to an afternoon without.

"YOU'RE VERY GOOD, YOU KNOW," EMMA SAID, SITTING on the hillside, collecting daisies. "Your paintings capture more than the shapes and the colors. They capture the feeling of the countryside."

He quirked a brow her way, pleased at her compliment. "I thought you said you weren't a critic."

"I'm not, but I have eyes, do I not?"

"You have beautiful green eyes that can cause a man to lose his soul." He kept his voice low so as not to carry to the young girls further down the hill.

Emma lowered her gaze as if disbelieving of his words. Damnation, what did it take for the woman to realize she was a prize and not some plain-Jane cousin?

"Why aren't you painting?" he asked. "Is it because my brush inspires you in a different way?"

Although hidden beneath an oversized sun hat, her blush betrayed her memory. And the memory was a good one if the tiny quirk of her sweet lips was any indication. Good. Any misgivings she might harbor after their last lesson had not overshadowed her enjoyment of the event. He selected the sable brush and extended it to her. "Perhaps this time, you'd like to employ a variety of brushes on my canvas?"

"Sir!" Her eyes widened, confirming she understood his innuendo. His smile broadened. *Smart girl.*

"The girls are not far beyond hearing," she hissed, casting a quick glance down the hill. "You must be discreet!"

He chuckled, enjoying her mock outrage. "Ah, Mrs. Brimley, I so miss our earlier discourse. Ask me a question. You still have so much to learn."

She plucked a daisy from the field and threw it at him. The flower head bounced off his shoulder.

"Discretion has never been one of my virtues," he teased. "You should have considered that before you invited your young charges to join us."

"You do yourself an injustice. You have been discreet." She gazed up at him through lowered lashes, making him feel like a cad for his suggestive teasing. "Not a word has returned to me that would suggest anyone knew the true purpose for my visits. For that discretion, I shall be eternally grateful."

"Emma, I hardly think—"

"Ssh, no more need be spoken. You have guarded my secrets and assisted in my . . . tutelage. I wanted to express my gratitude now that my education is at an end."

"An end! My dear Emma, you have only just begun!" What nonsense was this? He attempted a laugh, but as her lips offered not a hint of humor, the sentiment died in his throat. "If you are upset about my behavior at our last meeting, I assure you I am most contrite."

Alice waved at them from far down the hill. She held up a paper that was too distant to see. Emma and Nicholas returned her wave, to all apparent a couple engaged in acceptable social conversation.

"I apologize for my ungentlemanly behavior, but I think—"

"Miss Darlington has a talent for artistic pursuits. Don't you agree?" Emma interrupted, shifting her position. "She has sketched many pleasing views of the school and has even attempted a few portraits of the girls."

Perplexed, he turned toward Emma, studying her profile. "I am a wretched scoundrel for saying those things. Don't you agree?"

She refused to take the bait and, instead, squeezed her eyes closed, shutting him out. A horror clawed at his chest.

"Madam, is this your way of telling me you won't entertain the prospect of returning to my studio?" Shocked, he felt a tingling in his forehead. He knew his callous comment had hurt her, but he thought he could charm his way back into her good graces.

She bit her lip and nodded with a barely visible inclination of the head. She continued to observe the girls down the hill, not even giving him the benefit of her full countenance.

"What will you do when the spinsters wish to see the projects you've been working on all these months?" he asked, casting at straws to have her reconsider her decision.

She frowned. "We've discussed so much about art and painting, I believe I could teach much of the subject without censure."

He smiled. "You, of all people, should realize that discussing a subject is far different than experiencing it for oneself."

Pink infused her cheek, reminding him of that other pink beneath that hideous attire. Desire stirred at the memory. He shifted uncomfortably. Damnation, as much as he was agitated by her refusal to return to his studio, she still had the power to arouse him.

He focused his attention on his painting, hoping the diversion would calm the ache between his legs. Beneath his brush a dab of ochre yellow turned into a sun hat.

Emma abandoned her spot in front of him, taking a stance behind his left shoulder. Her sun-warmed skin released a fragrance of faint rosewater and feminine essence unique to Emma. Remembering his own uniqueness in recognizing that scent, he swallowed hard.

"That's Alice," she said, as the dab took shape. "You painted Alice into the picture. Why, she isn't even in your line of sight, yet her presence appears so natural in that spot."

Her exuberant praise and close proximity did nothing to alleviate his condition; if anything, his discomfort worsened. She stood behind him yet he could well imagine her green eyes brimming with admiration and mischief. Her moist succulent lips would part with her smile, displaying even, white teeth, perfect for grasping the fingertips of a glove, or for nibbling sensitive body parts. He glanced over to Alice and Charlotte happily chatting down the hill. If it weren't for those two, he'd have Emma flat on her back learning a few more valuable lessons. He gnawed his lip, stifling an internal groan.

"Were you in love with her?" Emma asked.

Confusion momentarily blinded him, stilling his hand. Had he missed some thread of conversation while allowing his fantasies to run riot? He straightened, pulling back from the canvas. "Could you hand me two of those rags, please?"

Emma handed him two clean cloths. One he used to clean his brush; the other he let fall to his lap, hoping it hid the evidence of his wayward thoughts. He glanced over his shoulder. "To whom do you refer?"

"Alice's mother. Were you in love with her?"

His brows lifted in surprise. Then, he remembered their discussion the night of Charlotte's disappearance. He relaxed, remembering he had mentioned his acquaintance with Alice's mother. Why she should wish to discuss history, he had no idea. However, she was talking to him, and for that he was grateful.

"Love takes many forms." He turned back to his painting. "I was very young at the time. Yes, I suppose I loved her."

"Are you the child's father?"

"Child?" What the devil was she talking about? Annoyance swiveled him around to face Emma. "What child?"

"Alice, of course," she said, her face deathly serious, framed in the lace from her widow's sunbonnet. "She has your talent, and her hair is as black as yours."

His hands stilled. Anger gathered like thunderclouds in his consciousness, squeezing out the previous confusion and desire. He waited a moment, gaining control over his words.

"Think carefully about what you suggest, madam." He jabbed his brush at the cloth, no longer caring that the action could ruin the future effectiveness of the instrument. "Do you think I have so little honor as to father a child and then abandon it on its mother's deathbed? Do you suppose me to be the worse kind of cad?" Nevermind that half of the district blamed him for the existence of bastards in the area. He had expected more of Emma. "How old is Alice?"

"Fifteen."

A vein beneath the delicate skin on her neck pulsed with her heightened heartbeat. His reaction frightened her. He grimaced. Good.

"Fifteen," he repeated. "So at the ripe old age of thirteen, you assumed I was off impregnating the countryside."

"Your voice, sir," she cautioned, obviously embarrassed. Apparently, mathematics had not been her strong suit. No poetry in that. "The girls will hear." Indeed, two interested heads turned their way.

"I don't give a bloody fig who hears," he roared. "You've credited me with far more experience than I have and far less honor than I deserve." He threw down his rag and tossed his brush in an open box of supplies. The action helped assuage his anger, leaving only disappointment. "I thought you were different," he said, rising from his stool.

A rag fluttered to the ground. He stared at it a moment. No need to worry about appearances now. Emma's accusations had performed admirably in that regard. Disgusted, he turned his back on her and removed himself from her presence.

She stood stunned, much as if someone had knocked her in the head with a croquet mallet. Surprised that he had taken umbrage with the very image he seemed to cultivate, she visually followed his withdrawal with a devastating sense of loss.

He was right, of course. Even though the stories and

rumors of Chambers's exploits had been almost legend, she shouldn't have let the opinions of others sway her from what she knew was true. He had kept her secrets and edicts, even in difficult times. He had been her confidante, friend, and a gentleman when she was fully dressed. It was those other times that had influenced her thoughts.

She followed his path and found him sitting on a boulder, his black hair mussed by an April breeze. Shadows of clouds raced on the emerald countryside below them, a velvet field sliced by a fast-flowing stream.

"I'm sorry, sir," she said. "I had no right to suggest the things I did."

He looked at her, narrowing his eyes. "My name is Nicholas, Emma. Not lord or sir, just Nicholas." He turned back to the tranquil scene in front of him.

She lowered her head. Everything she said seemed to turn out wrong. She wanted him to know she regretted her ill-chosen words, but didn't know how to begin.

"Katherine, Alice's mother," he said, apparently accepting her silence as encouragement, "was the one who taught me how to draw, how to see things as they actually are, and not how we imagine them to be." He smiled, a far distant look in his eye. "She was two years older than I and I idolized her."

Emma noticed his eyes spark at the memory and felt a brief stab of jealousy. Ridiculous, she scolded herself. As his model, she hadn't the right.

"She took little notice of me, though, other than that as a rapt pupil. No, Emma"—his lips twisted in a grim smile—"I am not the father."

But he wished to be, she heard it in his voice. He was carrying a torch for a one-sided love. The condition felt vaguely familiar.

"Alice's father was a friend of my older brother, William. He was handsome and witty." The smile faded.

"Some would say charming. All the young girls admired him, including Katherine."

He pulled a knee up and wrapped his arm around it. She wanted to comfort him, put her hand on his arm to remind him she was close, but refrained. She could be seen. It wouldn't be proper.

"Katherine was not much older than fifteen when she discovered she was carrying his child. The charming boy left her to join the King's army, while she faced the disgrace of carrying his bastard alone. She died of loneliness with only a young lad to hold her hand."

"You were there," Emma whispered, hearing the catch in his voice.

He nodded. "I was."

"And the father, where is he now?"

"I had heard Cogswell was in Africa, fighting the Zulus. I don't know if he's alive or dead." He scowled. "But I hope for the latter."

After a few moments of silence, he sighed, then slapped the rock. "So warn your young ladies not to waste their gloves on men who won't give them a proper wedding night."

"You sent the gloves." Relief accompanied the light turn of conversation. "I had suspected as much."

His lips turned in a sad smile. "I felt responsible for the rash of clothing mishaps. I hadn't expected you to be such an adept instructor."

She lowered her gaze, feeling heat sweep across her cheeks. "I don't wish the girls to follow in my footsteps." The truth of that statement stabbed at her heart. "If your instructions will help them avoid spinsterhood, then the sacrifice of a few gloves is of small consequence."

And what sacrifice could she make to avoid the path that lay before her? She was doomed to spend her days at Pettibone, teaching others how to reach out and grab at life, while she watched from her place beside Beatrice and Cecilia.

The mental image of a line of dowagers reminded her of another mission. "I almost forgot!"

She poked in her reticule until she found the crisp white envelope.

"What's this?" Chambers asked, accepting the extended offering. He opened it, scanning the contents. "A ball at Pettibone? Is there no end to the commotion you bring, Mrs. Brimley?"

She smiled. If he was back to calling her by her alias, then the storm had indeed passed. "What do you mean, commotion? You'll attend, of course."

"I certainly will not." He scowled. "I will not preen and strut for the benefit of the spinster sisters and their stable of breeding stock." He glanced over at her. "You will be there, I suppose, in your insufferable black."

She nodded. "It's part of the role I must play."

"I treasure my solitude, Mrs. Brimley. It's the reason I came to Yorkshire instead of following some predetermined road in London. Pettibone has left me comfortably alone. Since your arrival, I have had unconscious women in my parlor, uninvited children in my stable, and now unwanted invitations to parties. What is next, Mrs. Brimley? Visits from the old biddies themselves?"

She frowned, knowing how Beatrice had originally hoped to deliver the invitation herself. "You won't come?"

"No," he repeated. "I won't come."

"Then I suppose your brother will stand in your stead," she replied lightly, then turned to retreat to the easel. The girls would be concerned by their absence.

"You know of the Marquess?" A soft thud reassured her that he was following behind. A sense of power flashed through her.

"Miss Higgins speaks very highly of him. She sent him

an invitation over a week ago." Emma pushed some stray tendrils up under her hat before chancing a look his way. "Of course, there is no guarantee that he'll travel all the way from London."

Chambers hesitated, his eyes slightly narrowed, one brow arched.

So the invitation to the Marquess of Enon troubled him, she noted with an inward smile. Fine. Let him stew in his family difficulties, just as he had dismissed hers.

Emma glanced at the clouds building in the sky. "I think it's time we return. I had promised the sisters we'd return before tea."

ONCE EMMA'S BACK HAD TURNED, NICHOLAS BEHEADED an innocent daisy with the tip of his stick. Bloody hell! Guests at Black Oak would limit his opportunities with Emma. His servants would honor his edict not to speak about Emma's visits, but he couldn't trust his brother or any of his traveling companions to do the same.

He glanced at the sway of Emma's bustle as she collected her young charges, imagining for the moment the curve of her derriere without the artificial enhancement. A smile tugged at his lips.

"You can't hide behind their skirts forever, Emma." He kept his voice low so only the breeze that pushed at his face could hear. "Guests or no guests, I'll have you and your enticing pink corset back in my studio to complete your education or my name isn't Lord Nicholas Bedchambers."

· Fourteen ·

WITH ALL THE PREPARATIONS FOR THE BALL, NEITHER Cecilia nor Beatrice managed to participate in Emma's classes, much to her delight. The class had moved upstairs to the Higgins sisters' large bedroom, while preparations continued underfoot on the first floor. In the sanctity of the sparsely furnished room, the girls discussed kissing techniques at great length. Mentally reflecting on her first kiss with Nicholas, Emma warned that the timing of a kiss might not be of their choosing, then she suggested the possibility of an unfamiliar type of kiss.

"Ladies, I'd like you to stick out your tongues as far as they can go. Now move them to the right. Move them to the left. Up to the top and down."

All the girls stood in a line with their tongues rotating in a well-ordered drill.

"Why do we have to do this, Mrs. Brimley?" Alice asked.

"Because sometimes when kissing, men like to do battle with their tongues. You should be prepared to accept your husband's tongue if he chooses to explore with it."

Accept it, pray for it, demand it, she thought, remembering that internal explosion the last time Nicholas chose to explore her with his tongue. A quiver rimmed her feminine core and rippled up through her chest.

"Mrs. Brimley, are you all right?" Charlotte's eyes opened to wide circles. "Your face turned pink all over."

"I shall be fine." Retrieving her mother's handkerchief from her sleeve, she dabbed at her forehead. "I'm just excited about the ball."

The girls readily accepted the mistruth, and after a brief giggling fit, returned to the tongue exercises with renewed vigor. Emma smiled with affection. Silly girls, they had so much to learn.

"But if a man wishes to explore with his tongue," said Elizabeth, pausing long enough to scowl, "why are *we* doing this?"

"Because some men find it stimulating if you explore their mouths with your tongue as well." Three of the girls groaned, the other two laughed. Emma clapped her hands for order. "Therefore, we are doing tongue dexterity exercises."

"This does not seem ladylike," Elizabeth said, although it sounded more like "adie-ike" with her tongue extended.

"It's not meant to be ladylike, Elizabeth. Once you are properly married, many of society's rules are forgotten for purposes of more earthy concerns."

"Urte kaherns?" Charlotte asked.

"Procreation," Emma answered. "Production of heirs. That is, after all, why we are having this class." Her stern look silenced the anticipated snickers but did nothing to curb her own regret. She would most likely never sample the earthy concerns found in a marriage bed.

"Now I want you to roll your tongues in a tighter circle like this." She demonstrated. "And to help you, I've brought you these candy sticks." She produced the assortment of striped sugar confections that she had purchased in town. She placed one in each outstretched hand. "Pretend the candy is the man's tongue and swirl your tongue around it, just so."

"What does a man taste like?" Elizabeth asked, a faraway look in her eye. "Does he taste as sweet as this candy?"

"If he does," plump Hannah added, "I'm going to collect all the kisses I can." The girls laughed and Emma smiled indulgently.

"No, a man doesn't taste sweet." Emma glanced out the window at the wide green lawn bordered by woods. Black Oak lay just beyond, out of sight of the school. Not far in distance, it would be forever closed to her, now that she had decided not to return to Chambers's studio. Longing rose from her heart and congealed in her throat causing her voice to drop. "He tastes a bit like . . . warmed brandy. Powerful . . . potent, yet soft and gentle, all at the same time."

She closed her eyes and pressed a handkerchief to her nose, inhaling the faint scent of oils and turpentine.

The girls giggled. The sound jolted Emma back to reality, and in the process, knocked her glasses askew. She readjusted them just as Cecilia knocked on the doorframe.

"I'm sorry to intrude, Mrs. Brimley, but you have a visitor."

Emma hesitated. "A visitor?" Only Chambers knew of her presence at Pettibone, and he certainly wouldn't call for a visit.

"Yes, an old friend who is most anxious to see you once again." Cecilia bestowed one of her rare smiles, increasing Emma's already heightened anxiety.

"Girls, continue practicing your exercises," Emma said,

tucking the handkerchief back in her sleeve. "I'll return shortly."

She tried to keep concern off her face, but her heart quickened its pace. Had she become too comfortable here at Pettibone? Had she let down her guard and unconsciously let her past intrude? She no longer kept a packed valise handy in case she had to flee on a moment's notice. Of course, even if she exercised that plan, she had no where to go.

The two women descended the main staircase. Whereas Cecilia tended to be the more somber of the two, the lightness to her step left Emma mystified. She hurried Emma along as if she were a prized ewe brought to market. Cecilia led Emma to the very salon where she herself was first entertained. Beatrice obscured her view of the visitor, but judging by the rich trimmings on her fashionable overskirt, the mysterious woman was not only wealthy, she was also not local. At least the visitor was female and therefore not her uncle. She issued a soft sigh of relief.

"Here she is, Lady Cavendish, our own Mrs. Brimley," Cecilia announced.

Emma stopped, a smile of greeting frozen on her lips. *Lady Cavendish!*

Beatrice stepped aside, allowing full access to the very woman whose signature Emma had forged on a glowing letter of reference. What should be a reunion of acquaintances was truly a meeting of strangers. Emma's tongue felt too thick to offer a greeting. Her heartbeat pounded in her ears. She waited stiff as a board for an accusatory finger to denounce her as a fraud.

Lady Cavendish was an older woman, perhaps five or six years beyond her mother's own age. Her keen eyes leveled on Emma, and her lips curved in a knowing tilt.

Lady Cavendish dipped her head, reminding Emma to do the same. Indeed, Emma scolded herself; as the younger party, she should have been the one to initiate the greeting, if shock and dread hadn't robbed her senseless.

"Mrs. Brimley," Lady Cavendish said, "it is so good to see you again. I was most pleased to hear of your position here at Pettibone."

Emma just smiled. What else could she do? Though she longed to ask how Lady Cavendish managed to find her, her tongue apparently had forgotten how to work. A vile sickening swirled in her stomach.

Beatrice, however, after imploring all to sit and be comfortable, supplied the explanation that Emma lacked. She twisted toward Emma.

"My sister and I were so pleased with your abilities that we wrote to Lady Cavendish to thank her for her letter of reference." Beatrice twisted back to Lady Cavendish. "We had not entertained the hopes of finding someone of Mrs. Brimley's refinement. Once we saw your letter we knew at once that Mrs. Brimley would be perfect for Pettibone, and we certainly were not wrong." Her voice bubbled with enthusiasm. "I don't know how we managed before without her."

"A school of this nature needs an experienced woman," Cecilia continued, "to offer guidance of a more worldly nature."

"Indeed." Emma felt Lady Cavendish's intonation go right through her. "I'm pleased that my *dear* friend has filled the role so admirably. But I wonder if Mrs. Brimley and I may speak in private? We have much to discuss."

"I wish I had known you were coming," Emma offered tightly, maintaining the appearance that she knew this lady. "I could have rearranged my teaching schedule. As it is I have so little time . . ."

"The indiscretion was mine, I'm afraid." Lady Cavendish continued the hoax, pretending that they were not absolute strangers. "I didn't realize that I would be traveling this way till quite late. I could not send advance notice."

"But you will stay for the Pettibone Ball?" Beatrice asked, lace bobbing with her emphatic nod. "I'm sure it will not be as grand as those to which you are accustomed, but the girls will want to make your acquaintance. You will be our honored guest."

"But I . . ."

"Please, Lady Cavendish," Cecilia intoned. "We are hoping to introduce our ladies and demonstrate the skills they have learned at Pettibone. Your presence at this event will guarantee its success. Our reputation shall be greatly enhanced to have a guest of your social caliber."

"I suppose I could ask my host if I could extend my visit," Lady Cavendish demurred with a slight smile in Emma's direction. A cold chill of premonition settled over her. What game was in play here?

"Where are you staying?" Emma asked a bit urgently.

"At Black Oak," Lady Cavendish replied. "The Marquess of Enon was traveling in this direction, and I thought I might share his carriage so that I might visit with my old friend."

"You have an old friend at Black Oak?" Beatrice asked gaily. Emma tensed. Chambers had not mentioned friends in society's circles. Was there another deceit afoot?

"My old friend is you, Mrs. Brimley, not anyone at Black Oak." Lady Cavendish's smile did not reach her eyes. "Miss Higgins's letter stirred my curiosity about *my old friend.*" Her emphasis carved an awkward pause.

Cecilia looked to Emma, then to Lady Cavendish, and back to Emma. "I suppose we should leave you two alone to discuss private matters." Her tone suggested she and Emma would later confer privately. "The tea is still hot. Let us know if we can make your visit more enjoyable."

Emma freshened Lady Cavendish's cup and poured one

for herself while listening for retreating footsteps down the hall. Once satisfied that they were quite alone, Emma left her cup cooling on the saucer and turned to Lady Cavendish. "Why are you here?"

"I was curious," she said, a calculating gleam in her eye. "I don't seem to recall writing a letter of reference for a young widow. You can imagine my surprise when I received a highly complimentary letter on my excellent referral. Why, quite naturally I wished to meet this enterprising young widow who has capitalized on my reputation." Lady Cavendish smiled ever so slightly, then gazed at Emma over her cup.

"I didn't mean any harm," Emma whispered. "Teaching here at the Pettibone School for Young Ladies provided a much needed opportunity to escape London. I knew they would require validation for the position." She pulled her mother's handkerchief from her cuff, crushing it in her hand. Lady Cavendish's gaze followed the gesture.

"Why me?" she asked.

"I'd heard my mother mention your name," Emma said. "And, of course, you are well known in society, thus your name carries a certain prestige. I never imagined that you'd travel this far north. Even if you did, I supposed that the Pettibone School for Young Ladies would escape your notice."

Though Emma had hoped otherwise, her compliment made little impression. Lady Cavendish tilted her head and narrowed her focus. "Your mother spoke of me? Do I know her?"

"My mother died shortly before Christmas." Regret at lost opportunities settled in Emma's stomach. Her gaze dropped to the crumpled linen in her palm.

"I'm sorry," Lady Cavendish replied before squinting her eyes toward the window. "Brimley . . . Brimley . . .

that name has a ring of familiarity, in an obscure way." She glanced back at Emma. "Did I know your husband?"

"I'm not a widow, Lady Cavendish." Emma correctly anticipated Lady Cavendish's look of surprise. "The school specified that the proper applicant be a widow, and so I invented a husband."

The admission brought a smile to Lady Cavendish's lips. She leaned forward. "I believe those invented husbands are often the best kind."

They shared a laugh that violently shook the ribbons and silk flowers attached to Lady Cavendish's hat and eased Emma's fear of condemnation. She breathed a bit easier.

Lady Cavendish's smile narrowed. She studied Emma's face while appearing to reach some internal conclusion. "While I do not condone the appropriation of another's reputation to serve one's own purpose, I am inclined to believe that the gratitude of Miss Higgins and her sister shows you have served my reputation well. However," she added, her face taking on a stern bent, "if I am to be a participant in the charade you have constructed, I must know if you have invented more than just a husband."

Emma hesitated, reluctant to place her fate in this woman's hands.

"You mentioned that you needed to escape London," Lady Cavendish prodded. "Are you a criminal, Mrs. Brimley?"

"No, not at all," Emma gasped, never expecting one could conceive of such a question. "I needed to escape my uncle who had dubious plans for my future."

"Your uncle's name would be?"

Emma chewed on her lower lip. Once her uncle's name was revealed, it would be a simple matter to trace back to . . .

"Speak up girl, or I shall call back those two droll sisters and explain that you are a liar and a charlatan," Lady Cavendish snapped. She tapped the tip of her parasol on the floor, reminding Emma of another who used a walking stick to punctuate his thoughts. He held her secrets as well.

"My name is Emma Heatherston," she said, summoning her courage. "My uncle is Mr. George Heatherston."

"And the name Brimley? Quick girl. Where did you find that particular name?"

"I had heard both my uncle and mother mention it. I thought perhaps it might be . . ." She dropped her head, her voice little more than a whisper. "My father's name."

"Silly girl, your story twists and turns like Parliament's temper." Lady Cavendish shook her head. "A child does not 'borrow' a father's name unless—" Her eyes widened in sudden comprehension. "A by-blow?"

Emma's throat tightened; she nodded.

Lady Cavendish pursed her lips in a thoughtful manner.

"What is the nature of this dubious plan your uncle has designed?"

"He seeks to barter me for money. I left London before I became part of his nefarious scheme."

"Barter you? Whatever nonsense is this?"

"It is not nonsense, I assure you. I know what I overheard. It is best that I remain hidden from him."

"For how long, child?"

"Until he loses interest in finding me. Until I no longer have value."

"This is a sordid story, Miss Heatherston." She pushed on the handle of her parasol in consternation. "I shall daresay attempt to get to the bottom of it when I return to London." She dropped her voice to conspiratorial tones. "I'm considered a bit of an amateur sleuth, you know."

"No!" Emma cautioned. "You mustn't do that. My uncle will only become suspicious and renew his efforts to find me. Please don't stir the waters! And may I prevail on you, Lady Cavendish, to refer to me as Mrs. Brimley? If the sisters expect otherwise, I shall be cast adrift."

Lady Cavendish seemed surprised. "Those two? Why, did I not just hear them say they could not function efficiently without you?"

"The sisters would feel betrayed if they learn I have been less than honest with my identity. They would feel honor bound to insist on my departure." She dropped her head. "And I have no where else to go."

The wrinkles around Lady Cavendish's eyes softened. "I would open my home to you, my dear, but that might prove difficult given Lord Cavendish's delight in attractive young women."

Emma blushed. No one had ever referred to her in those terms. No one but Chambers, she amended.

Lady Cavendish stood, causing Emma to rise as well.

"I am not unfamiliar with the scandalous way in which society treats women such as your mother." Lady Cavendish met Emma's gaze. "And yourself."

The affection in her voice melted Emma's apprehensions. Little had she expected that her deception would earn her an ally.

"I will keep your secret as long as your actions warrant such secrecy. Do not dishonor my recommendation, Mrs. Brimley, and I will do no harm to yours."

NICHOLAS SAT ALONE IN HIS STUDIO, ADDING THE FINAL touches to Artemis's veil. The necessary garment swirled behind the goddess as if caught in the breeze, allowing one end to conceal the feminine virtues considered too risqué for the times. Nicholas smiled. Although he disagreed with the popular trend of hiding such detail, he admitted he preferred to keep this aspect of Emma his private domain.

Emma's natural beauty radiated through the layers of

oil and varnish. His brushes had captured Emma's innocence and sensuality in a way he had not envisioned. Few
people viewing the painting would even notice the figure
Actaeon hiding in the bushes. Without question, this repre-
sented his best work, his masterpiece.

Of course, Emma had often repeated requests to see the
work while in progress; each time he had been careful to
keep it draped from her view. He remembered her distress
when she first viewed her half-naked body in the mirror. A
smile teased his lips; of course, part of her distress was dis-
covering that he had watched her artless removal of garments. He suspected she would disapprove of the
full-frontal nude.

After their long afternoons of "instruction," if she
viewed the painting with even the smallest reproach or regret, it would cut him to the quick. Her beautiful sea green
eyes, most assuredly, would never again gaze at him with
trust and compassion. She'd shun him just like the prissy
Pettibone headmistress. Her heart would harden against
him. He gnawed on his lip. Why hadn't he considered this
before?

Because it was easier not to, an internal voice answered.
He never expected to care so much for the scrawny black
scarecrow that conveniently appeared on his doorstep. Ah,
but she had plumped up nicely. He smiled, appreciating his
reproduction of her luscious, inviting curves.

Abandoning this painting, or allowing her to view it,
would mean an end to her visits. Deserting fashionable
London society for the wilds of Yorkshire had dubbed him
"strong willed," but even he wasn't strong enough to for-
swear Emma's visits. So he kept the painting covered and
in so doing, denied himself the opportunity to see appreciation of his mastery in her eyes. That penance was almost
as bad as the other alternative.

An idea swirled in his mind of a new portrait with

Emma again as the model. Even though she had indicated an unwillingness to return to his studio, he knew that wouldn't last. He'd find a way to bring her back. His art and sanity demanded it.

Footsteps pounded down the hallway behind the closed door of his studio. Too heavy for Emma, he thought with disappointment. He quickly pulled a cloth over the painting.

The studio door swung open without the courtesy of a knock. William, bright and shiny as his new spit-polished boots, strode into the room.

"I don't know what is more shocking, old man: to find you here alone or to find you sober."

"Hello, William." Nicholas swiveled on his stool to face his brother. Other than a new crease or two about William's eyes and a general softness that attested to London living, the two brothers shared more similarities than differences. Nicholas sighed. His father dominated all things in life; it should be no surprise that he dominated the gene pool as well. "What foul wind blew you this far north?"

"A pretty young miss whose mother schemes to snare a title for the family tree." William stepped forward to greet his brother, leaving a flustered Thomas in the doorway. Nicholas signaled all was well with a nod of his head. Thomas silently closed the door. "The going rate for a marquess is substantially more than her family coffers, so I thought it best to leave London before the mother concocts an entanglement from which I cannot escape. I'll wager she'll turn her sights on another before two weeks have passed."

"So you intend to be my guest for the next two weeks?" Nicholas didn't bother to hide his irritation. His brother's visit would mean two more weeks without Emma.

"If you don't mind . . ." William's critical eye glanced around the studio, alighting briefly on each exposed painting.

Of course he minded! But for the life of him, Nicholas wasn't sure how to explain the situation to his brother without calling undue attention to a certain masquerading widow wary of discovery. He couldn't send him away without explanation and could not keep him without discomfort. Sighing, he chose the latter. "What are brothers for?"

"I envy you, you know," William said, inspecting a pile of painted canvases stacked against the wall. "Living out here where no decent civilized man, or woman, would think to intercede. No scheming mothers or . . ."

"Meddling fathers?" Nicholas asked with sudden intuition. "Did he send you? Is that the real reason for this visit?"

"No. I told you the reason." William's expression mimicked injury. "But he does send his warm wishes and inquires as to when you will return to London."

Nicholas picked up his paintbrush and swirled it in a murky jar. "I have no desire to return dragging my tail between my legs like a hound off the scent."

"It would not be like that, Nicholas. He misses you. He's just too stubborn to admit it."

Nicholas made no response, letting the awkward silence suggest his discomfort with the topic. William's gaze settled on the draped painting. "What are you working on? Is this for the Academy exhibition?"

Nicholas put a restraining hand on William's arm. "It's still wet. I wouldn't want the cloth to smudge it."

"You know, you should consider venturing away from those quaint little landscapes of yours." William backed away from the easel. "Oh, they're pretty enough, but there's no meat to them, no purpose."

"Are you an art critic now as well, William?" Nicholas raised a brow. "And you wonder why I prefer a residence far away from family comments?"

William scowled, then picked up a sketchbook from Nicholas's desk. "I was only trying to be helpful, brother." He flipped through the pages. "You know I believe in your talent. You just need challenge."

He paused on one page; his lips pulled to a wide grin. "Now here's something with purpose. Some local miss, I'll venture. There's something to be said for a woman without finery, feathers, and baubles. Something elemental and pristine."

Nicholas rose and calmly removed the drawing of Emma's face from his brother's fingers. "Would you care for a brandy after your long trip?" He slipped the drawing in a drawer.

William pursed his lips briefly as if to protest, then thought better of it. "A brandy would be just the thing. Naturally, you will join me?" Nicholas nodded and set about to pour two drinks from a cut-crystal decanter.

A gray and white cat ambled out of its hiding spot beneath the desk, stretching his long legs and splaying his claws. William's eyes lit with discovery. "What ho! Is this a new addition?"

William scooped the cat up and tucked him into the crook of his arm, scratching the appreciative cat between the ears.

Nicholas let a smile tip his lips. The discovery of his cat appeared to end William's inquiries about the picture in his drawer. Clever cat. He'd instruct Henry to round up a special treat for a reward. Nicholas approached William with a glass of amber liquid.

"I should warn you that I've brought a houseguest with me," William said, cat in one hand, drink in the other. "Lady Cavendish, a harmless matron from the fashionable set. She's off visiting a relative or acquaintance at Pettibone while her third husband cavorts in London."

"Hardly your usual company, William." Nicholas sipped at his drink.

"I know, but her social position is such that I could not readily refuse. I shall make my calls on the spinster sisters a bit later today."

Nicholas grimaced. "Why do you pander to those two old ladies?"

"Because they love me, brother." William smiled. "Almost as much as they despise you."

"My reputation has earned me the isolation I need to paint." Nicholas scowled. "The last thing I want is for those two withered cows to march their stock by my door every few minutes."

"Judging from that drawing"—William nodded toward the desk—"someone has marched through your door. Who is she?" He leered over the edge of his glass. "Perhaps the country miss would prefer the company of a well-mannered gentleman over that of an insolent rogue."

Nicholas gripped the handle of his stick so hard he noticed his knuckles whitening. He willed his grip to lessen. "I know you, brother. You've been threatened with matrimonial pursuits before. Why are you really here?"

"I received an invitation." William put down the cat and fished in his jacket pocket.

"Not from me you didn't."

"Of course not from you, brother. Parliament would go up in flames before I receive a social invitation from you. No, this is from your neighbor, the Pettibone School for Young Ladies." He retrieved a white envelope. "Ah, here it is. The pleasure of my company is requested for some sort of ball they're hosting. Don't tell me you weren't invited?" He laughed. "I knew they despised you, but a cut direct to someone of your standing is truly extraordinary."

"I received an invitation," Nicholas conceded, irritated

by his brother's inference. "But I had planned not to attend."

William tapped the corner of the envelope. "This arrived about the same time as the scheming mother. It was a sign from heaven and a convenient diversion." He smiled broadly.

"Let's toast to convenient diversions then." Nicholas raised his glass in a mock salute before drinking deeply.

"Perhaps your visit is fortuitous." Nicholas squinted in thought. "If you are planning to return to London, perhaps you can spare me a trip and deliver my recent work to the Academy jury for consideration."

"Why not return with me and visit Father while you're in town?" William suggested.

"He has no wish to see me." Nicholas scowled. "I refuse to live up to his dictates. You know that."

"He only wants what is best for you, Nicholas. He believes this period of pleasure-seeking indulgences away from family and society has run its course. You know he's never taken your art seriously. It's time to move on to familial responsibilities and obligations."

"I'm the younger son. Familial responsibilities and obligations are your ballywick, are they not?" Nicholas smiled.

"He wants an heir, Nick. A woman with proper lineage is most likely in London."

Nicholas scoffed. "All the more reason to stay away." He couldn't fathom a more ridiculous reason to return. "I hadn't realized Father and the Pettibone spinisters had so much in common."

William lifted an eyebrow and picked up an older sketchbook, one Nicholas recognized as the one he took to various taverns.

"It is all relative, old man. Don't think that he hasn't exerted similar entreaties on me. As I said earlier, I envy you your distance." He flipped through the pages, pausing periodically.

"You're still recruiting prostitutes for your models, I see." He turned the page to another. "Either you are very quick at your art, brother, or their talents are costing you an arm and a leg. Tell me, do you study their luscious bodies with more than your pen?"

Nicholas exercised his most practiced leer. "Are you envious of more than my distance, dear brother?"

William laughed, then tossed back the rest of his brandy. "Seriously, Nick, you must attend this Pettibone affair. I need someone other than Lady Cavendish to talk to. Good Lord, man, I don't know how you can understand the dialect up here."

"Is that what you mean by familial obligations? I should attend a ball and stand about so you'll have a ready ear for your witticisms and observations?" He glanced toward his brother's legs. "I suppose I shouldn't object. I'm of little use on a dance floor, unless someone is needed to tap out the count." He emptied his glass.

Pity filled William's eyes. The very expression Nicholas thought he'd left behind in London. After a brief pause, William quietly crossed the floor to retrieve the cut-crystal decanter.

"You should never have chased after Cogswell. You knew he was a superior horseman. You weren't more than a lad."

"I knew he was leaving behind a woman with child, his child." Nicholas palmed the handle of his stick, attempting to ignore the ache in his leg. Strange. Throughout all the changes in weather in the last five months, the old injury lay dormant. Now that his brother had arrived, the ache flared up. "I shouldn't have raced through that pasture, but—"

"If you hadn't, the horse wouldn't have fallen on your

leg, and we wouldn't have had to put down the poor creature—"

"Whether to fault the horse, the rider, or the surgeon
who couldn't set the bone properly is of little concern. The
conclusion remains that I will not attend that bloody ball!"
Nicholas felt his face warm and dismissed the eyebrow
raised in his direction.

William glanced around the studio. "Which of these
paintings are you entering in the competition?"

"I have not decided." Nicholas glanced at his drape-
shrouded easel. Unquestionably, *Artemis's Revenge* repre-
sented his best chance for the Royal Academy exhibition.
Never before had he achieved such a subtle blending of
technique and emotion. However, the subject matter on
display for the general populace made him a little uneasy.

"With the exhibition so close at hand, I would have expected you'd have the chosen piece framed, packed, and
ready to go." William shook his head. "This is exactly what
Father means by not taking responsibility seriously. You
procrastinate even in the things most important to you."

"William, you sound just like him." Nicholas's lips
curled in a tight smile. "Come, let's have another brandy
and you can tell me about the charms of London and the
lady who has chased you so far north."

· Fifteen ·

ONCE CECILIA RECEIVED WORD THAT THE MAR-
quess of Enon planned to attend the festivities, no expense was spared transforming the school into an imitation
of a fine London estate. All the furniture, except the piano,
had been moved from the music room to create a space
sufficiently large for dancing. The carpets were rolled up,
exposing hardwood floors that amplified the sound of tapping toes and scurrying footfalls. Both the library and the
salon had been cleared to accommodate the many anticipated patrons. Several villagers had been engaged as servants. Even Cook had been persuaded to wear a new gray
dress under her wide white apron and a maid's cap over her
tidy gray-streaked bun. Already, faint notes from the hired
ensemble warming up their instruments drifted up the
stairs to Alice's room.

"Oh, Mrs. Brimley, isn't this exciting? A real Marquess

is coming to our ball. What if he asks us to dance?" Charlotte preened before a mirror.

Emma's thoughts turned to someone else whose seductive smile she'd rather see across the room, but wisely held her tongue. "Then you shall take care not to step on his toes."

She wove alyssum through Alice's hair. "There should be many young men at Pettibone tonight. Take care not to ignore them for hopes of a dance with the Marquess of Enon." She caught a movement from the corner of her eye. "Charlotte, that ribbon was meant for your hair, not to entertain the kitten."

"You look so beautiful tonight, Mrs. Brimley. What if the Marquess asks you to dance?" Alice asked. "Would you?"

"It would be impolite to refuse," she answered briskly. In truth, the likelihood was rare. Although Nicholas had convinced her she was not the ugly cousin that her uncle had suggested, there remained the issue of age. Her prime years had passed, her youth spent playing ladies' maid to Penelope. Her fingers hesitated in Alice's deep black locks as she recalled doing something similar with Penelope's golden hair. Had she unknowingly been apprenticing for a future of service?

Alice must have felt Emma's hesitation. Her anxious glance in the mirror elicited Emma's confident smile. When Emma caught the affection beaming from Alice's eyes, she corrected herself. A world of difference existed between these girls and the selfish Penelope.

"Now come, Charlotte, let me finish your hair. Alice, run and see if Elizabeth and Fanny are ready. The musicians have taken their places by the sound of it. Miss Higgins will want you all downstairs to properly welcome our guests."

After she had sent Charlotte off to follow the others,

Emma glanced in the oval mirror on the wall. Earlier in the day, Beatrice had presented her with a beautiful gray satin gown, hand stitched by the two sisters to thank Emma for the skills she had brought to the girls. By no means would the garment challenge a Worth gown for high fashion, but its simple lines and lack of trim presented an elegant, refined reflection.

"For the image of the school," Cecilia had said when Emma offered her gratitude. The pair had grown so dear to her over the past months, it was easy to forget that she was their employee.

A year ago, Emma imagined she would have been too self-conscious in the low-cut gown. Indeed the bodice barely covered the top of her corset, exposing the small strawberry birthmark on the lift of her left breast. However, after posing for long hours in less attire for Chambers, Emma found herself surprisingly comfortably in the rich fabric.

She retrieved the long glove box sent by "the mysterious stranger" and removed the black lace gloves, pulling each to her elbow. Nicholas may not attend the ball, but her thoughts would fly to him every time the lace would cross her field of vision. Earbobs and a jet necklace completed the ensemble. She straightened her spine, wishing he could see her. She may not be the prettiest flower in the garden tonight, but she no longer played the role of a weed.

Emma descended the stairs into the organized chaos that signaled a successful gathering. Young men with freshly scrubbed faces and imaginative cravats buzzed about the lower floor like bees mining blossoms. Cecilia and Beatrice tended to the older couples, the parents of the girls, she assumed. The music room was alive with swirling satins and lace. It was truly a night of enchantment.

"Mrs. Brimley, there you are. I've been looking all over

for you." Beatrice broke away from a small gathering. "Some of the parents have specifically asked to make your acquaintance."

Emma allowed herself to be led from couple to couple, politely acknowledging the introductions and taking care to comment on each girl's assets to her parents. Over the months she had come to know the girls by their talents and faults, the sound of their laughter as well as the sound of their tears. She faltered on her curtsy to Mr. and Mrs. Barnesworth at the sudden realization. The girls were her family. She loved each of them as one would love a child or a little sister. No matter the circumstances that brought her to Leighton-on-the-Wold, she would be eternally grateful for the privilege of being a part of Pettibone.

The music paused, yet the noise level heightened. Cecilia, who had stood by Emma's side throughout the endless introductions, glanced to the entrance of the room. Her face brightened. "He's here," she pronounced with no small measure of awe.

Nicholas! Emma's heart increased its tempo. A giddiness swelled in her throat. He must have reversed his decision not to attend. She turned, expecting to see him in that same formal attire she had witnessed the first night they met, and stared.

From his top hat, to his complicated cravat the color of freshly fallen snow, he was easily the most handsome man she had ever seen, the epitome of a fashionably dressed gentleman. Had she been in London, the ladies would plot and scheme for an introduction. He carried the look of money about him, in his attire as well as in his lofty expression, which left her disinterested. Still there was something intriguing about his dark coloring, the sensual fullness of his lips and the elegantly tapered hands encased in fine kid gloves. If his upper lip hadn't been completely devoid of facial hair, she might have mistaken him for . . .

"Chambers," she said, quite surprised to hear she had spoken aloud.

"His older brother," Beatrice corrected. "The Marquess of Enon. We're honored by his attendance. Come, Mrs. Brimley, you should make his acquaintance." Beatrice tugged on her arm, but Emma stood her ground.

"This night is to showcase the girls, not their matronly instructors," she said, hoping to dissuade Beatrice. If the Marquess of Enon had newly traveled from London, it was possible he might know of her uncle and hence be on the lookout for her.

"One could hardly describe such a young widow as matronly," Mrs. Barnesworth observed. "Why if I were younger and open to the marriage mart, I would insist on an introduction."

Mrs. Barnesworth's high-pitched voice must have cut a swath through the festive current, for at that precise moment, the gentleman in question caught Emma's glance. He squinted slightly, then turned to speak to someone blocked by a small gathering in her line of vision.

"Exactly my point," Beatrice agreed.

"Excuse me," Emma interjected, "I have an unbearable thirst. I believe I will check on the girls at the lemonade table."

She skirted along the back wall, hoping the crowd that had gathered around the Marquess would hide her from view. She had almost reached the safety of the side exit, when Lady Cavendish's voice stopped her retreat.

"Mrs. Brimley, please do not run off. I have someone here to meet you."

Emma turned, facing the apprising eyes of the Marquess of Enon. Lady Cavendish performed the introductions. Emma extended her hand and curtsied.

"We have met before?" he asked. His voice, so similar to his brother's, startled her. She glanced up expecting to see intriguing brown eyes lit by humor and shared secrets, but instead found a questioning gaze that left her unaffected. The stirring about her rib cage dissipated.

"No, sir, I do not believe I have had that pleasure," Emma replied. She started to pull her hand away when his fingers closed over her glove.

"You're from London." A warmth poured into his voice, his smile broadened. "Your accent is music to my ears, and your face . . ." His eyes narrowed. "Your face is familiar to me. Have you been to London recently?"

Emma bit her lip, looking anxiously toward Lady Cavendish for assistance.

"Mrs. Brimley has been an institution at Pettibone for some time now," Lady Cavendish interrupted with a toss of the ostrich feather hairpiece that dangled close to the Marquess's head. "Indeed, *I* was her sponsor."

Emma smiled her appreciation.

"She hasn't been at this institution long enough to lose her educated tones," the Marquess said, his gaze never leaving her face.

His toothy smile raised the fine hairs on the back of Emma's neck. She tugged her hand from his grasp. His gaze dropped to her lace gloves, before returning to her face.

"We have met," he said. "I'm certain of it. I have a keen eye for faces, you see. It will come to me in time."

Emma's throat tightened. Although she knew for certain that they had never met in London, the Marquess's memory could prove a problem if he encountered her uncle. "If you'll excuse me, I was just on my way—"

"May I have the honor of a dance?" he asked. "The musicians are about to begin the second set."

Panic seared her skin. To refuse would embarrass Pettibone, to accept would publicly demonstrate her lack of grace. She leaned close to the Marquess so as to make herself heard over the discord of the instruments' tuning.

"I am not a skilled dancer. Please don't ask me to demonstrate. I beg of you, sir." Her lack of abilities on the dance floor had followed her throughout her adolescence, much to Penelope's chagrin.

"I am delighted you wish to demonstrate." He smiled. Clasping her elbow with a firm hold, he led her out to the floor. She glanced about hoping other couples would join them, but her students all watched with envy in their eyes. She was all alone and on display.

The musicians struck a tune; the Marquess smiled his approval. "Are you familiar with the Glide Waltz?" She shook her head. "Then allow me to show you."

He placed his hand on her waist and with subtle pressure, directed the way she should go. With his firmly extended arm and the strong hold on her waist, he provided a sturdy frame of support. Soon, she was swept up in the dance, counting the steps out silently in her mind, appreciating that he failed to notice that she often took two steps to his one.

"I'm going to turn you now," he warned, and true enough they spun to the music. Laughter bubbled from her lips. His eyes acknowledged her delight.

"I find it difficult to believe that such an attractive young woman as yourself yet remains a widow," he said before signaling another turn. "Do you not care for these country gentlemen?"

"I have been married once, sir," she replied, prepared this time for the sweep. "I feel no urgency to repeat the process." Of course it was a lie, but to Emma's mind, the response sounded smart and appropriate.

"Hah," he laughed, "you sound like my brother. He sees no benefit in the arrangement. Perhaps if he did, he would have come this evening. I'm afraid he is so involved with his artistic endeavors that the procurement of a proper wife quite eludes him."

His phrasing caught her so off guard, she missed a step and took two to catch up.

"As you know, sir, we at Pettibone try to teach the girls the qualities they need to obtain the title of a 'proper wife.' What characteristics do you believe would be necessary to appeal to your brother?" Artfully done, she congratulated herself.

"You are rather young to play at matchmaker." He laughed. "I would expect the two spinsters to wile away their time on such folly." The music ended. They bowed and curtsied appropriately before he led her from the dance floor.

"Very well," he said after a pause. " I'll play your game, although some qualities, unfortunately, cannot be learned in school, but must be instilled through birth and upbringing." He led her in the direction of the refreshments. "My brother has an appreciation of art, so I imagine the woman he chooses must be beautiful beyond the pale. Once he outgrows his current predilection with painting and accepts his family responsibilities, he'll need a wife who can move throughout society. She must have proper carriage and be a witty conversationalist as well as exhibit genteel manners. She should have excellent bloodlines as well, in the event of offspring."

"With the possible exception of a witty conversationalist, I believe you've described all the attributes of a racehorse," Emma said, accepting an offered glass of lemonade.

"And so I have." He laughed. "I suppose I have something of a predilection of my own in that regard." He leaned closer to her ear. "You know, Mrs. Brimley, that I am a widower myself. I understand what it means to lose a close companion. If ever you feel the need for—"

"Conversation?" Emma interjected. Now that she understood so much more about intimacy, she was quite sure she did not want to share such experiences with this man. Racehorses, indeed.

His smile broadened while his eyelids lowered. "Conversation would be a part of it, surely. But I was suggesting something of a more physical nature." He positioned himself in front of her, shielding her from the ball participants by his broad back. "I'm sure a widow such as yourself understands both the needs and *the opportunities* in such a venture."

"You have given me much to think about," she said, wondering how to disengage herself from this odious man without harming the school's reputation. The door to the terrace beckoned a few steps to her left. If she could effectively excuse herself . . .

He stroked the side of her face with a knuckle. Her stomach roiled. "Perhaps we may discuss this under more private circumstances?" he asked.

"I believe there are a number of young ladies present who are hoping for the favor of a dance." She hoped her smile hid her revulsion. "I've been remiss in keeping your attention far too long."

He lifted her gloved hand to his lips. "I shall look forward to enjoying your 'conversation' at a later date, Mrs. Brimley."

She curtsied, as was his due, and kept a demure smile until he turned and walked back toward Lady Cavendish. Gaiety deserted her. Smiling became a bit of a chore. Emma glanced to her side. Dark solitude on the terrace lay just beyond the glass panes. Her hand extended, she turned the knob. A breath of fresh air would clear her troubled thoughts.

• • •

NICHOLAS WATCHED FROM THE SHADOWS IN THE GAR-
den. His silver flask opened and near empty. The multi-
paned glass doors provided a clear view of the frivolity
within. Almost three weeks had passed since his last
glimpse of Emma. Her absence had brought him to this
degradation: formally attired, fully foxed, and spying from
the bushes.

After his brother and that flighty Lady Cavendish left
for the ball, Nicholas decided to hang his bloody pride and
come as well. Perhaps Emma would consent to talk with
him as he stood apart from the jostling crowd. Maybe he
could tease a rosy blush to her sweet cheeks once more.
That hope carried him to the Pettibone School, but the
sight of the crush at the door chased away his bravado. He
slipped around to the deserted rear terrace with his flask
for company.

Just as he decided to trust the sturdy trunk of a tree for
the support his wobbly walking stick lacked, Emma appeared in the window, a vision in a gray satin gown that
bared parts of her unseen by any man other than himself.
His breath caught. He stared, afraid that she might vanish
if he so much as blinked.

Look at her! A goddess stepped down to earth. His eyes
burned in their sockets. What he had imagined to be skill
in reproducing her image, now, when faced with her reality, seemed uninspired.

What happened to that insidious black dress that covered every square inch of enticing flesh? She knew he
hadn't planned to attend. Why did she choose tonight to
share that soft skin with the fawning likes of . . . his
brother! Nicholas gnashed his teeth. A searing pain burned
through his gut. Other eyes, interested masculine eyes,
viewed the prize that he regarded as his alone. Almost in
insult, his brother put his hand on her cinched waist, gazed
at her sweet breasts, trussed up like plump pigeons on a

platter, straining at the top of her gown. Nicholas clenched his fists.

Perhaps she'd prefer the company of a well-mannered gentleman, William had said. She certainly was enjoying one now. Look at her smile and twirl and laugh, a proper lady dancing with the equally elegant Marquess of Enon. And her eyes, they positively glistened when William stroked the side of her face.

"Bloody hell." He slumped against the rough bark pressing his back. "She dances to his fiddle all right. Doesn't she realize what he's about?"

He drained his flask, disappointed to find insufficient liquid to burn away the image of his love in his brother's arms.

He should leave; he should turn away and crawl back to the carriage if his leg refused to cooperate. But the sight of Emma kept him transfixed. Just as in his painting Actaeon couldn't turn his head away from Artemis, Nicholas could not turn his gaze from Emma. There was irony in the comparison, he thought. Perhaps he should have used his own likeness for Actaeon rather than that of Thomas.

A cool breeze blew, making him wish for the comfort and solitude of his carriage, when Emma ran to the terrace door as if she knew he waited. If he were to leave now, she'd see him sulking away. Just like the goddess, she'd turn him into a wild stag with just one glance, he thought in his alcohol-induced state. He smiled, or tried to smile. It would serve him right to be a wild, rutting stag.

EMMA STEPPED OUTSIDE, WRAPPING HER ARMS ABOUT her shoulders, hoping the cool air would chase the memory of the Marquess's suggestive proposals from her mind. How could he consider such an arrangement? Was there something about her that suggested she might comply?

Her lace-clad hand brushed at the corner of her eye, knocking her spectacles slightly askew.

"You appeared to enjoy yourself."

Chambers's voice startled her. Squinting in the dark, she located the white points of his collar. As her vision adjusted, the whole man separated from the surrounding night, from his narrowed accusing eyes, to the underlying grace of his nonchalant lean against the trunk of a substantial tree.

Relief bubbled through her. The Marquess's remarkable resemblance to his brother had only served to remind Emma how long it had been since she enjoyed Nicholas's company. She had missed his wit, and charm, and . . . Suddenly recalling the reason she chose not to share his company, she quickly reined in her emotions.

"I thought you were not planning to attend the dance," she said, steeling her spine.

"I changed my mind." His words carried a slight slur, probably not noticeable to someone not as familiar with the cadence and timbre of his voice as she. He advanced a bit awkwardly on her position near the terrace wall. Light spilling from the inside activities captured him briefly. Her breath caught. With the exception of his loosely tied cravat and his high collar, he wore all black, allowing him to blend into the very night. Indeed, she felt surrounded by his exotic expansive presence. Tremors raced down her spine.

"I had thought to come here and ask you to dance, Emma." His step was unsure. She noted he leaned a little heavier on his walking stick as he approached. "Would you have danced with me?"

Her gaze shifted from his leg to his face. "Of course. Naturally, I would—"

He placed a glove-clad finger to her lips. It lingered a moment then slipped beneath her chin, raising her lips as

if for a kiss. It had been so long, her lips parted in anticipation.

"Would you have allowed me to slide my hand down
your side like so?" He placed his hand under her arm at the
top of the satin and slowly dragged his fingers down her
side till they settled on the cinch of her waist. Heat burst
from the path like sparks from a smoldering log. She sa-
vored the sensation, remembering her foolish edict against
his touch. How could she have denied herself this simple
pleasure?

". . . as you allowed my brother?"

Oh, but his brother's touch did not reach deep inside
her, causing her breath to turn short and choppy the way
Nicholas's did.

"It was a necessary posture for the dance," she explained, though in truth Nicholas's talented fingers made
her skin tingle as if nothing separated him from her flesh.
His touch barely seemed proper. "If we were to dance, you
would—"

He raised his brow. "I saw him study your breasts just
so." His lids lowered seductively, calling forth an answering heat across her chest. "Was that a necessary posture as
well?"

The slant of his brows combined with a hardened edge
to his tone registered a warning. She gasped, stepping
backward to force distance between them. Yet he advanced
as she retreated, his fingers tightening on her waist. Although they moved beyond the arc of light from the ball-
room, music from within merged with the night air, a
reminder of guests just inside the door.

Damp stone brushed her back. Trapped in the shadowed
corner of the terrace wall and the school exterior, she could
retreat no more.

He pushed forward till the satin-covered tips of her

breasts brushed the front of his black vest. A brandy scent coated his words.

"You laughed and smiled in his arms." His fingers pressed tight on her waist like ill-placed stays. His lips grazed her cheekbone. "Why aren't you smiling for me, Mrs. Brimley?"

"Because you are frightening me." Her voice shook, the constriction in her throat making words difficult.

"I could take you here, Emma. We're alone in the dark. Can you feel my desire?" He guided her fingers to the bulge in his trousers. "That's what arousal feels like. That's what you do to me, Emma."

"Lord Chambers—" she gasped.

"Ssh . . . Nicholas. Say it Emma." His voice turned soft, pleading. "Say my name."

She forced her tone to be calm, soothing. "I should return inside. I'm bound to be missed. Someone will come looking for me. You should come inside as well. It would be an honor to—"

"There is a coupling posture I hadn't mentioned before." His provocative words overrode hers as if she had never spoken. In this place, at this time, his words frightened her more than his nearness. She tried to remove her hand from where he pressed it, but he wouldn't allow it.

"The lady sits here on the wall with her skirts trussed up and her legs spread wide." His knee nudged between her legs, the ample fabric offering no barrier. "I'll stand and insert my manhood through that small slit in your drawers. You remember that small slit, don't you, Emma?"

Shivers raced up and down her spine. How could she forget? The memory of his tongue exploring her through that opening triggered a pooling in that very spot.

"Spread your legs for me, Emma. Let me into your heat."

His repetition of her name lulled her into an almost

hypnotic trance. Her legs felt weak, incapable of supporting her weight. Heavens above, she wanted to yield to her desires; she longed to experience him inside her once again, but not here. Not on the terrace with so many people nearby.

"You won't compromise me here in the dark," she said, trusting that her instincts were true. Although he had the means to do otherwise, Nicholas had protected her thus far. He wouldn't harm her. Though part of her hungered for him to do just that.

"Are you so very sure?" His nose stroked the length of hers. She closed her eyes, hoping he wouldn't see the desire burning there.

"Isn't that what my brother wanted?" Nicholas's fingers caressed the side of her face just as William had done earlier, only this time she pressed toward the soft caress.

"Isn't that why you smiled, dear Emma, because you wanted a man of courtly manners to find his pleasure deep inside you?"

She shook her head. "I want only you."

His body stilled. He pulled back, studying her face. "What? What did you say?"

The door handle clicked. Chambers quickly pushed Emma deep into the shadows, shielding her body with his.

"Mrs. Brimley, are you out here?" Alice called.

Emma opened her mouth to respond, but Chambers's lips covered hers first. His kiss stole her breath and response.

The door clicked shut, but his kiss continued. No longer resistant to his pursuit, she slid her hands up his chest and twined about his neck. She tasted him deeply, drawing on the strength of his desire with a reassurance of her own.

With a sound akin to a low growl, Nicholas pulled her closer, tighter against his chest, locking her in the security of his arms.

She could have stayed locked in that embrace forever, but she was needed, else Alice would not be searching for her. She pulled back, sucking gently on Nicholas's lower lip as if to sample the intoxication that lingered there.

"You seductive minx." His heated breath bathed her face, yet she heard a smile in his voice. "You must have had a very good teacher."

"The very best," she answered, still breathless from his kiss.

He leaned forward to whisper in her ear. "Don't let him touch you."

If she hadn't heard the plea in his voice, that soft chord of desperation that exposed a rare vulnerability, she might have felt insult that he would even harbor such a notion. She smiled against his shoulder, recognizing that he had just claimed her, just as she had claimed him earlier.

"Never," she said, but her response, muffled by his many layers of superfine, was lost. She pulled back so her words would be clear. "Dance with me?"

"I believe we already have." He smiled, the whiteness of his teeth cutting through the night. He kissed her cheek, lingering for a moment. "You'd best return to the party. You've been missed."

"And you?"

"No one will miss me. Thank you, dear Emma. I don't think I shall ever enjoy a dance more."

He turned and silently crossed the terrace, his walking stick tucked beneath his arm. The deep shadows swallowed his retreat.

"You're wrong," she whispered to the sweet musical strains drifting from the ball. "I already miss you."

· Sixteen ·

FLOWERS ARRIVED THE NEXT MORNING. BOUQUET upon bouquet of daisies, rosebuds laced with ferns, violets and lilies arrived for the girls who attended the ball. The local hothouses must have been quite emptied by the demand. Even Emma received a full bouquet of roses with a note of gratitude signed by "W" for which she cared little, and a bouquet of daisies, which thrilled her greatly. The blank white card said more than if it had been signed. Nicholas.

"It must be a mistake," Cecilia said. "Who would send a message of innocence to a widow? The bouquet must be meant for one of the girls."

"With so many gifts to prepare," Emma replied, tempering her excitement with difficulty, "it's likely the florist made a mistake." When no one was looking, she slipped one of the daisies inside her dress to later press inside a volume of Lord Byron's poetry.

Beatrice combined bouquets so as to utilize Pettibone's few available vases. When she resorted to borrowing Cook's favorite milk pitcher for some fragile blossoms, Cook created such a fuss that Emma was beseeched to borrow some vessels from Black Oak when next she went for a lesson. Emma agreed, deciding that very afternoon she required immediate art instruction.

Borrowing the school's open rig, she drove herself to Black Oak, pondering how best to phrase the question that had kept her awake long after the Higgins sisters were snoring in their beds. Was there a way to prevent the conception of a child, if one was to succumb to one's desires? The gables of Black Oak loomed before her; she flicked the reins to speed up the pony.

"Hello, Thomas, I don't believe Lord Chambers is expecting me, but I had hoped I could prevail upon him for a lesson?"

"I am quite sure his lordship will be delighted to see you, Mrs. Brimley. It has been too long since you visited Black Oak." Thomas smiled and stepped back from the door, allowing her entrance. He took her cloak and led her down the hallway toward the studio. "I'm told the festivities last night were a success?"

"Oh yes," Emma exclaimed, knowing that she could never admit the results of the ball far exceeded her expectations. She had thought she had turned Nicholas away, yet his presence last night proved otherwise. "The Higgins sisters were most pleased with the attendance."

She explained their need for vases. Thomas offered to see what he could find to alleviate the crisis.

"Lord Chambers will attend upon you shortly, madam. Please make yourself comfortable. I'll return with some tea." Thomas left the door slightly ajar.

She had never waited long in the studio before. Without Nicholas's commanding vibrancy, the room held a cool, empty resonance. She rubbed her forearms, as though a spring breeze had wound its way into the studio.

Then she spied the draped easel set before the dais and all thoughts of temperature evaporated. Curiosity pulled her to the canvas Nicholas had kept hidden from view.

She approached it silently, solemnly, as if entering the village church. Her initial embarrassment, her long tedious hours of posing, her fabrications to the school, all culminated in this work. She had wondered sometimes whether Nicholas was seriously painting anything at all or just splashing colors on a canvas as an excuse for her "education." Excitement tingled to the tips of her fingers, but reverence held her cautiously at bay. Looking back once more to make sure her indiscretion would not be noticed, she carefully lifted the drape.

Her gaze shot immediately to the nude woman holding a long narrow cloth that streamed behind her in an imaginary wind. Awed by the painting's artistic beauty and refined talent, she didn't immediately recognize the model. She certainly had never remotely resembled this heavenly creature. Unlike Emma, the goddess apparently had perfect eyesight as she didn't wear spectacles, but Artemis's striking green eyes, rich brown hair, and birthmark above her left breast seemed familiar.

She tossed the drape over the back of the easel so as to view the entire painting. Her breath caught. The colors! The textures! Nicholas's skill was undeniable. Although she noted a man in the woods and a stag running in the background, her gaze continued to return to Artemis.

Oh, she would have been wrong, so wrong, to have believed Nicholas was without talent. Emma did not credit herself a critic, but to her eye, the painting was a masterpiece. The painting could well be placed on exhibition and viewed by thousands of people. Her eyes widened, panic surged beneath her corset. What was she thinking!

Footsteps pounded in the hallway. Thomas must be returning with refreshments. Emma quickly tugged at the drapery to recover the painting. Unfortunately, it had been much easier to remove then replace. The cloth snagged on the point of the easel, falling over half of the painting. Although she had effectively covered the goddess, a portion of the painting remained exposed, providing evidence of her tampering.

"Mrs. Brimley!" The Marquess of Enon stood in the doorway. Alarm fled the confines of her stomach to lodge in her throat.

"Thomas mentioned he had situated you in the studio." He carefully closed the door behind him and approached. A knowing smile tipped his lips. He rubbed his hands together as if beset by the same chill that tripped down Emma's spine.

"I see you've wasted no time considering my proposal."

Compared to the thump of Nicholas's stick, the Marquess's silent continuing approach seemed both unearthly and villainous.

"I believe there must be a mis—"

"I enjoy a woman who knows what she wants," he interrupted. "And doesn't hesitate to seek it out."

His gaze raked the length of her from hat to hemline in the manner of a dandy accustomed to such liberties. Emma stood her ground, remembering the disappointment when such dandies rejected her in favor of her cousin, Penelope. This time, however, she would feel no disappointment. The Marquess's interest held no sway.

"A houseguest, however, should never presume upon his host's hospitality to provide for the occasional tryst, don't you agree?" William asked.

"Sir, you are mistaken as to my purpose," Emma insisted.

He pursed his lips, then lifted a brow, and still advanced.

"I extended an offer of companionship, and here you are unannounced and alone. What is there to misunderstand?"

Emma began to retreat. The man was as persistent and stubborn as a devil incarnate. "Your brother has been giving me lessons in this studio. I'm here for a previously arranged appointment."

He chuckled low in his throat as he pulled even with the easel. "My brother gives art lessons?" He laughed outright. "I'd more likely believe he offered lessons of a different kind."

Heat blossomed in her cheeks. She would have been concerned about the Marquess's ability to translate that blush, but his gaze had been caught by the disheveled drape.

He turned toward the easel. "Were you peeking, Mrs. Brimley?" he teased. "I must admit a certain curiosity on my part, as well."

The blood rushed from her head, leaving her faint and queasy. She tried to rush forward, to stop him from removing the top of the proverbial Pandora's box, or in this case, a drape.

"No!" she cried, although the words couldn't squeeze past the constriction in her throat. They emitted as a whisper.

The Marquess firmly grasped the edge of the remaining drapery and tossed it back over the easel without effort.

For several seconds there was no sound, save that of her racing heartbeat pounding in her ears. The Marquess stepped back, crossed his arms, and studied the work, his face devoid of expression.

"Magnificent!" He said, awe evident in his voice. "This is far superior to any of his previous work. Why, this is bound to be accepted by the Academy." He leaned forward, his nose almost touching the oil, then straightened and stepped back, viewing the work from several angles.

Emma withdrew until the solid wall pressed her back. Her stomach roiled, threatening to expel its contents. Her throat tightened. She could barely breathe. Perhaps he wouldn't recognize the model. She hadn't at first. She was the least likely candidate to be painted as a goddess.

"The overall composition is masterful, wouldn't you agree?" he asked.

Fortunately, he didn't look her way for confirmation; the painting captured all his attention.

"Look at the brushwork, the detail . . ." He turned toward her, his face exuberant.

Her lips trembled. His broad smile lessened. He narrowed his eyes and glanced back to the painting.

"It's you," he said, softly. "You posed for this painting. I can see it now." He turned back to Emma, studying her as if she were a complicated stanza of poetry. "I knew I recognized you, but I hadn't seen this painting until just this minute. How could that be?"

Please let the ground open up beneath me and swallow me whole, she prayed. Humiliated, she remained fastened to the wall like one of Nicholas's framed landscapes. Perhaps if she were still enough, quiet enough, he would forget she was in the room. She recognized the absurdity of that notion but saw no other viable course of action. The door was on the opposite wall. Besides, she could never escape the damage caused by viewing that painting.

Her body numbed. All that was meaningful in her life drained out through her pores and floated about the room like a spirit, leaving behind a cold, empty shell of bone and ash.

The devil Marquess of Enon tapped one elegant finger against his cheek. "Unless . . ." His eyes widened. He quickly crossed the floor to rummage in the desk drawer.

She could escape now. The path was clear, but what was the use? Everything she had hoped for—a longtime position at Pettibone, a happy family consisting of two spinster sisters and a flock of giggling girls—now appeared impossible. Her reputation ruined, she would soon be tossed out like old, moldy bread.

The Marquess found a sketchbook and fumbled through the pages.

"I knew I had seen your face." He stopped midway through the book, then gazed back toward her. "Of course, you're the country miss."

He held aloft an opened sketchbook displaying a charcoal drawing of a woman with flowers and ivy in her hair. Some spark of memory fought ineffectively against the cold fog that gripped her mind and body. When one had no future, of what value are memories?

"The sly devil." The Marquess laughed. "I can well imagine the lessons my brother was teaching you."

Emma turned her face away from his mockery. *What did you expect?* Her uncle's voice taunted her. *You knew what society demands of respectable women. If you were respectable you wouldn't have succumbed to Chambers's bargain.*

Deep within she felt a tiny protest against her uncle's words, a tiny flame that sputtered in a cold unfeeling body.

"At least my brother has progressed from the tavern whores to country widows." The devil's voice loomed closer, impossible now to tell the difference between her uncle's leering tone and that of the Marquess of Enon. But then, what did it matter?

"Leave her alone, William."

She knew that voice. The sputtering flame fought back against the pressing cold. Her eyes began to focus, searching for the source.

"Nicholas!" The devil voice cried in greeting. "You

should have told me. I never would have presumed to interfere with your sport."

The comforting tap of Nicholas's stick crossed the room as if in a dream. With each tap, the flame brightened, but he was coming too late. Too late.

"Your painting is marvelous, masterful, destined to earn accolades for your talents. And the fact that your model is a finishing school teacher will surely attract attention in London." The Marquess's exuberant praises failed to stop the rhythmic tapping. "Your painting will be the hit of the exhibition."

"No one is to know that Emma is the model."

Nicholas's soft voice surrounded her. The pulse in her veins strengthened. She recognized the touch of his fingertips on the underside of her chin by the quickly generating warmth radiating outward, bringing her back to life.

He lifted her chin until she focused on his searching, deep brown eyes. Awareness stabbed at her with a million tiny pricks as if she had become Beatrice's human pincushion.

"I'm sorry." Nicholas's words were spoken too softly to extend beyond her ears. She lifted her fingers with the intent to touch his face, to make sure he was real. He captured her hand midpath and brought her fingertips to his lips for a gentle kiss. The flame burning within her multiplied, banishing the cold mists to distant memory.

"Emma, is it now?" The Marquess shook his head as if remnants of sleep had fogged his perception. "I swear, little brother, you could charm the stars from the heavens if they were female. What difference will it make in London who the model is? The painting is the important thing."

"It matters to me," Nicholas said in a tone not to be ignored. His lips tilted in an apologetic smile, then he patted her hand and replaced it by her side.

Pivoting on his stick, he turned away and approached the easel. "Besides, this painting will never see London."

Hope pulsed through her veins. She should never have doubted him. He had always protected her.

Nicholas pulled the drape back in place, concealing the treasure beneath. "I'll send another, one of my landscapes."

"Don't be a fool, Nick," William argued, all mirth gone from his face. "The Academy doesn't want landscapes. You'll be rejected again."

"Then I'll be rejected. There are worst things." He nodded toward Emma. "I won't have Mrs. Brimley's reputation harmed in any way, either by idle gossip or public display of this painting."

If her legs had strength, she'd rush over and throw her arms around him. He was willing to sacrifice his well-earned recognition to preserve her reputation. Tears of gratitude burned at the corners of her eyes.

"Bloody hell, Nick." William cast a disparaging frown in her direction, waving the sketchbook as if to punctuate his words. "She's used goods. A painting like this could boost her popularity as well. She'll be a novelty. You've painted her with a shy, self-conscious quality that is outright titillating. No one will deny your talent."

Nicholas's lips thinned. "Yesterday I had a preoccupation, today I have a talent." He glanced her way. Her rigidity melted in response. "I'd rather have neither if it hurts Emma."

The Marquess dropped the sketchbook, letting the binding bounce on the floor. The book flipped open to Emma's goddess sketch.

"Not a word, William," Nicholas warned. "Do you understand?"

The Marquess scowled but nodded assent. He marched across the studio floor to the door, leaving a boot print across Emma's sketched cheek in the process.

As William's boots echoed down the hall, Nicholas turned to Emma.

"I'm sorry," he said. "I tried to keep the painting hidden."

Nicholas fished in his pocket and removed a handkerchief. "I suppose I should have packed the painting away the moment he arrived, but I couldn't."

He dabbed at her cheeks. Had she been crying? She couldn't remember.

"I just couldn't." He opened his arms, and she stepped into his comfort. "The important thing is that no one will ever see that painting again. Trust me, Emma. It shall be our secret, and our secret alone."

"It's my fault," she said. "I uncovered it. I just wanted to see . . ." Her voice faltered, then disappeared altogether. Tears ran uncontrolled down her cheeks.

"William would have seen it eventually. It's not your fault." His fingertips soothed the hair back from her cheeks.

"I know." His voice lightened. "I shall hide it in the root cellar with the potatoes, if you like. I'll cover it from view, although I suspect Thomas would want his likeness to be revealed."

His gentle teasing brought a smile to her lips. "Thomas?" The words forced her throat to open to accommodate them. "The man in the woods?"

Nicholas nodded, gently squeezing her shoulder. He shifted toward the easel. "I'd prefer to hang it, though, in my private quarters." He glanced down to her. "With your permission, of course."

Emma sniffed, not a refined sound, but necessary. "I thought this studio was your private quarter."

He sighed and hugged her tighter. "That was the original plan when I moved to Yorkshire. My family and houseguests apparently consider this a public gallery of sorts." He pulled back a bit to see her face. "You're the first to recognize how much of my heart and soul reside in this room."

"After these last few months, I think a bit of my heart resides here as well." Emma sniffled.

He held her in silence a few moments longer then stepped back. "I suppose you didn't come here today to pose for my next great work."

His humor pulled at her heart. She rubbed the last traces of tears from her eyes and straightened her spectacles on her nose, then took a large settling breath. "Your brother is correct. It is a magnificent work."

"The next one will be even better." Nicholas smiled, and moved over to his stool. "You shall see."

"I had thought that now that this project was complete, you could teach me about art in earnest." Emma followed him back to the center of the room and stepped up on the dais by habit. "The sisters still expect me to teach painting to the girls."

"Emma, everything we have done has been in earnest." Nicholas picked a brush from a jar and held it aloft to inspect it. She recognized the sable brush instantly and smiled, remembering the silky texture on her skin.

"I'd wager you know more about art now than all of Yorkshire," Nicholas said.

Emma sat on the divan, too drained to argue or even agree. She tried to believe Nicholas's light banter, but the draped easel remained her focus. What she once considered a freeing experience had become a trap.

"You don't believe me?" Nicholas pulled a mock frown. "Then I suppose we should get to work. Let us begin with the topic of negative space."

· Seventeen ·

THE PAINTING CHANGED EVERYTHING.

Once she returned to Pettibone, Emma feigned a headache and retired early. Even an invitation from Alice to indulge in a game of cards could not lift her spirits. Cecilia audibly supposed that the excitement of the dance had tired her unduly and urged her to seek rest. The girls would be distraught if illness would to befall their favorite teacher.

Emma smiled to acknowledge the compliment, then quickly escaped to her room to think.

She trusted Nicholas to keep the painting private, but servants talked. It wouldn't take long for the rumors and gossip to travel from Black Oak to Pettibone. The Marquess's words echoed in her mind. *At least my brother has progressed from tavern whores to country widows.* How quickly would people begin to associate her with the former group and not the latter?

She had to leave. A sullied reputation would ruin Pettibone. Cecilia had said as much the day she had arrived. Leaving her newly found family would be difficult, but leave she must. The question was, where to go?

She could teach to earn a wage. Her time at Pettibone had taught her that much. She had an affinity for the young girls that resulted in their acceptance and learning. Perhaps she could secure a position in a finishing school in Switzerland or Paris. No, not Paris, she decided. Loyalty to God and country wouldn't allow her to teach in that godforsaken hovel. That meant Switzerland would have to be her destination. Her past surely wouldn't follow her that far.

She had done well in her widow portrayal. The next time, she would do even better, now that she was armed with the lessons Nicholas had taught her.

So it was settled. She would approach Nicholas at the first opportunity about securing transportation out of the country. He was a reasonable man, an intelligent man. She had recognized that from the very first when they met in the carriage.

Memories of that night pulled at her heart. She could travel the world over and never meet another man like him. Tears leaked from the corners of her eyes. She swiped at them with a corner of the pillowcase.

With her departure Nicholas would be free to exhibit his masterpiece. She couldn't deny the world of its next great artist. Her heart ached at his proposed sacrifice. She couldn't allow it.

He had given her so much. He had taught her how to appreciate art, and herself. He had awakened her heart to what it felt like to love and to be loved. This was the only gift she could give him in return, her absence. Her chest tightened, making it difficult to draw breath.

He would see the logic of her plan. It was a brilliant plan. This would benefit them both.

Then why were tears streaming down her cheeks at thought of her future?

"NO." WITH ONE HAND, NICHOLAS SNAPPED HIS BOOK shut before shoving it into place on his library shelf. "Absolutely not."

"You must see the necessity of this move," Emma pleaded, crossing deeper into the book-lined recess. Normally she would stop and savor the smell of old leather and musty paper, but not today. Not when she was pleading for an opportunity to never stand in this library again. "I don't wish to go, but I have no other choice."

"I see no such thing." Nicholas crossed his arms in front of him. "I will not assist this foolish venture in any way."

"Foolish venture!" she gasped. How could he not appreciate that circumstances had changed? "Don't you see that it's only a matter of time before gossip travels to Pettibone?"

"Emma, if those in residence at Black Oak were interested in spreading gossip, don't you think the spinster sisters would already know the nature of your art lessons?" Nicholas's voice riled her with his calm logic, the complete antithesis to her own current sensibilities. "Despite his obvious faults, my brother is an honorable man. He can be trusted not to divulge the nature of the painting."

She rolled her eyes, not sharing his appreciation of his brother's virtues.

Nicholas's lips turned in the slightest of smiles. "I've been my family's black sheep for so long, I've forgotten that some may not hold my brother in as high esteem as the family is wont to do."

Nicholas must come from a family of fools if they respected the eldest brother over the younger, she thought.

"Nevertheless, the painting is again under cover in my

studio." He selected another leather volume and slammed it home on the shelf. "The marquess and Lady Cavendish are departing for London early tomorrow morning. I see no reason why our paths cannot carry on, just as they had before the unfortunate unveiling of *Artemis's Revenge*."

"I cannot go on as before." Emma shook her head, despondent over his lack of cooperation in this endeavor. "I am no longer in desperate need of your knowledge, and I refuse to continue to lie about my visits here. I've become a part of so many deceits, I have difficulty recalling where the truth begins."

"Emma, I would give anything in my power to rectify this injustice." He soothed his hands down her arms, as if to stop her sudden retreat. "Please don't ask me to assist you in leaving." He studied her beneath shuddered lids. "I don't want you to go."

"Then ask me to stay," she whispered, searching his face for answers.

"Have I not done that very thing?" Frustration tinged his voice. "What more can you expect of me?"

Tell me you love me, she silently begged. Give me the only kind of protection a woman has against a sullied reputation. Give me a ring and a vow.

He studied her a moment more, his gaze flickering over her features as if to seal them in his memory. His mouth opened as if he had more to say. Yet nothing issued forth. He turned abruptly away, and in doing so, turned away from all they had shared the past five months, all the intimacies and past histories, all the unburied emotions and discoveries. He turned away.

"I see," she said quietly while her heart screamed in the void of her chest. Numb, she stepped back, then dipped in an expedient curtsy. "Thank you for your time, Lord Nicholas Chambers. Good day to you, sir."

Her eyes burned; a sob twisted in her throat. But she refused to cry in front of him. A proper lady had to have some pride, even when her heart had been torn asunder. She turned toward the door and hurried toward the manor's entrance.

"Emma, wait!" His voice trailed behind her, but she continued to her waiting rig. She untied the reins, stepped up to the wooden seat, and urged the horse forward.

"Emma!"

She refused to look back. Her heart lodged in her throat, pulling forth great, shaking sobs. The horse attempted to twist his head, as if he didn't understand the direction her quivering arms dictated. Indeed, she was unsure herself. Tears blurred her vision. Once she had pulled beyond sight of Black Oak, she reined in the horse to a stop.

Tears flowed freely beneath the hands raised to her face. Was it any wonder he wished for things to continue as they were? She had allowed liberties, admitted emotions that a proper lady would have kept hidden. She was unsuitable to be more than a convenient distraction. Unsuitable!

She fished for her handkerchief and dabbed at her eyes. She would have to leave on her own, away from Black Oak and its painful memories and away from Pettibone and its fond ones. A fresh sob shook her shoulders. She pushed the handkerchief to her mouth to muffle the sound.

Dear heavens, she could taste his scent on the linen. Instantly, his face appeared in her mind, sympathetic and compassionate. In one quick motion, she clenched the linen into a ball and tossed it to the narrow stone wall that bordered the road. Where she was going, she wanted no more remembrances of Lord Nicholas Chambers.

A moist wind, rich with the promise of spring and changing weather pushed at her face. Though tempted to remain on the road through the pending rain as a way to explain her distressed appearance, she decided against it. Poor health due to a sudden chill could delay her departure

from Pettibone. Better to return quickly so as to quickly
leave in turn. She swiped the tears from her cheeks with
the hem of her skirt before setting the horse to motion
again. Barely able to control her own life, she was in no
shape to direct a horse. Hopefully the fellow would trot his
way home and drag the rig behind.

"MRS. BRIMLEY," CECILIA GREETED HER BEFORE SHE
could disembark from the rig. "I'm so glad you're back. I
need your advice on some correspondence I received from
an applicant."

Emma tilted her head in the hopes that the brim of her
hat would hide the proof of her tears, but Cecilia clasped
her arm as she approached and faced her directly. Cecilia
squinted.

"You've been crying. You saw the younger brother,
didn't you?" she accused. "I knew that man was no good.
What did he do?"

"Nothing. He did nothing," she said flatly, pushing her
way past Cecilia. "May we continue the discussion of your
recent correspondence a bit later? I'd like to go to my room
for a few moments, and—"

"One would suppose that the man would be more man-
nerly with his refined older brother in residence," Cecilia
grumbled following behind.

Emma stopped, a defense of Nicholas poised on the tip
of her tongue. Her gaze snapped to Cecilia, but she didn't
speak. What was the point? Any words of rebuttal would
soon be forgotten in lieu of condemnation of her own behavior. She continued to the front door.

"Mrs. Brimley." Fanny waited just inside. "Charlotte
shouldn't be allowed to have a cat. The vicious beast just
destroyed the lacework on my best petticoat. I demand
something be done about it."

The refuge of her room appeared more distant with each step Emma took toward it. With one hand on the staircase newel, Emma directed Fanny to take the ruined petticoat to Beatrice for repair.

"But the cat—" Fanny whined.

"I'll talk to Charlotte. Now go," Emma snapped.

"Mrs. Brimley?" Hannah called from the top of the stairs. "What color ribbon goes best with my complexion?"

"The blue," Emma responded with barely a glance. If she could just gain the stairs without any more interruptions, she could—

"Mrs. Brimley?" She heard Cook call in the hallway below. Emma quickly rounded the top of the stairs and hurried the last few steps to her room.

IN FIVE SHORT MONTHS, SHE HAD EVOLVED FROM someone whispered about in the hallways to something of the resident authority. The success of the ball, Lady Cavendish's visit, and the Marquess's apparent interest elevated her in the esteem of the school. Even Cecilia gave her the occasional nod of approval and respect.

Her heart tugged deep in the chest. Just when she had earned their respect, she would lose it all as soon as they learned the truth. She couldn't stay to watch. Her eyelids burned for want of tears; she had cried them all out by the stone wall. She pulled her old valise from under the bed, just as the threatening cloudburst erupted outside.

Without Nicholas's financial help, she would have to leave with just the essentials she could carry. Her jewelry might be bartered for passage for somewhere far from Pettibone. She emptied her drawers, spreading her entire wardrobe out on her bed. The last time she had done this, she had donned all these garments to confront Nicholas. A fluttering in her chest reminded her of the outcome of that adventure. No, she chastised herself, she wouldn't think of him. She wouldn't remember the concern in his eyes, or the power of his grip as he held her to the mattress, or the desire to feel the caress of his lips while at his mercy.

A rumble of thunder brought her back to the task at hand. Even if the temperature weren't too warm to accommodate all those garments, her figure had expanded after sharing too many teas at Black Oak. She could never fit all those clothes onto her frame.

"Mrs. Brimley, what are you doing?"

Emma glanced up. Alice watched from the doorway. "You're going away, aren't you?" Her lip trembled.

Emma sat on the bed, crushing her mother's black crepe. "I don't expect you to understand, but circumstances have forced me to—"

"Take me with you," Alice said. "It won't take me long to pack. Just let me say good-bye to Charlotte and I'll be ready."

Emma's heart twisted. "I can't take you with me, Alice, as much as I want to. I don't know where I'm going, so it wouldn't be responsible of me—"

"I don't care about responsible." Alice rushed in the room and clasped Emma's hands. "I don't want to be alone again. You and I are family. You said so. I won't let you leave without me. I won't." A tear carved a track down the young woman's cheek. Emma brushed it away with the tip of her finger.

"Why do you have to go?" Alice cried. "Is it something I've done? Did Miss Higgins find out that I put Charlotte's kitten in Fanny's room on purpose?"

Emma smiled, pulling the girl's head onto her shoulder. "It has nothing to do with the kitten, or with you." She stroked the girl's back, soothing away her tears.

"Then why do you have to leave?" Alice looked up at

her with puffy eyes. "Everything has changed since you've been here. If you leave, it will all go back to the way it was. Please stay. Don't leave us."

Was that true? Two days ago, Emma had complimented herself on how much she'd changed since arriving at Pettibone. Had the school changed as well? She hugged Alice, gently rocking her forward and back. Things were different now. Someone wanted her, needed her. How could she turn her back on the Higgins sisters or their brood of young girls without explanation?

The old Emma would have run away, but maybe this new Emma could find another solution. The thought took root and strengthened. Perhaps Nicholas was right. She knew him to be an intelligent man. Maybe life could go on just as it had. Not those modeling sessions, those would have to end. But if the painting were concealed, and the Marquess of Enon returned to London without revealing her secrets, maybe she could stay and continue teaching.

"You are wise beyond your years, Alice," Emma said, watching hope blossom on the young girl's face. "I suppose there's no real reason to leave. The sisters don't know that I had thought of running away. Can we keep this a secret between us?"

"Do you promise?" Alice asked. "If you change your mind, do you promise to take me with you?"

"I don't know if I can promise that." Emma pursed her lips. "But I promise that if I change my mind, I'll tell you about it first. No more surprises."

"No more surprises," Alice repeated, then broke into a wide smile. "I'm glad you're staying because I wanted to ask you about a note I received from a boy."

"One of the boys at the dance?" Emma began to fold the garments she had laid out to pack.

Alice nodded, and handed the folded garments to Emma to put away. "I couldn't tell Charlotte about it because she might be jealous. I need another woman's perspective."

Emma smiled, shelving her plans to run away along with fantasies of a life beyond Pettibone. This was where she was most happy, and this was where she would stay.

LATER THAT EVENING, EMMA WRAPPED A SHAWL TIGHTLY about her shoulders, contemplating how one small decision could affect one's entire outlook on life. She told the sisters that she was going for a walk, the fresh air would help to clear her mind. After all the demands and excitement of the preceding week, they agreed. So she privately reassured Alice that she would stay on school grounds, and slipped outside into the cool welcoming air.

After the sudden midday storm, the sky had cleared and slanting rays of fading sunlight lent an enchanted quality to the atmosphere. Emma couldn't remember London ever looking this beautiful, nor were its gentle breezes ever this sweet. Now that she had resolved that Pettibone would be her home, everything glowed in a magical shimmer.

Deep in pleasant reverie of this phenomenon, she failed to note the dull thud of a horse's hooves fast approaching. As soon as she felt the ground tremble beneath her feet, she turned to see who galloped so urgently across school grounds. However, a man's arm reached down and swept her off the ground and onto his horse.

Only one man would steal her in such a fashion. Her uncle!

· Eighteen ·

TRAPPED IN HIS FIRM GRIP, EMMA THRASHED AND struggled; her very life depended upon it. Her spectacles dislodged and teetered awkwardly on the tip of her nose, but she didn't need sharp sight to pull at the arm wrapped tightly about her waist or punch at the damp thigh at her side.

"Emma, stop it or I'm liable to drop you."

"Nicholas?" she gasped. Instantly, she stilled her kicks and jabs, squinting instead at her capturer's clenched jaw. Although her fear fled at the sound of his voice, her heart still beat a fierce rhythm, leaving her breathless. "What are you doing?"

"I told you I wouldn't let you go." The firm muscles of his legs shifted and the horse slowed, but his iron grip around her waist kept her bottom firmly planted between his thighs. "I knew you were determined to run away and that you'd try on your own if necessary. I've been watching and waiting for your attempt."

Her mouth dropped open. "I was not running away."

"What?" He pulled on the reins, slowing the horse to a walk. "I thought most definitely . . ."

From her close proximity she watched his eyes narrow. "Bloody hell, woman, you looked the part."

"I was out for a walk," she protested, stiffening her spine. If one's looks purported to have meaning, one might conclude that Nicholas was the one in flight. Green leaves clung to his disheveled brown superfine; the folds of his cravat hung limp and shoddy. A man could ride to Scotland and back and appear less bedraggled than the one who scooped her from the path.

"I meant that you looked determined this morning when you proposed that ridiculous scheme," he said with irritation. "You've run before when in a stew. I thought you'd run again."

She averted her gaze. "I was convinced otherwise." She saw no reason to explain that he was not the one who had convinced her. "I have decided to rely on your promise that my reputation will remain unblemished as a result of that painting."

"So it shall." His jaw set in defiance of argument a moment before he loosened his hold on her waist. She remained trapped between his arms, causing a delicious heat to spread through her veins. A subtle pressure on her backside suggested he was similarly affected. The horse ambled to the path separating the two manor houses.

"Where are we going?" she asked, aware of the increasing distance from Pettibone.

"It appears Lord Byron has decided to return home." He glanced down at her briefly from beneath shuttered lids.

"Lord Byron is your horse?"

"Why not? A horse is as fluent and balanced as a well-written poem." His lips softened from their previous tight line, bringing a slight smile to hers. How could she have ever thought to leave this man? Who else would have the temerity to compare a horse and Lord Byron?

"Both the man and beast are known for their gallantry," he continued. "Lord Byron, the horse, has certainly visited as many taverns as the revered poet."

"Have you forgotten that Pettibone is in the opposite direction?" Emma glanced uneasily at the passing greenery. She suspected she had already broken her promise to Alice.

"I haven't, but Lord Byron has pressing concerns."

"Those concerns being?"

"A bag of oats, a comfortable stall, fresh hay . . ." Nicholas's brow lifted. "Did I mention that Lord Byron and I have waited for your flight from Pettibone since you left Black Oak?"

"Even in the rain?"

His lips thinned, but his attire answered her query. All the while she had assumed he felt she was beneath his concern, he was waiting in the wind and rain to stop her flight.

"We found a bit of shelter under a tree." The forced lightness in his voice made her suspect otherwise. Her heart expanded. No one had ever sacrificed personal comfort on her behalf.

"Is there a Keats or Marlowe in the stables waiting to take me back to the school?" She forced the question around the constriction in her throat.

He frowned down at her. "I will see you safely back, provided you promise you will stay at Pettibone and you won't suddenly disappear over some foreign border."

"I promise." Twice in one evening, she had made the same promise. That two people cared so much about her to demand her oath filled her heart to overflowing. She could give her oath freely, she would never leave.

They dismounted just outside the stable. Nicholas tended to his horse while Emma admired his smooth efficient motions. She hadn't thought of Nicholas's capabilities beyond his artistic talents. He obviously knew his way around horseflesh as well, even with the disadvantage of a slight limp. He was a man of surprises. "I rather expected someone would tend to your horses for you."

"Henry does, when needed. He's not here today, though. I sent him off to tend to his wife."

"I'm afraid the preparations for the ball took a toll on Cook," Emma said. Thoughts of the dance brought to mind another question. She glanced up, uncertain. "You sent me the daisies, did you not?" His dimple deepened, granting an answer.

"You shouldn't have done that," she lightly scolded. "Miss Higgins thought they were meant for one of the girls."

"But you and I know better." His low seductive voice slammed into her heart, tingled down her spine and set her nerve endings vibrating. Nicholas finished his tasks and closed the half door to the stall. "Come with me, Emma. I want to show you something."

His hand grasped hers with firm determination, leading her to a back stall, the same one she had visited with Alice the night they had searched for Charlotte. A lantern hung from the rafters casting a yellow flickering light over the straw bedding.

"What is it? A new batch of kittens?" She looked around the empty stall, but saw nothing out of the ordinary. "The one you gave Charlotte is causing some mischief at the school."

He closed the door, then leaned against it, barring exit. "Ask me a question, Emma," he commanded, low and masterful.

"What do you mean?" She stumbled backward a bit, desire flooding her senses. "What kind of question?"

His eyelids lowered. "You know what kind of question. Ask me."

She tried to think. Dear Father in heaven, she tried. But all her thoughts riveted on the rich timbre of his voice, the building passion in his eyes, and the increasing bulge at the juncture of his thighs. Her nipples instinctively tightened to hard buds that scraped the washing silk shielding them. Moisture dampened her thighs. He stood in arm's reach, broad, hard, and demanding. Her voice took a husky note. "What if I already know all I need for the girls?"

"You don't." He kissed the side of her neck just under her earlobe, sending vibrations down to her curling toes. "But if you can't think of a question, I'll ask one of you and you can undress me."

Her one glimpse of his broad expanse of chest had haunted her for many sleepless nights. The little moisture remaining in her throat evaporated at the thought that she might experience such a sight again.

"What if someone sees us? You have houseguests, do you not?" The touch of his lips a bit lower on her neck pushed spasms of tingling sensation throughout her shoulder and chest. She tilted her head to give him greater access.

He smiled. "That's two questions." He shrugged off his coat, then his cravat, tossing all into a corner. "My houseguests can entertain themselves. I told them earlier that I'd be out for the day. No one will come out to the stables this late."

Nicholas pulled her shawl, letting it slide smoothly across her shoulders before he rolled the wool into a ball and placed it on a bale of hay. A chill slipped down her back, though she certainly was not cold, quite the opposite.

"Ask me another," he whispered, turning his attention to the row of buttons on her blouse.

Her mind melted to mush, liquefied by the intensity of his gaze on her chest. His fingers deftly revealed skin and bits of the ribbon and lace on her chemise and corset. Her breath quickened. "What are your intentions?"

"Right now?" His brow lifted in time with the corner of his mouth. She nodded, her throat too dry for words.

"My intentions are for you to receive a different kind of flower in the future, one that does not denote innocence." He pulled the bottom of her blouse from her skirt, then slipped the sleeves off her shoulders, catching at her elbows. Using the pleated muslin as one might use a rope, he pulled her close till her breasts pressed firmly against his chest. "Now, I have a question for you." His voice swirled in her ear, rich and seductive. "Which of these kisses do you enjoy the most?"

His lips descended moist and demanding. She opened wide for him, wanting him deeper, closer. Her arms slid around his waist then up his broad shoulders, holding on as her legs dissolved to jelly. All of her intended resistance, all of her supposed control, evaporated in the heat of his kiss. Their tongues mated, allowing her to enjoy the hard, firm press of him. His hardness pressed other places as well. The jut of him pushed into her fig leaf apron, moisture pooling between her thighs.

Much too soon, he pulled back, allowing a few inches of heated air between them. She struggled for breath, feeling the pinch of constricting whalebone. His gaze slipped to the top of her corset, where her chest rose and fell with her labored breathing.

"Where's the pink?" he rasped, surprising her that he was similarly afflicted by lack of breath. Before she could answer, his fingers teased the white satin, enticing her nipples to tighten and push at the restraining lace. Other parts of her body answered his call as well, eliciting ripples of anticipation and desire. He bent down and kissed the birthmark on the rise of her breast. Two moist lips barely cooled the heated flesh beneath. She wanted more. Where once she clung to the fabric barriers between his gaze and her body, now she cursed the impediments denying her release.

"I have to choose between those two kisses?" she asked, struggling to keep her voice from shaking.

"Between these three." He knelt, lifting her skirts to reveal the narrow band of skin between her stocking and drawers. One hand reached under the lace of the drawers, reaching to the top of her leg, while he kissed the sensitive skin on the inside of her thigh. Her knees shook. His gentle tug on her hips brought her down to the yielding hay.

He extricated himself from her billowing skirts. "Well?" he asked, breathless.

"I enjoyed all three," she said, reaching for the buttons on his trousers.

He laughed. "I thought you wanted to deprive me of my shirt. You tugged it free from the waist when we kissed."

She hadn't realized that, but no matter. She shook her head. "I want to see your manhood," she said, ignoring the warning bells sounding in her head. If she were to remain at Pettibone, she must remain as a widow. Innocence was not expected of her, and at this moment, no longer desired. Her hand stroked the length of his protrusion. "I want to see flesh and blood, not a drawing or a painting."

"Then you shall." In short order he tugged free of his trousers and drawers. His man's flesh rose in a slant from a nest of thick coarse black hair. Although his drawing had proved factual, his reality manifested much thicker and longer than she had anticipated. Her breath caught. It stretched toward her as if it had a mind of its own.

"May I touch it?" she asked, enthralled at the way it stretched and pulsated.

"You know the price." His eyes smoldered with passion, daring her to take the lead.

Holding his gaze with her own, she stood before him, then unfastened her skirts, letting them fall to the stable floor at his knees. She stepped out of the pile of petticoats and fabric, then bending low so her breasts would dangle free of their satin support, she moved the clothing aside. Emma approached Nicholas with reverence, much as she imagined Artemis would have done. She knelt beside him, then carefully wrapped her hand around his shaft to measure his thickness with her thumb and forefinger. His heated flesh moved rhythmically against her hand. She stroked its length, marveling at the velvety smoothness of the reddening head.

"If you teach your girls to handle their men like that, they should have no difficulty arousing them for the purpose at hand." His voice sounded strained, giving her a perverse form of pleasure. She tightened her grip. He gasped.

"Did I hurt you?" She let go, afraid her experiment had been too brutal.

"Only with pleasure, my sweet." He led her hand back to his shaft. "Examine me as you will."

She relaxed, using her other hand to explore the various textures of his skin. "What is this drop of moisture at the very tip? Is that your seed? I had thought there would be more."

"There will be more if you keep studying me so thoroughly." His eyes narrowed to mere slits. His breathing turned shallow.

Emma slipped the drop of moisture onto her finger and raised it to her lips.

"Oh God, Emma," he groaned. "Who taught you to do that?"

She sucked the tip of her finger, sampling the salty taste of his seed. Did all men taste this way? Or just the extraordinarily talented ones? She smiled down at Nicholas, who writhed in apparent discomfort. "All in the pursuit of knowledge, my lord."

"Again," he demanded, but she shook her head.

"You've answered my question and deserve your forfeit." She stood, planting her feet on either side of his knees, then released her stockings from the corset's garters. Arching her back, she reached behind to unfasten her corset.

"Let me," he offered, but she shook her head.

"Don't touch," she whispered. "I wish to do this for you." She loosened the back lacing until she could pull both the whale and underlying chemise free overhead. She tossed them on the growing pile of clothes.

Nicholas appeared mesmerized by the sway of her bosom once freed of the constricting cloth. She bent forward to roll her stockings. Her nipples strained toward his chest.

"My God, you are beautiful," he said, awe evident in his voice. "Is there any wonder that my best work is of you?"

His tone, his words, and his gaze exorcized her uncle's insidious whispers. An artist could recognize beauty, and never had she felt more beautiful. Nicholas reached for her breast, and she leaned into his grasp, letting her fullness fill his palm. He paid homage to her by touch and tongue, before slowly drawing her down to the hay.

"I want you to feel my manhood inside of you," he said with difficulty. "But only if you wish it as well. There's no turning back, Emma."

"Yes," she said. Already anticipation exploded through her body. No matter what else may happen, if she were to be a spinster like Cecilia or Beatrice, she would have this moment, this knowledge, this experience to carry the rest of her life.

He removed her drawers. For the first time, she lay totally exposed to his eyes. A brief moment of apprehension melted in his smoldering gaze. He began as before, massaging her feminine core with his fingers. She wanted his words. He had always patiently explained what was happening before. However, her throat, as dry as the scattered straw around them, couldn't utter a plea. All her body moisture gathered between her legs, proclaiming both need and desire. He guided his shaft to her waiting sheath. She stiffened.

"Relax, my dear Emma," he whispered, easing his body down till he covered every inch of her. Never had anyone touched her so thoroughly, so intimately. She rejoiced in his nearness, accepting his weight. His lips grazed on hers, then he pressed his man's flesh to her wetness, just as he had in her hand, once, twice, then . . .

"Oh!" His mouth captured her cry of pain, far more than the pinprick she had hoped for. Nicholas held still, waiting for her body to accommodate him, before pressing on. Her hips discovered his rhythm and parried, in effect pulling him deeper. An internal pulsing ebbed and flowed with each of his thrusts, as if some lofty goal beckoned just out of reach. Just as she strained to reach it, a great tension shattered in rippling waves of pleasure.

He pulled on her shoulders forcing his way up to her womb. A moment later, he arched, forcing a guttural sound between his lips, while Emma lay triumphant beneath, accepting all he had to give.

His body sagged heavily upon her, while a part of him remained inside. Such an astonishing sensation, as if a part of his talent, compassion, and determination all lingered inside her, mingling with her own body's juices. Her breasts nestled in the hair of his chest, his hips pressed into hers. His heartbeat pounded fast and solid in her ear. Such an ancient posture listening to another's life force. Never had she felt so new, so alive, so purposeful.

Purposeful? Yes, she decided. There was the purpose of

need, *her* need to give of herself to this man. Their interlocking bodies felt both correct and absolutely necessary.

"Why are you smiling?" he rasped in between gasps for air.

"You can't see me." She hadn't realized that she was, but then with so much joy and love inside, how could she not? His shoulder hovered a fraction from her nose. "How do you know I'm smiling?"

"I can feel it," he said. "I can feel every movement of your luscious body as if it were my own."

She delighted in the vibration of his words rumbling through his chest. Her fingers idly danced across the bare skin of his back. Bathed in his heat and attention, she could lay here forever, even with the bits of hay and straw stabbing her in unusual places.

"I should get you back to Pettibone before a horde of females come looking for you," he said, though his only movement was to kiss the top of her head.

"Yes," she reluctantly agreed, more concerned with one young female in particular. One to whom she had made a promise. Nicholas shifted his weight, and Emma released him, instantly mourning his loss.

He stood above her like a Greek god, one carved from veined marble. Perhaps if he would model for her, she would complete those painting projects he teased her about.

"The next time, Emma," he said, smiling down at her prone body, "I promise we'll make use of a proper bed." He offered his arm and helped her to her feet. "Unfortunately, with houseguests—"

"The next time?" She smiled, pulling a shaft of straw from his hair. She hadn't considered beyond this evening. "Doesn't this complete my education?"

He laughed. "Emma, my love, it's just begun."

My love. The words rippled through her brain, making

her giddy. He had known her in the most intimate way conceivable, yet he still loved her! The thought expanded inside her while she dressed, making her feel featherlight and bright as the sun. In her current condition, she could easily have held her shawl aloft and floated back to Pettibone. Nicholas, however, completed dressing and readied a horse for a more conservative approach.

After he had mounted the chestnut mare, he reached for her waist and swung her up into his lap. All her petticoats couldn't protect her from the stab of pain on her sensitive bottom. She almost jumped off the horse, but Nicholas held her in place.

"I know it must hurt." He jiggled the reins and set the horse in motion before kissing her cheek. "But it will pass. Do you remember when we talked about the ways to alleviate the pain of the first time?"

Already, the ache was receding. Emma leaned lightly against Nicholas's chest, adjusting to the sway of the horse's easy walk.

"I remember," she answered, thinking less of his actual advice than the incident that had preceded the conversation. He had undressed her and held her to the bed. What a fool she was to have been frightened. Nicholas wouldn't have hurt her. Remembering how his gaze had appeared fixated on the rise and fall of her pink corset, she felt a low tingling building once more in her feminine core. Perhaps they could try that scenario again, only this time—

"You're so quiet," he said, brushing his lips across her forehead. "Have I displeased you?"

She heard the catch in his voice. "No," she hastened to reassure him. "I am not disappointed. I was just . . . thinking."

He nodded his head. "I expected as much." He shifted in the saddle. "Emma, if our coupling brings forth issue . . ."

"Issue?" A shiver of dread sliced through her soft fantasies of attachment with Nicholas. She jerked upright.

"A child, Emma," he soothed, trying to nudge her back into her former position. "There are precautions one can take. We'll talk more about them the next time we meet. But if our coupling has resulted in a child, I wish to reassure you that I will not desert you as your father did your mother."

A coldness settled in the pit of her stomach. What had she done? She knew the consequences that befell a woman carrying a child out of wedlock. Had she not lived those very consequences? Why had she not considered the possibility she could conceive a child earlier?

"I'm a commoner," she whispered, already feeling a rift in their magical experience. "A lady bred, perhaps, but I'm still—"

"There's nothing common about you, Emma." His chin nuzzled the side of her face. "I will hold you to your promise." His voice carried a warning tone. "No more running. You will stay at Pettibone."

But if indeed she carried Nicholas's seed in her womb, how long before the sisters at Pettibone forced her to leave?

The horse stepped free of the woods. Through the fog that gathered at this lowest point, she could see the looming structure of Pettibone at the top of a gentle slope.

"Emma, look at me," Nicholas commanded with a sense of urgency.

She tilted her head up and his lips crashed down upon hers. His tongue filled her in remembrance of an earlier shared intimate posture. Her hands slipped around his waist, needing to feel the protective wall of his chest. He groaned in response before pulling back and resting his forehead on hers.

"Promise me, Emma. You won't leave."

In that moment, she knew without question that
Nicholas would protect her and her child if need be. He
would never hurt her. He loved her. *Just not enough to
marry,* an internal voice whispered.

"I promise," she replied, trusting in his protection of her
future. "But I should dismount here, while the fog covers
your presence."

After another quick embrace, he lowered her carefully
to the ground. She gathered her skirts and started up the
hill, feeling the heat of his gaze measuring her progress.

· Nineteen ·

NICHOLAS COULD BARELY FOCUS ON PREPARING his Academy submission for transport to London. Barely two hours had passed since he had returned her to Pettibone and already he missed the soft press of her sweet body, his flesh-and-blood goddess sent to earth. His gaze slipped to Emma's compassionate smile in his completed portrait. She had accepted his passion without demand or complaint. She had accepted him as an artist, not as a connection to peerage, nor as a means to an unlimited supply of Worth gowns. She brought out the best of him as an artist, as a man, and as a . . . father?

His fingers fumbled the nail that he had positioned on the wooden transportation crate. Was it possible that Emma could even now carry his heir? That thought, as distasteful as it may have been with other women, felt somehow right with Emma. A smile pulled at his lips. He could imagine Emma with a swollen belly. Fumbling on the floor for the dropped nail, he imagined her reading long passages of Wordsworth and Coleridge to their unborn child, and he'd paint her every expression. A deep warmth crept up from his soul. He repositioned the nail and tapped it with his hammer. She would be a loving mother, just like his own, and he'd be a . . . A vision of his own father slipped into his mind.

The hammer missed its mark and caught Nicholas's thumb. "Bloody hell!" He slipped the sore finger between his lips. The action reminded him of Emma sucking ever so sweetly on his seed that she'd collected on her fingers. His manhood stirred and his lips lifted in a smile.

"Look at you." William strode into the studio, his eyes widened in astonishment. "There you sit with a finger in your mouth, grinning like a half-wit. Is this delirium due to the advent of our departure, or a result of your earlier activities in town?" He lifted a brow. "You were plying your talents in the local tavern this day, were you not?"

Nicholas simply smiled and finished pounding the nail home. Best let his brother imagine what he may. In truth, he hadn't visited that tavern in months. Not since he had found his Artemis.

"I thought as much," William said, a knowing tilt to his lips. "And I must say I'm pleased to see you back to your old self."

Nicholas lifted a landscape fitted in a gilded ornamental frame off the easel, then held it up for his brother's viewing. "Do you think this will be accepted in the exhibition?"

The smile froze on William's face. His eyes narrowed slightly, and his words slowed as if carefully chosen. "You plan to enter two paintings, then?"

"This is the only painting I'm sending to the competition."

"Surely, you jest!" William scowled, pointing to the

similarly sized, framed painting leaning at the easel's feet. "*Artemis's Revenge* outshines that landscape in depth and substance, as well as in pure artistry and emotion. You can't seriously intend to submit that, that . . . sheep pasture in its place."

Nicholas looked with mock horror at the landscape in his hands. "Do you really think it is that bad? I rather thought the inclusion of some of the Pettibone students made an interesting contrast to the rural scene."

Indeed, he had no doubt *Artemis's Revenge* would have secured a place of honor in the juried exhibition, but that was no longer his concern. Emma had already secured a similar placement in his heart. *Artemis's Revenge* would serve as a private reminder of the levels to which he was capable. There would be another year, and another painting opportunity for Academy recognition.

"Are you sure, brother?" William dropped his outrage for a confidential inflection. "*Artemis* would win the respect you've struggled years for. *She* wouldn't need to know."

"I would know and that's enough." Nicholas hoped his tone conveyed the end of that discussion. "I've made my decision, William. Let it stand."

Nicholas slipped the framed landscape carefully in the crate, then hammered home the carefully placed wooden lid. "There," he said once the task was completed. "It is all ready to be loaded in the morning."

William shook his head in disagreement but didn't say another word.

As an afterthought, Nicholas draped a gray cloth over the framed *Artemis's Revenge* destined to stay in his studio. As long as guests tarried at his house, his masterpiece had best remain covered. Emma would never forgive him if Lady Cavendish viewed the painting.

Once *Artemis's Revenge* was properly draped, he

wrapped his arm around his brother's shoulder. "Let's adjourn for a nightcap. My work here is finished."

NICHOLAS GREETED THE DAWN WITH AN ENTHUSIASM not often displayed at this ungodly hour. His brother and Lady Cavendish were leaving. The household fairly hummed with the bustling necessary to pack up the guests and send them speedily on their way. Nicholas located William in the dining room finishing his breakfast.

"What is that awful smell?" William asked, wrinkling his aristocratic nose. "It smells like burnt cork."

"Coffee," Nicholas replied, immediately drawn to the special pot Thomas had left on the sideboard. "It clears the mind, energizes the spirit." He wafted his hands over the pot, pretending to inhale a magic elixir.

"It chased Lady Cavendish from the room. She thought she'd suffer an apoplexy and dashed away with linen covering her nose." William turned to regard Nicholas over his shoulder. "I seem to recall that you usually indulge in another type of spirit in the morning."

Nicholas poured his dark brew into a cup. "I am a reformed man, William. Emma has taught me the need to keep my wits about me, even at this abominable hour."

William harrumphed, then patted his mouth with a napkin. "Lady Cavendish wishes to make her farewells. I didn't think it wise for her to traipse back to the studio looking for you. I suggested she wait in the salon."

"Thank you, William. That was most considerate." And surprising, given his brother's sentiments last night. Perhaps he was learning to respect his little brother's opinions. Nicholas smiled. By acknowledging the talent behind *Artemis's Revenge*, William appeared ready to forge a new relationship with Nicholas, one based on mutual respect.

William waved him toward the door. "Go on. I'll see that the crate is properly loaded on the carriage."

"Thank you." Genuine affection for his brother's improved attitude warmed his heart. For an instant, he wished William would delay his departure so they could discover more common ground. But Lady Cavendish waited, and he didn't want to delay *her* departure by a single minute. Her constant questions went beyond idle curiosity to barely tolerated nuisance.

"Where that woman finds the energy at this unnatural hour is a mystery to me," Nicholas said, sipping from his cup. "I don't envy you the trip back to London. I'll be back to bed five minutes after you leave."

And scheming to lure Emma back to Black Oak, he mentally added. Now that his houseguests were leaving, he could instruct her in all the various coupling positions without interruptions.

"While you lay in your bed," William intoned, "I'll be listening to the lady's endless chatter. I'm hoping she'll talk herself into a nap so my ears can rest." William waved him out of the room. "Go along now. Allow me to postpone the inevitable prattle as long as necessary."

Nicholas repaired to the salon to smile and nod at all the woman's continuous observations and lamentations. His brother's eventual arrival brought not only relief but also pity for poor William. Together they all walked out in the early dawn, where the horses steamed in anticipation of the long journey south.

After William and Lady Cavendish were settled, his brother called from the window. "Come visit us soon in London, Nicholas. You know Father would be delighted."

Nicholas offered his obligatory curt nod and waved them off. He walked through the house, hesitating at the door to his studio. The crate was gone; the draped painting leaned against the empty easel. Later he would determine the proper location for *Artemis's Revenge*, then he would return to block out a new painting. He had already chosen the title: *Seduction*.

HOURS LATER, THOMAS PULLED BACK THE HEAVY VEL-vet drapes, flooding the bedroom room with rich afternoon sun.

"They didn't come back, did they?" Nicholas asked in a sleep-laden voice. "I only closed my eyes a few minutes ago. What did Lady Cavendish forget?"

"No, sir, they are gone," Thomas replied with a satisfied air. "Black Oak is once more a haven of peace and soli-tude."

"Long overdue," Nicholas muttered into his pillow.

"You asked last night to roust you at this hour, just in case you were inclined to sleep overly long." He walked briskly to the hall and returned with a tray.

"That's right, I recall." Nicholas rubbed sleep from his eyes. "Thomas, there should be a covered painting in my studio. Could you bring it to me, please? I'm debating the best spot for it here in my room."

"Very good, sir. I shall return in a moment."

Nicholas busied himself with his morning rituals. Now that William and that Cavendish woman had departed, he could work on his art without secrecy or avoidance. He would also be able to teach Emma the pleasures to be had in a proper bed. That thought chased the sleep-induced cobwebs from his brain. Just knowing the delights that awaited him made rising a pleasant task indeed.

He counted back to the last time Emma had arrived for a lesson, frowning to discover that she wasn't due for one today. At least not a scheduled lesson, he reminded him-self. All he needed was some excuse to lure her to Black Oak, some reason . . .

"Is this the painting to which you referred, sir?" Thomas asked, struggling with a large, drape-covered rectangle. His nose poked over the top of the frame, while his white-knuckled fingers grasped the two sides.

"Yes, that's it." Nicholas walked to the wall across from his bed. From this position, he'd be able to see his Emma first thing in the morning, and the last thing at night. "Careful, now," he said. "Bring it over here. Gently, gently . . ."

Once directed to the proper spot, Thomas lowered the painting to rest on the floor. Nicholas yearned to rip the covering off his masterpiece but felt a small measure of caution might be prudent. He glanced over to Thomas, who rapidly shook his hands attempting to hasten circulation back to his fingers. A warm gratitude slipped through Nicholas. "Thank you, Thomas," he said. "I'd be lost without you."

"My pleasure, sir." Thomas nodded crisply.

"Now then." Nicholas turned his attentions back to the draped canvas. "I realize this is not necessary, but before I undrape this painting, I need to have your vow never to share the subject matter of this painting with anyone. It's to remain a secret from all outside the household."

"Of course, sir," Thomas replied. "You have my word and that of the rest of the staff." He paused, biting his lower lip for the briefest of seconds. "I am surprised, however, you feel the need to ask."

Nicholas smiled. "You'll understand when I remove this drape."

With a quick jerk, Nicholas whipped the covering free in one deft movement. He gathered the stiff white fabric into a ball and tossed it aside. Pride in his work filled his heart to bursting. He glanced first at Thomas, surprised to see his lack of reaction. Then he glanced down to where his latest Yorkshire landscape sat amid the dancing dust motes.

Shock rendered him motionless. A faintness caused no doubt by blood rushing from his brain tingled about his temples. What had happened to *Artemis*?

"Well, sir," Thomas said, tightly, "I can see why you'd want no one else to view this painting."

"He switched it!" Nicholas said as realization dawned. "Bloody hell, my brother switched the painting!"

Barefoot and without the assistance of his stick, Nicholas rushed from the bedroom down to his studio, Thomas close on his heels. Hopefully, William had merely hidden *Artemis's Revenge* as a parting jest. Nicholas rummaged through the many clean and partially painted canvases to no avail. The truth settled like five-stone lead on his heart. He sunk onto his stool with a groan. "He doesn't know the damage he's done."

"Beg pardon, sir, but is there anything I can do to help the situation?" Thomas asked.

"The only thing that will help is to retrieve that painting before it goes on display." Nicholas sunk his head into his hands. The day had begun with such promise, but now . . .

"He's got a seven-hour lead." He glanced up at Thomas. "Does the train leave for London this late?"

"Only arrivals come this late, sir, but there should be a departing train in the morning."

"I don't think I can wait that long," Nicholas said. "I'm not sure that I can catch him before London, but I might be able to intercept him before he submits *Artemis's Revenge* to the jury." He slapped his thigh. "Have Henry prepare Lord Byron. There's no time to waste."

"Yes, my lord." Thomas turned to leave.

"Thomas, one more thing." Nicholas paused, already feeling guilty over his next request. "Mrs. Brimley is not to know that *Artemis's Revenge* is en route to London. I intend to retrieve the painting before any harm is done."

"What if she should inquire, my lord?" Thomas asked.

Guilt stabbed at Nicholas's heart, but he saw no other option. "Lie."

BY AFTERNOON, EMMA REMAINED A BIT SORE FROM yesterday's "lesson," but otherwise was in high spirits. She supposed she should feel differently, *used* perhaps, or maybe *violated*, and most certainly *ruined*. Unless those words meant floating through the day with little thought other than the exact color of Nicholas's eyes or the precise way his lips turned when he smiled, she felt none of the things society suggested she should.

By her defiance of the major tenet of *The Ladies' Guide to Proper Etiquette*, the tenet in very large bold print, she had joined the ranks of womanhood. Was this how her mother had felt? So much in love with her young man that society's rules no longer mattered? In her heart, Emma felt a peace and kinship with her mother that she hadn't experienced while her mother lived. She wished she could talk to her now and tell her that she understood.

Today, the birds sang sweeter, the romantic poets expressed far greater passion, and she, Emma Heatherston, was more worldly and knowledgeable than any preceding day in her life. She was confident, and she was experienced, especially with regard to one talented artist.

In spite of her preparations, one aspect of yesterday's lesson had completely surprised her. But she had an idea for a remedy. With a little collaboration, her girls would be better prepared for their first night of passion.

She waited till after the evening meal, when the girls had instruction with Cecilia, to seek out Pettibone's talented seamstress. She found her alone in the parlor.

Beatrice glanced up. "Look at you, dear, you are positively glowing. Our country air has done wonders for your complexion." Heat rose to Emma's cheeks. Was it possible that her very appearance had altered as a result of last night? Did they suspect the reason for the change?

"Come sit next to me, dear. I'd enjoy some company while I work on my embroidery." Beatrice padded the cushion beside her.

"No, thank you. I'd prefer to stand," Emma added quickly. Sitting on a hard bench earlier in the day had taught her one of the consequences of a sore bottom. She made a mental note to mention that to the girls. Padded seat cushions were a necessity.

Emma drifted her fingers over the lacy antimacassars draped over the backs of the parlor chairs. Studying the handicraft, she tentatively approached her request. "Beatrice, do you recall that drawing I presented months ago of a gentleman's aroused manhood?"

"Oh yes, indeed," Beatrice responded, color rising in her parchment-thin cheeks. Her eyes never left her project, but Emma suspected her attention may have deviated from her brightly colored threads.

"I've been thinking . . . that drawing alone may prove insufficient for the girls, when they finally confront the real object." Emma watched the spinster carefully, unsure of her reaction.

"I thought your drawing most informative," Beatrice said, her voice rising an octave. "In what way was it insufficient?"

"It doesn't adequately present size and thickness . . ." Emma attempted to demonstrate with her fingers. Beatrice's glance drifted upward. Her needle remained poised in half-stitch, while her eyes widened to the size of salt cellars.

"I thought perhaps you could use your sewing talents to craft a suitable model out of fabric," Emma explained.

Beatrice's jaw dropped. "Of a man's . . ." She fumbled for the appropriate term, her voice falling to a whisper. "Sabre?"

Emma fought the temptation to smile. Beatrice had more difficulty with the terminology than the topic itself. Her two high spots of color slowly spread across the rest of her cheeks.

"I . . . I'm not sure how to go about such a thing." After unsuccessfully attempting to place her embroidery needle in the proper spot, Beatrice abandoned the project in her lap. "I've never seen a pattern for a man's . . . personals."

Emma closed the distance between them so as to lower her voice. "I thought that if you could form a tube"—Emma rounded her thumb and forefinger to indicate diameter—"and stuff it tightly with cloth till it was stiff, that might suffice."

Beatrice hadn't moved, not even to blink, though her eyes remained fixed as if watching a specter dance before her. Emma frowned. "It doesn't have to look exactly like the item in question, you understand. Just project the appropriate length and thickness."

"That big?" Beatrice tried to match Emma's circle with her own fingers.

Emma relaxed. "It's surprising, isn't it? That's why I think it's important the girls are adequately prepared."

"They'll be frightened out of their minds!"

"Ssh," Emma cautioned, glancing toward the doorway. "Let's keep this our secret until the project is complete."

"By all means." Beatrice nodded. She frowned briefly, then glanced up at Emma. "What about the baubles at the bottom. Will you be wanting those as well?"

Emma thought for a moment. "No, let's stick with the . . . sabre for now." She kept her smile to herself, imagining Beatrice's creative use of trimmings. "We can adjust the model later."

Beatrice squinted her lively eyes. "I have some flowered chintz that might fit the bill. A tube shouldn't be difficult to fashion. I'll put something together and let you have a look."

"Excellent." Emma beamed. Nicholas had been correct when he had said, "Discussing a subject is different than experiencing it for oneself." For all their discussions, her recent experience still proved shocking. If nothing else, she now had a better grasp on how to instruct the girls.

Grasp, she chuckled to herself. *What an appropriate choice of words.* She glanced down at Beatrice, who twitched her fingers, mentally measuring lengths of cloth for their project. Love and gratitude for the older woman seized Emma in an unanticipated surge. Thank heavens above that her uncle's debauchery had forced her to find Pettibone. She smiled down at Beatrice. "Perhaps we can meet after my lesson at Black Oak in two day's time to discuss the model."

Beatrice glanced up. "Oh, I doubt that you will have a lesson in two days."

Surprise stiffened Emma's spine, followed by a keen stab of disappointment. "Why not?"

Beatrice returned to her embroidery. "I heard Henry tell Cook that Lord Nicholas Chambers rode off for London earlier today."

"Oh." Emma relaxed. "Henry must have meant the Marquess of Enon. Both he and Lady Cavendish were to depart rather early this morning."

"No, Henry said it was the younger brother that left. The Marquess and Lady Cavendish left in the Marquess's carriage, but Lord Nicholas Chambers took off on his horse like he was racing at Newmarket." Beatrice glanced up. "According to Henry."

"That is most strange." Emma frowned. "I wonder that he didn't send a note to cancel our lesson."

"Nothing's strange at all when you consider it's Lord Nicholas Chambers." Beatrice smiled smugly.

"Did Henry suggest why Lord Nicholas Chambers might leave for London?" Emma asked, feeling an uncomfortable lump settle in her stomach.

"Mrs. Brimley, I'm surprised at you. One never inquires of servants as to their master's business." Beatrice feigned offense, although Emma guessed she had probably asked Henry that same question and received an incomplete answer.

Emma waited the following day for a note from Nicholas. Henry had to be mistaken, she reasoned. Nicholas hadn't mentioned a need to leave Black Oak. Hadn't Nicholas himself implied he wanted to see her again to continue her education? Of course, the sensible thing would be to confront Henry, but a lingering fear held her at bay.

When the time for her art lesson arrived, no carriage waited at the door. As the day was still young and bright, she walked the back path to Black Oak. Troubling thoughts spoiled the otherwise glorious day. Now that Nicholas had taken her innocence, had he lost interest in her? Had he abandoned her just as her father had abandoned her mother?

Thomas provided no further information. His lordship was simply not at home. Emma narrowed her eyes. Either Nicholas had not divulged his destination, or he had instructed Thomas to remain mute. Of the two, she suspected the latter, which only further complicated the mystery.

That night, she took to her poetry books, hoping to focus her mind on the words before her, and not on the man who so very recently had inspired her to verse as well.

She closed her eyes and opened the book, letting the

pages fall where they may. Opening her eyes, she read: "Be warm, but pure, be amorous, but be chaste." Her glance slipped to the poet's name: George Gordon Byron, otherwise known as Lord Byron, Nicholas's favorite poet.

She groaned. Was that her mistake? Did he consider her unchaste, and unfit for his continued company? Was he indeed running away from her?

She thought of Beatrice's lament, that at least Emma had known physical love at least once in her lifetime, but that made for small comfort. The only man who had treated her as a complete woman, one of intellectual pursuits as well as physical needs, had left—injuring both aspects of her being. Her heart cried out in pain, but there was no one to listen.

· *Twenty* ·

HIDDEN UNDER THEIR UMBRELLAS, MEN AND women scurried down the crowded London sidewalks with little thought to the rural treasures beyond the city limits. Nicholas shook his head in wonder. How could they live everyday in a place where coal dust fell along with the rain, staining the limestone buildings and the people bustling past them? Hansom cabs and dray wagons clogged the streets, even in the dismal rain that had followed him in from Coventry. Although his first priority placed him in a rented cab en route to the Royal Academy, arranging for a hot bath and a dry bed promised to be the next consideration.

A long queue of hopeful artists, juggling umbrellas along with well-protected paintings, lined the approach to Burlington House, the home of the Royal Academy. Nicholas well understood their hopeful determination. Last year, well over three thousand paintings had been submitted for consideration and only three hundred accepted. In the past, he had hoped that one of his paintings would be accepted and thus validate his talent. Today he prayed for rejection.

Although his brother would most likely be admitted directly into Burlington House, Nicholas scrutinized the faces of his fellow artists waiting in the rain for their chance at fame. Some would wait a lifetime; some already had. Last year, Nicholas would have eagerly joined their ranks, but not today. Fame and accreditation paled in light of Emma's situation. The painting must not be put on public display. As soon as the cab pulled to the front of the Italian Renaissance façade, Nicholas exited and ran up the steps, ignoring the protests of those in line.

Given the large amount of artwork submitted, the selection process to determine the few pieces to earn a spot in the exhibition began even before all the paintings had been reviewed. Nicholas followed the sound of raised voices to a crowded meeting room where the selection jury already sat in judgment. Five Royal Academicians sat in a semicircle before a swiftly moving parade of paintings. With barely a glance at the presented work, the judges would vote whether to accept or reject the painting before them by motioning with a metal wand. If three of the five judges accepted a piece, the work would move to a "doubtful" room to undergo a second round of judging after the preliminary reduction. If *Artemis's Revenge* was not immediately rejected, it would wait in the doubtful room.

After asking directions to the holding area, Nicholas found the chamber a ways distant from the jury. A clerk, a bored art student from the looks of him, guarded the door with a ledger book in the crook of his arm.

"One of my paintings," Nicholas said, "was submitted for the exhibition." He glanced over the student's shoulder, hoping for a glimpse of *Artemis*. The paintings, however, were stacked five deep, facing the wall. "Can you tell me if it was accepted?"

"Name?"

"Chambers, Lord Nicholas Chambers."

The clerk glanced up, startled. A corner of Nicholas's mouth pulled back; it wasn't the first time his title brought that reaction.

A stubby finger slipped down the column of names. Sculpture, Nicholas thought, noticing clay under the clerk's fingernails. *We all must wear little telltale signs of our passion.*

"I'm sorry, sir. I don't see your name listed."

Fatigue lifted from Nicholas's shoulders. His lips spread in an unrestrained smile. "Thank you, my good man." He laughed, pumping the hand of the young clerk hardly seemed enough. "If you were a woman, I'd kiss you."

The clerk's eyes widened before he ventured a step backward. "There is a possibility that your painting was rejected, my lord. Most are." The clerk offered a sympathetic smile. "The rejections are held in the store, but I believe there's a bit of a crush right now."

"Can you point me in the proper direction?" Nicholas asked, almost giddy that he didn't have to worry about the exhibition. The poor student must think him totally mad.

The clerk pointed toward the right, without leaving the safety of the room.

"Thank you, again." Nicholas dipped his head, then followed the lad's directions. Just as he had hoped, this hurried excursion to London was proving unnecessary. Ensuring that Emma's future remained at Pettibone, however, made the trip worth the trouble. He supposed the reality that his best work had been rejected would settle in eventually, but for now, his good fortune buoyed his spirits. He fairly sailed down the hallway in search of the store.

"I'm sorry, sir," said the gentleman in charge of the

store, reviewing his listings. "I don't see your painting listed, but as you can see we have hundreds in storage. It could be here, but we won't know for several days until the bulk of the rejections are collected."

Nicholas was not all that surprised. In all likelihood William would have used his influence to have the painting evaluated immediately. He probably took it back to his London town house, or worse, his father's house. Which meant he would have to go there to pick it up. Nicholas's euphoric bubble deflated. Damnation. He had hoped to avoid his father on this trip.

UPON ARRIVAL AT HIS BROTHER'S TOWN HOUSE, NICHOLAS was ushered into the library. William greeted him a few minutes later. "When I extended an invitation, I hadn't expected to see you so soon."

"Bloody hell, you didn't." Nicholas tried to muster a scowl, but his recent joy over his rejection prevented anything convincing. "Did you think I wouldn't notice that you switched the paintings?"

"I thought it might take a bit longer." William held aloft a decanter of brandy. Nicholas nodded and William poured. "I suppose you have already heard that the oil was rejected."

"It wasn't on the doubtful list, so I assumed as much." Nicholas accepted the offered glass. "May I assume as well that you have the painting?"

William nodded. "I secured it back in the crate. I'm sorry, Nicholas. I truly expected the Academy to recognize the merits of *Artemis's Revenge*."

"I must say I've never been overly concerned about the Academy's approval." Nicholas held his glass aloft as in a toast. "But this time their rejection positively elates me."

William studied him over his own snifter. "Does the widow mean that much?"

The slow burn of the brandy settled on the back of Nicholas's tongue before warming a path down his throat.

"Yes," he answered unequivocally. But how could he explain Emma's uniqueness to his brother? He wasn't sure where to begin. It was more than her appearance, though he could spend a lifetime looking into her gentle green eyes. It was more than her companionship, though there wasn't another with whom he'd rather spend an afternoon. It was her acceptance, her compassion, her curiosity, her wit. He didn't think his brother would understand. He wasn't sure he understood himself. He just knew Emma was special in a way no one else could be.

"She is . . . rare," he said, though he knew that didn't do her justice.

William stared at him as if he expected Nicholas to say more. When the silence stretched out overlong, his brother frowned, then shifted uneasily. He lifted his glass in a salute. "Well then, here's to the rare ones." He tilted his chin toward Nicholas. "May there be many more."

No need, Nicholas thought. No need for many, just for the one. They both upended their drinks.

"Now that you've come to town, you might as well stay for the exhibition," William offered. "They're hanging a week from Monday and opening two days after. You'd enjoy it."

"I suppose now that I know that my picture is in no jeopardy of being viewed, I would rather enjoy the exhibition." The brandy blossomed in his stomach, spreading pleasant warmth and cheer throughout his body. It would be good to view the Academy's choices and maybe call upon some old acquaintances in town. Emma's reputation was safe, and she had promised not to run from Pettibone. Yes, he could afford to bask in a bit of his brother's hospitality.

"Then it's settled." William took his empty glass and

placed it on the sideboard. "You'll stay here. You look exhausted and I have spare beds aplenty." He clapped him on the back. "Good to have you home, brother."

Nicholas smiled. "Thank you, William."

FORTUNATELY, MOST OF THE TON HAD LEFT LONDON for the summer, preferring to dwell at their country estates. William introduced Nicholas to his social clubs and favored gambling hells to fill the social void. Nicholas begged off after only a few nights, preferring to use his daylight hours to sketch the city's landscape rather than sleep off an evening's frivolous pursuits. His brother had scowled but accepted his decision without complaint.

A parade of women, orchestrated no doubt by his brother, found their way to Nicholas as well. Pasty-white, social aristocrats whose passions consisted of little more than fashion and gossip. Nicholas supposed they could read. They were rumored to be educated. Yet not a one could quote a line of poetry or entertain a novel thought in their empty heads. They could never stand up to a Yorkshire winter, Nicholas reasoned. No backbone.

Then his thoughts would turn to Emma, who had a magnificent backbone, and many fine front bones as well. He smiled. She read for more than just pleasure and actually retained what she had consumed. Would any of these silly sheep be willing to defy society and undress for him for the purpose of modeling?

Well, yes, at least one of them would.

At the Haddocks' party, Lady Cavendish seemed most anxious that Nicholas be introduced to her new charge, a Miss Penelope Heatherston, a comely creature whose best attributes were amply displayed in her low-cut gown. No intelligence, however, registered behind her attractive and vaguely familiar visage. Something about her name pulled at him, though he couldn't make the connection. Undoubtedly the copious amounts of alcohol he had consumed might explain the lapse.

Nevertheless, he smiled at the appropriate intervals and feigned interest in conversation, just so his boredom would not cast unfavorably upon his brother. Surrounded by all these people, Nicholas was lonely, there was no denying it. Back home in Yorkshire with only Emma in his studio, he had all the company he needed.

Indeed, he'd be back there now, his desire to see Emma again even stronger than his desire to view the Royal Academy's summer exhibition, if not for his promise to his brother.

He wrote to Emma to tell her of his change in plans so she would not arrive at an empty Black Oak for painting sessions. There was no need to mention the switch in the painting. No need to upset her that a remote threat to her reputation had ever existed, now that it had been thwarted.

After two weeks, the grand day for the opening of the exhibition arrived in some of the foulest weather to hit the city that week. Traffic around Piccadilly Circus came to a complete standstill as a horde of wet, black umbrellas thronged to the exhibition.

"It's really quite a crush on the first day, old man," William said to Nicholas as they waited impatiently in the carriage.

"We could walk," Nicholas said. "It's not far."

"I refuse to walk a single block in this downpour. Look at it. We'd be soaked through and through before we took five steps." A low rumble of thunder confirmed his displeasure.

"In Yorkshire—"

"Oh please, no more comparisons between London and Yorkshire," his brother groaned. "I've heard little else these last two weeks than how beautiful the scenery, how sweet the air, and how hardy the women. You forget I was just there myself, dear brother, and I'm afraid I don't share your appreciation."

Nicholas chuckled beneath his breath. The criticism was just, his preferences apparent.

"I say we come back tomorrow," William said. "The day will be drier and the crowds thinner."

"I had planned to leave tomorrow," Nicholas replied with a bit of a growl. He could feel the pull of Yorkshire, the pull of Emma, even as he sat in this ridiculous little carriage waiting for other ridiculous little carriages to move forward.

"The trains will run the day after as well. Come on, brother. Did I tell you Arianne is here?"

His sister? "No. You failed to mention that."

"She arrived yesterday and is staying at Father's house. I propose we go visit there instead of the gallery. This can wait for another day."

"As opposed to visiting Father?" Nicholas frowned. "If I didn't know better, I'd suspect you planned this standstill so you could propose this venture."

"Seriously Nicholas, what kind of brother doesn't go visit his sister on the rare occasion when she's in town?"

Nicholas sighed. "Let's go and get this over with. Of course I want to see Arianne again, but Father?" He shook his head and glanced up at his beaming brother. "You appear quite pleased with your artful manipulation."

"I am, dear brother. Believe me, I am." He tapped on the roof and redirected the carriage to his father's residence.

WILLIAM AND NICHOLAS WERE DIRECTED TO THE FAMily salon, where Arianne with her delightful humor and effervescent chatter already entertained the dour Duke of Bedford.

He looked considerably older than Nicholas recalled, he

thought with a twinge of guilt. Even the full white beard trimmed meticulously to the top of his collar failed to hide the deep bags gathered under his father's eyes. His skin had paled to a papery thinness, but his eyes retained their hawklike stare. The rich satin dinner jacket tied at the waist emphasized the Duke's vivid blue eyes now directed in assessment of his youngest son. Nicholas cast a quick glance to his brother, who solemnly nodded in return.

Arianne rushed forward, encircling him with her flowery scent and demanding his attention until dinner was served and throughout the many courses. Finally, the three men retired to the library with their brandies. Nicholas waited for the inevitable attack to begin, on his lack of character, on his lack of responsibility, on his lack of talent.

"Nicholas, as you are well aware, we have had our differences in the past," the Duke began. "I suspect those disagreements are the primary reason why so much distance has gathered between us."

Nicholas just sipped his wine. To say anything would add fuel to his father's fire.

"That is why it gives me great pleasure to admit to my fallacies. I was wrong about you, Nick. Grievously wrong. I have seen your work and can now acknowledge that all that time spent with your paintbrush has not been wasted. I wish to offer a toast to your talent."

"Hear, hear," added William with a lifted glass.

Stunned, Nicholas fumbled for words. "You have me at a disadvantage, sir. On what occasion have you viewed my work?"

His father laughed, a hardy sound Nicholas couldn't recall having heard before.

"All of London is lifting a glass to your talent, my boy. It isn't everyday that one's painting is accepted into the Royal Academy's summer exhibition. Why, your work will hang in museums and galleries long after I'm buried and forgotten."

Nicholas jerked as if punched in the gut. He looked to William for answers.

"I told you Father would be pleased to see you." William beamed.

"What painting is hanging in the exhibition?" His tone alone could have turned the June rain beating against the windows to hail pellets.

"*Artemis's Revenge*, of course, the one with the naked woman." His father chuckled. "I must admit, I thought you were just having your fun with those women, not painting them. I attended the private showing yesterday for the artists and guests. I'm surprised you didn't attend, but William said you were busy with one thing or another."

· Twenty-one ·

NICHOLAS LOOKED FROM HIS FATHER TO HIS brother and back. A cold, blind fury settled around his heart. He'd been tricked! Manipulated by the very brother he had trusted. His eyes bored into William.

"I tell you that painting was the talk of the show," the Duke continued, oblivious to the rising tension between his sons. "I understand a new record was set for attendance today. Why, half of London must have come to the opening."

"You told me the painting was rejected," Nicholas stated with deadly calm. "You lied to me."

"You would have pulled the painting if I hadn't," William replied. "A few pounds appropriately placed can buy a good deal of silence." He met his brother's stare. "I did it for your own good. *Artemis's Revenge* is a masterpiece. It deserves to be seen."

"You thought your painting was rejected?" The Duke of

Bedford laughed again. "This is too rich. A jest played by your brother. Well done, William." The Duke's glance darted between his sons. "Look at Nicholas! Why, the boy's in shock. Drink up, man. The brandy will bring you to your senses. Then we can discuss you moving your studio to town."

"Excuse me, sir." The Duke of Bedford's butler stood at the door. "Lady Cavendish desires a word with Lord Nicholas Chambers."

"Lady Cavendish?" the Duke roared. "What in the devil is that busybody doing here?"

The butler extended a note to Nicholas. He quickly unfolded it: *Emma is in danger.*

"Lady Cavendish remains?" he asked.

"She waits in the green salon, sir."

Nicholas stood and crossed to the door.

"What goes on here?" His father demanded. "Where are you going?"

Nicholas glanced back. "I must see this woman." He scowled at his brother. "No amount of apology will justify the damage you have done. I expect you to retrieve my painting before the exhibition opens tomorrow."

William sputtered. "Don't be ridiculous. The show is hung. They won't remove a painting once it's on display."

Nicholas replied over his shoulder. "Then have it covered. I won't have the populace gawking at my Emma."

"She's just a—"

Nicholas turned, ice dripping from his words. "Be careful choosing your next word, William. Your very life may well depend upon it."

William gulped his wine. His father's wide smile faded.

Nicholas hurried to the green salon near the front end of the manor, perplexed as to how sweet Emma could possibly be in danger in tiny Leighton-on-the-Wold. What he recalled of Lady Cavendish did not suggest she would engage in a cruel jest. No, that remained the realm of his brother. His teeth set on edge. Of course, Lady Cavendish had traveled with his brother. The two could be partners in crime.

He found Lady Cavendish pacing furiously in the salon. "You sent for me?"

"Why?" Her gaze knifed through him like a finely honed rapier. She shook a lace-covered fist at him. "Why did you do it?"

"Madam, I haven't a clue to your reference. Nothing I've done affects your household." He narrowed his gaze. "Why did you send me that note? What kind of danger?"

"Why did you paint that picture of Emma and then submit it to the summer exhibition?" she countered.

"I did not submit a painting, although one was submitted for me. However I fail to see—"

"I attended the opening with Emma's uncle, Mr. George Heatherston. He recognized his niece immediately." Her scowl suggested an attachment to Emma of which Nicholas was previously unaware. He was suddenly enamored with the constantly inquisitive Lady Cavendish. In this household of backstabbing relatives, he recognized an ally.

"Your note said she was in danger."

"Heatherston was very upset. He's been searching for Emma for months and months. Did you not know? He was leaving to reclaim her as soon as he left me. She must be warned before he finds her."

Nicholas called for his hat and then scribbled a hurried message to his family. "Even if he recognized Emma, how would he know where to look?"

"I am afraid that may be my fault." Lady Cavendish grimaced, averting her eyes for a moment. "I had mentioned that I had visited Black Oak, not realizing at the time that the details would put Emma at risk." She waved her hand in front of her face as if dismissing the matter. "We turned a corner and saw your *Artemis*. But enough of this. We must hurry."

Nicholas paused in his writing. "Does the uncle know that she teaches at Pettibone?"

"I don't think so," she answered with a pensive look. "But it wouldn't be difficult to find someone who recognized her in Leighton-on-the-Wold. It's such a small village, and Emma is memorable."

That much is true, Nicholas thought ruefully.

The butler appeared with Nicholas's hat in hand, as well as Lady Cavendish's wet umbrella. For one brief instant, Nicholas was glad that she had checked her weapon at the door, else he suspected the umbrella would have been bashed across his head. He didn't understand the origin of the woman's loyalty to Emma, but he was grateful for it.

"Did you come in a carriage?" he asked.

"I have a cab outside."

"Madam," he said, "I have no time to concern myself with society's transgressions. I wish to take your cab to the train station. Will you ride with me and tell me all you know?"

She smiled. "At my age, I don't have many opportunities to set tongues wagging. Let's be off."

Twenty-two

ALICE SUGGESTED THEY PACK A PICNIC LUNCH and share it out in the garden while reading their favorite passages aloud from Mr. Shakespeare. Emma suspected the ploy was meant to lift her spirits. Ever since Nicholas had left for London, doubts about the wisdom of her actions, and the sincerity of his, had left her muddled in a cloud of despair.

Once, while reading a dated copy of the *Times*, she noticed mention in the society column of Lord Nicholas Chambers in the company of a debutante. A sharp pain had stabbed at her heart, and she was tempted to retrieve Mr. Copland's *A Dictionary of Practical Medicine* from the top shelf in the library. But she doubted she would find a sufficient remedy for a broken heart even in that copious work.

Still, she couldn't resist scouring the society columns for his name. She found frequent mention of the parties and dances he had attended. The knowledge rankled. He would not dance with her at the Pettibone ball, but he would dance with the society ladies at the fancy parties of the polite world. Her temperament grew sullen and irritable.

"I'm so glad you remained at Pettibone," Alice repeated for the umpteenth time. "Especially now that all the girls have left for the summer. My past summers were always so lonely."

"You weren't alone." Emma tried to focus on Alice's conversation rather than Nicholas's social opportunities. "Miss Higgins and Miss Beatrice were here."

"Yes, but they never knew what to do with me. I endeavored to stay out of their way as much as possible. I believe they vowed to stay out of mine as well."

"That does sound like a lonely existence," Emma said quietly, gazing down the hillside at the crisscross hedges and the fields of ripening grass. Lambs bleated in the distance, their cries carried on the same breeze that chased cloud shadows across the valley. She kept her back turned to the path on the left that led down to the woods and beyond to Black Oak. Too many memories lie in that direction. She hadn't even hope that Nicholas's issue would break the heavy mantle of her loneliness. Her monthlies had arrived last week, an event she welcomed with a bit of relief, but also mourned as one might a lost dream. She sighed heavily.

"At least you had this glorious countryside for your own. I can see a hundred magical reading spots right from this hill." Emma smiled. "That's what helped me through my lonely spells when I was your age. My books."

"Still it's good to have someone to share a book with," Alice observed.

"That it is," Emma agreed.

"Mrs. Brimley!" Cecilia called from the terrace. "We must see you immediately. You have a visitor."

"A visitor?" Emma smiled at Alice. "I can't imagine who that could be. Shall we go see?"

Visitors no longer terrified her as they once had. Ever since the Pettibone ball, several of the village men made their way to the school, dressed in their Sunday best, to call upon the young widow. They were kind, she was polite, but none of them stirred her passion as Nicholas did. Indeed, she often hoped the caller in the parlor would wait for her with a wicked grin, a tilted mustache, and a dancing dimple. However, the likelihood that Lord Nicholas Chambers, noted recluse and rake, would present himself at Pettibone as a suitor was beyond even the fantasies of the popular light novels.

Hand in hand, Emma and Alice walked back toward the school, chatting like sisters. However, once they reached the terrace, Cecilia stopped them from entering together.

"Alice, I think it would be better if you went to your room," she instructed with a nod.

Alice's forehead wrinkled in concern.

"It's all right," Emma reassured. "I'll come get you after meeting whoever has come to call." Alice departed, leaving Emma and Cecilia on the terrace.

Cecilia frowned. "He's waiting in the sitting room."

Only one person could earn Cecilia's scowl. A smile crept to Emma's lips. Nicholas was back! His letter had indicated that he'd return in two weeks, and so he had. Although Cecilia had softened her criticism of Lord Nicholas Chambers after his assistance in locating poor lost Charlotte, that frown proved her reluctance to drop old grudges.

Emma brushed errant grass off her dress, then crossed the music room to the front hallway, trying to keep a dignified pace and not break into a run. He returned for her! All the excitement and glamour of London couldn't keep him away. Her heart surged with gratitude and love and delicious anticipation.

Cecilia's footsteps sounded two steps behind Emma, as if she were guarding against retreat. Emma stopped and glanced back, but Cecilia's face proved unreadable. A shadow of unease dampened Emma's enthusiasm.

Beatrice waited in the sitting room. As soon as she spotted Emma approaching, she became quite animated. "Here she is, Mr. Heatherston. This is our Mrs. Brimley. As you can see, she is hardly a young, innocent runaway."

Bile rose to Emma's throat, even before she saw her uncle on the far side of the room. Cecilia took up position beside her sister.

"My dear Emma," he said, smiling from ear to ear. "I've been searching all over London for you. I'm so glad to find you safe."

Emma nodded stiffly. "Uncle George."

His appearance hadn't changed since she last saw him. The buttons on his yellow silk vest barely closed over a stomach that never missed a meal. His long white sideburns crawled down his pudgy cheeks like milk running down the side of a pail. His tiny black eyes beetled out from bushy tufts of disorderly white eyebrows.

"This man is your uncle?" Beatrice gasped. "He said as much, but we didn't believe him."

Emma nodded, keeping a steady eye on him. How much did he know? How much had he confided to the sisters?

"May I have a few minutes alone with my niece?" Her uncle effused a false sort of charm. "We have so many things to discuss." He never broke eye contact with Emma even as his words addressed others.

"We shall be nearby." Cecilia stiffened, then ushered her sister out the door. Thank heavens for Cecilia's general mistrust, Emma thought, not wishing to be left alone with the man, but accepting that privacy would be best.

Once the door clicked, her uncle advanced, lowering his voice to a whisper. "Mrs. Brimley, is it now? And a widow by the looks of that black dress? Is this some masquerade, or did you marry some poor bloke just to cheat me out of what's mine?"

"How did you find me?" she hissed.

"There's a painting hanging at the Royal Academy." His gaze swept her from toes to shoulders. He sneered. "A real show-stopper it is too, if you know what I mean."

"A painting?" She gasped. There could only be one painting that might merit his leer: *Artemis's Revenge*. Cold comprehension chilled her blood. Nicholas had promised that no one would see that painting, yet he had taken it to London to put on display for the entire civilized world. Suddenly, she understood the true purpose for his urgent London trip, as well as the true extent of his respect for her reputation. What a fool she had been. A bloody, blasted, stupid fool.

"An enormous painting of a naked woman thinking she's some kind of goddess. She has a striking resemblance to you, even to that strawberry birthmark right about—" He lifted his hand as if to touch her breast, but she knocked it aside. He chuckled. "Still have a streak of rebellion in you, I see."

"What do you want here?" Her lip curled. His touch was still as revolting as she recalled.

"You." The laughter left his face. "I want you." He held her stare for a moment, then looked away, sneering. "Actually, I want money. I need it for some debts I've accumulated. I haven't got the coin, but I do have you, and I've found me a buyer for your womanly charms."

"You no account, gutter-thriving flesh peddler. Surely, you don't think I'll just go off with you."

"Now isn't that the pot calling the kettle black." He

circled around her as if he were looking for a weakness. She turned on her heel to keep him in her sight.

"Do those old biddies know about that painting of you displaying your privates?"

Her entire face heated. He sneered again, obviously pleased with her confirmation. "No, I didn't think so. You wouldn't be stashed away in this cozy place if they knew, would you?"

He edged over to a table decorated with a variety of porcelain knickknacks. "Do they know that you're no more a widow than a newborn babe?" He glanced up at her. "That one's got me pickled. Why are you pretending to be a widow?"

She didn't answer. Rather, she edged around to the far side of the room, putting as much distance between them as possible.

He shrugged. "No matter." He slipped something into his pocket. "Now, here's my proposition. If you come with me quietly, I won't share our little secret. If you make a grand fuss, I'll set them straight as to the type of woman they have teaching at this fancy school. You won't be able to hide out here away from your own relations, that's for certain."

"Where are you planning to take me?" She slowly backed up to Cecilia's desk. Her fingers searched frantically for something that could be used as a weapon.

"Right now, I'm planning to take you out to my waiting carriage. You'll know the final destination soon enough." His lips opened in a sickening parody of a smile.

Emma's stomach turned even as her fingertips touched Cecilia's letter opener. She slowly turned it on the table behind her, so she could slip it into her hand.

"The old biddies left us some tea. Would you like a cup?"

She shook her head.

"No? I hope you don't mind if I pour some myself."

The instant his back was turned she dashed for the door. He lunged and caught her wrist, twisting her back against his chest. The hand with the blade flailed ineffectively in the air above her head while he clamped a cloth across her mouth.

"I knew you would be trouble. That wasn't tea I was pouring, missy."

Her eyes bulged open as a sickly sweet vapor filled her lungs.

"That's right. Breathe deep. We'll be on our way in no time." His voice drifted in and out of her consciousness. Something metal clanged to the floor seconds before her knees crumbled. The last thing she remembered was her uncle's ugly, sneering face. Her eyelids refused to remain open. In a matter of seconds, her world simply dissolved.

His niece's limp body weighed heavy in his arms. "You've been eating well, I see."

Heatherston chuckled at his own wit, then laid her gently on the floor. His laudanum-soaked handkerchief disappeared in his pocket. With a swift kick, the useless letter opener slid under the skirts of a chair. After visually checking to make sure he'd removed all appearance of a struggle, he yelled, "Help! Help!" He flung open the door. "Something terrible has happened to my niece!"

"Oh dear!" Beatrice tumbled into the room first. "Whatever happened?" She knelt beside Emma, placing a hand on her forehead. "Saints be praised, there's no fever. I know she's not been her vital self lately, but she shouldn't have collapsed."

Cecilia looked over Beatrice's shoulder. "Bea, go run and get your smelling salts."

"No, no," Heatherston protested. "She needs a doctor. My carriage is just outside. Help me settle her inside and I'll take her to the village."

Cecilia sniffed the air. "Do you smell something peculiar?" When no one responded, she turned back toward Heatherston. "I don't think she should be moved. The doctor will come out to see her. Perhaps by then she will be recovered and can tell us what happened."

Heatherston reddened. "She's my niece and I know what's good for her. I will take her to see a doctor and that's that. It could be too late by the time the doctor found his way out here." He scooped her up in his arms, heaving with the effort. "If one of you ladies will see to the door, I'll take her to get proper medical attention."

"I'll go with you," Cecilia said.

"No!" Heatherston turned to face the two of them. "Who knows what you've done to my poor niece already. She's better off with me. I'm family."

The two sisters exchanged a glance, then accommodated the stranger.

"Emma did say he was her uncle," Beatrice observed sadly. "One family member would not hurt another."

"I'll get the door," Cecilia said.

· *Twenty-three* ·

A FAINT SICKLY ODOR LINGERED IN HER NOSTRILS and clung to the back of her throat. The side of her face bounced repeatedly on a stale cushion. Although her eyelids refused to open, her ears registered the familiar creak and rumble of a carriage in motion. Emma smiled. Why else would she be in a carriage if not to travel to Black Oak? Still, at this pace, she'd be lucky to arrive whole.

"Henry, slow down." Her voice drifted back to her ears, slurred and distant as if from a fog. "One rut in the road could kill us all."

"It's good that you're awake," a frighteningly familiar voice said. "If you behave yourself, I won't have to administer another dose of laudanum."

Uncle George! What was happening? Her stomach roiled in a surge of nausea. She tried to retrieve her mother's handkerchief, but her arms wouldn't move. Panicked, she forced eyes open, only to see what she thought might be her uncle's knees.

"Your hostility forced me to tie your arms. You gave me no choice." Uncle George hoisted her to a sitting position, then leaned her body toward the near side of the carriage. "There you go." He grinned. "All upright and proper."

"Proper? You consider this proper?" The dry, scratchy texture of her throat robbed her of enunciation. Her spectacles were missing, robbing her of focus. If only this were a nightmare, she'd soon wake up and the world would be right again.

"Wait. You'll need these I suppose." Her uncle reached over and pushed her missing spectacles in place. "Thought you might break them, bouncing on the seat the way you were."

Emma blinked, seeing clearly that this was not some horrible dream. Her heart sank. How could she possibly extricate herself from this?

The corner of her uncle's lips twitched. Reaching into his jacket, he removed a silver flask and shoved it under her nose. "Drink this."

Emma clenched her lips tight and shook her head.

"The water will help with the nausea. Drink." He held the metal opening to her lips, but the liquid ran down her chin to drip on her dress bodice.

"You don't trust me, is that it?" He lowered the flask. "Well, I can't say that I blame you." His eyes brightened. "Tell you what. Look at me." He tilted the flask to his own lips and swallowed. "See it's only water."

"It would be easier if you freed my hands," Emma said, still not sure she believed the man. Her arms and shoulders ached from their forced confinement. While she was tied, she was at his mercy. That, she could not abide.

"You won't cause me any trouble?"

She shook her head, although she felt no obligation to honor her response.

"I suppose there's nothing you can do." He cast a quick look out the window. "At this speed, you'd break your neck if you jumped from the carriage."

He pulled a small knife from his pocket, then sawed through the rope. Once free, she rubbed her chafed wrists and shook her aching arms. Accepting the water flask, she sniffed it first, then sipped the water, letting the refreshing moisture soothe her mouth and throat.

"Where are we?" she rasped between sips. The water did nothing to settle her stomach, but it did lessen the pounding in her head.

Her uncle settled back in a corner of the swaying carriage, a satisfied smile across his face. "We're miles from Pettibone. No one can hear you if you scream. No one will come to your aid."

Scream? Just the thought made her throat ache more. No, that would do no good.

"Where are you taking me?" She braced her arms on each side, trying to stay as still as possible to settle the protests of her stomach. Burning bile still rose in her throat.

"Scotland. We're not that far." He smiled. "It is fortunate indeed that you ran someplace so close to the border. At this pace we can stop for a right proper supper, then drive on and reach our destination before the cock crows."

Emma frowned, trying to will her swirling thoughts to some order. Scotland . . . There was something important about Scotland.

"Cheer up, Emma. You should be happy. I could have left you in that convent to become a shriveled-up old prune like those other two."

Dear heaven, his smug smile told her he supposed he

was doing her a favor stealing her away from the very people she loved.

"Do not pretend you are my benefactor. You wouldn't have bothered with me at all unless there was some profit in it for you."

"Aye, you were always the smart one, you were." He winked and stretched out his legs. "It's a shame Penelope isn't more like you that way. Maybe if she were smarter I wouldn't have had to hire that chatty Lady Cavendish to find her a proper husband."

"Lady Cavendish!" Emma couldn't have been more surprised than if he had said Beatrice was assisting Penelope. What was going on?

"She sought me out, she did. Said she could help find Penelope a wealthy husband with her connections and all." He leered at Emma. "Come to think of it, that's what I'm doing. Helping you find a husband."

The Scotland connection suddenly made sense. She recalled old stories about eloping couples dashing off to Gretna Green in Scotland. The place was legendary for quick nuptials. However, laws were passed to change all that about the time she was born.

"You can't force me to marry someone against my will." Now it was her turn for a smug smile. "You'd have to hold me hostage in Scotland for three weeks before I could marry there. I think that would be difficult even for you, to say nothing of the expense."

If her uncle had a vulnerability, it would be in his purse.

"That would be true enough, missy, if you hadn't had the good fortune to be born in Scotland." His rat face almost split in two by the size of his grin. "Your mother never told you that, did she? She was so afraid you'd run off and leave her that she kept the truth from you."

"I don't believe you," Emma snapped.

"Believe what you will." He shrugged, then leaned

close so that his nose bobbed mere inches from her own. "But know this. Enough coin in the right palm will buy a proper marriage whether you agree to it or not. There's ways to make a reluctant bride eager, if you know what I mean."

Her jaw dropped. "You'd drug me!"

He laughed. "I did it once already, didn't I? What do you think?"

Emma sank back on the cushions. What was she to do now? She had no doubt that her uncle would stoop to just about any measure to ensure his nefarious scheme.

"If all goes according to plan, you'd be a right proper married woman within the week. You should be grateful to your old uncle. Looking out for you, I am."

He had someone in play; she could see it in his beady little eyes.

"Who?" She managed with a grimace.

"Do you remember Mr. Perichilde?"

"The old man from Sussex?" Emma recoiled at the memory. They had met at one of the dinners she attended with Penelope. Now that she recalled, Uncle George did sequester himself with a tall thin man who resembled the grim reaper himself.

"That old man is desperate for an heir. Desperate enough to pay handsomely for a young untried bride like yourself. He's waiting for us in Gretna Green."

"He's so old!" Emma gasped.

"I wouldn't divest of those widow's weeds, if you know what I mean." He laughed heartily. "Perichilde will wear out long before you will."

"Why are you doing this?" she asked.

"I told you, it's for your own good. Who wants an old plow horse when there are young fillies on the market? You're lucky to have an uncle like me. Besides, the fee Perichilde will pay will clear some debts."

"I'm not an untried woman," Emma said, desperate to make her uncle reconsider his plan. "Perichilde may not pay when he discovers that I'm no longer a virgin."

Her uncle's mouth dropped open. "That artist! You gave him your maidenhood? You silly chit. Did you think he would marry you?" He laughed, a harsh, cruel sound. "Why, he's gallivanting around London looking for his next conquest. He even gave Penelope a twirl around the dance floor." His eyes narrowed. "You didn't believe he really loved you, did you?"

Penelope and Nicholas! Emma felt like she had been punched in the stomach. Her eyes burned; she struggled for breath.

"You did, you did. I can see it in your face." He cackled, then shook his head. "I should have known. I always said you were just like your mother. I thought you might have had more sense than lifting your skirts for the first pretty man that came sniffing."

Her cheeks burned. Is that what she had done? Given herself to a man who chased after a woman's virtue as another would hunt down a fox. In her mind, she heard his voice. *I have no knowledge of anything but debauchery.* She gasped. He had warned her on her first visit to Black Oak, yet she had refused to listen.

"I should have sold you to a brothel when I had the chance," her uncle muttered, oblivious to her turmoil. He glanced up at her. "I would have, if you hadn't run away. I gave my word to your mother that I wouldn't harm you while she was alive. I waited all these years, watching you grow, spending good money on your education. I even chased off those two sorry suitors who came asking after you. All my scheming and then you up and disappear. You lifted your skirts for what? A bit of paint?"

He shook his head as if in true misery. Good, Emma thought. If nothing else, she had ruined her uncle's plans.

She had given her heart and her virtue for more than a "bit of paint," as he so cruelly suggested. But her uncle wouldn't understand that.

"Still," he continued, "I gave my word to Perichilde, and a gentleman's word is his bond." George frowned, staring at her stomach. "If you're lucky, you've already got a baby planted in your belly. If I don't miss my guess, Perichilde will leave you alone once an heir is on its way."

"A gentleman does not sell his relatives to the highest bidder. Your word is worthless," Emma scoffed.

Her uncle scowled. "You think you are too good for the likes of a common man, but let me tell you, missy, there's nothing you can do to change your fate."

Emma crossed her arms and sank into silence. Perhaps a year ago she would have accepted his decree that this was to be her destiny. Marriage to an old man might even prove attractive to an inexperienced girl who hadn't tasted true passion. But she wasn't that inexperienced girl any longer. She refused to accept what her uncle called "fate."

The nausea had passed, along with the lingering scent of laudanum. Emma sat up and arched her back and lifted her shoulders to ease the aching of her constrained position.

"What are you doing?" her uncle demanded. "That's no posture for a lady. You're acting like a servant who's been on hands and knees all day. Behave. Someone might see you. Don't force me to restrain you again." He looked right and left as if through some miracle of nature, a stranger had affixed themselves to the side of the racing coach for the sole purpose of watching Emma flex her muscles.

"It's the constraint that makes such movements necessary, Uncle." Her protest made no mark on his dour expression. Until she determined some method of escape, she had best play along with his scheme. Escape would be easier with her hands unbound.

"Very well," she said, with a sigh of resignation. "Perhaps you are correct. I am grateful that you have rescued me from Pettibone. I was tired of playing nursemaid to a bunch of snotty girls. I suppose marriage to an older, more experienced man is better than no marriage at all."

His face brightened. "There you go. You were always a bright one. Now you'll see that I'm right."

"How much further to our destination?" she asked.

"We made great strides while you were sleeping. I'd estimate three more hours to cross the border, but we shall stop before that to pick up Perichilde."

"He's waiting for us?"

"I sent word to him as soon as I saw that painting. I didn't give twenty-odd years of my life letting you and your mother live under my roof without learning to recognize you with or without your clothes."

"You . . . you . . . spied on me?" she gasped. Was there no level to which this man would not sink?

"Not often, only when the opportunity presented itself." He sneered. "I'm a man, after all."

Not much of one, she thought.

"I never touched you. That's more than you can say about that Lord Nicholas Chambers."

The carriage pulled through the arch of an old stone inn with a sign in front proclaiming it "The George." While the picturesque ivy climbing up half the building spoke of longevity, the subtle signs of disrepair indicated hard times. Like many of the old coach inns, this one had apparently suffered from the railroad diverting its previous revenues.

"There's no one here that can help you, so there's no sense in you trying anything. Do you understand me?" her uncle warned. She nodded as expected. "Good. Because if you do anything at all, I'll tie you back up and haul you across the border quicker than you can say Jack Sprat. Now act the proper widow and behave yourself."

Even with the loss of traffic, The George handled a bustling business as evidenced by the horses tied to the rail and the hardy masculine laughter that reached outside. The aromatic waft of a stew issued an invitation difficult to resist. Emma entered by her uncle's side, her head demurely lowered but her mind alert for opportunities to change her fate. She needed time. Time to plan. Time to execute. If she could just get a message back to Nicholas, he'd help her. He may not love her the way she did him, but they had shared a bond. He would come to her aid much as he had to Charlotte's.

But he was in London. The thought pushed her deeper in despair. He had mentioned in his letter that he planned to return to Yorkshire any day now. However, that letter was written before he became a constant news item in the *Times*. He might choose to stay in London indefinitely.

No, she had to think for herself if she was to avoid a life tied to a shriveled-up specter of a man.

A white-haired gentleman who looked to be as old as the inn itself manned the front desk. Her uncle stepped forward for the purpose of negotiating a room. Emma looked toward the large public area off to the side. She doubted she could find much assistance among the drunken male patrons. A serving girl, not much older than Alice, moved down the rows, filling tankards and delivering plates, without seeming to mind the occasional hand that fondled her backside.

Poor Alice. She'd believe Emma had run off and left her behind. The thought twisted Emma's heart. Oh, to be back at Pettibone in the heart of female companionship. Female . . . that inspired an idea.

"We'll be needing a private dining area as well," Uncle George said, with an eye toward the public room. "Can you tell me if a fine gentleman by the name of Perichilde has arrived yet?"

Emma laid her hand on her uncle's arm. "Uncle, I need to speak with you privately."

"Time enough for that when we get our room. I'm checking now to see if your groom has arrived." The clerk raised an eyebrow in her direction but otherwise appeared enthralled with his ledgers.

"I don't think I can wait that long," Emma whispered. "I have need to confide in another woman. You rushed me off from Pettibone without items necessary for female needs. I fear my monthly has begun."

Her uncle cursed under his breath and yanked his arm away from her touch as if she had confided that she had the plague. "Saints above woman," he hissed. "You don't have to inform the general public. Don't you have your ladies' necessities?"

"I have them back at Pettibone. Had you given me time to pack . . ."

"Well, I couldn't very well do that now, could I?" He looked around to make sure no one had heard him raise his voice. "What do you propose to do about it?"

"If I can talk to one of the women here, I'm sure they would give me what I need."

"All right. Make it quick. Don't offer to pay for anything. Until Perichilde arrives, our funds are low."

She nodded, acting the obedient niece, and glided into the public room. The loud cacophony died down a bit upon her entrance. Whether it was the result of her widow's attire or that she was the only woman fully clothed from head to toe, she wasn't sure.

"Are tha' lost?" one of the serving girls asked with an abbreviated curtsy and a dubious smile. "Not many ladies come her' at this hour."

Emma leaned close to the girl's ear and whispered, "I'm

not lost but I need your help. See that man standing by the clerk's desk?" The girl nodded. "I'm being kidnapped. I need to send a note to Lord Nicholas Chambers in Leighton-on-the-Wold to—"

"Nicky?" the girl's smile lit up her face. "Tha' know Nicky?"

"Ssh!" Emma cautioned with a quick look over her shoulder. Uncle George appeared in deep conversation with the clerk, probably bargaining over the cost of the room. "Can you take me someplace quiet and less public?"

The girl nodded. She led the way up the back stairs to a dark corridor. "All the rooms are in use right now. But this'd be as quiet as tha'll find this side of the inn." A loud groan from behind one of the doors spoke of the activity inside. The girl smiled with a nod to the door. "That room'll free up real quick."

"I need a pen and some paper to write a note," Emma said, squinting down the hallway. "I don't suppose you have . . . ?"

"Not much call for writin' up here." The girl looked at her askance. "How do tha' know Nicky? Thou one of his girls?"

"His girls?" Emma asked, annoyed. Maybe she could direct the girl to get the necessary writing supplies from the clerk? Would Uncle George get suspicious? Could this girl manage to slip her out of the inn to safety?

"Tha' know, one of th' girls he paints. He's painted Rosie and Annie. I've always wanted him to paint my picture, but he says I'm too young. Do tha' think I'm too young?"

Emma looked at the girl anew. "What's your name?"

"Daisy, just like th' flower. My mama says it means innocence." She smiled, exposing a gap in yellowed teeth. "But I ain't been that for near two years." She couldn't have been older than sixteen, certainly no older than Elizabeth. Emma bit her lip to hide her frown. Such a young girl to have so much earthy exposure.

"We ain't seen Nick . . . Lord Nicholas Chambers for nigh on six months. I don't know when I can get a message to him. If tha'ld be a friend of his, we—the other girls and me—we'll help tha' out if we can."

"Well, Daisy, you're right. I'm one of 'Nicky's girls,' and I'm in trouble." Emma hated to involve such a child in her scheme, but she saw little choice. "That man downstairs is trying to sneak me across the border into Scotland to marry me to someone I don't like. Lord Nicholas . . . Nicky . . . is in London, but he would stop—"

"London!" Daisy's eyes widened before she shook her head. "It'll take a week or more for us to get a message that far. I don't suppose thou's planning to stay a week?"

"No. I think my uncle plans to leave tonight." Emma glanced at Daisy's loose attire, a glimmer of an idea taking root. "Maybe you could hide me until the note gets through?"

"No unused rooms to hide thee in." Daisy studied her. "In that getup, tha'll stand out like the Queen herself come callin'."

Emma glanced down at the widow's garb that covered her as efficiently as a burial shroud. In contrast, Daisy displayed more skin than fabric.

"If I could blend in, my uncle might not notice." But could she bare that much skin in public? She'd bared much more in private, she reminded herself. She could do this.

"May I borrow some of your clothes?" Emma asked, completing a mental inventory of her appearance. "And maybe you can help me with my hair?"

Daisy's face split with a toothy smile. "Sounds like we's got ourselves another girl."

"WHERE IS SHE!" GEORGE HEATHERSTON BELLOWED. Patrons paused in the lifting of their tankards. "I saw her come into this room. Where did she go?"

"There's only one exit on this side of the inn and you were standing right by it," the elderly clerk patiently explained for the third time. "If we allowed other methods of egress, we'd lose half of our revenues."

"Then she must be here somewhere." Heatherston charged into the public room, rousing some sleeping patrons, who protested the disturbance.

Emma concentrated on pouring ale into the tankard of a lone man in the corner. She had shed her spectacles to complete her disguise, making the task of aiming the liquid more difficult. Her hair, loosened from its braided bun, flowed long over her shoulders. She tilted her head, hoping the curtain of hair would hide her face from her uncle as well.

"What's up here?" Heatherston asked at the base of steps.

"That's our entertainment quarters," the clerk said with a nervous glance upstairs. "I'm sure the young widow would not go up there. No decent lady would."

"Decent, my foot." Heatherston stomped up the steps. "Emma, you come down here."

The man at Emma's table slipped his hand along the back of her skirt, pressing the backs of her thighs. "Rosie, me love," his voice slurred. "How about tha' givin' a poor sot a free un."

"Ssh!" Emma whispered. "I'm not Rosie. Mind your manners." She slapped at his hand.

She could hear her uncle's heavy tread and billowing voice overhead. Her heart raced. If she made a mad dash for the door, her exit would surely be noted and reported to Uncle George. Besides, he'd be down those steps in a thrice if he had cause. Patience, she cautioned. If she merely worked her way toward the door while he was engaged upstairs, she might be able to slip away unnoticed.

She heard him pound on a door. "Emma, come out of there, you little slut. I know you're in there."

Her drunken patron's errant hand journeyed round her backside, the trespass all the more personal without the benefit of her bustle. "Come on, be a sport." Although with his elongated "s" and lack of a definite "t," she could be mistaken as to his meaning.

With a glance toward the doorway, she continued to pour until the ale overflowed the tankard, then spilled over the table and onto the patron's lap.

"Ey! Whot the devil!" He stood in a hurry, swiping his hand over the damp material.

"So sorry," Emma crooned. At least his hands were no longer her concern. "Let me get a rag to wipe up."

Overhead, her uncle's insistent knocking was followed by the sound of splintering wood. Emma used a corner of her apron to wipe off the table, casting a furtive glance to the inn's entrance.

Sounds of a scuffle erupted overhead. Before she could move toward the door, a body tumbled down the steps to land in a heap at her feet. Emma quickly glanced at the man on his backside at precisely the same moment that a gleam of recognition lit her uncle's eyes.

"Enough of the table. Whot about me pants!" Her customer grabbed her arm and pulled her around to face him. "Yur not Rosie. Who are you?"

She tried to pull her arm out of his grasp, but his grip tightened. A drunken leer spread across his face.

"You're a feisty one, ain't ya? How about being feisty with me upstairs?"

She could hear Uncle George scrambling behind her. But the harder she struggled against her captor, the tighter he held. "Please!" she begged. "Please let me go."

"Not till ya wipe off me pants." The drunkard sneered. "Wipe them off real good."

"Let her go," Uncle George said from behind her.

"I saw her first," the stranger protested.

"Well maybe I'll let you have her when I'm through with her." Uncle George pushed some shillings into the man's hand. "Here. Buy yourself another whore."

The man's face lit up. He released Emma's arm and walked at a tilt toward the middle of the room. Emma tried to turn and run, but her uncle was faster. He grabbed both her arms and held her in front of him.

"You cheap bit of trash." His foul breath heated her ear. She turned away, fear racing through her. "Perichilde is too good for the likes of you."

He piloted her further into the room's shadows. "You with your head buried in books. You and your mother always thought you were too good to wait on the likes of me. Now look at you. I have a mind to take you upstairs, strip off those rags, and teach you just what you are good for."

"I think you've taught her enough for one day."

Nicholas! Her heart recognized his voice. She tried to twist round to see him, but her uncle blocked the way.

Apparently Uncle George hadn't her talent of recognition. "I thought I told you to leave us alone." He growled over his shoulder. "You've got your money. Now get out of here."

"Let the lady go."

Uncle George laughed. "You must be blind. This is no lady. This is nothing but a bloody whore."

Emma heard the sound of splintering wood and a cry of pain, then felt her uncle releasing her arms. She spun about in time to see Nicholas's fist crash into Uncle George's face. Her uncle sank to the floor in a sprawl alongside a broken walking stick.

Nicholas stepped awkwardly toward her, then lightly took her arms. "Are you all right?"

His voice poured over her like warm chocolate. Her

heart threatened to burst from her chest with its fierce pounding. Emma fumbled in a pocket to retrieve her glasses. Once she could see clearly, she threw her arms around his neck.

He staggered back half a step, then wrapped his arms around her, pulling her close. His fingers pulled back her curtain of hair, exposing her neck. His light kiss on her sensitive skin sent tremors of ecstasy straight through to her toes.

"Did he hurt you?" he asked, holding her tight.

"No, but I think he might have if you hadn't arrived." Giddy with relief, she could barely stand.

"That's me." The soft chuckle in his voice rekindled a spark in her that had lain dormant for several weeks. "Always in the nick of time."

"How did you find me?" She pulled back so she could see his handsome face. Latent desperation caught her, an awareness of what almost had happened. Her hand trembled where it rested on his shirt. Her throat burned, making speech difficult. "I . . . I thought I'd never see you again."

A shadow of uncertainty flashed across his face. He squeezed her arm, then released her. "We'll have time for answers later. Let's get you out of here before your uncle wakes up."

She hesitated. "Are we just going to leave him here?"

Chambers looked down his nose at the bundle at his feet. "Yes," he said simply. "I think he can find his own way back to London."

She looked down at the stained garments that barely covered her chest. "What about my clothes? I can't leave like this."

Chambers pulled off his riding jacket and wrapped it over her shoulders. He leaned close to her ear. "Are you still wearing that pink corset?"

She nodded. Indeed, she had selected it this morning in memory of him.

"Then you're wearing all the clothes you need."

Delicious ripples tingled through her chest. She wasn't convinced her attire was appropriate, but they had no time to argue. She wrapped her arm around his waist so she could assist him in their progress to the front door. After a moment's hesitation, he accepted her help.

As they approached the entrance arm in arm, a withered old man stepped up to the clerk's desk.

"My name is Perichilde," Emma heard the man say behind her. "I believe I am expected."

· Twenty-four ·

ONCE OUTSIDE, EMMA IMMEDIATELY RECOGNIZED Lord Byron tied to the rail. A gruff man stroked the horse's head with great affection. Nicholas helped Emma up into an open two-wheel gig before speaking privately with him. The man nodded approval and waved them off.

The vehicle hadn't the shine and sparkle of one of Nicholas's well-kept carriages, but held more of the country sturdiness that defined Northern England. Nicholas climbed up next to Emma, clicked the reins, and engaged the horse in a brisk trot back through the arch and over the stone bridge spanning a nearby river.

Emma stared at the back of an unfamiliar bay. A million questions bubbled from her brain, but the one that raced to her lips surprised even her. "Why are you leaving your horse?"

"I rode him hard to reach you in time. He's gaining a well-deserved rest while we put some distance between you and your uncle," he said, expertly guiding the bay away from the inn.

"You intend to return?" Bile rose in her throat. Was this to be a temporary reprieve?

"In due time, of course, but only after the threat from your uncle has been dispensed. I must return the gig, Emma."

Nicholas directed the horse to turn onto a side road.

"I can't go back to Pettibone," Emma stated, panic near the surface. "I fear the Higgins sisters know that I am not, and never was, a widow. I'm afraid their opinion of me has been irreparably altered."

She remembered the look in Beatrice's eyes when Emma acknowledged Uncle George. He obviously told them he was seeking his innocent, unmarried niece. Even if her uncle had not mentioned the painting on display in London, and he very well could have while she was unconscious, it would not take long for the two sisters to question, then condemn her visits to Black Oak. Tears blurred her vision, but she hadn't even the comfort of her mother's handkerchief to blot them away.

"Perhaps Lady Cavendish will permit my temporary residence," she said, grasping at a faint hope. "But even she might turn away a social pariah."

"Emma, I swear to you, I never meant for that painting to go on public exhibition," Nicholas pleaded.

Emma's heart softened with compassion, but his sincerity did little to alter her situation. She still had no home. She glanced quickly over her shoulder, half expecting to see her uncle in hot pursuit.

"I may have begun with that purpose in mind," Nicholas admitted, "but as I came to know you, to respect you, I planned to substitute another painting for *Artemis*. I had crated up a landscape for London."

The catch in his voice twisted her heart; she placed her

hand on his arm. "Your painting deserves the accolades it received," she said, softly reassuring him. "Your talent belongs on the walls of the Royal Academy. It will be my honor, in the years to come, to say that I knew one of the Empire's finest talents."

She managed a smile for him, even though her world looked as bleak as a Yorkshire winter. His star was rising, even as hers had flamed out. "You have a brilliant future before you."

She squeezed his arm in support before she let go, taking a moment to quickly glance over her shoulder. "I, however, cannot seriously be considered a steward of young girls."

"Nonsense," he exclaimed. "You belong at Pettibone. You were meant to teach. Have you not noticed the change in spirit you brought to that school? Have you not noticed how the girls look up to you?"

He glanced her way. "No, I suppose you haven't. You've been so busy maintaining that false charade of yours that you haven't noticed how much has changed since your arrival." He hesitated. "How much you have changed since your arrival."

She twisted around again to check the road behind them.

"You can rest easy," Nicholas said. "He won't follow for quite a while. The manager at The George promised to lock him away in his room. That should give us an advantage."

An advantage for what? Where could she go? Perhaps if she had thought about her uncle's solution with her head instead of her heart, she would have allowed that marriage to an old crony might have provided her with at least a home. For that matter . . .

"How did you find me?" she asked.

"Lady Cavendish sent an urgent message to my father's house."

"Lady Cavendish! My uncle mentioned that she was working to procure a husband for Penelope."

"Apparently she accompanied your uncle on a tour of the exhibition and saw his reaction to the painting. She suspected you would need assistance. From what you have told me of your uncle, I had no doubt which direction he would take. Scotland is too close for those on nefarious business to ignore. The George is a frequent stop for travelers. Had you not been there, I would have continued to the next inn until I found you."

"You were at your father's house?"

He smiled. "One positive result of my brother switching the painting destined for the exhibition is that my father and I are now in accord. He supports my artistic pursuits."

"Why, then, did you come? My uncle said your painting was a grand success. Your talents have finally been recognized. By your own admission you have reconciled with your family. You have everything that you have ever wanted."

"And you were a vital part of it." Moonlight caught in his flashing smile. "You were my inspiration. I couldn't very well let another man cart off my inspiration, could I?"

Emma felt as if a gaping hole had just swallowed her up. She was no more than a good luck charm, a rabbit's foot, an evening's pleasure. Nothing more. Her lips refused to return his smile; her soul cried out in pain.

"I was miserable in London, Emma." He spread one arm out toward the orderly hedgerows defining the land. "I missed the gentle peacefulness of the country and your warm engaging conversation. We belong out here where we make our own society." He subtly glanced over toward her. "Tomorrow, we can head back home. I have in mind a new painting. I think I shall call it *Seduction*."

"Tomorrow?" A note of panic struck her voice. "Where are we heading if not Black Oak?" She tried to remember the direction they had turned after leaving the inn. At the time of actual occurrence, her mind had been too occupied with other thoughts.

Nicholas glanced at her, a bit pensive for his earlier joviality. "Have you never wondered that the school shares a common boundary with Black Oak?"

"Miss Higgins implied that Pettibone exists as the result of your brother's generosity." Emma vividly recalled Cecilia's adulations. "This, however, does not explain our destination."

"My brother's beneficence extends only to his appearance at Pettibone's social affairs. I established Pettibone School for Young Girls so that my reputation would not taint that of my orphaned godchild."

"You?" She felt her mouth gape. She wasn't sure what to question first. "You have an orphaned godchild?"

Emma mentally dashed through a list of the school's residents and recalled only one orphan, the student most dear to her heart. "Alice is your godchild?"

He nodded. "Her mother entrusted her baby in my care when she feared she would not survive the birth. Unfortunately, her intuition proved accurate. She died within one week. I was not equipped at the time to assume the responsibility of rearing a small child, so I established a school to do it for me. In fact, as Alice was coming to an appropriate age, it was my anonymous suggestion to procure someone to teach the girls about intimacy."

"You are responsible for my position at Pettibone?" Just as she thought she knew all, Nicholas released one revelation after another. She sat dumbfounded. No wonder he never questioned the appropriateness of the class instruction. She glanced over at him. Just the appropriateness of the instructor.

He nodded. "In a manner of speaking. But I had envisioned someone older and experienced. You took me quite by surprise."

She took *him* by surprise? She could honestly state that he returned the favor. She had never envisioned upon embarking from London that she would have experienced so much of life in a remote country village.

"Does Alice know?" she asked, remembering the other unexpected pleasure of her move to Yorkshire, that of gaining Alice's confidence.

"About me?" Nicholas's brows rose in that boyish expression she loved. "No. As the years passed, I felt it was in her best interest not to be associated with my household. Some people believe I would be a poor influence on the girl and thus limit her prospects for a worthy marriage."

"That is ridiculous," Emma protested. "Only those people who have not bothered to know you would make such preposterous suggestions."

"Thank you for your championship." He tilted his head in a mock bow. "Nevertheless, as the years passed, it became more difficult to broach the topic with the girl. I had become a complete stranger to her. So I avoided her altogether. I have discovered that avoidance is one trait at which I excel."

She worried her lower lip. He wasn't the only one who practiced avoidance. She herself had avoided most of her conflicts with a creative lie, except when it came to Nicholas.

She hadn't managed to avoid falling in love with him.

"But we digress from the issue at hand," he said. "Given my financial backing of the school, I can assure you of a position at Pettibone as long as you desire it to be so."

Emma shook her head. "You can demand that Pettibone retain my services, but you cannot make similar demands of the parents of the students. They will not entrust the education of their daughters to a woman who has removed her clothing for an artist, now matter how exalted that artist may be. Pettibone would become a school without students." She shook her head. "No, that avenue is closed to me now."

"Women disrobe for men other than their husbands every day," Nicholas protested.

"But they are not on exhibition in the Royal Academy."

"What of extenuating circumstances?" he pleaded.

"You make no sense." She shook her head, still shocked at all his revelations.

"I am serious, Emma. I set out for London in hopes of retrieving *Artemis's Revenge* before it was shown to the jury. Throughout the entire journey, I could think of nothing but this: I can create other paintings, but I could never replace the bond that has formed between us. I arrived too late for the substitution, but not too late for the celebration. I couldn't enjoy the accolades because you were not there to share them with me."

"Sir, a lady could never participate in the celebration of the public display of her private person." In spite of her rebuke, she still felt a warmth spread through her. He apparently missed her, as she had missed him. Still, to think she could have participated in a celebration of *Artemis's Revenge* . . . She shook her head. Truly, it was difficult at times to remember that Nicholas was of the noble class. He apparently had forgotten the restrictions and refinements of the privileged society.

He took the reins in one hand and slipped his free hand in hers. He squeezed. "I was thinking more of a private celebration."

Desire knifed through her. Heat rose on her cheeks. He wanted to bed her, and dear heaven above, she wanted him as well. She concentrated on the backside of the horse before them.

"Every day apart from you made me realize how much I need you," he said.

Desire tingled the tips of her breasts, pulling a yearning from her chest.

"When I received that message from Lady Cavendish about your fate, I knew I had to act."

"I am grateful that you did, or I would be bound for Scotland right now," she said, remembering she had never thanked him for arriving when he did.

Nicholas's silence was disconcerting. He stared straight ahead over the horse's ears as if he could see far into the night. Discomfort settled in her stomach.

"Sir, where *are* we going?"

"To Scotland."

"Scotland! But I thought—are you doing my uncle's bidding?" Shock riveted her to her seat. Of all the possible roads they could take, this was not one she had envisioned. "Are you part of his scheme?"

"No!" His face twisted in a frown. "How can you suggest such a notion? This is the only way you can be truly safe. If I were to take you back to Pettibone, he would come after you again."

"Then take me somewhere else. I have already explained why I cannot return to Pettibone. Were you not listening?"

"Of course I was listening. And I heard that marriage is the best solution to your problems."

"And who have *you* arranged for me to marry?" she snapped. Indignation replaced her earlier desire. She had spent so many years alone. Why did every man now feel an urgency to see her wed?

"Me."

She would have been less shocked if he had suggested Thomas.

"This resolves all your difficulties," he explained. "It is

the perfect solution. As my wife, there should be no out-
cry over you teaching, nor can anyone object to how I display my wife's virtues—although I assure you that
Artemis's Revenge will be promptly removed from all
public venues."

He must be joking. She was a commoner. Hardly the
daughter-in-law a duke would welcome into the family, especially one whose assets have already been displayed for
all of London.

"Furthermore," he continued, oblivious to her shock,
"you will be removed from the marriage market, thus rendering your uncle powerless in this regard." He grinned as
if he had just eaten the last spoonful of the brandy bread
pudding and was quite pleased with himself.

Emma sat stunned, not sure if she were more aghast at
his proposal or his logic. Granted, marrying Nicholas
would mean her wildest fantasy had come true, but for the
wrong reasons. As her employer, he wanted to keep a val-
ued employee. And as a man, he felt it necessary to protect
her from her uncle, rather than letting her protect herself.

Nicholas's smile faded. He clicked the reins in a most
agitated manner. "I had thought this solution would make
you happy, Emma."

"I am, sir," she responded tightly, "exceedingly happy."

"Will you please favor me by calling me by my familiar name." He scowled. "I confess I find 'sir' and 'lord' ref-
erences disturbing."

"I am exceedingly happy, Nick . . . Nicholas." She
could not bring herself to call him "Nicky."

They rode in silence a bit longer. He continued to
glance at her, as if he expected her to break out in tears. Indeed, his expectations may yet prove true, she realized,
feeling the constriction in her throat.

"You will consent to be my wife?" he asked without
mirth.

"Yes," she whispered. He wanted more, she could hear it in his voice, but she had hoped for so much more herself. She struggled hard to appear at least pleasant while deep inside her heart was breaking. Closing her eyes, she inhaled deep draughts of blooming heather, fertile rot, and Nicholas's unique combination of exotic oils.

The horse's steady gait and the rattle of the harness clapped a rhythmic lullaby. For a moment she wished they would never arrive at a destination. Decisions and painful examination of emotions waited at their journey's end. For now, she would enjoy the sweet breeze, the spacious accepting landscape, and the freedom to determine her own destiny.

"WAKE UP, EMMA. WE'VE ARRIVED."

Nicholas guided the tired horse to a small black and white cottage with a swinging sign in front. Inviting light from gaslit rooms spilled a welcome to exhausted strangers.

"We can rest here for the night. I'll find a justice of the peace in the morning."

"My uncle?" Emma asked. She looked about, suddenly alert.

"If he follows, he will arrive too late. Come now, let's put you to bed." He sounded fatigued, more so than she.

He jumped down from the gig and tied the horse to the post. He walked around to her side and attempted to lift her into his arms. She batted his hands away.

"That is unnecessary, sir."

He raised his brow.

"Nicholas," she quickly amended. "I'm not too tired to walk, and your leg may not be up to it."

He scowled, then offered his hand to help her down. "You slept on my shoulder most of the way here. Now that

I have you in Scotland, I don't want to chance you disappearing as you did to your uncle."

"Oh no. I wouldn't try such a thing." Scotland! They were in Scotland?

"Based on your warm reception to my proposal, I'm not so sure." He grasped her arm, pulling her tight against him.

Her heart twisted. If only he loved her the way she did him, then she could entertain his proposal with the enthusiasm he so obviously expected. Perhaps in time, he would learn to love her. But could she promise herself to him knowing he had made no similar promises to her?

He led her to the room indicated by the manager, then saw her properly inside.

"I have arrangements to make, but I won't be far away," Nicholas said, standing by the door. "Sleep, dear Emma. I'll be back soon and our problems will be resolved." He hesitated a moment, then delivered a chaste kiss to her forehead.

No! She wanted to scream. What happened to the passion he had demonstrated in the stable? The scandalous temptations he offered in the studio? Had he tasted her passion and found her wanting? Was she doomed to a lifetime of chaste kisses?

"Thank you," she murmured as manners would dictate. The door closed behind him as he left. She threw herself across the bed, allowing her tears to flow free until exhaustion lulled her to sleep.

THE SUBTLE CLICK OF A LOCK BROUGHT HER EYES FULLY open. Her mind snapped to attention. The dim light of dawn flowed through the window, bathing the room in a soft gray hue. She was alone. The bed had been disturbed only where she had slept, yet something was amiss.

Then she saw it. A beautiful long-stemmed rose lay on

the pillow beside her, along with a scroll tied with a ribbon. She slipped off the ribbon and carried the paper to the window. The gentle light flowed over a penned verse.

To Emma, with apologies to Christopher Marlowe

Come live with me and be my love
And prove to all and God above
That love transforms the basest of men
And brings them back to the light again.

And I will lie thee in a bed of roses
And paint thee in a thousand poses
Each will proclaim thy beauty and grace
After each, we shall love and not in haste.

Share with me a world of art and oil
Loving you shall be no toil
For love and learning will ensue
And perchance a babe or two.

I love you Emma with all my heart
I should have mentioned this from the start.
If my promises to you delight,
Come live with me and be my wife.

"Yes," she said softly to the empty room, letting joy awaken every nerve ending. "Yes," she called louder, but received no response. She dropped the poem, then pulled a blanket from the bed, wrapping it over her shoulders.

No one waited for her outside the door. She crept down the stairs of the slumbering inn. No one occupied the lobby, but a light from the public room caught her eye. She crept to the doorway and saw Nicholas bent over a piece of paper illuminated by the light of an oil lamp.

"Yes," she said.

He glanced up, hope lighting his eyes. "Emma?"

Her heart flipped over. The poor man looked absolutely exhausted. She walked straight into his arms and kissed him till he could have no doubt as to the depth of her desire. His arms locked around her back and pulled her tight to his chest, molding her body into his. Never had she felt more safe and more loved.

"What are you doing down here?" she asked, too content to pull away.

"I wanted to make certain we had no unwanted visitors." Nicholas pulled back enough to kiss her neck. Delicious shivers tingled down her back.

"I wrote you a poem," he said before slipping the blanket off her shoulder. "Did you see it?"

She nodded, stretching her neck to offer him more skin to sample. His lips blazed a path down her neck and across her shoulder. Her terse nipples strained at the flimsy material of Daisy's blouse. She arched back slightly, hoping to direct his attentions to their need.

"It was the most beautiful poem I've ever read," she said, breathless.

"That's because you haven't read my most recent attempt, 'Ode to a Pink Corset.'" He pushed both the blanket and the short sleeves of Daisy's accommodating blouse down to the crook of her elbows. His lips and tongue paid homage to her breasts. Sensation arced straight to her feminine core. Her head fell back, her knees threatened to buckle. She felt a moment's hesitation that someone could walk in on them at any second, but then, she didn't care. As long as she was in Nicholas's arms, the world, the school, her reputation, none of it mattered a fig.

"If you want me," she rasped, "I will be yours, no matter the circumstances. But I must know why."

She steeled her heart in anticipation of his answer. Although she had read his verse, she was all too aware that false sentiments could be used to make a rhyme or fill a meter. She needed to hear the words and know his true intent. If he wanted a lifetime model or a convenient mistress, she would do it, but at least her eyes would be wide open. There would be no delusions of love or happy endings. She would share his life as much as he would allow and that would be enough.

His lips stilled. He glanced up at her, then straightened.

Suddenly, she wished she hadn't asked. Her heart might not survive his answer. Biting her lip for her own stupidity, she turned her head away.

"I love you, Emma." His fingers guided her chin back to him. "I never realized how much I loved you, until I had almost lost you." He kissed her gently. "I had planned on living my life alone with only my canvas and paint for company, but you've made that impossible. I can't lose you again. I don't think I could survive it."

Had he truly said he loved her? Her heart expanded, squeezing out all the breath in her rib cage. She wanted to hold him so tight, their flesh would meld and they could never be separated. Her lips sought his in a kiss that would return all the love and passion he had given.

"I want you," Nicholas said, "as my wife."

Her head giddy with joy, she thrilled at his smile and the desire burning in his eyes. "I love you, Nicholas. I have since that first night in the carriage."

She wanted to shout and wake up all the patrons in the inn. Instead she leaned close to his ear and whispered, "And you shall have me, corset and all."

· Epilogue ·

CECILIA CLAPPED HER HANDS TO BRING THE ROOM to attention. "Girls, girls, settle down. As you are aware, we at the Pettibone School for Young Ladies pride ourselves on preparing our girls for all the eventualities that you may encounter as a new bride. To that end, we are delighted to have Lady Nicholas Chambers conduct a series of classes on this very subject.

"As you can see by her developing form, she is very knowledgeable about the successful procreation of heirs. Now I want you to pay close attention. Previous graduates of Mrs. Brimley's . . . Lady Nicholas Chambers's classes have reported that this information has served them well in securing a husband as well as maintaining a satisfying relationship for all involved.

"After this class, Lord Nicholas Chambers will be conducting a session in oil painting out in the garden. A well-mannered lady must have a talent, be it music or painting, to make her stand out in the crowd. I advise you all to take advantage of the knowledge of this talented artist. His work hangs in the Royal Academy, you know." Some of the girls found this to be an invitation to giggle. Cecilia clapped her hands for order.

"One final note: a picnic will be held tomorrow afternoon at nearby Black Oak, hosted by Miss Alice Darlington. It promises to be a beautiful day and I encourage you all to be on your very best behavior.

"With that I shall turn the class over to Mrs. Brim . . . er, Chambers. The girls are yours."

Emma confidently moved forward from her position in the back of the library, her protruding belly leading the way. She was no longer a weed among flowers; her pale blue and golden yellow ensemble rivaled any of the girls in the room. A hush of expectancy settled over their eager faces. Emma smiled. How very like the faces of last year's class. This year, however, she had ready answers and more.

"Let us begin with your list of questions."

Turn the page for a preview
of the next historical romance
by Donna MacMeans

THE TROUBLE
WITH MOONLIGHT

Coming soon from Berkley Sensation!

London, 1876

IF HIS LIFE, ALONG WITH THOSE OF SO MANY faithful agents of the Crown, didn't hang in the balance, James Locke knew he would turn and escape Lord Pembroke's study as silently as he had entered. The mission, however, demanded his legendary skill at cracking safes, a skill now more myth than reality.

The narrow, stuffy room opened before him and was seeped in darkness, much like a tomb. He shuddered, reminding himself he wasn't in a hellhole prison cell, not this time. Ignoring the clamminess of his palms, he looked for a window, knowing he couldn't risk opening it but needing to know one existed all the same.

Yes, thick curtains hung on the wall to his right. He parted the heavy velvet, letting bright moonlight flood the room to reveal a Milner holdfast safe near the desk. By his calculations, he had little more than one hour before the servants would be roused to welcome their employer back from the gambling hells.

Kneeling before the hinged black door, he slipped a skeleton key and a holding lever into the narrow slot, letting the delicate tips of his fingers signal the lift of a tumbler. Twice the slight tremor in his hand caused the lever to slip, forcing him to start the process from the beginning. He cursed silently but knew he couldn't abandon the mission; not with so much at stake.

Finally, the lock clicked and he allowed himself the luxury of a deep breath of relief before turning the latch and swinging open the heavy iron door. Inside a series of small compartments held the valuable treasures Lord Pembroke believed secure. James checked each, methodically moving from the top down, searching for the list of British operatives that had presumably fallen into the wrong hands. Just as he had examined the last drawer, the sound of light footsteps in the hall caught his ear. Damn! He carefully closed the safe door, but did not turn the latch as the sound of resetting tumblers might signal his presence. He slipped behind the velvet draperies hoping the footsteps would pass by, but no. They stopped. Holding his breath, James peeked through the gap in the heavy panels.

The door to the study opened, then closed. Footsteps softly padded across the thick Persian carpet in the direction of the safe. James squinted through the narrow opening but saw . . . no one. Mystified, he carefully pushed a small measure of the dusty velvet aside to give him better visibility. Knowing his opponents could be as valuable as locating the elusive list. But no one appeared to be in the room. How could that be?

The heavy safe door slowly swung back. One by one, the compartment drawers slid open, then pulled back. Stunned, James watched a jewelry case from one of the drawers levitate and hover in midair. Logically, he knew there had to be some explanation for the unbelievable event transpiring before him. But his eyes provided none, and no flute-playing Indian fakir had suddenly taken residence in the study.

The jewelry case opened and a necklace of finely cut rubies escaped from its housing, flashing bloodred in the moonlight. The empty case returned to the drawer, the drawer slid into the safe, the heavy safe door swung back on its hinges, and the latch turned all without benefit of a human hand. Had he not been cold sober, James would have thought he was deep in his cups. Were his eyes playing tricks, or was some fiendish jest afoot? His nose pushed further into the drapery, unsettling the accumulated dust. James fought the tickle deep in his nostrils. His eyes burned and watered yet he followed the necklace's silent flight across the room. As it passed the desk, the corners of the papers scattered there lifted briefly as if in silent salute. An unusual scent, foreign to that of the study's wood polish and book leather, floated on a stirred current. What the devil?

He couldn't restrain the sneeze any longer. He tried to swallow the sound but a strangled harrumph escaped beyond his best efforts. The necklace swung momentarily in his direction. He heard a swift intake of air, almost feminine in nature, then rapid footfalls to the door. The study door flew open. The necklace darted through.

"Wait!" James called in a hissing whisper. Fool. As if a necklace had ears to listen. He dashed from his hiding place in pursuit, of what he wasn't sure, but he was determined to find out. He followed both the sound of running footfalls down the hall and the lingering trail of a sweet floral scent. No time to think about that now. The heavy jewels bounced and swayed in their flight toward the kitchen then flew in a high arc around a corner. James followed, his hasty exit generating far more noise than his earlier entrance; his heart pounding as if he were the fox and not the hound.

The kitchen doorknob turned, allowing the wooden

door to open. The necklace flew into the night. A gasp to
his right warned him that he was not alone. He glanced at
a wide-eyed scullery maid whose open mouth and frigid
paralysis suggested he wasn't the only one witnessing a
flying necklace fleeing the household. Even with her validation, he still wasn't sure he believed what his own eyes
told him to be true.

The necklace proved more elusive in the dark. Only the
chance spark of moonlight reflecting on the jewels allowed
him to follow in shadow. He had spooked the necklace
once, he didn't intend to do so again. Dashing from hedge
to tree to bush, he silently followed the necklace through
the back garden to a waiting brougham. It was an older
model, but obviously serviceable. The door opened, and
the carriage body sagged as if a passenger had boarded, but
naught but the jewelry entered.

The driver clicked the horses forward. Without hesitation, James raced for the back of the brougham, even
though his own hack waited around the corner. He caught
a handhold on the edge of the moving conveyance and
braced his feet on the fenders above the spinning wheel
axels so that he was tenuously attached to the back of the
vehicle like an overgrown street urchin.

After several minutes and near fatal turns, the carriage
slowed and Locke dropped off. He dashed across the street
to a park to avoid detection and allow the blood to flow
back into his whitened fingers. Although he attempted to
appear unobtrusive, his gaze was clearly focused on the
brougham. The driver hopped down and rushed to open the
carriage door.

Although he half expected to see a necklace fly from
the carriage and up the townhouse steps, a widow emerged
from the depths of the brougham. A young widow at that,
judging from her pleasing waist and saucy bustle. A jet-
black reticule with a bulging bottom swung from her wrist.

Locke smiled in spite of himself, imagining a fat ruby necklace nestled inside. He strained to see beneath the black-lace veil that contoured a narrow face with distinctive cheek planes, but she was either too distant or the lace too dense. How did she do it? He never saw a woman anywhere near Pembroke's study. One had to admire such talent, even if it was used for common thievery.

She mounted the steps toward a town house door framed with blooming white flowers. Odd to see flowers blooming at this hour, he mused before dismissing the thought. The widow paused then turned to look straight at him, as if she knew he'd be there. He should turn away. Play the role of a drunken sot stumbling down the pavement, but instead he remained rooted to the spot. He raised his arm as if to tip his hat, but then he remembered that he'd left it in the waiting carriage at Pembroke's residence.

She quickly turned and entered the house. What to do now? He was tempted to storm the house and demand to know how she had palmed the necklace. However, storming a widow's home at such a disrespectful hour might raise a bit of unwanted attention. Better to observe the mysterious widow, make a few inquiries, and discover which way her allegiances lay before making any rash moves.

A welcome breeze surrounded him with the strange floral fragrance he'd noted earlier. He took a deep breath, reliving the fascinating memory of all he didn't see in the study. The widow's techniques would certainly make her a formidable spy. That gave him pause. He glanced back up at the residence, noting the address. It shouldn't be difficult to gather a bit of information about her tomorrow once the working world was about. He noted a shift at the draperies then turned to retrace the path to Lord Pembroke's house, where his own carriage waited.

• • •

"HOW DID IT GO, DEAR?" AUNT EUGENIA ASKED.

Lucinda Havershaw hurried to the front window to peek out between the drapes. The lacy veil obscured her vision but she didn't dare move it until she was certain . . .

"Someone saw me tonight."

"Oh dear!" Her aunt, a thickened, older version of Lucinda herself, hurried to the window to add her scrutiny to the street. "Were you followed?"

"I'm not certain." Lucinda began to pull off her black gloves. "I had thought I had lost him once I reached the outside of the house, but there was a strange man on the pavement just now. I think he was watching me."

She pulled off her hat and veil and tossed them to the well-worn settee. The grandfather clock in the corner tapped out two bells. Aunt Eugenia readjusted the draperies before turning toward her niece. She gasped. "Dear Heavens, I don't suppose I'll ever become accustomed to seeing you like that."

Lucinda smiled, although she knew no one could see it. She had peeked at a mirror once when she was in full-phase. Viewing the headless dress reflected there had shocked even herself. She had avoided mirrors while in phase ever since.

She opened her reticule and retrieved the beautiful ruby necklace she had liberated from Pembroke's safe. "Mrs. Farthington will be very happy to see we reclaimed her necklace. I hope she can keep it out of the hands of her foolish husband this time."

"I hope she doesn't." Aunt Eugenia took the necklace from Lucinda's invisible hand to store in their parlor safe hidden beneath a chintz table cloth. She lifted the flowery fabric and inserted an ornately carved key into the exposed keyhole. "We make more money if he gambles it away. A woman on her own can never have enough money, dear, especially with four mouths to feed and a household to run."

"Lucy?"

Lucinda turned quickly to see her youngest sister, Rhea, in the hallway. The sight of the three-year-old clutching a bedraggled velveteen kitten tugged at her heart.

"I'm here, my sweet."

"But I can't see you," the little one said with a yawn.

The child's lament pulled at Lucinda's heart. It was bad enough Rhea would never know her own mother, and then to add a sometimes invisible sister to the situation must certainly lead to insecurities. Lucinda swooped the sleepy-eyed toddler into her arms while her aunt hastily closed the family safe. "You can feel me all around you." Lucinda nuzzled the top of her sister's little blonde head. "Why aren't you in bed?"

She cast a disapproving glance to her aunt, but of course, her aunt was oblivious to her expression.

"I had a bad dream." The child reached up and touched her face. "I thought you were gone."

"The moon is still full and the stars are awake." She kissed Rhea's fingers. "Go back to bed, sweet angel, and tomorrow morning you'll see me just fine."

"Come on, little miss. I'll see you back to bed." Aunt Eugenia patted the child on the back.

The little girl puckered her lips in a kiss, while Lucinda moved her cheek to meet them. "Good night, Lucy." Rhea clenched the ear of her bedraggled kitten, then proceeded to climb the stairs using hands and feet.

"Your blessed mother would be proud of the way you've taken care of the girls," Eugenia said as she passed by Lucinda, "as I am."

"Thank you, Auntie." Eugenia's appreciation of her efforts warmed her like a welcome cup of tea. She stooped to kiss her Aunt's cheek as well, but as the older woman couldn't see her, Eugenia continued by without pausing to receive the kiss. Lucinda's pursed lips met only air.

A familiar jab of frustration stabbed at her heart, reminding her of the loneliness that went hand in hand with her unique ability. She had no choice but to accept her fate. She sighed. Anger couldn't change what God had made. Better to concentrate on providing for her family, which brought her thoughts back to tonight.

Lucinda doused the lamps on the mantle and on the wall, before returning to the parlor window. She'd been spotted. Consequences always followed a sighting. At best the rumors of ghosts and headless horsemen would reappear, at worst they would need to once again find a new home. What would it be like to not have to schedule one's existence to the phases of the moon? To not constantly worry about being labeled the devil's child or a witch? Perhaps she was being too vigilant. Perhaps there was nothing to worry about. Still, an uneasiness settled heavy about her heart.

THE NEXT MORNING, JAMES SPOTTED THE QUAINT TOWN house easily enough. Although the flowers that had bloomed so enchantingly in the moonlight were closed and twisted tight, he remembered the location and the glimmer of the brass plaque by the door. How could he forget this location? Late into the wee hours of the morning, he had contemplated the mystery woman and her magnificent feats of magic—if, indeed, they were magic. One way or another, he was determined to find out.

Already he had learned through inquisition of the neighboring merchants, that a widow, Mrs. Eugenia Gertrude, and her three nieces had rented the residence. The information pleased him as it validated his sighting of a widow the evening before.

The town house faced a park, so he found an empty bench and watched the front of the house. The day stretched on with no remarkable activity. Indeed he had invested enough time on that hard bench to have read his copy of the *Illustrated Times* five times front to back. He stood to stretch when a closed carriage pulled up in front of the town house. Watching with interest, he observed a rather broad Mrs. Farthington exit and climb the few steps to the townhouse with difficulty. She was ushered inside without incident.

James crossed the street, moving closer to the front of the house. Mrs. Farthington's husband, a gentleman who, it had been rumored, had fallen on some desperate times, was well-known around the gambling hells where Lord Pembroke frequented. James would be willing to bet that the Farthingtons were the link between the mystery widow and Lord Pembroke's safe.

When Mrs. Farthington reemerged thirty minutes later, Locke was ready. He hailed a cab to follow her home. The mystery widow did not realize it, but the noose about her enchanting neck was about to tighten.

JAMES HADN'T ENGAGED IN DISGUISE SINCE HIS TRAVeling days with a caravan crossing the Karakum Desert in Central Asia. He affixed a bushy mustache that made his upper lip all but disappear, then added bushy eyebrows as well. Padding thickened his waist and gave him a bit of a belly before he covered it all with an unfashionable tweed jacket, knickerbockers, and gaiters. He checked his image in the mirror, confident that if the widow had glimpsed him in Pembroke's study, she certainly wouldn't recognize him now. With spirited determination, he journeyed to the widow's address and rang the bell. He glanced at the brass plaque by the door, "Appointments during daylight hours only." What in the devil did that mean?

A cat, black as the widow's gown, jaunted up the steps

and wove its lithe body between his legs. "What have we here?"

He scooped the cat up in his arms and was giving it a good scratch between the ears when the door opened.

"Oh my." The stout woman held her hands out for the cat. "Has our Shadow been digging in your gardens? I'm so sorry."

"Not at all." Disappointment clawed at his throat. Although the woman at the door was dressed in widow's weeds, she certainly couldn't be the same woman he had observed leaving the brougham. Her height was about right. He would have taken an oath that she had been a bit thinner last evening, but perhaps that was a trick of the moonlight. He cleared his throat. "No, this fellow just joined me on the step." He handed the cat over to its owner. "I had hoped to see the lady of the house."

"I suppose that would be me, sir." She stroked the cat's head and studied him from her position in the doorway.

"Oh!" He snatched the brown bowler from his head. "I'm Laurence Langtree." He cast a nervous eye to the street. "I'm told that we might be able to do business."

"Is that so?" She cocked her head, and frowned. "And what kind of business would that be?"

Mrs. Farthington had prepared him for this very question. He leaned forward and lowered his voice. "Recovery business."

Her face brightened. "Then I suppose you should come in so we can talk." She moved back from the doorway, letting James cross the threshold.

An ornate grandfather clock complete with a lunar phase dial immediately caught his attention. It was clearly the most valuable piece of furniture in the cluttered room. However, if he wasn't mistaken, that bump beneath the flowery tablecloth hid the lock mechanism for a small safe.

He smiled, remembering his last encounter with a safe and his reason for being here.

"I have been advised that you possess, shall we say, some remarkable attributes in the area of recovery."

"I, sir?" She smiled, though it did not reach to her eyes. "Whoever told you that?"

"I am loath to name sources. I wish to respect privacy whenever possible."

"In that case, I'm afraid you are mistaken, Mr. . . ."

"Langtree. Laurence Langtree."

Footsteps sounded behind him. "Aunt Eugenia, I wonder if you would mind—"

James turned toward the voice and stood stunned. This was the one. This had to be her. She had a proud, straight nose with just the slightest uplift on the end and the high cheekbones that had molded the veil. Yet, there was so much more. Her eyes were the deep blue of the evening sky just before the sun slipped from view, made all the more striking by her almost luminous skin. It had been wise of her to wear a black veil, he thought with appreciation, for skin like that would outshine the moon.

"Mr. Langtree, this is my niece, Miss Lucinda Havershaw."

"Miss Havershaw." Even her name suited her, Lucinda with hair the color of moonlight and a curtsy borne of good manners.

"Mr. Langtree believes he has need of your recovery services."

"Oh?" Her head cocked and intelligent eyes assessed him. He felt a stirring in his bones. Yes, this was the talented one he'd encountered the previous night. She wiped her hands on a handkerchief she removed from her serviceable pinafore. "I apologize, sir. I was doing a bit of gardening in back." She motioned for them to sit. "What precisely did you wish recovered, Mr. Langtree?"

Not surprising, her voice was as enchanting as her appearance. He was in the presence of an angel. Even her scent was bewitching. Something floral, something familiar . . .

"Mr. Langtree?"

Pull yourself together, man! She'll think you're a drooling idiot. He cleared his throat. "A pocket watch of great sentimental value."

"You've lost your watch?"

"In a manner of speaking, it is in another's possession." He watched her amazing eyes. He could almost see the clockwork of her mind, the tumblers clicking . . . Her eyes narrowed.

"I'm not a thief, Mr. Langtree."

"Of course not." *Liar. A thief is exactly what you are, and one of the best I've ever seen.* He smiled, ever so slightly. "The watch belongs to me even though it currently resides in another's pocket."

Her brows lifted. "How could such an injustice have ever occurred?"

Sarcasm! He swallowed the grin that threatened to spread across his face. "The watch was initially . . . my father's." He feigned sadness hoping to appear sincere. "As I mentioned, it has great sentimental value." He accepted an offered tea cup from the aunt and sipped. "My mother decided to gift it to her paramour even though it was not hers to give."

"Have you asked your mother to retrieve the watch for you?" The slight tilt of her lips suggested she thought he was a bit addlepated, which was his intention. However, he was sorely tempted to drop the pretense just so he'd stand taller in her eyes. Still, he needed to finish the game.

"She wouldn't hear of it. Mrs. Farthington suggested I come to you." The name had registered with her aunt, but the only hint of recognition in the niece was the faintest separation in her enticing lips. She was competent at hiding her emotions. Thank the powers that be that the likes of Miss Havershaw would never be admitted to the gentlemen's clubs for the purposes of a card game. He'd lose his shirt. Of course, if he lost it to Miss Havershaw, that might not be the worst experience. "Mrs. Farthington mentioned that you had retrieved an item for her for which she is very grateful."

"Yes, well, I would have preferred that Mrs. Farthington had not shared that information." She narrowed her gaze, studying him with an air of skepticism. He concentrated on the tea cup, hoping to avoid her scrutiny.

"Are you familiar with Lord Pembroke, Mr. Langtree?"

What the devil? His disguise must be failing! He delicately touched his napkin to his upper lip, just in case the steam from the tea had weakened the spirit gum. He used the moment to regain his poise before resuming the facade.

"No. I'm afraid not." He balled the napkin in his palm. "Of course, I expect to show my gratitude with a financial boon for the return of my watch."

She studied him a moment longer, her distrust still lingering, then glanced at the tall parlor clock. "How much of a boon, Mr. Langtree?"

"Shall we say, twenty pounds?" Her eyes widened and he hastened to add before she questioned his generosity. "It is a very dear and rare watch."

Judging from the state of her brougham and the parlor furnishings, it would be a difficult offer to decline. Besides, he hadn't the social boon that she had extracted from Mrs. Farthington.

"Perhaps you should tell us more about this watch, Mr. Langtree," the aunt interceded with a piqued interest. "Where do you suspect it to be?"

And so he did. Their tea finished and the bait set, he

stood to take his leave. "When do you suppose I'll see my dear watch again?"

He noticed the aunt's eyes shift to the tall clock in the corner, while Miss Havershaw kept him firmly in her gaze.

"I imagine before the week is out," the aunt said.

He nodded. "Good day, ladies."

LUCINDA ATTEMPTED TO DISCRETELY PEER THROUGH the draperies at Mr. Langtree once he had left the town house. There was something about the man. Something that just didn't register true. His clothes and mannerisms seemed at odds to the sharp glittering acuity in his eyes. There was something familiar about him. The fine hairs at the base of her neck prickled.

"This has certainly turned into a profitable week." Aunt Eugenia could hardly contain her excitement. "First, Mrs. Farthington and then Mr. Langtree, we shall have enough funds for the household expenses and a little extra to put aside for the winter."

Winter, Lucinda grimaced, Aunt Eugenia's euphemism for living on the street. Fighting starvation while avoiding detection, without a shelter to call home and with hungry mouths to feed . . . Yes, she understood her aunt's joy at avoiding that dire turn of circumstances. But still, there was something about that man . . .

She recalled his expression when she had first entered the room. A delicious warmth had spread beneath her corset at his appreciative stare. Even now, at the memory, a strange fluttering pushed at her stays. Then he spoke, his voice soft and deep, like a childhood lullaby meant to seduce the listener into doing one's bidding . . .

"Lucinda? Are you listening to me, dear?"

Her aunt's voice chased Mr. Langtree's pleasant attributes from her thoughts. "I'm sorry, you were saying?"

"I was noting that you only have about two more nights of full moonlight left. When do you propose to retrieve Mr. Langtree's watch?"

She bit her lip. On one hand, the unsettling contradictions about Mr. Langtree's person could cause her to dismiss the notion of retrieving his watch. However, should she do that, she would miss the opportunity of seeing and hearing him again. Then, of course, there was the question of financial need . . .

"Tonight," Lucinda replied, with a nod to her aunt. "Best to keep the winter at bay."

Before beginning her writing career in earnest, **Donna MacMeans** kept books of a different nature. A certified public accountant, she only recently abandoned the exciting world of debits and credits to return to her passion: writing romances. Her debut novel, *The Education of Mrs. Brimley*, won the 2006 Golden Heart for Best Long Historical. Originally from Towson, Maryland, she currently resides in central Ohio with her husband, two adult children, and loyal canine protector, Oreo.

Donna loves to hear from her readers. You may write to her at P.O. Box 1981, Westerville, Ohio 43086.

Visit her website at www.DonnaMacMeans.com.

Enter the rich world of *historical romance* *with Berkley Books.*

Lynn Kurland

Patricia Potter

Betina Krahn

Jodi Thomas

Anne Gracie

Love is timeless.

penguin.com